NOTHING SACRED

Elizabeth Ann Scarborough

SPECTRA ™

BANTAM BOOKS

NEW YORK · TORONTO · LONDON · SYDNEY · AUCKLAND

All of the characters in this book are fictitious, and any resemblance to actual persons, living or dead, is purely coincidental.

This edition contains the complete text of the
original hardcover edition.
NOT ONE WORD HAS BEEN OMITTED.

NOTHING SACRED
A Bantam Spectra Book / published by arrangement with
Doubleday

PRINTING HISTORY
Doubleday edition published March 1991
Bantam edition / January 1992

ISBN 0-553-29511-X

Published simultaneously in the United States and Canada

Bantam Books are published by Bantam Books, a division of
Bantam Doubleday Dell Publishing Group, Inc. Its trademark,
consisting of the words "Bantam Books" and the portrayal of a
rooster, is Registered in U.S. Patent and Trademark Office and
in other countries. Marca Registrada. Bantam Books, 666 Fifth
Avenue, New York, New York 10103.

PRINTED IN THE UNITED STATES OF AMERICA

RAD   0 9 8 7 6 5 4 3 2 1

Merridew put his face so close to mine I could almost see it even in the dark. "Okay, young lady, I am going to assume that you are new to the enemy's penal system and give you a little short survival course. Here's the drill. We stick together. It's as simple as that. Each of us has been in and out of other prisons and in and out of other cell arrangements in this one—including years of solitary in some cases. If you do betray us, we will at some point all betray each other and this place will be even more of a hellhole than it is right now. Do I make myself clear?"

"Yes, sir," I said. "I understand. I just want to make sure before I promise anything that we're all on the same side. So with all due respect, sir, which side are you on?"

"We're Americans, of course," Danielson said.

"But who are you with?" I insisted.

"We've been here a spell," Thibideaux said. "Things may have changed some. There were some pretty strange new policies brewin' before Marsh and me were taken. Who's the U.S. helpin' now, ma'am?"

The U.S.? God, maybe we were just having a little communication problem. "The U.S." was considered a separatist designation these days.

Praise for Elizabeth Ann Scarborough

"Scarborough is a writer towering above most of her contemporaries."   —*The Houston Post*

"Moves . . . to a mystical denouement that is both fully prepared for and wonderfully surprising."
                                            —*St. Louis Post-Dispatch*

". . . this book stands as a high achievement of the metaphoric art. Scarborough deserves a round of vigorous applause."   —*Analog*

NOTHING

SACRED

PART ONE

KALAPA COMPOUND, TIBET.
Late September,
2069.
DAY 11?

✗ The guards gave me this paper with instructions to write about my career as a war criminal, starting with my life at age eight. This is fairly standard practice in these places, according to what I've read, and to what the Colonel told me when I first got here. He also said they "haf vays off" not only making you talk but making you believe it after a while. So before my brain gets too well washed, I am saving out some of this paper to keep a true record of what happened, just to keep it straight in my own mind and give me something to fill up the time. The Colonel and the others told me some of the jargon the interrogators like to have included in a confession and I think I get the drift. It behooves the smart prisoner to indulge in a lot of verbal self-flagellation before the authorities decide to flagellate said prisoner in a more literal sense. There's a very strict prose style involved. No problem, though. I'm a good mimic and can write the most incredible bullshit as long as I don't have to keep a straight face.

My name is Viveka Jeng Vanachek. I am currently, albeit reluctantly, a warrant officer in the North American Continental Allied Forces, 5th Cobras, attached to the 9th New Ghurkas at Katmandu. I was captured September 15, 2069, following a plane crash near the Kun Lun Mountains while on a mapping mission. Not that I am this great cartographer, but I do know the section of the file in the program that allows the computer to reconfigure existing maps while scanning the countryside

3

from an eye in the bottom of an XLT-3000 high-altitude reconaissance aircraft. Anyway, I'm trained to use that knowledge, although that flight was the first actual mission I've been on. Right up until the crash, I'd been having the best day since I sold out and joined the military.

Major Tom Siddons was a very nice guy, and I think he must have enjoyed working with me as much as I did with him. I suppose he got as far as he did in the military just by being relatively good-natured and an exceptionally good pilot. Unlike the other pilots, he could express himself not only in words rather than in long strings of symbols and numbers, he could even express himself in words of more than one syllable. He also liked poetry, and I think he liked me chiefly because he was impressed with my ability to recite dirty limericks in Middle English and translate Chinese verses.

I hadn't been in Katmandu very long, but I had already told him over a beer how much I hated the monotony of knowing one section of one file of one program. Each of the other warrant officers in Katmandu with the same rating knew another section of the same file of the same program. If anyone was transferred, died or committed suicide, he or she was replaced by a brand-new specialist in the same section—specialists were never cross-trained, so the left hand never knew what the right hand was doing. It made me feel like a not-very-expensive microchip. Here I had spent almost twenty years, off and on, studying the humanities and what do they do with me? Stick me in computers, because I'd once taken a class to fulfill a math requirement. My art history background and the one drafting class I'd gotten a C in qualified me for the mapping section. I told Siddons all of this and he sipped his beer slowly and nodded in most of the right places.

I forgot all about griping to him until one morning when he strode into the hangar office, decked out in a silver suit with so many pockets he looked like a walking shoe bag.

"Grab a flight suit and your kit, Ms. Vanachek," he told me. "We have us a mission."

It didn't occur to me to bring a weapon. I'd been in what was technically considered a combat zone for the best part of six months and had yet to see more than a fleeting glimpse of an indigenous civilian, much less an enemy.

I gawked through the canopy as we climbed to 19,000 feet, then settled down to the keyboard and punched up my section. Siddons had explained that the plane's computer would do just as mine did back at the hangar, except that while the computer in the hangar usually had to make do with adjusting data, inputting new topographical information from a graphic mock-up to existing map data, this one had a special adapter that translated the terrain passing through an eye in the bottom of the plane into a graphic image and instantly altered the corresponding map data accordingly.

We need map updates frequently because the terrain constantly changes so that it no longer conforms to earlier maps. And while our hangar-bound graphics adjustments are fine for recording the changes our own side wreaks on the local scenery, our allies and our enemies are not so conscientious about informing us of all of their destructive activities. Furthermore, the war precipitates natural disasters—earthquakes, avalanches and floods—that also make unauthorized and, worse, undocumented alterations.

We overflew the pass, into the Tibetan Autonomous Region. The more heavily populated areas had been kept up to date, but the whole central plateau was still a battleground. New valleys are dug daily and mountains of rubble make strategic barriers that need recording.

The problem with fast travel through or over any country, of course, is that it so thoroughly objectifies what you're seeing that you might as well be looking at a holovid screen. The landscape of Tibet, vast plains with mountains pinched up all around the edges like a fancy piecrust, seemed highly improbable to me and I returned to my screen after about fifteen minutes of admiring the view. Siddons wasn't about to let me ignore it, however. His voice crackled into my headphones saying, "Nah, don't bury your nose in your goddamn graphics yet. Take a gander out there at the real world."

I stared down over and through a swath of cloud. The tail end of the cloud snagged on the ragged snow-splattered tops of raw-rock mountains, but beneath it spread a lake covering—I checked my screen—twenty square miles. It cupped the plane's shadow in waters that looked like a huge opal, milky with shots of blue and red fire reflecting off the surface. "Gorgeous," I said. "What makes it look like that?"

"Poison," he said. "Check your coordinates. This is where the PRC dumped its toxic wastes before some of our forces helped India shoo the bastards back behind the border again. The lake's Tibetan name is Lhamo Lhatso. It was sacred. The holy men saw the birthplace of their last spiritual leader in it."

With an innocent-looking twinkle, the lake passed under our starboard wing and away.

"We're going to veer over India way now, toward Karakoram Pass. Between the avalanches the saturation bombing triggered and the floods this spring, the area is useless to ground troops."

"Not to mention a little tricky for the local inhabitants," I said.

"There aren't a hell of a lot of those left, except guerrillas," Siddons said. "And they're tough bozos who play their own game and don't kiss anybody's ass."

"Sounds like you admire them."

"Well, hey, when you have been in the service of our beloved organization as long as I have, little lady, you too may come to admire anybody who doesn't basically sit back and leave all the fighting to *our* troops wearing *their* patches. The Tibetan guerrillas have to be about the only people on the face of the planet fighting anything worse than a hot game of Parcheesi who don't have NACAF allies specifically assigned to them, evening up the odds manpower- and firepower-wise."

"Major, I had no idea you were such an idealist."

"Doesn't mean I won't blow the little buggers off the face of the earth if I get a chance, you understand. There's no need to get sentimental about it. If we blow

up our fellow AmCans who are working for the PRC or
the Soviets, I see no particular reason to extend professional courtesy to anyone else."

I watched the high wild mountains sweep past our
belly and noticed how often the bomb pocks and avalanches showed up on the screen as a major change in
the landscape. I remembered that before NACAF entered the three-sided conflict among China, India and
the USSR, with all the territory in the middle, including
Tibet and the Himalayas, as the battleground, Mount
Everest had been the highest mountain in the world,
instead of the fourth highest. I told the major, "I once
took a course in myth and folklore. Did you know that
in the old days, Tibetans never climbed their mountains
much? They were afraid of disturbing the demons of the
upper air."

"Well, we got those demons good and stirred up
now," he said.

Soon we were past one range and once more flying
over a vast flattened plain, flyspecked with the ruins of
villages and monasteries, the jagged hills bursting from
the plains at times like the work of some giant gopher.
The flatlands were as pocked as the mountains, the earth
blasted and sickly tan, the whole thing treeless. NACAF-
made planes, NACAF pilots or pilot trainers, NACAF
defoliants and NACAF bombs made it all possible.

"Hey, maybe they meant us," I said to Siddons.
"Maybe they foresaw us."

"Who?"

"The old-time Tibetans with those myths. Maybe
we're the upper-air demons."

"Don't let the scenery give you an attitude now,
Warrant Officer. We didn't do all of that by our lone-
some, you know. This little old country's been a stompin'
ground for a good hundred years now for all kinds of
people who didn't like the way the local pope ran
things—"

"Dalai Lama," I corrected, remembering Comparative Religion and Central Asian Soc.

"Yeah, I knew that," he said, grinning back at me.
His grin was as jerky as a stop-motion film clip as the

aircraft hopped from air pocket to air pocket in a series of stomach-churning dips and bumps. I took a deep breath. My digestive tract preferred ground travel.

"Anyhow," he continued, "one thing good ol' NACAF does do is keep it all a clean fight. You got any idea what we need all these updated maps for?"

"Making sure whichever rock the enemy hides behind doesn't move before our side finds it?" I asked.

He ignored that. I think he began to feel at that point he was setting a bad example for a junior officer. So he said, "Nope, so we can still locate any possible covert nuclear devices, no matter when or where they were hidden, and send crews to disarm them. Fighting for Peace, just like the recruitment ad says."

I would like those words to be remembered as the major's last.

The XLT-300 model aircraft we were in flew very far, very fast and changed altitudes with very little difficulty. Ask a pilot why and how, or an engineer. All they paid me to know was that my Ground-Air-Geocartography program, or GAG as it was affectionately called, was specifically designed to keep up with the plane. We covered the plateau within about an hour and when we took the hit, we were on the far side of the Karakoram Pass, headed east for the Kun Lun Mountains. Radio transmission this far from base was damn near impossible, satellites or no satellites. The mountains didn't get in the plane's way, and they didn't get in the satellite's way, but they sure got in Ground Control's way.

The wind was fierce that day, and blew the little jet around as if it was a paper airplane instead of a real one. So when we took the hit, I thought for a moment it was just another gust of wind. Siddons caught on quicker, and I saw his hands fly across the switches and buttons on the control panel.

Suddenly the canopy popped and all those upper-air demons I'd been thinking about roared in and snatched us from the plane. Something kicked me in the rear. My seat bucked like the barroom bull-riding machine they keep in the Cowboy Museum my grandparents once took me to in Tacoma. Except that this bronco didn't come down again but blasted me through the shrieking wind, up and over the body of the jet. I screamed, not of my own accord but as if the scream was ripped from my vocal cords by the velocity of my plunge to earth.

When I haven't had worse things to dream about, I still see the bolus of flame spewing from the underside of the geometrically precise angle of the starboard wing, and I spin to face a maw of rock and snow yawning like a fast forward of some boa's jaws as it swallows prey. I bolt awake as once more the feeling of the automatic chute opening reminds me of being plucked from midair by a giant bird and I try to come fully awake before Siddons's body, twisting beneath a burning chute, plummets past me.

But my actual landing must have been a testimony to the parachute maker's technology. For though I had a bad case of vertical jet lag, my mind skipping a few beats between ejecting and landing, when I came to myself enough to take inventory, everything was intact—no broken bones or missing teeth. Encouraged, I attempted to stand, but the force of the wind complicated matters, billowing my chute against me so it molded to my face, blinding and smothering me within a wave of blue, red and white silon. I yanked the suffocating fabric from my head. The stench of burning metal, wiring and flesh pricked my nostrils before I focused sufficiently to visually locate the smoke.

Pulling off my helmet, I divested myself of the yard or so of chute attached to it and scanned the horizon for a telltale plume, but it was as if I was still swathed in some larger, grayer fabric, a bolt of wildly swirling gauze which obscured everything. The ground on which I stood was indistinguishable from the air in front of me. I was standing on some mountain plateau then, shrouded with cloud. Vaguely, near the toes of my boots, ghostly tufts of grass emerged and vanished as the wind whipped the ground cover. But I saw no sign of Siddons.

I've dreamed of his death since then, so I must have seen it, but I honestly don't remember seeing him die other than in the dreams. Shock probably. I tried calling to Siddons, but my words vanished in the cloud before they were out of my mouth.

As I gathered up the chute and uncoiled it from my legs, the wind whipped away a corner of the mist and I saw four people jogging down a mountain path toward me, carrying rifles. They all appeared to be Asian but I wasn't alarmed by that, since many of our NACAF troops are American or Canadian of Asian origin, or Asian allies. I even felt a small surge of relief, thinking perhaps we were being rescued. The rifles didn't alarm me either. There's a war on. Of course they carried weapons.

I waved a cautious greeting and would have shouted at them but they didn't return my wave. That was when I began to realize that the crash might be more than a temporary setback. Even if these were our people, I didn't know any passwords. They pointed their guns at me and one barked an order. He must have been used to talking over the wind or else the wind had died down because I heard him very well. He was speaking in Han Chinese, of which I had learned a smattering in Intro to Chinese Dialects 101. Before I could try to puzzle out exactly what it was that he'd said, the man who'd spoken pushed me down while a woman rapidly scooped up my helmet, then gathered the rest of my parachute. When she finished, the first man prodded my ribs with his rifle, forcing me to stand again, while a third covered me with another rifle, presumably to make sure I didn't over-power the guy with the gun in my ribs. A fourth man trotted through the mist toward us carrying two winter kits, slightly charred and smoky around the edges. A pair of jump boots dangled from his shoulder by their laces and bounced in rhythm with his gait. Siddons's helmet— I could read his name in black block letters across the front—dangled from one hand.

The woman tied my wrists together. I stared at them stupidly. Right then the tangible evidence that I was a prisoner cut through the shock of the crash. We had had a frightening little lecture about enemy torture in basic training, but the only advice about getting captured I was able to recall was "Don't." Each of us knew so little about each piece of equipment that almost everyone was expendable. People in my grade who got captured fell into the category of "acceptable losses."

We started walking, the wind driving against us. Even the tough silon fibers of my flight suit didn't entirely block the cold. The others were dressed in a motley assortment of winter garb, leather jackets, woolen sweaters and down vests, and wore sheepskin leggings over heavy trousers—the woman's trousers were an incongruously cheerful turquoise and I thought they must have come long ago from a ski apparel shop.

As we descended the first ridge, and out of the fog, the wind subsided to fits of gusting and between gusts I caught a few fragments of the conversation between the guards. Too bad I never got beyond Intro. My knowledge of the Han dialect was limited to numbers, the alphabet, and "Have you seen my luggage?" and "Please tell me where I will find a toilet." None of this erudition was applicable. I regretted the deficiencies in my education more bitterly at that moment than I have on the other recent occasions when I found it did not prepare me for life outside the university. After all, we of the NAC have been at war, or involved in several capacities in a series of wars, with the PRC, among others, for a little over a century now. Why in the hell couldn't my courses have taught me to ask, "When may I see the North American consul?" or to understand when someone said, "We will take this prisoner to Beijing by transport truck, but we must be careful because along the way we will pass her countrymen who could aid her in escaping if they know that she is with us." Something useful. *Why* couldn't I have learned something useful? Even their names would have been helpful. I hate groups, especially ones in which I don't know anyone.

My affiliation was announced to my captors by the patch on my flight suit. The New Ghurkas are, of course, allied with the Indians. We are not currently allied with the PRC. The PRC is not currently allied with the USSR. I now understand the black market trade in patches among NACAF troops. A Chinese dragon patch would have been a big help just then, instead of my cobra insignia.

These people wore no patches, which was, as Grandpa Ananda might say, good news and bad news. The good news was that they were probably irregular foot soldiers for the PRC rather than freelance body-looters looking for equipment to sell on the black market. The distinction was slight, true, but the guerrillas did have some sort of military structure and purpose, whereas the body-looters were the entrepreneurs of the war. The bad news was, these people did *not* wear a cobra and had guns pointed at me so they weren't on my side and since they had military objectives, I could expect to be interrogated (read "tortured") instead of killed outright. Maybe, I thought optimistically, they were body-looters but for the time being preferred my equipment on the hoof, allowing me to save them the trouble of carrying my gear.

Which was hardly reassuring because I was still bruised and stiff and shocky and slowed the party down. Every so often the guard in back of me would give me a jab in the spine with the rifle or a little kick of en-couragement, but such incentives did not improve my speed since I usually fell down and had to be hauled back onto my feet again. The air was thin and cold, needling my hands and face even when the wind wasn't flogging me, and each fresh gust ripped the fragile veil of oxygen away from my nose and lips before I could draw a breath.

By the time we stopped I was half crawling, my lungs about to burst. My feet and legs hurt clear up to my armpits and my throat ached from screaming against the wind and the effort of breathing.

I sank onto the rocky path we'd been climbing and went blind for a few moments while I tried to catch my breath. My ears roared constantly and when my eyes refocused, I saw my captors' mouths moving but I couldn't hear the words. The woman in the loud ski pants pointed down over the edge of the cliff the path skirted. A couple of hundred yards below lay the smoldering wreckage of the plane. Farther down, hidden by the haze and by a tumble of boulders, a bubble of parachute

swelled and collapsed, swelled and collapsed, one blackened edge fluttering in the wind.

I said a mental prayer for Siddons, including in my
entreaties all regional and international deities, from Je-
hovah, Jesus, and the Hindu bunch to the Collective
Unconscious and the upper-air demons, and finally the
soldier's God, who could not have been the same one
who lived in clean white churches and fancy cathedrals
and synagogues back in the NAC unless He was schiz-
ophrenic. The God out here presided over battlefields
and bombers and His name was apparently Damn.

The woman gave me another shove and I lumbered
to my feet, no easy task with bound hands on a steep
incline.

When we finally stopped climbing I hoped the worst
was over, but the descent was no better. Though the
mountains shielded us from the wind on the downhill
side, the trail was slippery and small rock slides hailed
upon our heads and boobytrapped the footing. My legs
and toes cramped constantly and I was so exhausted that
when we reached the ruined village at dusk I was more
hopeful that we would finally rest than I was fearful that
the rest, for me, might be a permanent one.

From a distance the roofless stone walls of the
bombed-out huts looked odd, deep and hollow, but as
we drew nearer I saw that black tents were pitched inside
the shells of the houses, the walls offering a form of
camouflage as well as extra protection from the wind.

Two people tended half an oil drum set over an open
fire. Steam rose cozily from the oil drum. Soon one of
the people ducked into the doorway of the nearest ruin,
then reemerged to signal us toward it.

My guards, not superhuman after all, had for the
last leg of the trip left me alone so that they too could
concentrate on walking without falling, but now they
rallied enough to manhandle me through the doorway
of the ruined house and into the tent.

A man who looked to be about fifty, his arm tightly
bandaged to his side with a strip of parachute silon, sat
on the floor in the midst of a clutch of snotty-nosed

children. A Coleman lantern hanging from the central mast of the tent provided a circle of urine-colored light in the middle of the gloom, but in the deep shadows around the edges, something moved and I caught the glitter of a dark eye in a half-glimpsed web of dusky wrinkles and a wisp of white hair.

The man spoke a sharp word and the children retreated to one side of the tent and stared solemnly at me.

Cute. The smallest one wrung the sides of her long coat in her little fists so it showed she wore not even a diaper underneath. Very cute, but standing back in the shadows like that, dutifully solemn and quiet but with their eyes shining with the excitement of having a strange creature like me among them, the children reminded me less of cherubs and more of wolf cubs waiting for dinner.

Remembering manners from my social anthropology texts and numerous old films of Pearl Buck books, I bowed and mumbled the Han greeting that meant something like "How kind of you to let me come."

The man flicked his eyes toward my guards, who pushed me to my knees and plopped crosslegged down beside me, rifles in my ribs. I wondered if they were going to execute me inside, in front of the children.

Nothing more ominous than supper occurred, however, and a rather good supper at that. Unless I'm mistaken, it was rice made into a stew with various packages of freeze-dried trail food.

When we finished the man amazingly offered me a cigarette. I was puzzled for a moment, thinking that they surely intended to finish me off in some quicker fashion than that, and then recalled that in some parts of the world, smoking was still considered a relaxing amenity. I refused with another very weary bow. For someone so imperiled I was having a hell of a time staying awake.

The man asked me a question in Han, but it was too rapid for me. In Mandarin, of which I knew a great deal more since there were more language programs available in that dialect, I carefully replied that I did not understand, please go slower, I spoke only a little Han.

The man glowered and the ancient in the corner grumbled a word to him, at which he flipped his hand at the guards who dragged me to my feet again and out to one of the few intact houses—or maybe it was an animal shed. There they deposited me. A tent would have made a more luxurious accommodation, for my little prison was riddled with chinks and drafts and stank faintly of manure. Someone threw in a blanket and I lay down.

For about five seconds I worried about all those stories of desirable AmCan women being raped by horny Asian men, but then the wind whistled through the nearest crack in the wall and I wrapped the blanket around me and decided that if someone did attack me I'd try to get him to stay the night just for the sake of warmth.

Each time exhaustion carried me over the precipice of fear into sleep, the wind sliced up my spine. Groggily, I'd pull the blanket tighter, try to squirm the cramps out of wherever they were gripping me and clutch my shivering body back into a tight fetal fist.

I was dreaming I was late for class and had to parachute down to Kane Hall to avoid flunking out when I looked up and saw my parachute was on fire. I sat up and opened my eyes to the glare of a flashlight.

"Well, I'll be damned," a deep male voice with a reassuring redneck drawl said. Abruptly, somebody plopped down hard next to me, almost on top of me, and the light withdrew. "Sorry about that, sweetheart. Guess you probably weren't expectin' company."

"No, but I'm glad to see you," I said. "In a manner of speaking, that is, because I can't see you and of course I'm sorry they caught you but it's good to hear another American voice."

"What outfit you with, sugar? What's your name?" he asked, his drawl dripping molasses in my ear as he pulled my shoulders, blanket and all, against his chest, so, as I thought, he could speak without being overheard by the guard.

"Viv Vanachek—Viveka actually, family name— from Bellingham, Washington. I'm a computer specialist in geocartography. We were just flying around updating our topodata when we were hit. What's your name? How did you get captured?"

"Call me Buzz, Viv. I'm with recon and intelligence, which is how I got here. Golly damn, baby, I'm sorry to see you in this kind of fix." He petted my hair with his hand. He smelled like a goat, or anyhow, as sour and strong as goats are reported to smell (I've never met one of the beasts myself) but he felt great. His hands were strong and a little rough and surprisingly not too cold, his breath stirring my hair and warming my cheek.

I offered him some blanket since it didn't look like they were going to throw him one of his own. He remarked then that I seemed to be the prize catch of the day and snuggled beneath the blanket, thought my hands were too cold and tucked them into his shirt. One thing led to another. It's a scientific fact that danger raises hormone levels and increases erotic responsiveness. It's also my personal scientific theory that a woman who expects to be shot at any moment is somewhat less worried than usual about little things like disease and pregnancy and is inclined to gather her rosebuds (or whatever) while she may. I developed the theory on the spot, thinking we were in the same situation and that sharing warmth and comfort on what might be our last night on earth seemed the only sane alternative. When we were finally both comfortable and nicely warmed up, he asked, joking (I thought he had to be joking), "How did a nice girl like you end up in a place like this?"

"The usual way, I guess," I said, and turned the question back on him, but he wasn't having any. He was the first guy I'd ever been around who, given the opportunity to talk about himself, preferred to hear about me. So I told him.

I explained how since my mother died and my grandparents' timber farm had been sold to a lumber company, I had been working on my undergraduate degree off and on for fifteen years, living on what small income was left from the sale of the farm after our debts and taxes were paid, until finally that too was taxed away,

then doing little odd jobs for crummy money to stay alive
and get tuition.

"Why didn't you just bite the bullet and finish up,
get your degree and get a job instead of coming into the
army?" he asked.

I asked him how long since he'd been in the academic system NAC-side and he allowed that it had been
at least fifteen years and even then, he wasn't much of
a college man.

"Things have changed some," I said. "It used to be
that a graduate degree was a pretty reasonable goal if
you made the grades, kept at it, and were able to spend
enough money on books and tuition to house an average
family. There used to be scholarships and grants and my
mother said once there were even government loans.
But—well, why did you join the army? Let me guess.
You couldn't find a job, right? Well, neither can anybody
else with what used to be an okay education. My poly
sci prof said NACAF was formed partly to overcome that
problem. The military is absorbing the excess population."

"I've been over here a long time," he said. "I'd like
to know how your professor has that figured."

"Simple. The country was going to hell faster every
year and there wasn't enough for anybody, not even the
privileged. Too many people, not enough jobs or resources, a weak economy, and so many well-educated
people who stayed in school to stay out of the lousy job
market that there was even more discontent than normal.
Uneducated people may resent the system but know
their place. Educated people are harder to handle. Of
course, these days it takes quite a bit of education just
to get by, so according to my prof the government was
responsible for raising tuitions for grad degrees to uphold
the Jeffersonian principles on which democratic society
was founded—his very words—meaning no more wast-
ing opportunity on the riffraff. So nowdays only the rich
can get the grad degrees needed to get richer—or even
get by. It takes a Ph.D. in transportation engineering to
drive a truck and a master's in restaurant management

to work in a fast-food joint. I have three undergrad degrees, but I not only can't afford to get a graduate degree, I am no longer qualified to do the two-bit jobs people like me used to be able to get to earn the money to get the degree it now takes to be hired for one of those same dumb jobs. So there I was, and it was my forty-second birthday, right?"

"You'd never know it," he said, pulling the blanket tighter and lighting up a smoke. I decided if he was so disadvantaged he'd had to spend fifteen years in the military he probably needed to smoke, so even though it made me cough when I was already having a tough time breathing I didn't object.

"Thanks, but *I* know it. And having collected my third degree and my one hundred and seventh thanks-for-considering-our-firm-but-no-thanks from the sanitation contractors, I took my tuition money for next semester, went to this place I know called Sammy's Bar, and got blotto.

"Sammy's a friend of mine, or I thought she was anyway. She'd been the teaching assistant for my psych class while she was in grad school, before she got her doctorate and started her own place with a no-interest loan from her folks—you'll love this, Buzz. Most bartenders and tavern owners I know are like Sammy now; they all have doctorates in psychology, at least a master's in business admin and a black belt in two or more martial arts as well as their mixologist certificates. She started telling me that my problem was I was having an identity crisis and I said it was more like a midlife crisis and I was just realizing it had taken me half my life to get nowhere. She thought I was touching her for a job, and tried to let me off easy with that stuff about being too smart and not having the right interests and how pretty soon I would leave for something better. Well, it's true, really. I've always been interested in history, language, literature, philosophy and so on—you know, humanities stuff. But there's no jobs in it. Anywhere. Unless you don't need a job. I told her if I could leave for something better I'd be long gone."

"So she says, 'If not a career, why not a merger—

you know, with a man. You're bright, perceptive, and very capable . . .' But, well, Buzz, no aspersions on your taste or anything, but back home everyone is so perfect now. There's all this money from the war economy and everyone, men and women both, who's able to stay home, seems to be able to afford fancy diets and cosmetic surgery to correct every physical aberration. I mean, not that I want to look like everyone else, but who wants to look worse just because you look like what used to be normal? And don't think nobody notices. They do. So Sammy allowed that maybe I should save a little to get contacts to make my hazel eyes a more fashionable green, a dye job to take the curl out of my hair and make this kind of dishwater brown color more like chestnut or auburn or maybe a pale ash, a diet for the old hipline and at least a cheekbone sculpt and a pinch off the schnoz because, as she said, a merger requires that you live up to the senior partner's physical image and obviously in my present state I would have to go in as a junior partner. And I said, sure, but a surgeon also requires you to pay and that was part of my problem. Besides, I'm almost past childbearing age. The women in my family seem to wait until the last possible minute to spawn. My grandma had my mother when she was forty-two and my mother had me when *she* was forty-two and now I'm almost forty-three. So I told her I'm overqualified to be nonthreatening and underqualified to be a corporate asset to anybody and I shoved another bill at her and had another tequila. I think she was watering them by then, so I skipped the salt and lemon. I was blathering on about the damn busybody pro-lifers from the nineties that my mom used to blather on about when *she* got drunk and what kind of a life did they think we excess populace were going to have anyway and Sam was telling me what I was saying was nothing but a sociological self-pitying cop-out and there were all kinds of things someone like me could do when I saw that poster. You know, the NACAF recruiting poster of the couple in the snappy dress dove grays?"

"Don't think I've seen it," he said, sounding a little impatient and taking another long drag.

"The woman looks a little like a Native American with Scandinavian genes and the man looks a little Hispanic but raised for generations on the West Coast—you know the type, blond and tall and with deep, natural noncarcinogenic tans? They looked so sincere with those blue eyes and outstretched hands following you around the room—well, hell. I was drunk. I knew all about the shanghai stations—"

"The what?"

"You *have* been over here for a long time. The twenty-four-hour recruiting stations NACAF has. Promise you anything but give you a one-way ticket to some Third World war. But boy, right then, they looked like they had it made. They had a job and I wanted one. I was sick of farting around with college and poverty. So I asked Sam did she think I could pass the physical and damned if she didn't say 'sure' and slip on that cute little gaucho-hat that goes with the dress grays.

" 'Did I tell you,' she asks casually, 'that I'm working part time as a recruiter? Just sign right here, Viv,' she says. 'And don't worry, hon. NACAF will have you in shape and teach you a trade in no time.' The manipulative, self-serving, upper-class bitch."

"Now, cheer up, baby doll. At least she didn't lie to you. You got a job, you said, and maybe it'll get you out of this. Did you think about that? Like, did your mapping expedition maybe tell you anything that might help with escape? Did you find out where these people might have other guerrilla camps or where the nearest Cobra support group is?"

His patting my shoulder and his persuasive voice made me realize what a tangent of self-pity I'd been on and I felt vaguely embarrassed. "I wasn't really looking for that kind of thing," I admitted, and explained what Siddons had told me about looking for bombs and so on. He seemed more interested in that than he had in any of the personal stuff I'd told him.

"Nukes, huh? Any other military objectives?"

"Knowing the terrain is a military objective, isn't it?" I asked, and scooted slightly back from him, so the smoke wouldn't blow right into my face. He puffed silently for a few moments and I asked, "Do you suppose they'll kill us?"

"Hard telling," he said. "Look, you sure there wasn't anything special y'all were lookin' for?"

I shrugged. "This was my first time up. Sorry I didn't learn more."

"Me too. But it was pretty good for starters." He stubbed out his cigarette and kissed me on the forehead, then swept the blanket aside, pulled up his pants, and leaned over to knock on the door. It opened and the guard quite courteously held it for him, then saluted as he brushed past her. "Sleep tight, sugar," he called back in to me.

I didn't feel the full weight of my stupidity until the next morning. The shock of the crash, the long airless hike, the anxiety and the exhaustion took over and it wasn't until I woke that I realized I had spilled anything anybody wanted to know about my identity, my attitudes, my occupational specialty and my mission without so much as anyone having to say "please," much less sticking burning bamboo splinters under my fingernails. Maybe I was wrong about Buzz. I thought the withdrawal I felt from him was just because of the premature intimacy or maybe because a man like him, who had been in the field by his own admission for fifteen years and, the way things now stood, could never expect to go home again, had little sympathy for the crisis I had faced at making a choice he'd made years before.

But then I remembered the guard's attitude and when I was taken into the sling-armed man's tent the next morning, I knew the salute had been no hallucination. There sat my male Mata Hari grinning pleasantly at me over a cup of something steamy, his dragon patch in full view on the pocket of his down vest.

"Good mornin', Warrant Officer Vanachek, sugar," he said. "I heard tell you gals from the enemy camp could be real nice and I'm here to tell you . . ."

I glared at him and he grinned wider.

"That's a low blow," I said. I wished I could address him by his rank but he wasn't wearing any. I was pretty sure the patch was purely for my benefit. "I heard tell you guys in the dragon horde aren't gentlemen about respecting a girl in the morning either and I'm here to tell *you*—"

"All's fair in love and war, sugar. I try to get a little of both if possible."

I tried to simmer down. After all, for somebody with as much training as I'd had, I hadn't been especially analytical about the situation of the previous night. And it was a pretty painless interrogation, if humiliating in retrospect. "So okay," I said. "Now that you've had your wicked way with me, what happens? Are you going to shoot me or what?"

"That's up to the allies, sugar. I can only make recommendations." He leaned back on one arm and flipped his cigarette toward his top lip with his bottom lip. I wished it would burn his nose or flip ash in his eye. In broad daylight he looked like the kind of man you might have found in a well-appointed prison yard in my grandparents' day—round-cheeked and jowly with limp, thinnish hair and small sly eyes of indiscriminate color under low-slung eyebrows. He was much more attractive in the dark, but it seemed an inopportune time to discuss that.

"Look," I said, "why can't I just switch services?"

" 'Cause you're a snake, baby, not a dragon," he said as if that explained away the fact that we both drew our pay from the same government. I began to realize that this man might possibly be crazy enough to think the whole NACAF military juggling act was not only sane and reasonable, but some kind of righteous cause.

Nuts as it was, in previous wars and civilian atrocities, people had dehumanized each other by calling one another Gooks or Redskins, Japs, Krauts, Kikes, Niggers, even Yanks and Rebs. This guy was telling me I didn't matter to him, despite all I'd told him that should have impressed on him what a superior-type individual I was, because my patch had a cobra instead of a dragon. "See, baby, you're different from us. Trained different, hang with different people, conduct yourselves different . . ." He let that trail off with an insolent glance up and down my flight suit. "If the People's Republic of China was to forgive you for the crimes you've committed against them on behalf of the warmongering Indians, you'd have to improve a whole bunch."

I wished I had something to throw at him. The man with the injured arm looked on as if willing himself to speak English and the raptor eyes of the old person in the corner took in every change of expression. I was embarrassed to be bandying words with this lowlife countryman of mine who had so little regard for any of us, who had taken advantage of my trust and misfortune to create a recreational opportunity for himself while betraying me and our common heritage.

Okay, so maybe the ally these earnest-looking folks had drawn for themselves might have been effective this time, with a green recruit like myself, but I thought he'd be just as treacherous with them as with me given half a chance. I wished I had enough knowledge of Han to tell them so. On the other hand, I had said entirely too much as it was. I stared at my boot hoping that the heat in my face would be attributed to windburn.

The ancient in the corner asked something which the injured man repeated to Buzz. Buzz said nothing to me but nodded to the guard, who grabbed my arm and marched me back to my makeshift cell.

I told him to wait a goddamn minute but the guard raised his rifle butt in the vicinity of my left ear so I ducked back into my cell and sat brooding, feeling scared and ridiculous at the same time but mostly pissed off not only at Buzz but at myself. I had volunteered information that usually had to be pried out of better soldiers with torture. I had freely relinquished any possible bargaining chips. I did not even understand why what I had been doing would be of any special interest to the enemy. Surely, since the PRC got comparable troops and equipment from the NACAF to that allotted the Indians, anything I could tell them about my job or equipment was redundant?

I spent the best part of the day turning this over in my mind, trying to convince myself that since I had been so cooperative and was so strategically useless they'd probably just let me go and the worst that could happen was I'd die of exposure.

But good ol' Buzz let himself in that evening, without the subterfuge, this time, of having another jailer admit him.

"What in the hell do you want?" I asked. "I told you everything already."

"Just saying good night, honeybuns. Not often I run across a friendly girl like you who still smells and feels good, even if you are a little long in the tooth . . ."

"Get the fuck out of here!"

"Or what? You'll scream? They'd enjoy that, out there. I didn't bring my pistol along but that fellow at the door's got one."

This time his goaty stench and my aversion to him were so strong I threw up. But he just avoided my head and was, if a lot rougher, at least mercifully quicker than the last time.

Early A.M.
DAY 2

When he'd gone I huddled shaking and sore in the blanket and tried to remember that rape is an act of aggression as surely as beating or torture, that it was practiced against men too. At one time anyone on the streets was fair game to be raped, mugged and/or killed by drug-crazed gangs of ruffians. That was before NACAF was formed and the drug-crazed ruffians were absorbed by the military.

Sometimes the underground newspapers my grandparents received contained atrocity stories of the nastinesses worked by these new "recruits," but the military countered any stories that reached broader distribution by reassuring people that discipline was being established. Of course, the truth was, most of the taxpayers didn't mind what happened abroad and were happy to allow the army to export so many of the problems that for many years kept everyone confined by rigid curfews and surveillance.

I was old enough that I'd received training since grade school about sexual abuse and violence. The first time I was asked to do a school report in third grade on how and who to tell if someone was trying to touch me inappropriately, my grandmother took one look at the little picture book, shook her head, and said to Grandad, "Holy shit, Ananda, will you look at this? Remember how it was when we were little kids and our folks were embarrassed to have to tell us the fairy tale about the birds and the bees when we hit puberty? I guess you got to give the pervs credit for promoting sex education at least."

In high school I'd learned all that stuff about how rape was a function of the rage of the perpetrator and should not be taken personally by the victim. I could believe that, because the quick and impersonal way the creep had dumped into me had more in common with the way someone would use a toilet than the way someone would make love with another person whose humanity he acknowledged. I used a corner of the blanket to wipe the tears from my eyes, the puke from my mouth and the semen, corrosive to me as acid, from my skin.

The wind howled in from a hundred holes and I felt as if I were in a magician's trick cabinet and the trick had gone wrong so the daggers were all piercing me. My clothes were about as much shelter from the cold as a particularly rotten piece of Swiss cheese. My only consolation through all this was that now I knew that even if I had not been so stupid as to fall for good ol' Buzz's subterfuge the night before, it wouldn't have made much difference.

Just as I was starting to turn the last thought into an indictment that said that by joining the military I had actually asked to be mistreated and in some fashion deserved what happened to me, plane crash, Siddons's death, capture, rape and all, the door swung open again.

The slight human figure outlined by the night was momentarily erased as the door closed behind it. A match flared quickly and dropped, then a light not much brighter than the match flame ignited with the smell of burning fat and a lot of rancid smoke. A yak butter lamp. The words from an anthropology text sprang into the disorder of my mind and connected with the glowing object. The text explaining what a yak was would probably have occurred to me next except that the figure chose that moment to speak. "Foolish woman. What is the matter with you, a person your age, who should be at home with your grandchildren instead of helping oppress my people?"

The voice spoke in raspy German, oddly accented, but it sounded female to me and that reassured me. "Do you understand me?" she demanded like an impatient instructor. I nodded slowly, wondering what in the hell was going on.

"Do you always have your prisoners raped to soften them up before you interrogate them?" I demanded in German that emerged harsher than hers only because my voice was stronger and the anger and hysteria I was fighting down made it hard to control the volume.

Oddly, she continued in French, except for one or two unrecognizable words which I thought might be Chinese or possibly, and it only crossed my mind because of the yak butter lamp, ethnic Tibetan. "What has happened to you is disgraceful but the *philing* is not within my control. You would have been killed rather than brought here except that we needed to know how you came to be in the area."

"I told whatsisname that," I said in plain English. "I help computers make maps. I know which buttons to push but I don't know how it works. You probably have somebody on your side who can do the same thing and doesn't know how it works either. They don't tell us. To figure it out you'd need all the equipment and maybe thirty people who know different parts of the program. No matter what you or that sonofabitch do to me, I can't tell you any more because I don't *know* any more."

"En français, s'il vous plaît," she said, and waited

while I repeated myself in French before she switched to Mandarin. "I wish to know something else. You tried to speak Chinese to Kunga yesterday. The *phling* soldier says that you have been highly educated."

As I suspected, that phase of our postcoital chat had not meant he was taking me home to mother. Unless this was mother. Nah. "For someone who is not very bright, I suppose I am," I admitted, which translated very well into Mandarin since there were all sorts of self-effacing phrases inherent in the expression of an ancient Confucian culture.

"And your education is in which subjects?"

"Things you can't earn a living at mostly."

"Be specific, please."

"World anthropology, sociocultural, four semesters, comparative religion, philosophy, psychology, languages—I like languages—look, I'd have sent for transcripts if I'd known I was going to need them. I was a student for a long time. My degrees are in history, psychology, and general humanities."

"Including scientific and military studies?" she asked, in Russian this time.

Maybe they thought I had learned a lot about NACAF military theory and practice and some of the technological applications beyond my own job. If they thought that, they naturally would want to keep me around. Perhaps with a little judicious fabrication I might have some bargaining chips left after all.

"Military history and theory, political science, some economics," I answered her cautiously in Russian, trying not to sound as if I was telling everything I knew. In fact, other than what I admitted, I had studied only the smattering of biology and basic physics plus the minimal math requirements necessary to support the rest of my curriculum.

The lamp was lowered, the flame directly across from my eyes, dazzling them, and I felt that my face was being closely scrutinized for—what? Honesty? Then, the lamp was raised, the woman pried the door open a crack before the wind pulled it from her hand and banged it open against the side of the shed. The lamp burst into oxygen-fed brilliance for a moment. I caught a glimpse of silvery hair above bright eyes, a hand translucent with age and delicately veined futilely shielding the flame that was almost immediately extinguished by the gale.

A short time later a plastic bottle of water and a sliver of soap were thrown into the shed. I washed, uncovering small portions of my anatomy at a time, rubbing an area clean with one corner of the blanket, drying with another, trying to protect myself against the relentless cold.

The room was so small I could not even pace for warmth, so I sat fully dressed, huddled in the dry parts of my blanket, hearing only the wind and hoping to hear nothing and no one else. I did not want to think about Buzz, or try to figure out which of the nasty little fantasies he'd confided during his last session with me were threats and which were plans.

Instead, I concentrated on the odd encounter with the old woman. The memory of it became surrealistic within a few moments of her departure and I would have thought I'd only dreamed of her but for the soap and water, which surely had arrived at her instigation, and provided proof that she was no dream or hallucination. I was pretty sure she was the same bundled figure I'd glimpsed in the shadows of the command tent. She must be someone's grandmother, I thought, since she was scolding me about staying home with grandchildren, but whatever relation she bore to these people she had the air of one who wielded considerable authority. She was Tibetan, I felt sure from her choice of words and the lamp, or maybe a Sino-Tibetan crossbreed. There were so few pure Tibetans left in this area anymore. The Tibetan diaspora of the 1950s and '60s and the subsequent colonization of Tibet by the PRC had taken care of that. And the people here weren't wearing Chinese uniforms, even though Buzz sported the dragon patch. Nor was it particularly significant that my captors spoke Chinese. The Tibetan language had been forbidden within Tibet for almost eighty years. And this woman had called the man with the bandaged arm Kunga—that didn't sound Chinese to me. Still, the woman was multilingual, and could have been from anywhere, though I wondered if it was significant that she had addressed me in both Chinese and Russian but not in any of the Indian dialects.

Much later I was startled from a fitful sleep by the scraping of the door. This time the sound was oddly distinct and loud, and I heard the creak of the hinges, the groan of the wood. The whining wind had blown itself out, and the air was oddly silent without it except for a distant noise like the rapid throb of a giant's heart, which gradually grew louder.

From the doorway a man's voice issued a sharp command in Chinese—an expression I recognized from the hike from the plane wreck, which seemed to mean something like "come along" or "hurry up." I tried to rise from a crosslegged position but my hands were still bound and my foot overturned the bathwater. Small impatient hands tugged me to my feet and shoved me out the door.

This time I automatically resisted being manhandled. Being dragged out of my cell in the middle of the night after the interrogation must have meant I'd flunked. I was going to be shot, I knew it, and I looked all around the encampment for the firing squad. Instead, everyone but the guard who shoved me in front of him ignored me, staring heavenward.

Something was wrong with the sky. The wind had blown holes in the night, allowing rays of light to escape through the torn fabric of darkness, forming a stark alliance with the pale peaks corrugating the horizon. The holes were only the stars, of course, and a snowball of a moon shining on the mountains that had been previously obscured by the storm, but I thought if I was going to die, it was a wonderful last glimpse of earth to carry with me into oblivion.

"Don't make 'em like that back in Bellingham, do they, sugar?" Buzz said from behind me. I stepped closer to my guard but didn't take my eyes off the sky, even to avoid good ol' Buzz. At least he wasn't lying this time. Even on the clearest night the mountains at home, stripmined and tunneled, denuded of timber and crisscrossed with ski runs and superhighways, were blanketed with a thick miasma from the cities far too impenetrable to permit a view like this. Grandma had some very old books with pictures in them from years ago, when the Cascades and Olympics resembled what I saw before me now, but this was more vast and beautiful than anything that could be contained on paper.

Buzz smirked over his cigarette at me. "Hell, it's so fuckin' romantic I'm sorry you're not going to be around a little longer so we could ignore it together."

Self-interest fought with revulsion and won, and I tried to ask him where exactly I was to be taken, but then the chopper that had sounded like a giant heart set down, its prop wash flattening the grass. As soon as the skis touched the ground, people began hauling boxes out to stack inside the aircraft while others hurried back into the tents to bring forth more boxes, which they also loaded.

The helicopter was one of the old kind, one of the first high-altitude types used, the kind with four blades rather than the top jet the sleek new models used. The deafening thud of its blades drowned out any answer Buzz might have made to my question, which was probably just as well.

A figure bundled in a thick hooded coat sprinted, head bent against the wind, toward the helicopter. The guard held my arm until the figure passed me, wisps of white hair flagging around the hood, sharp dark eyes acknowledging me briefly before she sprang up into the body of the bird and, holding on to the hanging strap beside the door, extended a hand to me. I scrambled awkwardly aboard after her, relief that I wasn't to be shot immediately making my heart pound as loud as the rotor blades. A few more boxes followed me, then the engine noise altered in pitch, the throb deepened, and we were airborne.

For a long time the old woman and I did not speak to each other, which I found reassuring. Apparently she was not going to interrogate me again while we flew and have me thrown out if she didn't like my answers. I remembered that in other wars, in other places, such

things had happened. I wondered how. We couldn't have
heard each other over the noise of the chopper anyway.
Besides, there were just the two of us and the pilot. He
had to fly the chopper and she was so much smaller and
older than I that I was pretty sure she would have
brought help if she meant to try physical force on me. I
could outmatch her by weight alone, even with my hands
bound.

She merely sat impassively on one of the boxes, her
mittened hands tucked into the folds of her sleeves, her
eyes staring steadily out at the mountains. From where
I sat her black irises were nothing but flat mirrored sur-
faces filled only with the reflection of the stars and moon.
I was happy to avert my own eyes from that expression-
less starry stare and, trying to ignore the circumstances
of the excursion, allowed myself to sightsee.

Maybe I'm not the greatest mapmaker in the world
without the help of a computer, but I wanted to get an
idea of the general lay of the land in case an opportunity
to escape presented itself. One thing I noticed, leaving
the camp, was that although three separate paths spun
from the hub of the village, none of them traveled in the
northeasterly direction taken by the helicopter. The
country we flew over was so high and rugged, other
routes would naturally be more favored for land travel.

We flew as a bird might, or perhaps more like a
bug, dwarfed by sheer vertical acreage, glacial fields
ditched with black crevasses, snow scalloping the slopes
in disorderly swoops like bunting three days after the
parade is over. Mountains soared above us and plunged
into abysses below our skis. Icy black lakes appeared
suddenly on the tops of ridges, or sparkled in deep valleys. Crystallized waterfalls gushed silently from hidden
streams, dripping like diamonds on the bosom of some
society matron.

The Kun Luns are not as high as the Himalayas, but
I haven't been on such intimate terms with the Himalayas. The helicopter was a much slower device than the
XLT-3000, and less powerful. The slower, heavier aircraft bobbed with the air currents, the rupple of the

blades breaking the starlight into a flickering strobe, distorting the chopper's ungainly shadow as it fell across the snow fields.

Spectacle after breathtaking spectacle enveloped us. Gradually the stars and moon dimmed and the navy of the sky grayed before blooming with rose from the tips of the peaks up, until the whole sky, the ridges and fields, the pleats and peaks of snow surrounding and high above us were bathed in amber, coral, and garnet light. The chopper banked for a turn and the glory of the mountains around us was abruptly eclipsed by a splendid cone, which would have soared far above the highest peak except that its tip had been scooped out and had tumbled down its leeward side. The sun crested in the middle of the scoop, and the mountain caught fire, ruby and garnet, gold, carnelian and pearly pink, looming ever higher above us, then disappearing as the pilot lowered the chopper into a ravine between two nearer ridges.

Setting her down gently, the pilot killed the engine and within moments the helicopter was surrounded by people in greasy sheepskin coats, who began unloading the boxes. I jumped unaided to the ground, landing on my knees in snow about six inches deep. One of the men reached up to assist the old woman, and she jumped lightly down beside me.

A man who seemed to issue from the side of the mountain plowed forward through the snow. He and the old woman exchanged remarks in an intense but unhurried fashion. They frequently bobbed their heads in my direction. Sometimes he sounded accusing while she appeared to defend; other times he was on the defensive. Finally, he paused for breath long enough for her to speak to him at some length in a surprisingly affectionate tone, and he reluctantly nodded. She turned back to me and in English said, "Come. We'll eat while they finish unloading."

She led me through the snow, some of it drifted waist high against the face of the cliff, to a cave half concealed by a rocky outcropping. Another of the butter lamps, nearly empty, suffused the center of the dark room with a soft glow. She poured liquid from a plastic

jug into two disposable hotcups and dropped something
into one of them—a battery-powered heating coil such
as campers used. She sipped the liquid while the second
cup was warming. I plucked the coil out when the solid
matter in the cup liquefied, although there was still a
congealed skim on the top that failed to blend in. The
drink was a hypertensive's nightmare—greasy and salty
both, in some sort of fluid that gave you an excuse to
imbibe the salt and grease. It smelled vile too but it
warmed the insides and warmth was welcome; even the
meager warmth from the cup between my hands felt
good.

"What is this?" I asked.

"Butter tea," she said in English. "Of course, the
butter is now an artificial product manufactured in Beijing, and is not as good as the butter we took from the
yaks before the soldiers destroyed most of the herds for
sport."

"I had some Comanche ancestors with the same
problem," I said. "Only it was buffalo, not yaks. I don't
suppose railroads were involved in the destruction of
your yaks, were they?"

"No, but the building of the roads didn't help. Of
course, your people with their big weapons have destroyed those roads too. Along with our forests and wild-
life and large numbers of our countrymen."

"It's no more than we do for anybody," I said flip-
pantly. Instead of yelling at me or threatening me, she
fixed me with that raptor gaze and allowed herself a slight
smile.

"You're a cynical woman, Miss Vanachek."

"These are cynical times, ma'am," I said. "But if
you think about it, NACAF hasn't done all the damage
here. We've been more or less Johnny-come-latelies. I
wouldn't be one to point any fingers or anything, but
the PRC did a good job of dismantling this country a
long time ago, if you want to take credit where credit is
due. And NACAF is not at all selective about who we
reinforce: we'll do it for anybody, and meanwhile we just
try to keep everybody's buried nukes from detonating."
I wanted to add something witty about how some of our

people even got so into their roles as allies of their adopted sides that they even raped some of our other people on opposite sides, but I couldn't frame the sentence and besides, I was afraid I might have used up her sense of humor.

Her eyes locked on mine. "Surely, you realize that your NACAF and the other major powers still produce weapons of massive destructive capability. They only disarm older weapons planted in earlier times and those owned by smaller countries."

I shrugged and tried to look away. I am not a missile scientist after all. It isn't my fault what NACAF does, or what they lie about doing. I just make my little maps. But the woman's eyes would not let mine drop and I didn't dare look away. She had the literal, if somewhat melodramatic-sounding, power of life and death over me. Looking at her, trying to find some less—you should pardon the expression—explosive direction for the conversation to take, I became aware that the cave was growing brighter, daylight from the entrance joining the lamp flame to wash the interior a paler gray. The woman's coat, I now saw, was standard issue Chinese infantry, and under the hood she wore a sheepskin hat. The impression of great age she had given in the guerrilla camp seemed largely to be a product of shadow and wind. Her face was weathered and lined, it was true, but in the snow-filtered light of the cave the wrinkles appeared shallower, the deepest being the crow's-feet sometimes called "laugh lines" at the corners of her eyes. Her high-boned cheeks were plump and rosy and the white wisps of hair that framed her face merely frosted the front and threaded through a predominantly glossy black bob. She may have been as much as thirty years my senior, but perhaps less, for some of her aged appearance—the hair thin at the top, the brown, crooked teeth, two of which were rimmed in little squares of gold—seemed to be the result of malnutrition or other deprivation rather than mere wear. Everything about her from her age to her rank to her national origin was ambiguous. "You know quite a lot about me," I said. "I'd like to know who you are and where I'm being taken and, if you know, what's going to happen to me."

"Yes, I'm sure you would," she said slowly, savoring her tea. "Very well, though my identity is of no importance, except perhaps to induce you to trust me to help you through a slight logistical problem. I am called many things, but what is relevant to you is that I hold the equivalent rank of a full colonel in the People's Army and I am a doctor."

"A doctor?" Well, counter my expectations! So much for the little old peasant woman. But why was a full colonel doctor assigned to a small band of guerrillas?

"Yes, and as to what is to become of you, that is up to you. We have communicated your presence and have received word that you are to be taken to a top-security facility for further processing. You should feel honored. Normally only quite important war criminals are assigned there. Part of the reason for this is that the facility is very isolated and can be reached only by a hazardous journey, difficult even for seasoned mountaineers."

"Can't we just fly?"

"I'm afraid not—for various security reasons. No, the only way is on foot."

"And it's a steep climb?"

She nodded once, briefly.

"I'll never make it," I said. I wasn't trying to be difficult. I didn't want to die. But one thing the academic life teaches you is your limits. Mine have always been severe when it concerns athletic physical activity. "I'm having trouble enough breathing just sitting here talking to you. Much as I hate to say so, you might as well go ahead and shoot me."

"Drink your tea," she said. "You will have ample opportunity to die later if you wish, but for now, I can help you. You have studied psychology, you said?"

"Yes," I replied cautiously.

"Then you are naturally acquainted with hypnosis, its benefits and purported limitations. You realize that a hypnotist cannot make you behave in a way that would be unacceptable to you if you were not hypnotized?"

"You can't really make me a Manchurian Candidate then?" I asked, risking a smile.

"I beg your pardon?"

"A film I viewed in the archives on mid-twentieth-century propaganda. About a man captured by the Chinese and Russians and turned into first a killer, then a presidential candidate while under hypnotic control."

The corners of her eyes and mouth tightened, the crow's-feet deepening. "And have you political ambitions?"

"No, ma'am," I said. "Except, perhaps, to change allies, as I told whatsisname . . ."

"Very pragmatic. But at this time, the only sensible thing for you to do is to cooperate while I prepare you to reach your destination. Finish your tea."

Despite the feeling that she was using the same tone the would-be fairest-in-the-land used to tell Snow White to eat the apple, it was good for her, I finished the tea. What was she going to do, poison me? Still, I felt a moment of panic when I realized that, yep, there was something in that cup besides high-cholesterol tea. She watched me as if there was a microscope between us, her hematite eyes glinting. When she spoke, her voice was gentle and her accented English took on a persuasive lilt. "The journey you are about to take is long and perilous," she began and I thought she sounded ridiculously like a parody of a Gypsy fortune-teller. "But you are a wonderful traveler. You love heights. Your body is very strong and you delight in movement. The cold invigorates you and the rarefied atmosphere lightens your step. You will be able to breathe deeply . . ."

That is as much as I recall. The next thing I knew I was standing and slipping into a stiff heavy coat. My tea cup was stacked with hers beside the plastic bottle and the old woman was boarding the helicopter. I left the cave to watch as it took off. The man with whom she had been arguing walked toward me carrying a rope and I thought, now that she's gone, maybe they mean to hang me, but he indicated that I should pass the rope around my waist and secure myself between him and another man. Everyone but me carried a box or bundle of some sort on his or her back but the doctor had apparently taken my lousy condition into account and granted me dispensation from being a packhorse.

Or—more likely—she and the others were afraid I'd fall into the first available crevasse and lose valuable supplies along with my relatively worthless warmongering carcass . . .

DAY 3.
AFTERNOON, THROUGH DAY?
The Trek

My watch had stopped, probably broken from the impact of my jump, so keeping track of the time of day other than in a general sense has been impossible. The combination of whatever "medicine" the good doctor used to spike my tea and the strength of the hypnotic suggestions disoriented me and I have no clear idea about the length of our little stroll across the mountains.

When we first set out from the drop-off point, even the first steep climb up the first pass seemed incredibly high above my head, ludicrously beyond my capabilities, but once on the trail I astonished myself by doing exceptionally well.

Of course, I was yoked to experienced mountaineers, but the trails were such that had I been exclusively under my own power I would no doubt have managed to drag all of us off the side of the mountain.

Many of the exact details of the trip are rather vague now, as if seen in a dream. This is no doubt because while my conscious mind was doing the sightseeing, it was actually my subconscious, still under the thrall of the hypnotist, propelling me over the trails on automatic pilot. But otherwise sheer terror would have prevented me from seeing, much less enjoying, views from the vantage point of the narrow paths where one could only place one foot at a time as one progressed toe to heel around steep cliff faces while freezing winds tried to sweep one into bottomless ravines. None of these obstacles daunted me. I seemed to sprint up the nearly perpendicular climbs and down the equally perpendicular descents as if I were not personally involved in the action but rather was watching it happen through tricky camera work. With no effort or fear, nor even a healthy amount of caution, I simply followed the man in front of me, putting my feet where his had been when his tracks were clear and blithely approximating otherwise, climbing one step at a time. The worst times were the walks through level spots and valleys in thigh-high snow. Without the necessity for absolute concentration, the posthypnotic spell was less powerful and I had to work much harder along such stretches than during steeper passages, for even though my breath came easily and my feet and legs lifted lightly, the snow sucked me under with each step and I was still yoked to less giddy people hampered by heavy loads.

But the climbing and walking mostly passed by in a daze and when we paused for a meal and calls of nature I gulped my tea, gnawed on the ball of grainy biscuit that was the sole sustenance at all meals, and paced on the end of my tether until we began walking again. The wind rose as the sky darkened and soon the blowing snow and the falling snow swirled into one massive whiteout—still we kept climbing.

Only when we stopped to sleep did my own reservations and fears fully return. My bulky clothing made it difficult for me to curl into a comfortable position and as I struggled to sleep, worries about frostbite caused me to compulsively keep touching and rubbing my hands and face, sure that the cold was damaging me even if I wasn't particularly aware of it most of the time. During these stops, the guards with whom I had been traveling all day frightened me by their laughter and the hard looks they sometimes cast my way, although they never mistreated me. Then too, as I tried to rest, I worried about where we were going, what would happen to me. And looking back toward the passes and mountains we had crossed that day, I grew absolutely horrified that I had done such a thing and became absolutely convinced that nothing short of an explosive charge under my rear end could induce me to continue. Yet as soon as the camp showed signs of stirring, I was ready and even eager to climb again.

My mother would never have understood it. No toilet, no bed, no blanket except the coat I wore, huddled together with all those strange people and God-only-knew what diseases and parasites, subject to the storms in the mountains, the blowing snow, the continual creak and sigh of rock and moisture resettling itself, threatening to fall down upon our heads at any moment.

But then, sometimes, it grew quiet and the peaks seemed to rise like a benediction, sheltering us from the night—perhaps not exactly protectively, but they were so awesomely huge and silent then that I forgot to be afraid, my life seeming no more significant than an amoeba's under the grand everlastingness of those immense snowy sails. The silence was crisp and electric at those times, with the clarity of a snapping icicle. The stillness was overpowering—anything louder than a whisper seemed irreverent, and even some of the guards seemed uncomfortable with normal tones, not because of avalanches, I thought, but just because silence seemed appropriate. Easy to believe, in a place like that, that souls had wings. Something inside you keeps wanting to fly free as a stringless kite, toward the pinnacles and the ragtag clouds, the blindingly bright stars. Easy to understand why such a land had been ruled by a theocracy, rather than some other form of government, for so long.

A blizzard caught us in the middle of one day and blew us into a premature night and on into yet another day and night. It slowed us down, but we made gradual progress. The snow sifted to a stop as we crossed a final plateau, then descended from the crest of the pass.

There we looked down into a great bowl, whose highest point was the horned peak I had glimpsed from the helicopter.

The last part of our journey was spent circling the bowl's rim. It took us all day and part of the night to spiral down into the valley, circumventing slides of snow and rock and huge, unstable boulders, areas where the cliff face has been gouged out by something that looked like a huge fist but was probably a bomb or a missile. By the time we reached the valley floor, I was feeling distinctly warm. I grew even warmer as we started to climb again, past an anemic pool half covered by thin ice and up a long rocky path.

As we climbed, my guards became more guardlike. Up until now they had pretty well ignored me, all of us being preoccupied by the task at hand. Now the one behind me gave me a little push once in a while and issued all kinds of useless commands I didn't understand. I ignored him. I had other things to worry about, because the closer we got to the prison, the slower I went. My heart and lungs were laboring as they had not since the beginning of the journey, and my legs and feet felt as if I was walking in casts of hot cement.

The prison was almost impossible to see until we were inside its walls.

A large part of the scooped-out mountain apparently landed at one time on the medium-sized mountain we climbed. The compound is camouflaged within this mountain, and is covered and surrounded by tremendous stones and piles of earth. It is further disguised by a snow-laden canopy netted across the tallest boulders. A stone wall surrounds the prison but its sides are irregular and blend with the rest of the rocky ground cover. The place must be virtually undetectable from the air.

Even within the compound, it is hard to tell how many people the prison holds, because all of the quarters and cells are contained in underground bunkers beneath the ruins. I first discovered this when my guards retreated through a door in a rock-covered mound and new guards, fresh, officious and rough, grabbed me and shoved me through another door, allowing me to tumble down a flight of stone steps into a passage that seemed to be less a bunker than part of an underground tunnel network.

I fell, landing on my side on a cold stone floor. As I tried to rise, the first cramp hit me, and I realized that since I was now at my destination, some posthypnotic signal in my surroundings must be releasing me from the spell that had propelled me so far. Apparently the good doctor forgot to include the standard part you always hear about how I would feel well and refreshed, because before I could gain my feet again the most horrible pain I had ever suffered wrenched my deluded body into one burning spasm.

My arms, legs, hips, feet, hands, even my chest, heart, neck and jaws shrieked with agony. Muscles and nerves I never knew I possessed ground and crushed each other as if my whole body were a huge self-compressing, red-hot vise. I was screaming too, blood pouring salty and hot into my mouth as I bit my tongue and cracked lips. My eyes burned. The guards thundered down the stairs after me, rolled me out of the way and opened a huge door, shoving me inside with their feet. I think they were laughing.

Laughing! My God, at home I'd have been rushed to the nearest hospital and sedated for pain, even if I couldn't pay. Someone, Sammy maybe, would have covered the expense. I couldn't think of anyone who would have found watching me suffer amusing.

Someone grabbed me. "Get his goddamn boots off, come on, hustle," a voice said and someone else said, "It's okay, soldier, it's okay, we got you now, babe. Only don't scream. Got that? Cool it with the screaming. Somebody give this guy something to bite on."

What felt like a stick was shoved into my open mouth but I spat it out and screamed anyway, then swore and kicked and landed a couple of blows as unseen hands tugged my coat, boots and flight suit off over cramp-contorted limbs.

"Holy shit, it's a girl," a new voice said.

"Get her right leg, Danielson. Marsh, you take the left. Colonel Merridew, sir, you and I'll get her arms." Even as he spoke, strong calloused fingers tore into the screeching pain, attacking it with swift, sure jabs that disintegrated its strongholds and sent it retreating to the right, the left, and straight through the limb where it met other relentless fingers.

"Okay, Danielson, now you start rubbin' them hands and feet, will you? Her goddamn boots weren't made for no mountain climbin'."

The hands that seemed to belong to the voice directing everything rubbed together above my nose and cupped it with pungent-smelling body heat. The hands weren't hot, but the warmth burned my face like a brand at first. As that pain faded, the hands worked their way along all my limbs to my shoulders, neck, hips and back. There was a little hesitation at chest level, then the voice said, "For medicinal purposes only, cher. Ol' Doc seen lotsa ladies, don't think nothin' of it, okay?"

"Fine," I whispered. My ears were still ringing from my own screaming, and everyone else's must have been too. My mouth tasted awful from the blood and I swallowed tears to dilute it, but the edge was off the pain.

"My back needs it worst now, I think," I whispered to the man, and rolled over onto my stomach so he'd lay off the ribs, which I thought might crack. He worked on my spine, shoulders, hips and upper thighs while the others continued massaging feet, legs and arms.

"Thanks," I managed finally. "I thought I was going to die. I didn't know prison camps featured masseurs these days."

"We had a little practice," Doc said. "I take it you didn't climb under your own steam? Fu Manchu's mother-in-law got to you, huh?"

"The doctor?"

"Uh-huh."

"She looked more like Fu Manchu's grandma to me," I said. "Yeah, she told me it would keep me from dying on the trip. I guess she didn't guarantee what would happen when I got here."

"Seems to be a trick they use a lot," another man with a voice soft and soothing as buttered rum said. "Other prisoners have fallen for it too. Different doctors, all female, but all hypnotists, promise to make the trek easier on people who would be a problem to the guards otherwise. I think it's a variation on an old Tibetan tantric discipline—except that instead of coming from your own training, which would prepare you for it, she induces it from the outside. They had another discipline that taught people how to keep themselves from freezing too but they seem to prefer to just bundle the prisoners up instead."

"Mr. Marsh here, he knows all these heathen things, dollin', but it ain't got him out of here no more than me or the others," Doc said.

"Only thing that's going to get us out of here is us and a few high-power weapons," another man grumbled.

"Sergeant Danielson, I'd take it kindly if you kept your opinions to yourself until after we've debriefed this lady." I didn't need Danielson's rather sheepish "Yes, sir" to know that it was the Colonel speaking. All but Marsh had southern accents. Ordinarily that wouldn't mean much—most people in NACAF, especially the men, particularly the enlisted men, including some from Canada-side, had southern accents. One of my profs who was a military history buff was asked about this by a linguistics major. He ascribed the phenomenon to the traditional preoccupation American fighting men seemed to retain at some atavistic level with the War Between the States, and the reverence still held for the Rebel soldiers. The linguistics student, who was from Toronto, said that seemed odd since the South lost. Ah, said the professor, but they lost with great style. People knew how to conduct a war in those days.

Sergeant Danielson's accent struck me as being one of those generic military drawls, but Doc's sounded real and regional. The Colonel's was more cultured and slightly less noticeable—more like a bass fiddle than the hoedown fiddle Doc's resembled. Siddons had an accent that was, like Danielson's, an acquisition (the major grew up in Portland), but like the Colonel's featured a broader vocabulary less full of Anglo-Saxon terminology than the average enlisted man's.

The auditory information was essential to me then because it was all I had. I couldn't see in the darkness, though the men moved around easily, albeit within a tight pattern that suggested the cell was small enough for the five of us to constitute a crowd. Danielson's remark indicated that the men were prisoners too, but I'd been fooled once and I was not about to wake up semi-clothed in a roomful of men to whom I'd bared my soul, so to speak; I'd already done that on an individual basis. This time I was the one who would ask the questions.

Doc gave my back a final pat and handed me my flight suit. "You gonna need this, dollin'. Gets cold here nights."

I struggled to pull the thing on again, but I was still too stiff and in too much pain. "Could you help me please, Doctor?" I asked.

"Yes, ma'am."

"I've been meeting enough physicians lately to staff a hospital," I said.

"I ain't exactly a physician, ma'am," he said. I noticed with relief that I was "ma'am" now that I was putting my clothes back on. "Perish the thought. I'm a field medic."

With all the slyness in my inconveniently transparent nature I asked, "And in what field are you a medic?"

"Ma'am?"

"To which allies did you administer aid? What's your patch?"

"Come again?"

"I think she means your unit, Thibideaux," Danielson said.

The Colonel's voice, unmistakable in its assumption of command, said, "Thibideaux, put a lid on it. You too, Danielson. I believe the time has come for some straight talk, don't you agree, Mr. Marsh?"

"Um-hmm."

"Now then, young lady, suppose you identify yourself."

"No."

"What?"

"I said no. I've already been tricked once. This time I want to know who I'm talking to and what your affiliations are."

The Colonel sputtered for a few moments, then Marsh cleared his throat and suggested, "Colonel, we already know who each of us is and the enemy knows who we are. I think you can tell her."

The Colonel said nothing and I could just imagine him standing there tight-lipped and unbending.

Finally Marsh said, "Well, okay then. My name is Keith Marsh. I'm not military. I was taken prisoner illegally while on a mission for the World Peace Organization."

"Nice to meet you," I said. Period. After the snide way Buzz had used my name and rank, I didn't even want to tell them that right away. Not even after the massage. Physical intimacy wasn't going to make an idiot of me this time.

There was a long silence, then the Colonel said, "Lady, I don't know if you're on the level or not but if you're a spy this is the oddest way of getting people to incriminate themselves I've encountered. What do you think, men? Shall we risk it?"

Thibideaux said, "Sir, I'm willing. She was in more legitimate physical distress than most spies would go through just to get us to say somethin' indiscreet. Hell, sir, we been here a coon's age and rougher places than this before. I reckon they've about beat outta this poor boy anything I got to tell already. Don't see what it can hurt to give her the basics."

"Danielson?"

"They haven't brought any ringers in on us here so far, sir. I'm inclined to think this place is too small and isolated for them to be able to shuffle people like that. She is new and she does appear to be an American. I say we take a chance and clue the little lady in. If she screws us over, we'll deal with it when we come to it."

"Marsh?"

"I guess I've already expressed my opinion."

Merridew put his face so close to mine I could almost see it even in the dark. I could smell his breath—a little toothpaste wouldn't hurt. "Okay, young lady, if my men are willing to put their asses on the line, so am I. I am going to assume that you are new to the enemy's penal system and give you a little short survival course. Here's the drill. We stick together. It's as simple as that. Each of us has been in and out of other prisons and in and out of other cell arrangements in this one—including years of solitary in some cases. The way the enemy gets to you is they break one person—often in what they call a struggle session or *thamzing*, they'll arbitrarily pick on one guy—maybe for instance me, since I'm the ranking officer, maybe you, because you're a woman, and beat the living shit out of you, accusing you of all kinds of stuff, and make the other prisoners beat the living shit out of you. Tell stuff on you. If you don't make up enough stories on the person getting beat, or if you don't beat hard enough, you're the next one that gets beat. Pretty soon, they got everybody spying on everybody else so no one can take a shit without all his cellmates telling just exactly how much it stinks and what color it was. There is only one way to survive these very effective interrogation tactics. A, you pull your punches at the beatings if you're beating; B, you pretend to be hurt worse than you really are if you're getting beaten; and C, under no circumstances do you ever betray your cellmates. They ask their questions and all they get out of any of us is dead silence. Got it? You scream all you want to when they start to hurt you, you make up all kinds of outrageous shit, but you never ever under any circumstances betray the rest of us and we give you the same courtesy.

"I know this seems rough, especially for a female, but I was never of the opinion females should be combat troops to begin with. And I want you to consider this, soldier. If you do betray us, we will at some point all betray each other and this place will be even more of a hellhole than it is right now, with the worst they can do to any of us coming from the outside. It will be as if your own brain has been turned against you, as if your very heart and lungs cannot trust each other. Do I make myself clear?"

"Yes, sir," I said. "I understand. I just want to make sure before I promise anything that we are all on the same side. So with all due respect, sir, which side are you on?"

"We're Americans, of course," Danielson said.

"But who are you with?" I insisted.

"We've been here a spell," Thibideaux said. "Things may have changed some. There were some pretty strange new policies brewin' before Marsh and me were taken. Who's the U.S. helpin' now, ma'am?"

The U.S.? God, maybe we were just having a little communication problem. "The U.S." was considered a separatist designation these days. "You first," I said, nevertheless.

"Never mind, Thibideaux, I made the command decision. I'll walk point on this. Besides, like Marsh says, the brass here in camp already know all this. So, young woman, I am the top ranking officer here, unless, of course, you outrank me. Merridew, George W., Colonel U.S. Air Force," and he rattled off a serial number at least six digits shorter than my own. "I was shot down several years ago during an airlift from Delhi to Srinagar when the Chinese had cut off northern India. Our official orders at the time were to lend no fire support to India, since the government was negotiating with Beijing, but we weren't about to let our people and our allies starve, so I was one of several officers who organized and carried out the lift. I've admitted that much already."

I didn't recall such an airlift, but then, as I've said, it sounded as if that mission had taken place somewhat before my time, and if the policy was somewhat questionable from an official viewpoint, NACAF wouldn't necessarily have reported it for the press or the history books to record. "You were allied with the Indians too, then?" I asked.

"That's what I said."

Marsh volunteered, "I guess you would say my position was nondenominational, politically, since my organization's mission was just to keep the peace. But I was on a fact-finding operation in Bangladesh with Thibideaux as my military liaison when we were captured."

"With all due respect for your civilian status, Marsh, I think you should let Thibideaux volunteer his own information."

"That's okay, Colonel," Thibideaux said. "Whatever

will help this sweet young thing relax. It's like Marsh said. I was field medic with the 616th Infantry Division and was detached to a special forces outfit assigned to help out with the flood situation in Bangladesh just before the Chinese moved in and all hell broke loose. At that time, the Chinese were supposed to be our allies but it didn't slow 'em down much when it came to openin' fire on our unit or beatin' the crap out of Marsh and me." As an afterthought he added, "Henri Thibideaux, Medical Specialist eighth class, U.S. Army, but like I said, you can call me Doc."

The last man simply said, "Sergeant Major Du P. Danielson, U.S. Army Special Forces. Your turn, lady."

Well, at least I wouldn't be giving anything away blindly, and this was about as sure as I could be in the dark without being able to inspect patches. From what these men were telling me, most of them were captured before patches were important anyway. "I'm Viveka J. Vanachek from Bellingham, Washington. I've only been in the military six months. I'm a warrant officer. I was just captured a few days ago and was routed here from what appeared to be a base camp for irregular PRC forces by a weird old woman who claimed to be a colonel in the PRC."

Can a person cower defiantly? If so, that's what I was doing while I waited for someone to demand more particulars. But after a long silence, Thibideaux asked, "Only in the service six months, huh? Then you were home six months ago?"

"That's right," I admitted cautiously.

"Then, can you tell me, do you know, I mean, I know some women still don't keep track of those things but, who won the last World Series?"

For a moment I thought it was a trap, like the codes used in the so-called world wars of the early twentieth century in which the names of ball players and actresses were used as passwords and military information was transmitted by Navajo Indians whose native language was employed as a cipher.

But then Danielson asked if I knew about the World Basketball Playoffs too and I realized that they very sim-

ply missed sports. They waited for the answers with a
certain boyish breathlessness that reassured me more
than the information they'd given me. They really had
been here—or at least somewhere out of touch—a long
long time. I hated to tell them the truth. Neither sport
had been played on a professional level since—God,
since the late forties, early fifties—because the players
and owners had tied each other up in litigation for so
many years that when sports fans spoke of who won in
connection with a particular team they meant who had
won the latest appeal on the latest lawsuit, or whose
lawyer had won the latest settlement. The sports/enter-
tainment field was in such turmoil that by the time I left
the university, basketball was played only in school gym-
nasiums and on playgrounds and what was left of the
sport of baseball was about to be exported to Korea where
an arms manufacturing firm was offering to buy up all
teams concerned, balls, bats and diamonds. I hated to
tell these men that, but I was afraid if I didn't, they'd
know I was lying and decide I was a spy after all.

As it was, they didn't believe me when I tried to
tell them the truth. Danielson said, "Oh, that kind of
rumors were always flying around. Who won the *last*
game?" I took a plunge and named a couple of teams
whose trials I'd seen on the holovid at Sammy's. My
fellow prisoners didn't seem to know the difference.
Maybe they would have if I'd been able to relate details
of the fictitious game, but as it was, they used my information to regale each other for a time about games
they had once seen played.

As soon as I realized my information was not going
to be challenged, I stopped paying attention. I had more
serious things to think about. Like, the reason my information wasn't being challenged was because the memories these men had of our continent were from at least
a couple of decades ago.

As they babbled maniacally on about strikes and
baskets they had known and loved, I sank deeper into
despair, realizing that these men had been prisoners for
almost half my life and that I was likely to be prisoner
with them for the rest of it.

INTERROGATION

The cell was checked with shadows from an over-head grille emitting frosty morning light along with the chill that wakened the cramps in my body to phantoms of what they had been the previous night. I'd dreamed of lions attacking me and woke feeling the wounds and listening to the roars. For two long heartbeats I lay still, not daring to stand and relieve the cramps—or my blad-der. The cramps themselves reminded me. A man with blond curls as sweet as any baby's lay flat on his back on the next bunk, snoring, his long square jaw sagging open. On the other side of me, a black man lay on his back, also snoring, though somewhat more mellifluously. The other two were on each side of them, dark forms huddled in the shadows. I carefully rose and filled the last inch of the pot on the all-too-near far side of the cell.

The guards rattled the cell door and my cellmates struggled up from sleep and straggled out. The steps were very difficult for me, and I moved as if I had aged three hundred years. A woman guard grabbed my arm at the head of the steps and hustled me in the opposite direction from that in which the men were being herded.

"Aw, ah. Be careful there, dollin'." Thibideaux's voice belonged to a raw-boned, balding redhead whose breath, like mine, clouded from his mouth like a cartoon balloon.

"Looks like your turn with the Dragon Lady," Marsh grunted, as his guard hissed reproach and shoved his back so that he stumbled down the path behind the others. My guard dragged me a few steps before I caught up with her.

She led me around boulders and ruined walls rib-bing the stony ground like mastodon bones. Dawn the color of carrot soup strained through the camouflage can-opy.

We stopped in front of a wall of sandbags. There was no building, just the sandbags with a door in the

middle, and it took me a moment to realize that earth-
works supported the sandbags. By then a sentry had
thrown open the door and I was being shoved down a
short flight of steps. White light exploded in front of me
and I tried to stop and let my eyes adjust. They'd gotten
well cooked in the snow on my little mountaineering
expedition and protested the violent changes in illumi-
nation. The guard nudged me again and I nearly stumbled over an orange extension cord. Following it upward,
I saw that it led to a work lamp suspended from a nail.
A series of these lamps were strung together with other
orange extension cords, the length of the hall. An unseen
generator muttered beneath a babble of bored voices
and at times the lamps flickered like candles from the
uneven flow of power.

Another extension cord grabbed my toe and I
lurched sideways, into a shoulder-high pile of rubble,
which slid toward me and tried to bury me. The noise
from the generator and the absorbent properties of the
dirt floor muffled the racket.

The place stinks. They need a good ventilation system down here or at least a few of those little squirt
bottles of air freshener. I'm a little more used to it now
but it smells like very dirty people sweated themselves
to death here and rotted until they disintegrated into air
particles. It also smells nauseatingly like rancid fat and
I kept swallowing hard to keep down the bile. Luckily,
I had had no food recently.

We wound through a maze of connecting corridors,
avoiding several in which collapsed walls or mounds of
rubble blocked the way. At two of the spots farther in,
work parties composed of both guards and prisoners
shoveled debris and shored up walls. I tried to map the
corridors in my mind but for a mapmaker I have a la-
mentable sense of direction.

But it seems to me we had made about three left
turns and one hard right when we reached the main
hallway, a broad spot with other corridors branching off
from it and doors, many of them open, some boarded
shut, on each side of the passage. A sentry stood at
attention beside the third door on the left and my guard

marched me through into a barn of a room. Plain OD wool blankets hung on the walls. I think they covered windows, which would indicate that maybe the room hadn't always been underground. I also caught a glimpse of what looked like the ruined, fancy frames of a pair of French doors peeking out from behind another stack of sandbags. A bare electric bulb hung from another orange extension cord looped across the top of a large, tarp-covered table. At first I thought it was a little girl sitting there, tapping away at the computer on the desk.

Then she looked up and smiled a sort of inverted smile, with the corners of her mouth turned down, and I saw that she was no child after all but one of those deceptively doll-like Asian women whose delicately sweet faces and butterfly-like fragility could conceal anything from an Olympic athlete to a chess champion to a despotic would-be witch-queen like Vietnam's historic villainess, Madame Nhu.

Nhu had also been called the Dragon Lady, after a comic strip about a pilot popular in the mid-twentieth century. The original Dragon Lady and Madame Nhu were both said to have had claws like a cat's but this woman's nails were short and serviceable, her hands even a trifle on the blunt and ugly side.

She smiled as if she were a receptionist in some business office and said to my guard, "Corporal Tsering, please bring tea."

The guard shouldered her rifle, did a smart about-face and marched out. The so-called Dragon Lady graciously gestured toward a beige metal folding chair. I slowly and stiffly arranged my collection of aches and pains into a folded position, realizing that this was the time when, had I been in any other condition, I should have tried to escape. The woman was so small I thought I could snap her neck with a well-placed blow but then what? If she was unarmed, which I doubted, I still had no place to go when and if I overcame her, which I didn't feel capable of doing right then anyway.

"A penny for your thoughts, as they say, Ms. Vanachek," the woman said cutely. Her voice lends itself to cute, among other things. It has a deceptively sweet

quality, like the silver chime my grandparents used to
ring before Sunday meditations.

"I am Commandant Wu." She consulted her screen,
tapped another key or two and said, still in English,
"Your name is Viveka Jeng Vanachek—Viveka, that's an
Indian name, isn't it? I thought you were North American."

"It's a family name, sort of. My grandmother was a
hippie—"

She arched an inquiring eyebrow.

"Hippies were like a mid-twentieth-century peace
and free-love activist movement," I explained. "They
also sometimes adopted Eastern philosophies and religions. Grandma Viveka was into Zen for a while and she
adopted a Sanskrit name. It means "discrimination." My
mom liked it so she named me the same thing." She
continued to look scornful and skeptical. "It's true. Look,
my grandfather was Czechoslovakian and Irish and I
never knew him as anything but Ananda, okay?"

Maybe I should have stuck with the name, rank and
serial number business but unless their communications
here were awfully poor she already had that information
from Buzz's report.

She continued to shake her head disbelievingly and
ignored me while she stared into the screen. "Why you
were spared to come here is beyond me. You are very
fortunate. The crimes of your people are so callous that
we've only admitted a very few others for our program."

"What program?" I asked. I know. I know. I should
have kept my mouth shut. But calling a prison camp a
program seems to me to be the ultimate in euphemistic
bullshit of the type the NACAF establishment likes so
much.

"Rehabilitation," she said. "But of course, as I keep
trying to point out to certain people, not all war criminals
are educable. Any people who could do what yours have
done to this country—"

"I know. That Chinese doctor already chewed me
out for that. But I'm not even a litterbug."

I didn't really mean to say that—it was a sort of a
little inside joke for myself. It kind of slipped out. It

shouldn't have. The Dragon Lady pounded both of her little fists on the desk, one on either side of the imperiled computer, and screamed at me with a face like a monkey-demon. "There! You see. You're denying responsibility! I knew you weren't worthy of our time. Do you know that before *your* people started scattering their bombs about, that mountain over there"—she pointed emphatically to the sandbags behind her—"had stood tall and perfect for millions of years and this valley was filled with a beautiful, sacred lake that nourished all who lived here?"

I shook my head.

"Of course you didn't. Yet it was your government who carelessly sanctioned such behavior, who supplied the weapons. Your government of, by, and for the people." She practically frothed at the mouth with fury, and just to make her point, spat at the floor, missed and hit the desk, which I guess is why the tarp is there. I tried to caution myself that this woman, like the doctor, had the power of life and death over me, and what kind of life and what kind of death at that. But it all seemed so damned melodramatic. I settled for hanging my head and trying to look contrite.

Making unintentional bad jokes is the height of my bravado. I may not intend to spy on the other prisoners, as they fear, but neither will I give in to any hysterical heroics. This lady does not especially scare me now, but I don't doubt that she can make me afraid of her if she wishes. I don't want to goad her into demonstrating her power. Insecure people in positions of bureaucratic power can be extremely cruel, as I have good reason to know from various encounters with personnel managers and professors.

"Just as I thought," she said. "You have no answer. You are utterly worthless, a waste of food and space. Nevertheless, you have questions to answer. You will be put in solitary confinement to mull over your crimes until the time, if ever, that I decide you are fit to return to society. In the meantime, I advise you to consider carefully your crimes, and the crimes of your accomplices, and also to try to think of any possible value your miserable life could be to this community."

At that point, the tea arrived but I was not offered any. Instead I was hauled away to my present cell, where I vegetated for an undetermined length of time until the guards brought me this paper with the instructions to write about my criminal career from age eight on.

PART TWO

THE CELL,
TWO SO-CALLED MEALS
AND TWO CHAMBER POTS LATER

I meant to keep a running record with this journal, writing every day, but I wanted to wait until I saw how the guards would react to my homework assignment from the commandant. I finished it and handed it in, and didn't even offer to give back any of the leftover paper. The guards were inscrutable, by which I gathered they either didn't notice the discrepancy in my supplies or they didn't give a damn. So far my assignment has not received a grade. An A undoubtedly means Alive and an F is for—let's not think about F. I trust my exposé of my criminal exploits will wow them.

So, although I continue to try to save paper, I also have to keep from going nuts. The physical environment is not worthy of attention except to say that it is a small stone room with a stone platform bench on which I recline if not actually sleep. I can stretch out full length on it and that's about all. I can almost reach from one wall to the other. They keep about a six-watt bulb burning in here all the time, strung on one of those damned orange extension cords. The generator mutters constantly.

The cruise director is definitely lying down on the job as the activity schedule is zilch. So far I have had my food—some kind of doughy rolls with stuff mixed in them—delivered to my door. These concoctions do not agree with me. I've thrown them up both times. The water, too, upsets my stomach. Maybe it's just nerves but I can't keep anything down. My chamber pot runneth over. The guard exchanges a full pot for a meal, a predictably unappetizing preprandial activity. The roof leaks and has a rotten spot about big enough to admit rats. Not big enough to escape through.

The stones do, however, contain hiding places for this diary. When I first arrived I inspected the whole joint, looking for graffitti ("The Count of Monte Cristo Slept Here," perhaps), the sort of convenient ventilation system you always see in old spy movies, or the sewer drain you see in others. Nothing. When the paper arrived I decided to try to make a cache for it by using a piece of the rock that fell from the ceiling to carve out the mortar from between a couple of stones. That's when I discovered the stones didn't have any mortar between them. They fit together so well that I broke all ten nails prying one from its slot, but finally made a nice little file cabinet out of the space below a chipped stone that fits under my left shoulder.

So, to whom it may concern, I hope you have a sense of humor. That's the problem with people like the Dragon Lady. Takes herself too seriously. Reminds me of a lot of the grandfolks' old cronies, the ones who didn't join the NACAF senior corps or request overdoses in their extended care facilities. Some of those other old ex-hippies, radicals, you know. Poor old dears, ranting on and on about the same kinds of things as our fearless leader here, not realizing it's just all too damned late. The oceans have been mostly dead for a long time. The rain forests are starting on third growth. We haven't used gas or oil on the continent in years. But to the end, the old fossils either didn't know or didn't care to admit that all of their best fights were over, either a total loss or solved by the reclamation industry during the first part of this century. But those codgers never had the ability to do anything more than bitch in their whole lives, and bitching was what they continued to do, with bitter, fanatic intensity. I often wondered what one of them would have done if they could have had someone specific to blame in their clutches. All that moral zeal always scared me. I tried to tell one of them once that the environment was cleaned up, at least where the nice people could see it, and had gotten cleaned up as soon as it became extremely profitable to do so. The poor old thing nearly stroked out telling me how my kind of apathetic young whippersnapper was responsible. That's what I mean. No sense of humor.

LATER

⚓ God, God, God, what an idiot I am. Just catching the line above makes me sick to my stomach. What kind of suicidal fool would make fun of Wu? On paper. Where it could be found. Jesus, she could keep me in this little room forever.

I think she knows about the paper. I mean, I'm sure she knows, but I think she noticed. They didn't bring my meal. I can't be sure, of course, with no watch and no daylight to go by, but the chamber pot is overflowing and I'm so hungry, even though I don't think I could keep anything down. What if they just stop feeding me to punish me? Why did I start this diary business? Where the hell do I think I am anyway?

Okay. All right. I know why I started it. I know. I'm in serious danger here of flipping out. It was just the dream, that's all. It scared me. Probably just the atmosphere of the place but maybe it was from some kind of mind control too.

Anyway, I had this dream. Nightmare. I was a Jewish girl (though we all looked Chinese, but that didn't seem strange in the dream) and my little sister and I, somehow, were the children of the commander of this Nazi prison camp. Our father was letting us live very much against his better judgment. He fought with our mother about it all the time.

Sometimes he was right on the point of sending us

into the ovens, and she'd hustle us off to a hiding place until he calmed down. I had these very clear memories of him killing my friends (or were they other brothers and sisters? other kids I loved, *loved*, that my mom loved too but couldn't save and all that were left, all that could be saved so far, were my sister and me). He murdered them in various ways, burning them in the ovens or locking them in the poison gas showers or using them for target practice for the firing squads; different methods. And I had no delusions. I knew it was real. I knew that if he flicked his finger a certain way, that was it. Final. So I had to stay out of his way and what was harder, keep my sister out of his way, because she kept feeling like he ought to love her and didn't understand that nothing she or I or Mom could do would make him any different. Once I remember the little sister saying, "Wouldn't it be great if we had come at the right time so Daddy would think we were his instead of just Mama's?" But that scared me too. Because somehow, with dream sense, our father didn't know that our mother was Jewish (like us), or he would have sent her to the ovens too, and that would have been the end of all of us. Even weirder, he didn't know that *he* was Jewish. Or if he had ever known he was so vicious that, like Hitler, he blocked out that part of him, but I couldn't think about his problems. I had to think about what I could do to stay out of his way, not attract his attention, or to please him when I did have to be around him. To do something he really wanted. Because if I didn't, and he noticed me in a negative way, there was nothing ahead but a void for both me and my sister.

Good. There, that's better. I guess that's why I risked keeping the paper. Writing helps—getting it on paper where I can look at it helps. So did throwing up again, except now I have to live with the smell. Thank God for the hole in the ceiling. I'm breathing okay again now, too, and I can't hear my pulse so loud—for a while it drowned out the generator, sounded like a damned drum.

Dream analysis time. This dream seems to me to be nature's way of telling me to watch my ass. My first

reaction was right on. I am an idiot if I trivialize Wu.
The men may talk lightly of being beaten into insensi-
bility during those sessions but I'm not some hero. I'm
not in good shape. I would die from it, or from the
complications, even something simple like a broken arm
if they made me keep working and wouldn't let anyone
help me. Nobody would have to torture me. I could die
slowly, from complications, with Wu and the others
cheering from the sidelines. Shit. Bad as the dream was,
waking up is not a hell of a lot better. Except that I'm
not a child, but almost as helpless. Like the little girls
in the dream, I have to try to please and stay out of their
way, find some reason for them to keep me alive, as Wu
said. I don't have a mother to protect me. The Colonel
and the others talk big, but they seem to be in the same
boat I am except that right now they're together and I'm
alone. Nope. They don't represent Mama. Maybe they're
the little sister—or, funny thought, maybe I am. Despite
all my intellectual understanding of why people might
hate me. I find the actual animosity of the people around
me almost as baffling as the little sister found her father's
hatred.

And why Nazis? There are more recent villains. But
then, of course, I read all that Nazi stuff when I was a
kid and thought that if I had been alive then I'd have
led a movement to whip their asses or some equally
moronic grandiose kid delusion. The fact that all of us
looked Chinese in the dream seems more significant. As
if it's just the same old evil in new skin. And the fact
that we were all Jewish, even the father, I think maybe
meant that we are all victims, casualties who have been
battered and abused by this whole big war network.

Was I a child in the dream because Wu seems like
such a child? Scary thought, but not likely. She's more
used to the business end of the whip. Maybe there are
other prisoners here whose vibes I was picking up.

But mostly, oh yeah, I have to be very very careful.
I have to not give Wu any excuse to flick her finger,
because if she does, I'm history, and such an unremark-
able bit that I won't even be missed. Nobody will remember who I was or care if I die here. It will be straight

oblivion. Unless maybe later, when this phase of the war is over and the co-belligerents buddy up for a while to figure out who to trash next, some tourists might find this, like Anne Frank's diary or the journals of the Civil War prisoners. God! What a concept. Listen to yourself, Vanachek. Even here you're trying to figure out how to get noticed, how to be a media star, even posthumously. But it's more than that. I just don't want to be wiped out, to go through all of this in a vacuum with nobody knowing or caring, now or later. Maybe at least this way somebody will get a thesis out of me.

ONE MEAL,
ONE EMPTY POT AND,
ALAS, SEVERAL MAJOR STOMACH
UPHEAVALS LATER

I have got to get control of my nerves. The dream was a good warning, but I can't let it scare me into this kind of state. What they feed me isn't so bad, but I can't seem to keep it down. Would they be awful enough to put an emetic in it? Surely not. Surely in some place this isolated they'd be more conscious of saving food than that, would just starve me instead. It must be my nerves. I'm sick all the time.

LATER

⋏ Had uninvited, unexpected callers. A pair of guards this time. Must be the fastidious type, got a whiff of the place and couldn't stand it. But anyway, thank God I was too sick and shook up to write much and had already hidden this again. So they found me flaked out on ye olde stone bunk, looking suitably subdued and vegetative. The woman, a hard-faced, thin-mouthed bitch who reminds me a lot of the head registrar back at UW, handed me a rag to mop up the mess and a cup of water to drink. The man frowned at the crumbs I was too sick to finish as if the sight of them personally offended him.

I took a cautious sip of water once they had gone and started to drag this out again, but then I heard more footsteps returning and got back into dejected prisoner mode, which becomes easier all the time.

The footsteps stopped, the door opened, and Wu stood there, flanked by the guards. "They tell me you are not feeling well," she simpered nastily. "You must take better care of yourself, Viv. You like to be called Viv, is that not true?"

Not that I didn't have more important things to worry about than embarrassment, but my ears burned. The last person I'd told that to was good ol' Buzz. I nodded though, remembering to keep a low profile and try to please.

"Yes, Viv, we are very far from the amenities here. Our resources are limited. You must take care not to get yourself into such a state that in order to take care of you, we would have to allot you more than your fair share. You do nothing productive here. You are a parasite."

"What—" I croaked, because my throat closed over and I tasted the burn of bile rising again, stinging my nostrils. I swallowed and took a deep breath. "What would you like me to do?" I asked her.

"For a beginning, you must correct this confession.

I want you to think more deeply about what you have written. You are so arrogant—your words are full of superior attitudes toward others, condescension. You will not be fit to mingle with others until you have mended your thoughts and accepted your responsibility." Then she took a step into the room, her doll's face childishly earnest and her voice lowered as she said, "Listen to me, Viv. I know how you are feeling. Once, like you, I was spoiled and pampered and believed my freedoms were all that mattered, that I was immune to the will of the common good. Unlike you, I did not live in a society that permitted me such selfish notions and I was nearly destroyed. I thought since your people said they believed in freedoms they would aid my cause, but no one came and my friends died all around me and I too would have died until compassionate people took pity on my ignorance and saved me. Since then I have seen my errors and renounced them. You must do the same. You must see how badly you have behaved, how inconsiderate you have been, how cruel and how naive. Only then can you begin to improve."

Abruptly, she cut off the sermon and snapped her fingers. The male guard handed her another sheaf of paper, which she handed to me. "Meditate on your errors and try again."

Paper must not be one of the scarcer resources. They seem to be pretty free with it—in order to spring a trap? Maybe they suspect what I'm doing and are setting me up. Morbid thought. Ah well, what's life without a little risk? I ask with a madcap cavalier air. (Life, I whimper in response.)

HOW MANY MEALS LATER? FOUR?

I'm not exactly acing my assignment. Vomiting every few minutes is horribly distracting, puts a—you should pardon the expression—cramp in one's literary style. Constant barfing, coupled with the panic that is no doubt causing it, makes me want to fill page after page with columns which read "Omigod," but I restrain myself. Neither will I waste paper, risk Wu's wrath, or bore posterity by recording my most frequent mental events—the multiplication tables, the lyrics to old songs, and dirty limericks I recite to myself to try to keep calm. This is a great way for the previously uninitiated to develop claustrophobia. I don't know how Wu expects me to improve my confession when she hasn't returned it. How can I remember enough to do it differently this time? Any kind of deep thinking is impossible in here—there isn't room to pace more than two steps and then I keep kicking the damned chamber pot.

I like to eat when I think, too, and there's certainly not enough of that lousy biscuit to use for study snacks, even if I could keep it down. The worst thing is the thirst, though—they don't bring me much water and the vomiting not only makes my mouth foul, it's also very dehydrating. Instead of writing, I, who was never much for math, count as high as I can count, and start over again, counting the seconds to pass the time until the next water. I keep hoping rain will come through the hole in the ceiling. Or melted snow. Or a giant eagle to carry me away. Get serious, Vanachek. I really do have to start that fiction piece for Wu now. Have to concentrate.

LATER

To whom it may concern: What I just finished of the second confession is total cow ca-ca and my Chinese grammar stinks but I did squeak out a few groveling phrases. I decided that the only way to please Wu is to try to think like her, really get into the role she wants me to play—method writing, no less. Try to think like the decadent war criminal I am supposed to be. Find the war criminal inside me. That is what she wants me to do and that is why I am now taking a prolonged break. Sitting here alone, in this cell, surrounded by people who either detest or mistrust me, is hard on an impressionable young thing such as myself. I start thinking, who knows, maybe they're right? Maybe some fatal flaw in my makeup is responsible for my being here. Maybe they've *finally found me out*. Maybe all of my past transgressions (real and imagined) have *finally caught up with me*. That's what they want me to think. That's what I have to think to write this damned thing, which is why Wu is being such a tough editor. She wants me to work so hard at writing a believable confession that I work myself up into truly believing it—these people are very good at this kind of mind control. I need to budget my time and intersperse focusing on the confession with thoughts about Great Literature or The Nature of Humankind or What Myth Means to Modern Society or How Can I Keep From Barfing for Ten More Minutes—anything to keep my balance.

They are, you see, controlling not only the information they give me but are attempting to control the information I feed back to myself. It's part of the whole brainwashing process, another patented mind-control trick. And dammit, after all the time and expense I've taken to fill my mind, I am very resistant to the idea that only by letting someone else control it can I hope to save myself.

MEAL 5—MOMOS

Aha! A small victory. My savory sustenance each
day is referred to as a momo. The guard slipped up and
told me so. I'm sure he was under orders not to talk to
me but I think he was sort of mumbling to himself.
Nevertheless, I have been eating and regurgitating
momos for some time now. Let's say five momos, at one
momo per day. It's about that many, more or less. Anyway, I shall count my time by momos. Today, inspired
by the austere presence of the guard, I dutifully wrote
about my warmongering transgressions from the time I
was ten until my fifteenth birthday. Nibbling the momo
instead of wolfing it down when it first arrives helps
mitigate the vomiting—my stomach has been confining
itself to dry heaves instead. So, after I confessed and
until I began feeling that I should save these people the
cost of feeding me by bashing my head against the wall,
I recited limericks to myself. Regrettably, constant vomiting is not good for one's recall, but then I have a lot of
time in which to recall. It is also difficult to hold on to
the pen. On the other hand, my journal is my only friend
so it is equally difficult to let loose of the pen. I just had
the most frightening thought. What will happen when
my pen runs out of ink? There are no insurance companies or automobile dealerships here to pass out new
ones. Maybe rat blood makes good ink? And a tiny little
rat bone for a quill?

LATER

† Too sick to work anymore. The Arabs are right in assuming the stomach is the seat of emotion—I'm beginning to think it's the seat of the soul, and I lose a portion of mine daily. Can't keep this up much longer.

MOMO 6

† I pointed to my pail and informed the guard I was ill and needed a doctor, in Chinese, which I don't think he understood. It seems to me that this meal was brought much sooner than the other one. More water too. Wish I had a toothbrush. My mouth tastes vile enough that it alone is good reason to toss my cookies.

MOMO 7

† Damn. I never understood why solitary confinement was such a horrible punishment before—all these years when I wished everyone would go away and leave me alone so I could study. I'm learning. Sensory deprivation is such a nice civilized term for being buried alive, like one of the old anchorites. What I wonder is why? And

why me? I didn't do anything to be punished for. I'd
already met the men. How could she know how badly
I'd need company now when I didn't even know? Guess
it must follow a pattern. She didn't seem stupid, exactly.
I can't figure her out. She looks so young—kind of an
avant-garde Red Guard, I suppose, the Chinese equivalent of the Hitler Youth or the Cambodian kiddie killers
of the Pol Pot. I wonder if their eyes looked like that
too—no lines around the edges, no furrowed brows, no
droopy lids to make them anything but wide and shiny
and yet old and hard, but with that kid's love of seeing
what will happen next—I saw that look on some of the
troops back in Katmandu. It reminded me of some old
tunes in Grandad's collection, songs with lines like "So
I took my razor blade, laid old Reuben in the shade.
Started me a graveyard of my own." Her eyes are like
that. Old and cold but with a little theatrical flair about
them, a little sensationalism, like a yellow journalist enjoying her own prose when she writes about a mass murder. Yuck. I tend to underestimate her when she
overplays the propaganda bit so that she sounds like some
kind of a missionary. I have to watch intellectualizing my
response to her too much. Abject fear is what she wants.
That's easy. What's hard is maintaining a little control.
It would be easier if I weren't so damned sick all the
time. Vomiting and stomach cramps are killing me. Can't
think about that. Think positive. Yeah.

So, okay, positive. I'm not as deprived of input as
she thinks. I have the paper and also have this dim bulb,
which may not let me sleep too soundly and keeps me
from telling day from night, but at least allows me to
find the paper with my pen. I have the generator's rock
and roll for company—I can make up all kinds of lyrics
to go with that beat, "Bin in this camp too long, whup!"
Then there's the scrabble of rats, the opportunity for a
sniff of fresh air my ceiling hole affords and my spacious
cell, which, compared to some of the little boxes I've
read about some POWs occupying, seems like the hon-
eymoon suite of solitary accommodations. Yes, my bless-
ings are legion but, I hate to say it, it doesn't cheer me
one fucking iota.

Okay, then. There's the changing decor as the ceiling hole dribbles a constant patter of rock and plaster and the companionship it affords when it shines, periodically, with bright feral eyes before little slick-furred bodies with long skinny tails plop to the floor to investigate my slop bucket for cast-off momo. Better the bucket than me. I do not discourage these visitors, because if I can ever digest anything again, I may decide to add meat to this vegetarian diet I'm on. Then too, a more enterprising prisoner might see the ceiling hole's potential as an escape route. But it is really very small and I ask you, escape to where? Those stalwart men I met when I first arrived, if they are truly prisoners, have been here years and years without finding a way back across the mountains. Far be it from me to show them up. But maybe with perseverance I can open the room up so I can see something else. I've memorized these damn walls.

LATER

Something's gone wrong. The generator has stopped. Could it have been what I did? I was trying to enlarge the hole and even though I didn't seem to be making any progress, all of a sudden all this dust and shit started falling into the cell, as if a whole room above was collapsing on me. I shoved my hands up against it and finally dammed the flow of debris, but I coughed so hard I started puking again. Damn, there's no air. I'll bet the generator pumps it in. I'll bet the guards are asleep and don't know it's broken. How far down *am* I, anyway?

Mixed with the rancid fat/B.O. stink there's another

smell, fainter, sweeter, sickening—toxic gas? That does it. I'm yelling for the guards.

AT LEAST A DAY LATER, MAYBE TWO (BUT NO MOMO)

So much for calling the guards. If the place burns to the ground, floods, anything, I'm dead. They came running when I screamed and I tried to tell them in Chinese about the generator and the gas, but the woman guard hit me across the mouth. I knocked her arm away and tried to get past her out the door. She and the man threw me back on the stone couch and all the time I'm struggling with them, trying to tell them about the generator. Finally, she pulled a roll of tape out of her pocket and taped my mouth shut. They tied me up and left me there. She made an impatient shushing gesture as she left the room, like I was a kid. Boy, I'd hate to have had a mother like that. Dust sifted into my eyes and nostrils and I couldn't move my head far enough to avoid it. The ropes bit into me where the stones didn't.

I felt my circulation shut off and my skin start swelling, ballooning out so that I pressed into the stone on all sides. I thought: anytime now I'll burst out of these ropes and the tape will pop right off my mouth and I'll start screaming again, sputtering around the room, spurting blood and breaking bones.

My gorge rose and I gulped and swallowed and choked down every drop of moisture in me trying not to throw up, because I would have choked to death, with the gag. The rats started trying to burrow into my clothing and all I could do was wiggle and make the ropes bite into me harder to try to chase them away. That made me even more nauseated. If they bit me, it would hurt and maybe the infection would kill me later, but if I vomited, I'd drown in my own juice.

I exhaled as much air as I could through my nose, blowing away the dust, held it, and inhaled, taking in as much oxygen as I could. Or toxic gas. If it was toxic gas as I'd believed, then it might be a better way to die. But the guards hadn't been bothered by it.

All at once the generator kicked in again, and the throb that had once seemed so faint reverberated like a jackhammer through the stone of the cot and walls, each beat booming through my body until my heartbeat was absorbed into it and my breaths skipped two, then three sputters, then four, lengthening, quieting, as I tried to forget where I was and lose myself in that mechanical pulse.

At some point another sound surfaced beneath the throb and mutter, a sound that had been there all along, surely, but that must have been drowned out by the rustle of my clothing and the sound of my breathing. Now it came deep and sonorous, a chant, rising at times then droning away.

Words. I heard words. Most of the chant was like a long groan, a long "oh" sound stretched to infinity, but then, underlying it, were the words. They grew louder, were coming closer.

And slowly, as I listened, I lifted my head, my neck, my shoulders from the cot, very carefully and silently so as to keep in touch with the sound. The chant was not Chinese, not Latin, and certainly not English, though at times the words, phonetically, seemed to be—"war-lord, war-whore, glory-war" over and over again. Then the key shifted, the pitch rose.

My eyes flew open and just for a moment I caught the wall in the act of breathing. It mimicked my breath. When I released mine, the wall released the breath it had been holding and folded in toward me, as if it was the inside of a great lung. Watching for it to expand again, I glanced down and saw myself still lying on the cot, bound and gagged, with my eyes closed.

"Oh," I remember thinking, "so that's it. I'm having

an out-of-body experience. Grandma Viveka warned me there would be times like this. Does this mean I'm dying?"

I decided it must because in the doorway sat the old woman doctor, the colonel, dressed in her guerrilla nomad garb and sitting crosslegged in a lotus pose, staring at me. As I watched, she retreated, never breaking the pose, through the closed door. In fact, she sat—well—with*in* the door for a long time, still staring at me. Her face was so perfectly composed that even her wrinkles were arranged in a methodical design possessing a harmonious beauty which would have astonished the surgeons at home who considered only youthful smoothness beautiful.

But whether I was dying or only dreaming I needed to get my astral—self—out, away from the cell. The doctor nodded a long slow nod that took as long as three phrases of the chant, which was now enhanced with what sounded like a brushed drum or cymbal. I stepped through the door and into the corridor.

Light and the music of the chant flowed through me. I was within the chant, my bare feet sliding along cool tiles instead of the rubble and dirt the floor had consisted of when I was first imprisoned. On graven beams of precious wood spanning the stone walls, animals played and lovers twined, the flickering of the butter lamps in sconces below lending animation to the carvings, so they danced in the smoky glow.

Within a horde of spectral figures, I glided past rooms glittering with filigree and swathed in sunlit smoke. Within the rooms people swayed gracefully as they moved about at their daily business. The windows and deep double doorways beyond them were filled with snowy mountain vistas.

Through one such doorway I entered a broad courtyard. Above and below it gleamed golden roofs and I saw that I was no longer in the underground prison, but in a palace with more tiers than a wedding cake or a California cliff house. The entire edifice was dwarfed, however, by the perfect, conical peak which rose thousands of feet above it. Gardens and rhododendron trees swept down the mountain path from the palace to the foot of the small mountain containing the buildings. Below the path an aquamarine lake spread sparkling to the foot of the peaks opposite.

Although tides of exotically dressed people rolled up the stepped pathway, I slid easily through them and ran toward the lake. But the farther I ran, down the hill and between the blossoming trees toward the cool blue expanse, the fainter the chanting grew until it was suddenly overpowered by a dull pounding, a faint jingle, a grating, and a sharp pain as something was yanked from my face at the same time my legs banged against a wall as I tried to keep running.

The transition from hallucination to reality blurred when I sensed that the guards who had just entered my cell, a woman in thick old-fashioned spectacles and a man I didn't see very clearly, were apparently trying to be human. The man thrust forward an orange quilted uniform that was very much like the blue outfits the guards wore, though theirs were accessorized with boots and belts and hats and such. The woman carefully finished untying me and even chafed my wrists and ankles, then handed me the uniform and indicated a dish of water and a sliver of soap she'd brought. Tentatively, she made washing motions on her own chest in case I was unfamiliar with the procedure. I swear the man even turned his back when I stripped and wiped up my mess with my flight suit. She watched, though, while I dressed in the orange outfit.

"Thanks," I said. "That's better. Anybody for a hand of canasta?" I thought she was almost about to smile. Instead, almost regretfully, she pulled out two pairs of handcuffs. With one pair she cuffed me to the man, with the other pair to herself, and the three of us sidled through the door and marched down the hallway, into another hallway, through a maze of ever ascending twists and turns until we passed a door I was almost certain was the one to Wu's office. That puzzled me, because I thought they were taking me to see her. Then I wondered if I was to be shot instead. They had to half drag me up the stone steps, my feet stumbling on the smooth gullies worn in the stones by the tread of many previous soles.

But I was too dazed from the dream to be very frightened. If they shot me it would relieve the tedium at least, part of me said. And as we emerged into the fresh air and canopy-shaded sunshine, it seemed worth the risk of being executed if only they would do it outdoors. The air I found so thin and oxygen-impoverished when I first arrived now seemed rich and winy compared to the miasma of my cell. I gulped it greedily, coughing out the stinking dusty stuff from my lungs.

We negotiated the ruins in a comical fashion, three abreast, until we came to the very edge of the camouflage canopy. Wu is quite the poser. The little scene she had set up resembled something from an old movie set in one of the resorts Mother used to write about, with the elegant worldly traveler, crosslegged and idle, sipping a drink at her table under a beach umbrella. She was waiting for a companion—me? Surely not. The table held two wine flutes, a bottle, and a bowl of oranges. Down the hill the miniature figures of happy peasants toiled in their fields. Well, actually these were prisoners pounding apart boulders and hauling them from one place to another, as I saw when I looked closer, but it was a nice illusion.

"Viv," she said, waving a wine flute at me. "Sit down. I've been reading your confession. It is a very confusing document. I believe a simple chat might help you clarify your thoughts."

I tried to sit, but the command was awkward to follow with a guard cuffed to each wrist so I had to sit with my hands suspended at shoulder level, while I suppressed an urge to bark.

Wu, however, was determined to chat. She even tried to sound helpful as she said, "I'm very much afraid you are still missing the point."

"Yes?" I had heard her bullshit before and even though it was bullshit vital to the preservation of my life, I was busy being dazzled by the sheer spiring sweep of the snow-laden landscape beaming down at us from its incredible height. More incredible, the prisoners work-

ing in the valley below were nude to the waist and waded
through green shoots, fronds, and lacy ferns proliferating
among the stones. A few hardy young trees sprouted on
the lower edge of the embankment, and small, coura-
geous splashes of scarlet, orchid, jonquil and a pale
tender pink that could only have been flower blossoms
raised their heads defiantly toward the sun.

She followed my eyes and said proudly, as if she
was personally responsible for the scenery, "Here in
Kalapa we are warmed by the sun caught in this bowl
and protected from the winds by the peaks." Distantly,
glaciers creaked and valleys hidden from us rumbled with
unseen storms. Wu listened with me for a moment, then
continued quietly. "Once this place was as beautiful as
its setting, with a lake below where you see now only
stones and many happy people living here and in the
valley until your bombs blew the mountain down on top
of them. Even now, after so many years of back-breaking
labor trying to recover some of what was lost, we have
barely scratched the surface."

"What was it like?" I asked her. "Were there lots
of buildings—were some of the rooms aboveground?"

"Oh, yes, I— How did you know? I will ask the
questions here."

"Excuse me," I said quickly. "I was only curious. I
saw photos once of some of the old lamaseries before
they were destroyed and they were quite impressive. I
wondered if this might be the site of one of them."

"I—yes, something like that. But now I must tell
you, in all seriousness, we have observed that there are
stages in an inmate's progress toward gaining an enlightened attitude and frankly, your confession does not reflect that you are receptive to these. You boast of no
militancy in your childhood, though I am sure you were
taught to oppress others from birth."

"I didn't have much of anyone to oppress, actually,"
I told her. "Except my mother, when she was home.
She wasn't crazy about motherhood. After she stopped
traveling—"

"She was on foreign duty with your NACAF?"

"No, she was on foreign duty as a freelance travel

writer. But then all the terrorist stuff escalated to the point where so many innocent people were being killed that—"

"What innocent people?"

"The ones killed by terrorists."

"There are no innocents. You are all responsible. Those who claim to be innocent by virtue of being apolitical are most guilty of all—it is their apathy that is the greatest crime of all. They are the ones who turn their faces from the slaughter of people in other lands to enjoy the profits your government reaps from supplying would-be conquerors with the wherewithal to oppress others."

"But what about the children? Surely they—"

"Many of the terrorists you speak of are themselves children who were allowed no childhood. But you were telling me about your mother."

I should probably have shut up then. But she was only asking about personal stuff. And I wanted to stay in the fresh air and I wanted to talk to somebody—even Wu. I also wanted her to give me some of the fruit on the table, and kept glancing at it as I talked. I told her how when the United States had first formed the North American Alliance with Canada and what was left of Mexico, Mom had been asked to join up and write propaganda for the draft-and-recruitment program. She had refused, joking that her mama hadn't named her Peace for nothing. She came home to Grandma and Grandpa's house and settled down with us, writing regional stuff. At first it was a little cramped, because the house was just a log cabin in what had originally been wilderness area around Mount Baker. All around my grandfolks' property urban sprawl from Bellingham, now incorporated into Greater Seattle, had taken over. The grandfolks, of course, had the timber ranch for our back yard.

"So," Wu said. "You helped rape the environment."

"We were too late for that. The old-growth stuff was chopped down a long time ago. But Grandad did have a stand of trees older than he was that he was proud of. I didn't do much myself. Mom's idea of raising me was that I read my books while she read hers. Other than that I helped the grandparents with craft projects—they were crazy about making their own soap and weaving things to wear and throwing kind of ugly pots, not that we couldn't have afforded to buy better stuff. They just liked doing it. They did chores by hand too. Not much was automated. It drove Mom crazy sometimes but she said that's how they'd always been. Good thing for me, I guess, because later on I sure couldn't afford a lot of luxuries. I wasn't nuts about helping with harvesting—too noisy—but I liked helping Grandad plant seedlings, even though he had some people he paid to do that."

"No doubt exploiting them," Wu said sourly. "And I understand that it is a particular kind of luxury in your country to do things as simply as those in other places are forced to do them for lack of adequate technology and a shortage of resources."

"Which are short," I finished for her, reciting by rote the rhetoric I had heard since childhood, "because we treated the trees like our personal property, buying and selling them, chopping them down and burning their stumps, leaving the country barren and making toilet tissue from them."

"You admit this?"

"My grandparents and their friends were always bitching—er, expressing the same viewpoint during their spit and whittle sessions." I'm not sure whether I actually said the last part or thought it. I'd noticed that among the bronzed backs and orange jackets a black torso earnestly stooped and straightened, stooped and straightened. The Colonel? As I finished my last sentence he stopped and stared uphill, straight at me. I wiggled my fingers a little but he gave no acknowledgment. A guard started toward him and he bent back to his work again. I felt myself sagging in the cuffs. He probably thought I was betraying the entire cellblock, though just how I could betray them in my present circumstances I had no idea. Good thing Wu didn't offer me one of those oranges to dish the dirt with her about my fellow prisoners. I might have made something up to get that orange. The very memory of the taste made me sick with hunger.

"You do not look very well, Viv Vanachek."

"I'm not," I said shortly.

"Impure thinking has been known to cause illness," she said primly. Then she surprised me by taking a tone that could only be described as defensive. "You are given good water from the same pool and food from the same pot as the rest of us. You have been allowed privacy and time to think and yet have offered offensive and unreasonable behavior to your attendants. We are not servants and you are not to be a spoiled princess as you were in your homeland. You have yet to present me with a good reason why we should continue to nurture you here."

I wasn't tracking too well by then. My stomach was cramping again and I was half afraid and half longing to barf all over her elegant spread. But two things in her last speech struck me with sudden, startling clarity. One was that she seemed genuinely offended that I didn't admit that I was actually thriving under her so-called care and that solitary confinement provided just the relaxing atmosphere I needed to contemplate the error of my ways. The other was the puzzled note in her voice. This woman, who was supposedly in charge of the camp, had no better idea why I was here than I did. Her rhetoric was an automatic spouting of dogma, but far from having me beaten or even seriously intimidating me, she seems baffled and irritated by my presence. Despite her posturing, I don't think she finds me particularly slimy or guilty of anything. But here I am for some reason we have both yet to learn and she's stuck with me. The writing, which she fortunately doesn't seem to keep very good track of, and the interrogations in the form of little chats, have seemed pointless for a very good reason, which is that she doesn't *know* the point. And neither do I. It just never occurred to me that there had to be one.

When she dismissed me I tried to burn the image of those mountains onto my retinas as the guards led me away, and I gulped deep breaths of the fresh air, trying to hoard it all the way back down to my cell.

LATER

I can't seem to think. I couldn't keep so much as a nibble down. The guards were pissed because my legs stopped working on the steps and I almost dragged us all down headfirst. I'll bet that sadistic bitch let me out just so the contrast between out there and down here would make me even more miserable. I wish she'd have these damned belly cramps and tell me it was *her* impure thoughts. Well, I do reject this whole mess and maybe I eject it too. Why the hell is she doing this to me if she doesn't know what I'm here for? Jesus! On the other hand, maybe I'd better hope she doesn't think about it too long. I doubt she'd bother chartering a plane to take me out of here if she thought there *was* no reason. In that case, the point is apt to turn out to be at the end of someone's bayonet. They probably don't waste bullets on people who have no purpose being here.

If only I could sleep again. Lately I just sort of drift in and out of daydreams, most of them fragments and abstractions—no more visions, no more real-seeming places like the one in the dream, the one I seem to have picked up from Wu's romanticizing about how this place used to be before the big bad imperialists spoiled it all. Not even any nightmares like the one about the children. When I close my eyes and try to bring back the mountains—both the real ones, outside, and those from the dream—I can barely remember them. Only their general shapes remain. The colors and detail wash away like an overexposed photograph.

God, a person shouldn't have to have an identity crisis in the middle of a prison camp. *I* don't know what my purpose is, here or in general. I've never made any sense out of anything. Oh, I used to be excited if something in a lecture or a book awakened some response in me, some sense of recognition, so that another piece seemed to slip into a huge puzzle, or turned the kaleidoscope another fraction so that I caught a glimpse of a whole new pattern. But none of it was any bloody good. Nobody ever asked me at job interviews what insights I'd gained from the sociobiology of the late twentieth century.

As for the facts, the vast piles of data I've acquired, I forgot it as soon as I no longer needed it to pass exams. As if I were climbing a sand dune, the little individual grains of information slid beneath my feet while I reached for more, so I never made any progress. I might be able to walk around the bottom of the dune, but I can't conquer it and even if I did, miles of other dunes stretch beyond that one. Just knowing that had once been a delight and a comfort but I have never grasped anything that was a solid foundation for anything else, something I can hold in my hand and show someone else. "Here. This is mine. I know this."

I joined the military because there was no other place for me, and I ended up here. Now it seems I have to justify my existence even here. Whatever happened to "I think, therefore I am"? What I think is that I'm too sick and too tired to deal with this shit. Oh, God. Back to the slop bucket.

LATER

人 Forget above. Cramps real bad. Blood in bucket. Can't track. Dying? Maybe.

God—hemorrhage at both ends. Hide this. I'll hide this so the next poor sap maybe won't be so iso . . .

PART THREE

DREAM, DEATH, AND (PARTIAL) DELIVERY

I must have fainted and fallen off the bunk, hit my head on the floor. Maybe I slipped in the blood. It was everywhere, gushing out from between my legs, sounding like a fountain splashing as it hit the floor, exploding against the wall as I vomited, choked, coughed and vomited again. Cramps sledgehammered my guts, pumping the blood out at both ends. One minute I was drowning in it, the next a blinding cymbal crash of pain reinitiated the soft, guttural chanting.

It rose and fell, rose and fell, timed to my belly's churning, its sonorous moan all the while descending in volume and pitch until it came from the guts of the palace, the dungeon, then from the earth itself. But as the last long "O" note faded, a high chiming note reinforced it, and the liquid tinkle of a single bell.

The tiled corridor reached out to meet me this time, fan folding away as I rushed through it, until I came upon an outer door so filled with mountain that not until I had left the confines of the building and walked several feet out onto the terrace, looking up and then higher and yet higher still, could I see the whole vast muscle of the earth, sleeved with white, immense and powerful. Below, almost straight down, the lake glittered as if sprinkled with blue and silver sequins, beckoning me. But I remembered from the other dream that when I ran straight toward the lake, I woke up. So this time I resisted my yearning for the lake and with an effort turned away from it to gaze at the palace surrounding me.

The golden roofs were not really gold, but tiles of lapis and amber the sun's blinding rays had melted into a honeyed glaze. Dragon gargoyles with elephant tusks leered through the rivulets of water running from their mouths down the corners of the buildings. Stone steps, geodes inlaid among the rocks, led from the terrace where I stood to another terrace and into another room and there a beautiful young Asian woman played what I would have thought was a spinet piano—except that the notes still rang like bells and chimes. The woman's slender hands danced on the keys, the curve of her long black hair flowing past her shoulders suggested serenity itself.

She didn't speak or acknowledge me and I accepted that I must be a ghost, or she was, and with the music somehow growing louder as I drifted farther from her, I entered another open doorway.

Beyond was no dreary corridor but a room bigger than the lobby of the Federal Building in downtown Seattle. The ceiling was painted, not carved, and inlaid with a design of silver-and-gold-rimmed ivory clouds. The walls were lined with bookshelves filled with everything from wood and leather-bound tomes to well-thumbed bright-colored paperbacks. At tables scattered throughout the room, people studied, worked puzzles, and played games like chess and checkers and others that were unfamiliar. The dice they used and the game pieces were beautifully sculpted from exotic woods such as zebra wood and vermilion. One chess set had pieces carved from amethyst on one side and garnet on the other. I fingered the books—the most beautiful were old sets of classics, many of them my favorites, others by unfamiliar authors; yet others had the titles and names in Cyrillic script, Hebrew, Arabic and other less common alphabets. Fiction, mythology, folklore, science, art, philosophy, mathematics, architecture, every imaginable subject and discipline was represented. I stroked the supple spines and read the titles yearningly, wondering if I could possibly stay long enough to read any of them.

But a perfume stronger than that of old paper, wood and leather led me on, with something of jasmine and something of musk in its fragrance. A wisp of white flickered through a set of double doors and I followed it.

And was suddenly swimming through a sea of billowing silken scarves. Like clouds flying past the moon, they played with the wavering light so that the rest of the room was even less substantial as to size, shape and feature than the scarves themselves. I might have been outdoors, with the scarves fluttering from tree branches, for all I could tell while I was among them. Filmy and deceptive, they concealed, then revealed, what usually turned out to be another wave of scarves. Once it seemed that they parted for a fraction of a fraction of a second and, as if through a distant well-curtained window, I glimpsed the moon, though a short time before I'd stood in sunlight. But the time was not an issue. No urgency existed here aside from that which mysteriously drove me.

The scarves fluttered tickling like moth wings or eyelashes and I breathed them in as if they were a cloud of insects. I knew that just ahead lay something beautiful, something—perfect, but as I strained toward it the scarves fell tangling in my hands and feet, dragging the ground, weighing me down and down until I sank back into something soft and spongy, sticky and sore.

"Viveka? Viv, now you stay with me, girl. Stay with me now." The voice was prosaic, dull and flat, the music gone. Thibideaux and Marsh swam into focus, looming above me like a two-headed monster.

Marsh patted my arm. "You should have said you were pregnant. These people can be human sometimes too, you know."

"How was she gonna know that?" the man with the childish blond curls, Danielson, snapped. "Look at her bruises. They probably beat her until she lost it."

I felt the bruises he referred to, deep, burning aches at my chin, forehead, cheekbones, knees and chest. I couldn't remember anybody laying a finger on me, though. Maybe my fall had preceded convulsions? I thought I ought to say something about it but my voice wouldn't work, so I closed my eyes and contented myself with listening.

Marsh responded in a withering voice, "If they'd done that, Du, why in the hell would they give us back Thibideaux's transfusion kit?"

Thibideaux interrupted. "You've lost a lot of blood but fortunately the Colonel and Marsh are both O-positive. How you feelin'?"

I hurt. That was how I felt. And I didn't want to talk. Besides the bruises, my gut ached, my vulva burned with pain, and there was a professional-looking white gauze bandage on my left arm. I felt as if I was floating about two inches above the cot and their voices were all coming from some distance away. I could barely lift my eyelids to look at anyone.

Colonel Merridew leaned over me, "We're sorry about your baby," he said, and handed me one of the pale pink blossoms from the valley floor. "Welcome back."

Baby? Was that it, then? The cramps, the vomiting—

The dream. The loss of a baby I had not known I carried is much less real to me than the dream. The guard noticing blood puddling under my door and finding me simply didn't happen. I was in the library at the time. I had never had a baby—I was gravida zero, para zero. Had been deliberately, chemically sterile since I was eighteen. Must have worn off. Nevertheless, the pregnancy was unsought and unexpected; the baby would have been a rapist's child to be raised by an inmate mother in a prisoner of war camp—no loss. Surely no loss. (But what would it have been? Boy or girl? What color hair and eyes? What would I have called it? Maybe it would have had the best qualities from my family and whatever good might have once been in Buzz . . .) Doggedly, I pursued the dream, sleeping at every opportunity.

The cell simply dissolved and re-formed into the palace or sometimes places remembered from home. The men's voices called me back periodically, then were gone

altogether. The guards left me alone, although one day
I rolled over and saw Wu staring at me from the door.
Her expression was one I carried back into the dream—
it reminded me of a programmer scanning the screen to
see if a new project would run, and finding many glitches.

The men's voices ebbed and flowed with the snow-
shadowed light dappling the dirty floor. The little room
was bare, filled with men or with grain. Once it expanded
and filled to capacity with mumbling people and a lifelike
statue that remained even after the people left, until
dust fell on it, and on me, and the day lengthened to fill
a span of years.

Another time something cold dribbled across my
lips, down my chin and neck, and I awoke to Danielson's
dulcet voice saying, "Come on, Vanachek, drink up.
There's a girl. Look, you got to make it. You can't just
stay down like that."

Why not? I wondered. The miscarriage had apparently promoted me, in the eyes of my fellow prisoners,
from potential spy to Fragile Flower of Thwarted American Motherhood. But I was a thirsty fragile flower, so
I sat up and took a swig from the plastic mug he held to
my lips. I almost gagged on it. "My God, it's fresh."

"From mother-fucking-nature's tap. We blew up a
boulder today and uncovered more of the buried lake.
The Dragon Lady was so thrilled she let me off work
detail to bring you a drink. They must think you're pretty
valuable—they've been keeping our bunker open during
the day so we could check on you. When I first came
here, she had me beaten until I thought I'd never walk,
talk, or pee without bleeding again and she sure didn't
have any kind of a compassionate nervous breakdown
over it. Same thing with the Colonel, though she's gone
a little easier on Thibideaux and Marsh, 'cause of Marsh's
political connections, I guess. None of us have heard of
her killing anybody yet, though, so maybe she's just
squeamish about killing little kids, though I'd have sworn
that broad doesn't have a soft bone in her itty-bitty
body."

The water was crunchy with rock and dirt but had
a sweet flavor that reminded me of flowers. What didn't

slide down my throat trickled outside my mouth and
down my chin, cooling my hot skin, making a little spot
of awareness that lingered until the water evaporated
and Danielson returned to work.

Most of the time, though, I was in that wonderful
palace where I listened to intelligent and esoteric conversations on subjects and in languages I should not have
been able to understand. Most people here wore Asian
clothing, not always the silks and satins which I thought
people who lived in such a place would wear, but often
simple cottons and woolens, comfortable and utilitarian.
Some did wear gorgeous costumes and there were even
a few obvious Westerners among them, some in rather
archaic costumes—I noticed one genuine 1960s flower
child, a middle-aged woman in a nineteenth-century
traveling gown, a couple of blocky blond men, one wearing what looked like Viking clothes, and a couple of dark-
skinned men wearing African textiles. Also, there were
several Indians, both saried women and men in historic
native garb. Sometimes some of the people were gathered at the statues, as if in religious observance, but
other times they simply talked in groups, attended what
appeared to be lectures, read, gardened, or did craftwork
of some sort. The same faces appeared frequently, lec-
turing, listening, praying. One monk was in almost every
group: a man with a face like a Mexican opal—stony and
rough-hewn—set with eyes radiant as smoky topaz, a
complex and tender intelligence firing their depths.

I drifted happily from one conversation to the next,
entered into the pages of the books and dreamed my
way through them. Pieces of plots and bits of information
blew through my mind like incense smoke when I woke
long enough to eat or drink and use the toilet bucket.
But as soon as possible, I dozed again and the palace
reappeared, great halls lined with sublime art treasures
my art history classes had informed me were long ago
lost in some war or other.

The rooms opened for me as if I were Beauty in the
Beast's palace, I thought, blending the dream with a story
from one of the dilapidated old books of fairy tales Mother

had given me as a present after she rescued it from a library burn pile.

Finally, I was jolted into the present by the palace bathtub. The sight of a chubby monk up to his ears in bubble bath in a green porcelain tub with a bronze plaque proudly declaring it to have been made in Akron, Ohio, was so comfortingly ordinary after the magnificence of the palace and the bleakness of the camp that I woke up smiling, cool and clear-headed, enjoying the daylight pouring through the grille into the little gray stone room.

And there I was, alone with a bucket full of turds and urine, a half-eaten bowl of food—no momo this time but maggoty rice with a few dried vegetables stirred in to provide three basic food groups—the starchy rice, the vegetables, and the protein in the maggots. The cell no longer revolted me. It felt warm and familiar. My head still hummed with images from the dreams, passages from the books, murmured conversations, wisps of songs and melodies, the surging rhythm of the chants, but I felt alert and perfectly content with the present experienced in the soothing wake of the dreams.

Alone, unguarded, and so full of sensation that solitary no longer held any terror for me, I began wishing for my papers and pen, and recalled that they were in my old cell. I blithely set out for the command bunker, expecting no problem since the door of my old cell no doubt opened easily from outside.

A tiny rational part of my brain rattling around somewhere in all the fairy dust and musk mist kept yelling warnings, but the rest of me ignored it. I felt serene and confident and besides, rescuing the journal seemed vital. It had surpassed all the reasons I had for beginning it and had become necessary to me. The time to fetch it was while the others thought me still too ill to move. Later, I might be locked up again or closely guarded as I worked with the men.

My real body was far clumsier than my dream self as I stepped out into the ugly sandbagged hallway and climbed the steps. The soles of my feet barely registered the touch of stones, as if they'd been numbed, and the door took all my strength to budge. It was heavily carved, obviously made for guarding grander things than a make-shift dungeon.

Air sharp and thin as pine needles pierced the door-way and shattered the spiderwebs whose strands shimmered in a rectangle of suddenly revealed sunlight.

Outside voices murmured from the end of the compound where Wu had erected her terrace table.

Within the baffling maze of ruins and boulders under the canopy I took two wrong turns, but after a third turn the command bunker was directly in front of my nose; the door had been left open, presumably to air out the stale, stinking passages below.

The warren of halls and rooms was dark and silent, except for the scrabble of loose rubble falling somewhere beyond the rectangle of light from the open door. No generator hum.

"This is crazy, old girl," I told myself, but down the steps I went, thinking I would figure out where I needed to go. But at the end of the hall that should have led past Wu's office was a collapsed wall. I felt along crumbly stone wall until my hands met open spaces flanking the rubble-cluttered wall on each side. Hopeless. I tried to turn back toward the entrance but after retracing a few steps ran into another pile of splinter and stone. This adventure was apt to lead to disaster without a light of some sort.

By that time, I'd begun to wake up and no longer floated around, feeling like my own ghost. Wide awake, I became more concerned—no, let's be honest, scared— that someone would find me here, unauthorized. If only I could find Wu's office I could snitch a candle or a flashlight from her desk. And maybe more writing paper and pens too.

But which door? Two corridors in and the third on the left, surely. But which two and which left? After a couple of tries, I thought I had found the right route, but another landslide of debris disabused me of that illusion.

Then suddenly voices called out, footsteps trotted

off in several different directions, and after a moment, the generator sputtered like a resuscitated drowning victim and the narrow corridors flooded with incriminating light.

With a measured scuffle one set of feet detached from the general melee and headed in my direction. I wedged myself behind the rubble, dislodging some of it. The steps paused and squeaked ever so slightly, the squeak of shoe sole on a hard surface as the occupant of the shoes turned. The occupant must have been peering into the debris but I crouched low behind it and closed my eyes, the better not to be seen, and after a few moments the footsteps scuffled away.

Okay. The light question was solved. But now how could I avoid detection while looking for my old cell? For that matter, how was I to return to my *new* cell without being discovered? Sliding from concealment, I tiptoed into the glare of the single bulb, my shadow stretching up the wall beside me.

Two corridors led into the central hall and its branches, and I hadn't really noticed the second one, the one I was in, the finer architectural details having escaped me on previous occasions when I was distracted by wondering if I was going to be killed or merely tortured a little. My corridor led into the other one from the side, just as it branched off. I had only to hang a right and I'd be headed straight back for the entrance now guarded by a cute couple sporting matching assault rifles.

My belly cramped again and I crabbed back toward the concealment of the rubble as I glimpsed two more guards headed up the second branch. One of them swung a finger this way and that, as if pointing out the color of paint he wanted on the walls, what fabric he wanted for the curtains, that sort of thing—renovation plans, in other words. When the first guard departed, the second extracted something from his pocket and made straight for my rubble pile. A flashlight beam passed over my head, into the corridor beyond. Where the beam penetrated behind the rubble, I was surprised to see that there was another corridor, relatively clear of debris, the ceiling still pretty much intact. Deep shadows cast by the white beam sank into a series of doorways, some seemingly arched at the top. When the guard left, I crept back, feeling along the wall until first one, then another, and finally a third door gave to my touch. Luckily for me the previous occupants hadn't believed in locks.

The room had the feeling of something vast—the air was less stale and smelly than in the hallway and I wondered if it contained an opening to the surface. If so, I had better find it cautiously, for the guard with the swinging finger looked as if he might be planning to work around here soon and any noise louder than that of your average well-fed rat would betray me.

I groped my way forward but felt nothing until my face ran into something fine and sticky, which clung to it. Spiderwebs? If so, I hoped the spiders were away from home and plunged ahead regardless, traversing the room as quickly as possible, expecting to see a flashlight beam and hear an order to halt at any moment. Perhaps I should have stayed near the door where I could mug the guard for his flashlight and escape back to the room before anyone else came, but no, if something happened to one of the guards Wu would probably not only find and punish me but vent her wrath on all of the other prisoners as well.

Besides, I wasn't here to mug anyone. I just wanted my journal.

My toe stubbed against what turned out to be a step, followed by a second and a third step, and finally by a platform that hit me at waist height. I felt the surface, my fingers encountering metal, cloth, stone and—eureka! paper.

The metal was a small noisy object perforated by cross-shaped holes. From the ringing sound it made I thought at first it was a bell, but at my touch it fell into two pieces and I recognized it as an incense burner like the ones the grandfolks had kept throughout the cabin until Grandad's emphysema made it hard for him to breathe the smoke.

Incense! Of course, that was the underlying sweetish note to the stink in the hall. Incense. I felt around some more, hoping there might be something more useful. When I found it, it took me a moment to remember what it was—a little book of matches that, when I lit one (after three tries), I saw carried the advertising legend of the St. Joe, Missouri, Holiday Inn.

Holiday Inn? The chain had been defunct since before Mother quit her job—I remembered her telling stories of the great motel chains that once spanned the country in the days when civilians could travel from state to state and even cross national borders without a pass from their city council, a written and notarized invitation from a friend or relative at the destination point guaranteeing a place to stay or an authorization to use a federally regulated hostel while visiting military personnel. Nowadays, people got around the regulations by having more than one home—one near their business and another, usually more comfortable, to escape to on days off.

But the matches harked back to a time when travel had been simple and fairly inexpensive, when anyone could travel anywhere. Before the random killings and drug traffic had become so ferocious and far-flung that even police in big cities *had* to know who everyone was and have addresses for all citizens at all times. Still, what a shame.

More remarkable than the origin of the matches was their age and the fact that they still lit. There were only ten remaining, so when the first one died and I lit another, I controlled my antiquarian's wonder long enough to discover an equally esoteric artifact near by. A ceramic bowl with a wick that looked as if it was made of dental floss lay a few inches away, buried in the dust as the matches had been until my hand uncovered them. Under the dust, the lamp still held a layer of congealed fat. After sacrificing a few more matches, I had a dusty-smelling, smoky light.

And saw that I held this open flame in a room filled with fragile, flammable objects. What I had mistaken for cobwebs were thousands of gauzy scarves, so old and rotted that they were as thin and transparent as any spider's handiwork. They hung forlornly from the ceiling, like the remnants of ghosts who'd caught their shrouds and torn them trying to get loose.

Luckily, as that thought hit me, I spotted the connecting door to the next room. Cupping the flame of the lamp in one palm, I bumped the door open with my hip and found myself staring at—the bathtub of my dreams.

The color was hard to discern, but it was dark, not white or pastel, and there was a little bronze plaque on it that, when I knelt to read it, proclaimed through the tarnish that the tub had been manufactured in Akron, Ohio.

Ooh. Déjà vu, as Grandma's old crony Autumn Dawn was apt to exclaim at odd moments. At that moment vertigo overtook me and I couldn't tell if I was in the dream with my body back in my cell or perhaps even dreaming this whole thing from a barracks or a dormitory room.

What was real was that I had a deep physical longing to fill the smooth cool curves of that tub with hot soapy water and take a nice long, preferably bubbly, soak. My muscles fairly wept as I resolutely turned my back on the object of my lust to examine the rest of the room.

Like the other cells, this one contained a stone sleeping bench but this was the deluxe edition, with a covering of some silky rotting cloth to which clung bits of dried grass. A faint smell of herbs clung to it, reminding me of Grandma's hiking manuals, in which she was wont to press various hapless plant specimens.

An expletive from the next room announced that someone else had entered and had encountered an obstacle.

The room contained no other door than the one through which I had entered. Funny place for an extra john. But then, perhaps it was a ritual bath for purification, prior to worship. Certainly I was praying for all I was worth as I crawled as quietly as possible into the tub. I thought about dragging the dried grass mattress over me but first I had to extinguish the lamp and by that time the connecting door was creaking open again.

So I lay still and waited, closing my eyes so their shine wouldn't give me away (okay, maybe I hoped it

would make me invisible). The incense burner, which
I'd stuck into the pocket of my prison uniform, rang ever
so slightly as I shifted in the bottom of the metal tub,
setting up a sympathetic vibration with other bells, other
chimes. *Not now*, I thought, then realized that the
chimes and bells were from the next room, where the
ritual was being celebrated.

And, sure enough, as I lay there, the monk with
the Mexican opal face rose from where he was bent over
the tub.

A flashlight ray brushed my eyelids, then a shadow
fell over it. I allowed one eyeball a squint, but I didn't
need my physical eyes to see the monk, still facing me,
standing between me and the soldier with the flashlight.
The monk stepped back and so did the soldier, closing
the door softly behind him.

And so I was literally saved by the bell. Or my own
delusions. Or the guard's nearsightedness, perhaps. His
glasses might have been fogged up. Still, one thing is
clear and that is that my dreams right now are the better
part of reality, if they are dreams. Maybe these are not
exactly ghosts, but memories I'm seeing. I used to read
stories about old houses with memories, back when there
were houses old enough to have such things. If this was
one of the lamaseries destroyed by the Chinese invasion
it was hundreds of years old. If all the monks had been
murdered by the Chinese, well, then their memories
might be sympathetic to another prisoner. Or maybe I'm
the ghost.

The room with the altar and scarves contained neither ghosts nor men when I peered back into it, my
panting breath loud and echoing in that vast place. I lit
the lamp again and started back for the hall. Then I saw
the other door, off to one side, beyond a pair of supporting pillars I hadn't noticed before.

Shielding the lamp flame, I slipped through the
door. The chamber was as large as the one I'd come
from, but this time the rustlings came from things my
feet brushed against. I lowered the lamp and its smoky
glow captured the translucent paleness of a crumpled
page covered in print. I scooped it up and heard a tearing

sound as I sundered the last connection it had to the book that lay beneath it. As I swung the lamp a little wider, I saw that the floor was all but impassable with great drifts and piles of books and papers.

By the butter lamp's light I could make out only a few characters, which looked like Arabic. Next to where the page had lain on the floor, however, sprawled an only slightly disheveled softbound copy of *Huckleberry Finn*. Odd, picking up something you first touched in a dream. I rescued the *Huck*, slipping it into my trouser band. Mark Twain will be good company in prison, something the men can enjoy too. No one will miss it. The mess on that floor surely hasn't been touched since whatever catastrophe befell it. From the actions of the guards and the pile of debris blocking most of the outer corridor, I gather that they have just uncovered this passage. I'm glad I found the books before some zealous revolutionary makes a bonfire of them. I've read about the atrocities the PRC committed against the literature of this region— throwing ancient hand-copied Buddhist scriptures into the streets so that people either had to stay in their houses or trample the sacred writings underfoot. Very clever and very *mean* to force people to destroy their own symbols. Not that *Huck* is much of a symbol of anything, but its value as humorous entertainment will no doubt be lost on these fanatics.

After a moment I realized that I now had the opportunity to leave my diary in its hiding place and take advantage of the paper all around me for further entries. With a little sifting, I found plenty of empty front and back pages, wide margins, and more reading material. On the bottom layer there were even broken pencils and old-fashioned ballpoints (ash dry). I stuffed two of the pencils into my pocket to keep the incense burner company and added the least-printed pages from several ruined books.

The dream ran true and there was a door where there should have been. It opened inward so I had to scoot back enough of the literary carpet to tug the door toward me and slide through to where the music room should have been. Instead, I stepped once more into a ruin, perforated by light and riddled with fresh air that blew out my lamp and sent the pages in the room behind me scuttling like road trash in the wake of a big rig.

Once beyond the rubble I was back in the open, with the ruined mountain looming moodily over me, its cleft full of mist, as if it had a cold that day. Below, my fellow prisoners including some who looked like women and children, worked up and down the ridge and in the boulder-strewn valley.

And up the slope, wending her way among her empire of boulders, slaves and minions, minced Wu, in earnest conversation with a companion whose gait was more straightforward but no less sprightly. The pair of them were headed straight toward me.

All of my instincts said, "Run" but every system in my body said, "No way." Logic said, "Run where?" Besides, I would have lost *Huck* and the lamp whereas if I bluffed it out . . . After all, the cell door hadn't been locked.

So I called out, "Commandant Wu, there you are. I was hoping I might get a chance to speak with you."

PART FOUR

ASSIGNMENT

人 "Ah, I see you are feeling better," said Wu's companion, none other than the peasant woman—doctor—hypnotist colonel. "Commandant Wu tells me you have been ill." The seamed face wore an overly solicitous expression—I almost expected her to click her tongue in a grandmotherly fashion.

"I can't think why," I said. "Fresh air and exercise are supposed to be so good for one and you did see to it that I got plenty of that sort of thing. The commandant considerately added a prescription for rest and quiet as well."

"Which you have disobeyed," Wu reminded me. "You have left your cell without permission." She all but hissed through her teeth. It is a particular refinement of torment to have such a woman for commandant because when she is at her harshest I still keep getting the feeling that after she makes such a pronouncement she will go backstage, take off her makeup, put on her party dress and go out dancing, a perfectly normal young woman. Her personnel manager style is more convincing, since I've known lots of apparently perfectly normal young women who turn into authoritarian bitches given that little bit of power. But a prison camp commandant? It would have helped if they could have gotten someone who naturally looked a little meaner.

I assumed my own role, that of thoroughly cowed

prisoner, even managing to hang my head a little. "The door was open. I assumed—".

"Assumptions of that sort have been known to prove painful," she said.

Now the old woman did hiss, in that admonishing way some older Asian women use. She wasn't hissing me, however, she was hissing Wu, who looked oddly wounded, a child unjustly admonished for fighting when her brother started it first.

Both reactions were intriguing—that the old woman should disapprove not of my leaving my cell but of Wu threatening me, and that Wu should listen to her, and react with more hurt than anger at such an obvious countermanding of her authority. Nothing further developed at that moment, however, because Marsh appeared from around a sandbagged corner.

"Ah, Mr. Marsh," Wu said in her Dragon Lady voice.

He steepled his hands in a short bow to both of them and with a sidelong glance at the old doctor, asked Wu, "You wanted to see me, Commandant?"

She nodded curtly but her pretty face was not quite as sour as it had been. Marsh's face was carefully bland and congenial.

"Mr. Marsh, we have uncovered a new passage which will require some delicacy in further excavation, cataloging and restoration. Perhaps you would like such an assignment?" She made the suggestion loftily, a queen bestowing a favor, but her eyes flicked nervously to the old woman.

Marsh surprised me. I would think he'd go for this more intellectual sort of job but for some reason he looked wary and shook his head. "I'm not really qualified for that kind of work."

Wu's china-doll face hardened a little. "Then perhaps you can suggest another more suitable applicant."

Marsh made another polite bow. I swear he was enjoying it. "Commandant Wu, I am a civilian and would of course have no idea about the capabilities of the soldiers. And segregated as we are from the other prisoners, I would have no idea of *their* aptitudes either. Perhaps

you should consult Colonel Merridew, who would surely
know if any of his men have the experience you require."

"Marsh, you are a spy and a liar," Wu said sweetly.
"You have been here many years and you are the sort
of man who makes it his business to know others. I fear
I—"

The old woman made a funny, throat-clearing hum
and said, "Miss Vanachek, I believe, has some training
in anthropology and related areas."

"Very good," Wu snapped, sounding disappointed
to be distracted from her game with Marsh. "She should
be good for something besides hysterics and lying about."
And to the nearest guard she said, "Take this prisoner
to Captain Taring."

Marsh winked at me as I turned to follow the guard.
We returned to the entrance to the bunkers, down the
corridors I had so recently traveled, and walked straight
up to the man I'd avoided by crawling into the bathtub.
This Captain Taring was bent over a rubble pile when
we arrived and when the guard presented me, he merely
nodded and waved his hand that I should wait.

The guard marched away and I duly shifted from
one foot to another and tried to peer over the man's
shoulder to see what was so fascinating. When he still
didn't seem inclined to take notice of me I leaned a little
farther over—cautiously, becoming very aware of how
badly I needed a bath. I still smelled of sweat and sick-
ness and my hair was matted and felt crawly. Fresh
patches of dust overlay the generally dirty condition of
my trousers. I hitched *Huck* up and brushed a cobweb
from my sleeve, then stopped moving around as I heard
the deafening crackle of the contraband paper in my
pockets.

My new boss handed me back something over his
shoulder and when it took me a moment to realize he
wanted me to take it, he turned and offered it more
openly, bouncing his hand slightly to indicate I should
relieve him of it and raising his eyebrows encouragingly.

But I could only stare at him, expecting to hear the
chanting and see my body lying dreaming below me.
His face was pitted with old scars and rough as a gravel

pit, but his eyes had the same clear topaz beauty as those of the monk in my dreams. The two men were so much alike it was hard to believe they weren't the same, but of course, this man could be a descendant or even a relative—or maybe just a fellow sufferer of whatever disease blemished the face so that the clarity and depth of the eyes made such a remarkable contrast.

"This humble person begs your illustrious pardon," I began in obsequious Mandarin, but he waved his hand and said, "Whoa there, little lady. Hang on to that thought until I am having me a closer look at this here piece of carving."

He sounded like a foreign version of those old John Wayne films my Great-uncle Medicine Bear Kowalski used to bring over to amuse Grandpa Ananda after Grandma died. He looked more like the other old films Uncle Bear used to bring over, though, the ones about the adventurous anthropologist with the name of the state, who was always hunkering over something ancient and valuable when he wasn't leaping over something or running from something.

Captain Taring handed me a splinter of the carving. "What are you thinking of this?"

"Ruined ceiling beam?" I ventured brightly. That wasn't hard. I'd seen the entire beam intact, in my dream. It was the one with birds soaring through stylized clouds.

He grunted, standing up and, oddly enough, offering his hand. "You are being new around these parts, are you not?"

"Yes. Yes, I am," I said, giving him my name and restraining my impulse to add that I was the new schoolmarm, providing rank and serial number instead. He vigorously pumped my hand, which he had had to retrieve from my side since I was too slow to offer it.

"Name of Lobsang Taring, but I am taking it kindly if you are just calling me Tea, little lady, like they did so back when I am getting my grad-yu-ate *dee*-gree at the Montana School of Mines."

This unlikely prison guard with what seemed a deliberately dopey accent (I had never heard another per-

son in the camp who spoke English speak it so strangely)
went on to explain that the "round-eye" boys at the
mining school had trouble with his name but the one tea
drinker in the crowd decided it was the same as Lapsang
Souchong tea. This explanation prompted the nickname.
Tea "reckons" I'd better call him Captain when others
are around.

We spent the rest of the daylight hours underground, clearing the rubble pile that blocked the en-
trances to the library and the room of scarves. We had
to sift through the rubble, rather than just shovel it away,
and anything that looked like it had once been ornamental or useful was laid carefully aside for cataloging,
which Tea explained we would do on the portable ter-
minal of the camp's computer.

Toward midafternoon, Tea left me to do the sifting
and began reconstructing the support structure of the
tunnel entrance. Two other men helped him with a hand-
saw and hammers, setting up notched logs on either side
of the rubble pile.

I'm tired and sore from bending and digging but
otherwise feel remarkably well. By the time we finished
today, the sun outside had given way to dusk, and wind
whipped my pajama top around me and sent showers of
snow flying from the rippling canopy. In the eastern
corner, two guards were scurrying around to shore up
an end of the net that had blown loose. From the mountain, snow blew from the horns of the ruined cone like
the veil on an elaborate medieval headdress.

Funny how quickly a person adjusts to anything.
The inside of the prison bunker feels almost like home
now. I find myself appreciating how the sandbagged walls
of the outer hall keep it insulated from the wind, and
the guard was not even surly as she nodded me inside
tonight.

And now it looks as if I'll have some opportunity to
be of use to the men and pay them back a little for taking
care of me—it seems that ever since I arrived they have
had to look after me. But my new boss seems like a
reasonable guy and I should be able to sneak more books
and things from the library, maybe even some more

matches and lamps. Not your major luxurious amenities maybe, but more than we have now.

LATER

🕱 The reaction from the men is not as unanimously enthusiastic as I might have hoped. They filed in shortly after I returned, while I was busily scribbling notes. I thought they would probably be glad to have me greet them cheerfully, relatively healthily for a change. "Hi guys, you are not going to believe the day I had . . . ," I began.

Thibideaux rolled his eyes at me and eased himself carefully onto his bunk before drawling wearily, "Mercy me, all recovered and chipper, are we?"

"Well, I *am* much better, thanks to the excellent care," I said quickly, hoping that flattery might improve his receptiveness, though his only response was a skeptical grunt. But then, he didn't know what I was going to say so he couldn't very well get excited beforehand. I plunged ahead, glad to finally have something to share with the others, after depending on them so heavily for so long. Once Marsh, Danielson and the Colonel were inside I began hauling my booty out of my pockets. "Look at this, will you? I found a lamp and these matches—from one of those old motel chains in Missouri, and this incense burner too—"

But Thibideaux was not the only one who was less than thrilled with my news.

"Great," Marsh said. "We can burn incense to disguise the smell of our wild dope parties. That way the guards won't suspect a thing."

I shrugged, puzzled by all this ennui. "Well, at least

it would be a change to have the cell smell like something besides shit, don't you think?"

Marsh was lying stomach down on his bunk, paring the dirt from his broken nails with a single long thumbnail. He told the others in a dry, rather accusatory voice, "Viv went to work with Lobsang Taring in the command bunker today."

"Oh, an *executive* position," Thibideaux said. "And so soon after you come here. My, my, it *is* an honor havin' you amongst us, ma'am. Do pardon the normal natural fragrance of our humble abode."

"What in the hell is eating you guys anyway?" I demanded, tossing the incense burner onto the bunk with a clatter. "I was just trying to show you this stuff to break up the monotony. And I don't know how you can be such an asshole about me getting the job, Marsh. You were the one who set it up. I've got a good mind not to show you my yak butter lamp and—"

"I've seen yak butter lamps before," he informed me in a withering tone.

"Is the lamp and the incense burner all that you found, Viv?" the Colonel asked.

"I'm sorry, sir. I looked for a file and a hacksaw but there didn't seem to be any handy. I thought at least it would be nice to have a little light once in a while instead of sitting around in the dark."

His prissy brusqueness was even more deflating than the grumbling from the others as he said, "If we're caught with these things we're not authorized to have, it will mean trouble."

"With all due respect, sir, what do you think we're in now?" Danielson snapped. Bless his heart, he sounded as disgusted with the others as I was beginning to feel.

"That's what I'd like to know," I said. "For Chrissake, I bring something that might be useful or novel and you guys act as if I was stealing your momo. You've spent I don't know how long looking after me and now when I'm trying to give back a little something you treat me like I've done something wrong. What's your problem?"

"We got no problem, dollin'," Thibideaux said.

" 'Cept we tired of bustin' rocks all day like we been doin' for Lord knows how long ever since we got here. You're here just a little while and got yourself a soft job right off the bat—looks to this ol' boy like you takin' care of yourself fine. You don't need no mama no more so why don't you just let us rest ourselves?"

The Colonel broke in, "No, no, I can see where it might be a good thing to have somebody down there, though I wish it were one of us so we could take the kind of things that will help with our escape attempt. We don't want to call attention to ourselves unnecessarily and these discoveries of yours might do just that if we don't hide them. If the guards thought we'd stolen something they might assume an escape plan and punish all of us. So you should return these things unless we can find some way to conceal them."

"That's no problem, sir," Danielson said. "We'll stick 'em in a sandbag in the hall during the day, retrieve 'em on the way into the cell. Even if there's a guard, one of us can create a diversion. Piece of cake."

Marsh changed the subject abruptly, asking if anyone had seen a new supply pack train come in. Thibideaux said he'd heard it had gotten in the previous night, after we were all tucked safe on our trundle slabs.

"Well, Dr. Jekyll was with them," Marsh said. "She was with the Dragon Lady today. She kept Wu from swallowing Viv whole when she caught her roaming around outside."

I was framing a reply to the next logical question, which should have been from someone asking *why* I was roaming around outside, when Danielson asked in an eager voice, "I wonder what came with the pack train. Do you think they might have finally brought our mail?"

Merridew shook his head in a hopeless kind of way and said gently, "Maybe so, Du. We'll just have to see."

Thibideaux's approach was more surgical. "Grow up, killer. We've been here how long?"

Danielson shrugged sullenly.

Thibideaux said, "A long time, Du, ain't it? A real long time. And in all these years have we got one letter, one message, seen even one little bitty empty envelope?"

"Thibideaux, put a goddamn lid on it," Colonel Merridew said amiably.

"Well, I *do* apologize if I undermine morale but it undermines mine having someone keep on remindin' me how we never hear nothin' from nobody all these god-knows-how-many years," Thibideaux griped, and rolled over to face the wall.

I suppose it's inevitable that five people in close quarters are not going to get along all the time, but when the men stopped sneering at me only to start bickering with each other I felt the same way I did the one time I saw my grandparents fight, shortly after I started living with them. It's a scary thing, seeing octogenarian pacifists breaking crockery and snapping "bastard" and "bitch" at each other. Mom said it was because of all the rapid changes they'd been forced into, all the things they'd cared about they'd watched die—the world just got on their nerves sometimes. But all the same I knew the fight was my fault, just as I knew it was now.

So I stood up and produced my final surprise, the torn and rumpled pages I'd folded into quarters to fit my pocket and the pièce de resistance—the *Huck.* "Look, though, there's something else. I found us something to read—" And I told them about the library.

Marsh looked pained. "If I'd known about that, I'd have volunteered to help Taring myself."

"Well, why the hell didn't you?" I asked. "Wu would have given it to you."

He shrugged. "I didn't know about the books. And I didn't want to work that close to Wu's office."

"I can get more books," I reassured him. "Just tell me what you want and I'll try. But some of these spare pages I want to use for writing paper."

"What are you going to write?" Danielson asked. "They won't take mail and we never get letters."

"I'm keeping a log about this."

"Oh, I can see where that would be real exciting," Danielson said. " 'Today I hauled rocks and ate a momo. Today I hauled more rocks and ate another momo'? Fascinating stuff."

The Colonel's eyes avoided mine and his mouth

tightened. I got the feeling he was uneasy about me keeping the journal, but he merely asked, "Did you happen to see any geography texts or maps from this area?"

"No. I didn't notice any. I'm not actually sure where exactly this area is. Are you?"

"No. Hell of a long march from anything else, and apparently north of the Tibetan Plateau, but that's about all anyone's been able to gather so far."

"When we crashed, we were heading into the Kun Luns," I told them. "So my guess is that's where we are now."

"That's more information than we've had up till now," Merridew said.

The prolonged tension was beginning to cause a fierce headache and right then I felt an unbearable pain in my temples and forehead as I asked, "Just how long is up till now?"

Danielson shrugged. "Long goddamn time, that's all any of us knows. I got captured after a shell hit near enough to knock me out and fill my ass full of shrapnel and so I was kind of out of it—the interrogations didn't help much either. I do remember the kid though . . ."

"What kid?" I asked, lying down on my own bunk and resting my throbbing temple against the cool stone. My head felt as if it had a constricting band around it.

"I don't know. Must have been one of the guards' kids or—who knows, the enemy gets younger every year—one of those runty little kid troops. Most of them make the punks and street gangs at home look like amateurs, but this kid seemed different. It was winter in the north of China. I was barefoot and they'd beaten me on the soles of my feet, among other places, so that I could hardly walk. Besides, I was wiped out with dysentery. The kid showed up, and I kept waiting for more to arrive with more of the whips and chains and bamboo rods business. She bent over my feet and I was wondering if I could wring her neck, just for the fun of it, before she started tormenting me, when I realized she was rubbing some kind of ointment on my feet, something that felt good. When she stepped back she handed me a pair of socks. They were so dirty they looked like they could walk by themselves, but they protected my feet. When she jerked her head for me to follow her, I hung back, thinking maybe I was being set up. Sometimes they use you for entertainment, fighting other guys, or seeing how much you can take. Once they tied my hands behind my back and put me in the ring with this little dog. It bit the shit out of me before I got its jugular in my teeth."

He fell silent and I said through a blur of pain that was beginning, just a little, to subside, "Well?"

"Oh, it wasn't that bad. She just took me to the edge of the compound and other soldiers met me. I thought, when she took me toward the fence, that maybe she was letting me go. At least she gave me something hot to drink before I left, and some rice balls. Next thing I knew, I was here, a lot warmer, but still in a cell. Food's better here, though."

"Anybody else remember him arriving?" I asked, and felt another sharp stab of pain.

"He's always been here," Thibideaux said, rubbing his eyes with his hands as if he too had a headache. " 'Course, they shift our cells a lot, we all been in and out of solitary. After a while the days all blur together— I tried keeping hatch marks once or twice but they moved me and anyway, every time I think about it, it gives me a headache. So I don't. Thinkin' about it won't get us out of here no quicker."

"It's bad for morale to dwell on it," the Colonel agreed, massaging his neck with his fingers. His eyes were clenched tight and he spoke through gritted teeth when he said, "The training manuals and texts all clearly state that personnel in past POW scenarios have found that dwelling on life outside is a good way to die or drive yourself crazy." After a moment he added, wincing, "Besides, I seem to have had a head injury when I came in. I don't remember much about my last assignment, which is lucky, because if I did they'd have broken me. Maybe they did, in that first camp. I hate to say it, but it can happen."

The headache returned with a vengeance, so awful

I couldn't seem to focus enough to remember the year or the month I was captured. I was going to tell them, so we could work backward, and I could almost picture the date on my watch before it broke, could almost see the first line in this journal before it got left behind in solitary. But the pain was too intense. Even now, as I write about it, I feel the first stab of that same headache and cannot for the life of me recall that date or any others.

I've been scribbling away by the light of my butter lamp. The men are all asleep and the flame of my lamp flickers to the rhythm of their breath and casts shadows on my paper, obscuring what I've written before. My cellmates' snores comfort me and somewhere within them are echos of the chants from my dreams. As I concentrate on the chanting, my headache begins to ease, but I'm too exhausted to write any more tonight.

TEA

My new boss is an odd duck, especially compared to the heroes here in the cell. His polyglot of Indian syntax and Wild West slang is so weird I keep forgetting he's a jailer, but even weirder is the fact that *he* seems to keep forgetting it too. For instance, he believes that whistling in the tunnels is bad luck and hums "Dark as a Dungeon" in compensation and also believes in coffee breaks and lunch hours, though the momos and tea take me only a few seconds to consume. During the first few of these breaks he kept asking me if Washington was not near Montana and if so, did I not know good old Joe Johannsen, by golly, or Mark Prokopovich or Brian Watson? Very fine fellows. He was obviously trying to put me at ease but if he's doing so to spy on us, as the Colonel seems to think, he has a funny way of doing it because he does almost all the talking. And most of it is so silly and inconsequential I can listen or not to the drone of his voice and it doesn't matter. I do nod in the right places and, at his request, occasionally correct something in his English—though if I edited his entire conversation *I* would be doing most of the talking.

He's somewhat different as we work—curious and intense when examining the structure and plotting how to reinforce it, grunting to himself when absorbed in some perplexing problem. He shows me these plans, drawing in the dirt, saying, "And this—it is originally belonging here, so. See?" He hands me some piece of debris and reconstructs it for me so that a warped gray board with what looks like flecks of phosphorescent fungus becomes a piece of carved cloud, once gilded and bordered with crimson. He guides the structural reinforcements, and examines the piles of crap with enthusiasm and tenderness. "Is a piece of lion, Viv, very fierce, guardian of this country. No more," he concludes sadly, and I catalog the lion and he tucks it away. There's a lot of this carved stuff, and stonework and tile, smashed and twisted but some still wearing most of its paint.

The Colonel glances in my direction when he thinks I'm not watching and if I catch him at it, gives me a tight little nod and pretends the whole exchange was my idea. Sometimes he drums his fingers on his knees and I know if I look, I'll find him watching me. I suppose that in spite of the fact that my job is forced labor the same as theirs, they don't like my being in such close contact with the enemy. But I truly don't think there's anything subversive about Tea. He's not the spy type. He's what Grandma would have called a nerd—just a simple cross-cultural mining engineer, so miscast as a prison overseer he doesn't even try to play the role.

NEW JOB, DAY 6

I'm writing this on my "coffee break" in the empty bathtub behind the big room with the scarves, all of which have been removed and cataloged now. Tea says they want to turn that room into a dining hall once it's safely shored up. He had to talk to some men about some logs so I have a chance to write in privacy, an all but extinct commodity for us these days. That's why I really prefer being here working on a one-to-one basis most of the time with Tea instead of among "my own kind" where the five of us are crowded together in the cell. I can't seem to get to know anybody—there's always an argument breaking out about something, usually sports or firearms or escape. Most often lately it's been escape. Merridew says—get this—now they have me to think of. Like they're all protecting me. Which wouldn't be so funny except in the next breath he tells me that since I have this new job in such a strategic location, I should be able to steal firearms, extra food, warm clothing and other equipment for an escape.

"I can't get that stuff," I told him. "I'm working in ruins, not as Wu's orderly."

"You're going to have to try, honey," he said as if his kindly encouragement changed the circumstances. "We sure can't procure the necessary supplies while we're working in the fields all day." There was, of course, an edge in his voice when he said that last to remind me that *some* people had to do *real* work. "Can't you trick your guard?"

"Maybe, but I still don't have access to anything useful."

"You could keep looking through those books," Marsh suggested. "There are probably maps in some of them."

"I wish I could. I'd love to get back into the library but nowadays there are guards and workmen around most of the time and when there aren't, Tea—Taring is with me."

"Someone sure got herself a cushy job in a big hurry," Danielson said, scratching his armpits.

"She was in no damn shape to haul rocks," Thibideaux reminded him.

"Just kidding. Just kidding," Danielson said, palms up. And I think he was but I was tired of the innuendos.

"How much do you know about excavations, Du?" Marsh asked mildly. The big man shrugged. "Well, she studied anthropology in college. They found out during the interrogation. Probably part of the reason they brought her here instead of killing her, though Wu played dumb and tried to get me to tell her something about the rest of you instead. I could tell her you're a fucking Ph.D.—better qualified than Viv here if you want the soft job youself for a while."

"Hell, no," Danielson said. "I can haul more rocks any day than you can in your best week and you know it. I'm glad she has the soft job. I'm just worried about her being over there with all the slants. Seems to me they must have some reason for being so considerate of her health."

NEW JOB, DAY 10

I'm beginning to long for the times when all the guys did was talk among themselves about the scores of long-defunct sports events or the calibers of obsolete weapons. The lack of privacy is driving us all nuts—especially me. I'd rather use the split trench the guards use—at least there're both males and females there and the Asians are much more casual about such things. It's

easier than everybody pretending to be looking else-
where, thinking deep thoughts, when I have to use the
can in the cell.

As a matter of fact, this is the first time I've had to
write in a few days as I seem to have developed an active
social life. It's taken time for me to recall exactly what
you call this phenomenon that seems to have crept into
our intracellular social structure.

The first inkling I had of it was when Thibideaux
spanned the space between our stone bunks with his
torso and rested his elbows on the unoccupied portion
of my bunk, while I was trying to enjoy a few more pages
of *Huck* before retiring.

"Gonna ruin your eyes," he said playfully.

"The light isn't going to get any stronger," I said.

"Maybe you should knock off reading then and—"

"If you think I'm going to go to all the trouble to
steal something and then not use it, you're crazy," I said.

"Maybe so," he said. "Crazy. Yeah. That sounds
right." But the next night, despite all their protests about
how they couldn't get useful escape equipment while out
there busting rocks, he had acquired a flashlight, which
he tried to give to me.

Colonel Merridew ordered him to hand over the
flashlight to him instead, for the escape, and raked him
over the coals for holding out on his cellmates. I thought
that was all there was to it until Merridew began performing various little gallantries that began to make it
clear he was considering himself my chief protector.

"Marsh, move a little to the right, will you? Viv's
trying to read and you're casting a shadow on her
page."

Just little, ridiculous stuff like that but it's all pretty
heady for me, when for years I've wielded zero sexual
power as gravity and grayness worked their wicked way
with my once comparatively lithesome form, while those
around me indulged in cosmetic and surgical antidotes,
as any sensible woman would do, instead of more books
and tuition.

And yet I am in no mood for a lover. For one thing,

in this cell, any liaison would end up as a gang bang or a spectator sport, which is distasteful enough even without the prospect of being perpetually barefoot and pregnant, at my age, in a prison camp with limited medical facilities. No thanks.

This is diabolical indeed. Had Wu been *planning* a situation that would produce more tension and inner torment than solitary confinement, she could have done no better.

NEW JOB, DAY 12

ㅅ Everything is going almost too well. Tea solved my paper problem by providing me with my own notebook and pen for field notes yesterday. He did not ask that I return them at the end of the day. This morning he left me alone in the corridor outside the room of scarves and the library. Somewhere in the building voices are raised—Wu's, from the sound of it, and Tea's. His doesn't sound as if he's angry, just as if he's talking loud enough so she will hear him over the sound of her own voice. There's a third voice too, never raised high enough to come to me as more than a murmur. There. That one stopped. Now I can hear only the throb of the generator, except that since my dreams began, it has never sounded like a simple soulless mechanical device. I cannot be aware of its throb without sensing the mutterings and deep groans of the chant beneath its beat. The three electric bulbs we've been allotted throw deep shadows into the corners, draping the doorways with black velvet, softening the destruction.

Here comes Tea, he's carrying something small and rectangular.

LATER

⚓ No wonder Wu raised so much hell! Tea brought a tiny computer, no bigger than the volume of *Huck*, with a monochrome screen but with graphics almost as sophisticated as the ones used with the GAG program.

"I am having a bad time convincing the commandant to let us use this," he said. "But you are needing to see what has happened here and what we are attempting to undo." He grinned. "The commandant is reprimanding me severely for being most unsecurity-conscious around such a desperado as yourself."

"I heard," I said.

So we sat together in the corridor, side by side on the ruins of a carved pillar, the urban anthropological equivalent of a tree stump in some sylvan glade, bending over the little screen and keyboard, our shadows blocking the bobbing light from the slightly swinging utility lamp overhead.

Tea tapped a series of keys. I paid careful attention, and also to his access code. He made no effort that I could see to hide it from me so it may be that his EARL GRAY opens only certain files to which I will need access. Still, it definitely bears remembering for future reference.

The screen cleared and the graphics lines began resolving themselves into a flash of blueprintlike diagrams flipping past like a more sophisticated version of the old children's books that, when riffled by a thumb, turned slightly varied drawings into moving pictures to demonstrate the elementary principles of animation and amuse the kiddies. Tea punched another button and the frame froze, then began filling in lines and shadings until the screen held two white mountains against a gray sky punctuated by fluffy white clouds. The mountain in the background was the shape of an inverted ice cream cone. The mountain in the foreground held what appeared to be the black and white photographic image of a great city, filled with people. The slopes below the buildings terraced to a broad bright lake which seemed to gleam despite the lack of color.

I opened my mouth to say, "But that's the city in my dreams," and barely caught myself. Tea looked at me curiously. "Nothing," I said. "What is this? Plans for a ski resort when the war's over?"

He held up his hand, then lowered it dramatically, forefinger first, and punched another key. The picture changed to a broad corridor with carved beams and a procession of robed people filing past. With a brief look between his knees to the pillar on which we sat, he gave a short grunt and pointed to a brocade-wrapped column on one side of the procession. Its top was embellished with the image of Ganesh, the god who was an elephant on top and a man on the bottom. "You see? Here we are sitting on this structure here?"

"You mean this is what's left of that corridor?"

"Yes."

He punched another key and we were back to the mountains and the city. With another punch, the image turned from a photograph into an old film and the motionless figures began walking, running, sweeping the front steps of buildings, holding merchandise aloft in the marketplace. Then, all at once, a point of light twinkled in one of the clouds, and although the flags continued to wave and the waters of the lake to lap on the shores, the people stopped in midframe, as if listening to some great voice. Then a tiny gray donkey in the marketplace pulled back on his reins and bolted through the streets, pulling strands of yarn from drying racks so that it fell onto his ears and tangled in his hooves, trampling fruits and vegetables on blankets on the curb, toppling towers of baskets and pots. The single donkey's movement was lost as yaks and horses, dogs and cats also began running. I was watching the animals and the people so closely that it was only when the people began first to point at the mountain, then to throw their arms up over their faces or to run, that I noticed what was happening to the taller mountain. I had seen enough avalanches on the trip here to know that that was what I was witnessing, but with the little plumes of snow rising from the summit and the sides of the great peak, it looked as if it was a smoking volcano, ready to blow its top.

Blow its top it did, but not with a great upward explosion. In silence, the top of the mountain poured down upon the city, seeming almost like a huge peaceful drift as it covered the buildings or knocked them down the terraced slopes into the lake. Of course, it would not have been silent. If the computer had sound, we would have heard the screams of the people, the groan the mountain gave as its top tore loose, the roar of the rushing snow, the thunder of the boulders smashing stone, timber and flesh, and the churning of the lake as its waters swallowed all of the avalanche and the city it could hold, before it filled to a dry hump, a foothill to a ravaged foothill of the familiar horned mountain that rose above me every day as I walked from one bunker to another.

"Then this *was* a lamasery?" I asked.

He grunted. "This is my home. A bomb dropping on the far border beyond the great peak is making the avalanche. Here is what we are doing to remedy this."

He showed me frame after frame of the manual clearing of the city site. The first two frames showed a handful of ragged survivors lifting rocks, clearing draped vaguely human forms, digging down with their hands to scoop out the tiny pool that was all that remained of the lake. A later frame, flashing by, showed a pack train with a party of weary-looking people in tattered uniforms led by a tiny dark girl. I thought one of the uncovered heads was blond and would have looked more closely but Tea rapidly punched to the next frame. Successive pictures showed the clearing of the boulders and the melting and runoff of the snow, the digging of the bunkers, the erection of the camouflage canopy. It looked a bit like the movies Mom used to show from her working vacations on ecotreks during the reclaim-the-earth kick when she was a beginning travel writer.

When the frames flipped back to the original picture, and Tea turned off the computer and closed the screen back over the keyboard, he rose and turned away from me without looking at me, but I had seen the ditch of moisture that tracked down the pits on his scarred cheek.

DANIELSON

‡ I resisted my first impulse, which was to tell my cellmates all about what I had seen on the screen immediately. I didn't feel like being rebuffed again or like listening to their cracks because my information had nothing in particular to do with escape. Now, if I could get another look at those blueprints, at a slower speed, I might have something to tell them they'd be interested in. Not that, lately, they have been uninterested in me at all, at least not as an object of competition and strutting. It seems to me, as I begin to have a little broader experience of this camp, that there are many other cell arrangements which could have been used in regard to me, but that Wu chose this particular one because of the way it would upset the men.

Not that I try to upset them. Their weirdness really has nothing personal to do with me at all. After the first rush of feeling flattered by the unaccustomed gallantry, I began to see that the competition for my attention wasn't so much romantic or even sexual as the sort of sibling rivalry I'd seen between Mom, Grandma, Grandpa, and Great-uncle Medicine Wolf during the last few years when Mom was stuck in the cabin taking care of all the older ones. On my infrequent visits from school and the city, each of them tried upstaging tricks worthy of the hammiest actors, if not open rudeness, to get my attention away from the others.

Even Merridew's charismatic leadership wore thin while he was under the influence of my novel charm. One evening, for instance, he suggested that Thibideaux, who had the best-looking rice bowl, ought to trade with me, since I needed to get my strength back after losing so much blood.

"For Chrissake, Colonel, you're not her fucking nursemaid," Danielson complained.

"Let's have none of that kind of language around here, soldier. There's a lady present."

I was beginning to feel like a piece of china in a bull shop. I tried to laugh it off, "That's right, Danielson, there's ladies present. What's your fucking problem anyway?" and firmly pushed away Thibideaux's proffered rice bowl.

Thibideaux shrugged and dug into his rice but Danielson, who is a literal kind of man, less humorous than your average antiaircraft gun, was nonplused. "Shit, Viv, I didn't mean—I mean, hell, I've got a wife and kids myself and I just . . ." He actually set his food aside to fumble in his pocket.

He pulled out a wallet devoid of anything except a picture of a woman and two toddlers. "That's them—Sherry and the twins." The color in the photo was faded and the woman's light limp hair and eyes were drained of color, but I could tell she would be pretty, even without surgery. Her smile was strained and I thought she was holding the two chunky curly-headed blond kids still from sheer force of will.

"They're gorgeous," I said, lying only a little.

He licked a pinch of rice from his fingers and gestured to his wife's picture with a little finger to which a grain of rice clung. "Sherry has that same trick you do of turning your head at a certain angle when she's trying to read," he said as if it were especially clever of us to do so.

"I guess I'll have to sue her," I said, trying to kid him into a little less intense a tone. The moony comparison with his wife irritated me when it seemed pretty clear to me that all we had in common was being female.

"What?" he asked, pulling himself back from his family to answer my silly remark. The picture was plasticized, but the plastic was yellow and cracked and had gray ground into the edges of the cracks from so much handling. Danielson's eyes were clear and pale around the pupils, so widely dilated to take best advantage of the butter-lamp light.

"Just a joke," I said quickly, reminding myself that it's a form of cruelty to inflict comedy on the humorless. "Tell me more about your wife."

He seemed at a loss for a moment and then said as if it was beside the point, "Oh, Sherry's great. A really good mother for the twins and when I was home, she always tried to make things nice for me—made nice meals and kept the kids quiet." That faint praise seemed to exhaust him, though he continued to stare at the picture, making me wonder what it was that made him long to hear from Sherry anyway, since she sounded very dull to me.

But I did want to know my cellmates as individuals and felt that it was vital to my sanity that I do so. So, although I was sure Danielson would have been more comfortable talking about his last body count than trying to articulate his feelings about his family, I asked, "How about the kids?"

"The boys—oh, they want to be just like me when they grow up." I thought, What—a prisoner? But this time I was smart enough not to say so.

Instead I asked their ages, which turned out to be another trap, which I realized with another quite physical pang as a pained look crossed Danielson's rugged mug.

"I— It's been a long time. I haven't even heard from Sherry since I've been here, and it's funny but I just realized, they could be grown already for all I know," he said. Then added bleakly, "Like the Colonel said, nobody knows how long we've been here."

We'd been over all that already and my head was beginning to throb again. Maybe I'm allergic to butter-lamp fumes. If so, it's unfortunate but I'll have to live with it.

Danielson swung down off his bunk to squat next to me, his back against the cell wall, his knees spread, rear resting on his heels, elbows resting on his knees. His skin was covered with a chalky smear from the day's labors and a scallop of mud gleamed moistly on the sides of his sandals. Still, he was pleasantly warm and didn't smell any worse than the rest of us and the room, which was at its most fragrant since we empty the bucket when the guards bring dinner.

Danielson kept his voice pitched low, as if he didn't want the others to hear, and I realized I'd been doing the same thing, though the conversation was not especially intimate.

Returning the photo to his wallet and that to his pocket he said, very earnestly, "I sure wish you could meet Sherry. She's my baby, all right. At least, I hope she still is. I keep saying I haven't heard from her but I bet she writes every day. God, I wish they'd just let us have our mail. They just do it to cut us off from our own kind." This speech should have been touching but there was a woodenness to it that didn't ring quite true, as if he was telling me what he thought I expected to hear— his feelings about his family, which seemed more a matter of concern to him than to any of the others, surely went deep and yet the trite stock phrases he used to speak of them were delivered in a colorless and mechanical way, albeit with a certain wistfulness. Has it been so long since he's seen them that their memory has grown too remote for real emotion? I suppose it's possible.

"Surely we wouldn't be kept in the same cell if they really wanted to isolate us," I said.

"Oh, well, that's so we won't mingle with the others. They've got other prisoners here too—most of 'em gooks and wogs, a few Russkies. Traitors probably—maybe defectors. We all haul rocks together but the guards are always watching to prevent fraternizing. Guess they're afraid we'll rally the others with our good old American know-how and gang up on them. There aren't that many guards, you know."

"Have you tried to escape before?" I asked.

"Yeah, I tried it once," he said grimly. "Thibideaux did too—tried to sneak out with a pack train, get back to our lines, send help for us. But they caught him before he'd been gone a day. Didn't even take him seriously enough to punish him, just laughed at him and put him back to work on the rock pile. Marsh would have tried at the same time, but he got frostbitten bad getting here and he can't take the cold out beyond the pass worth a damn. The Colonel has been trying to get together a plan to get all of us out but they've always guarded us way too close for anything that big. And now there's you. Even if the four of us could make it, we couldn't just go off and leave you with the slants, now could we?" He sat in angry silence for a while. "Bastards." He squeezed the bridge of his nose between a thick thumb and forefinger and for a moment his breathing was measured and heavy, the weeping equivalent of dry heaves. His evident despair did nothing to cheer me, and I didn't feel that his confidences had brought us any closer to understanding each other either. Instead, it made me wonder if he was more of a dolt than I had taken him for originally or if I was missing something in what he said.

So I patted him on the shoulder and said awkwardly that I supposed I had better turn in.

He took the comradely pat for what he wished it to be and abruptly exited the lonely-family-man mode and lurched into a pass which consisted of grabbing my hand and asking if I wanted him to tuck me in. I managed to refrain from jerking away and also from saying, "What? Here? You've got to be kidding?" and simply shook my head and crawled onto my bunk as the Colonel called to him to join a game they played with stones and wood splinters.

ANTHROPOLOGICAL BLACK LUNG

What a bore! As if being a POW wasn't bad enough, I seem to be sick all the time and unlike most of the camps I've read about in my history books, this one seems to have an uncommonly healthy inmate population and I have to be the puny exception.

It's the air, of course, and all the dust and dirt. As we dig through more and more of the rubble, we find more rooms intact, but Wu's wish is that we bypass the available rooms to shore up the hallway and clear the rubble to extend the passages to the lower reaches. We can, she says, study the contents of the rooms later. It's frustrating, but when I find something in a rubble pile and slip it into my pocket to examine later, Tea makes no objection, and sometimes I see him doing the same thing. Now and then he borrows the computer again to show me where we're heading, but I prefer the reality of the library to all of the computer's simulated secrets.

Every day we pass the door, leaving all of those mutilated books still crumpled on the floor, and we dive deeper into the maze of rooms and cells no bigger than the one I occupied in solitary. "Deeper" is a good term, for each tunnel-like passage leads farther downhill, and many small flights of stone steps must be excavated before we can continue to each new level, and that's what's done me in.

In the lower passages the dust and stink is even worse than it is above, since there aren't as many holes in the ceilings to admit air. We've swept and hauled dust and debris to the surface as if we were miners, and though it still isn't nearly the hard work hauling rocks on the surface is, my civilized respiratory system, accustomed in my youth to the healthful effects of being around trees and later benefiting from the cleanliness of the reoxygenated air prevalent on the NAC since the Reclamation, rebeled.

I coughed and sneezed until my head ached and my throat hurt, to the detriment of not only my health but my present assignment.

"Here, Viveka, what are you thinking of this?" Tea asked me one day, unrolling a delicate scrap of watercolor he had pulled from beneath a work stone. I bent forward, to let the beam from the work light fall on it without my shadow obscuring it. The tight feeling in my throat, the itch in my nose and ears, erupted into a sneeze spraying spittle over the pastel pigments, making the black ink run like a movie star's mascara. Another sneeze blew a fragile silk prayer flag to dust, while yet another caused a landslide within the pile caused by a collapsed ceiling and trapped us in a narrow passage until we dug our way out.

Wu chose that moment to make her inspection. She addressed Tea in Tibetan—I understood a few phrases by now—and he replied, gesturing to me.

"If she is not satisfactory, we can put her to work hauling rock with the others," Wu threatened in English, shrugging.

The doctor sauntered up then, just as I began another coughing spell and the three of them burst into a rapid conversation in Chinese or Tibetan, I couldn't really tell, the upshot being that despite what I gathered was Tea's protest, my cough and I were relegated to the chain gang.

It's not as bad as it sounds, however. The fresh air has helped my cough, and the cool breeze made short work of my feverishness, though initially I was dizzy when I bent to pick up the stones. As the day wore on, instead of getting much tireder I began to feel better, coughed less, and my chest and throat relaxed. Nobody made me pick up boulders, but I stacked medium-sized rocks on the wall all day and while my respiratory system felt better, every muscle in my body stiffened to immobility the moment I shuffled into the cell behind the men and stretched out on my cot.

That night, Merridew cut the courtly crap and pulled rank on me. "You know, Viv, my daddy and my grandaddy were career men like me. Back when Grandaddy served, they were only just letting women into the service. People had doubts about it then, and even though my daddy's second-in-command on the last manned space flight to Uranus was a woman, I confess I got my doubts about it still. And you're an excellent case in point. You were an out-of-shape mess when you rolled through that door and more than likely would have died of shock if we hadn't been around to help you and would have died from the trip if the old woman hadn't put that spell on you. And you were pregnant, which a male trooper wouldn't be, and then you lost a baby, which a male trooper wouldn't have done, and you got sick in a way that's impossible for a man. You're still peakedy and now you're sick again so you lost a strategic job that you might have been up to physically and are out there with us, where you can't pull your own weight. Not that anybody holds that against you, necessarily, but what if we do get this escape organized? You couldn't keep up, could you?"

"No," I said flatly. "But maybe you're overlooking other contributions I could make. I can speak a little of their language. I can find out their plans and where supplies are kept and—"

"You might have. If you'd kept that inside job. But even so, in return for that kind of help, do you expect one of us to carry you piggyback across the mountains?"

"Of course not."

"Well, then, lady. You wanted to be a soldier. Don't you think you'd better start acting like one and shape up?"

"This wasn't my idea," I whined, managing to produce another miserable cough.

"You volunteered, didn't you?" he demanded.

"I hardly think it's fair to call it that when all the other choices are made unavailable, or you're not qualified for them, and pretty soon you find you've been herded toward the only one they ever intended to let you take all along," I sniffed, feeling sorrier for myself than at any time since my capture. "Where the hell have you been, Merridew?"

"Here, mostly," he said, fixing me with a gimlet eye. "And so will you be the rest of your life unless you quit blaming people who are in no position to give a damn about what you think are injustices perpetrated on you and stir your butt to do something about helping yourself. I don't really give much of a shit how you got into this situation, Ms. Vanachek, I'm just telling you you'd better get yourself in good enough shape so you can leave with the rest of us if we make an escape."

"I'm in plenty good enough shape to die of exposure

and frostbite right now," I informed him in a withering tone that was somewhat spoiled by having to wipe my nose on the sleeve of my uniform.

"Well, and if anybody'd get it, it would be you," he said with a disgusted sigh. "I'm telling you this for your own good, Warrant Officer. Now I want you on a routine of calisthenics every evening before you dig into your rice."

"With all due respect, sir, fuck off," I said. "I am a prisoner of war. As far as I'm concerned that means I'm out of this war, and also as far as I'm concerned that's the best thing that's happened to me since I got *into* this war."

"Warrant Officer, it is the duty of every captured NACAF serviceman and -woman to attempt to escape. Now, in my judgment you are incapable of meeting the physical challenge this would pose. For the good of your fellow prisoners as well as for yourself, I think you'd better reconsider."

His voice was calm enough but his face was turning red.

"*Okay*," I snapped, turning my back on him and coughing as pitifully as possible into my fist. "As soon as I can breathe."

NEW JOURNAL, DAY 30

I coughed myself to sleep that night and had a reprise of the dream I'd had in solitary, but this time I wasn't a little girl and it wasn't Nazis: I knew I was Danielson, although I didn't look like him because I weighed about ninety pounds and was losing my hair. My rear was sore from continually being wet from dysentery and my stomach ached all the time as I trudged wearily from one end of a long kennel-like run to another, hauling rocks. I was building a castle, as in fairy tales, and I could just see the end of the long curly golden braid the princess had. I looked up and she waved. She was wearing a leotard and looked like my old buddy Sam and was telling me the health benefits of rock climbing. I wanted to answer back but my mouth was full of sores, and I knew these were from the disgusting stuff I'd been eating.

I was thoroughly ashamed of myself when I woke the next morning, to find an almost empty slop bucket, a healthy breakfast momo, and a trek out into a mountain meadow to do moderate exercise all day long in sunshine and fresh air, presided over by gorgeous scenery and guards who were at least reasonable enough to allow you to stop to relieve yourself when necessary or get a drink of water from a kid whose job was to carry a pail and a cup around all day.

I did not so much as whimper, however much my body creaked and groaned, when we began the exercise program this evening, though I didn't enjoy it any more than I ever have and the cramped space made it possible for only two people at a time to do anything which involved moving more than two inches in any direction. Still, I remain alive, mostly because despite Merridew's pitiless bullying I did only what I could bear.

The men were very funny, however, and apparently saw this new program of Merridew's as an opportunity to show the little lady how it's done. They stunk up the place royally working up a thoroughly goaty sweat while chinning themselves on an outcropping in the wall and doing situps on their bunks and moaning that boy, were they out of shape, why while they were in basic they could do twenty times as many as this. There was much earnest lamenting about the lack of sufficient room for side-straddle hops, something I am very grateful for, since my frontal tendency to floppiness makes me most reluctant to indulge in side-straddle hops in mixed company.

After bumping his head on the ceiling while too vigorously sitting up, Marsh declared that yoga would be a much better way to build strength, lung capacity, and properly condition one's muscles and tendons for the hard heavy work of the day.

That appealed to me much more than side-straddle hops. My grandmother could stand on her head until the day before she died and as a youngster I had been able to pretty well keep up with her regimen. Of course, as a youngster I could also run for miles, climb trees, and turn cartwheels. But yoga could effectively be done to the same slow and sluggish rhythm to which my blood seemed to circulate these days and didn't require all that bouncing. So I chimed in, "After all, Asians have been doing it for centuries and they lift enormously heavy bundles with nothing but a tup line across the forehead and run for miles with heavy loads and probably have less space than this to practice in."

"Sounds too much like 'If you can't beat 'em join 'em' to me," Danielson growled, but then Thibideaux reminded him of the classic martial arts movies they discovered they both used to watch as boys with lots of bloody ways of dismembering people with your bare hands and Danielson seemed considerably cheered.

Later, I asked Thibideaux where he had found such antiques as martial arts movies (of which Grandad and Great-uncle Medicine Bear had been so fond in their declining years, watching them on an ancient TVCR which they continually tinkered into operation with the same devotion young boys of affluent families devote to personal transport systems and young boys of less affluent families devote to rocket launchers and personal weapons) and he said, oh, you know, and looked at me as if I was crazy.

NEW JOURNAL, DAY 32—Work Detail

The Colonel could have made a fortune as a civilian exercise coach, judging from the way I feel. After only a couple of days, I can not only breathe but I'm actually enjoying the chain gang.

Partially, of course, it's the fresh air, brisk as whiskey and elusive as an easy dollar. Partially it's looking up from rocks now and then to see that great ruined mountain with its arms spread high above, as if blessing us for cleaning up the mess it made. For the first hour or so it's certainly the sunshine, which has been in plentiful supply and in which I revel until I become so hot and sticky with my efforts that I loathe it and long for a straw hat and sunscreen. And it's not all monotonous hauling of bits of shattered boulders. Perhaps that had been the case, but work parties have dug down now to a level where the ruins of the buildings Tea showed me are beginning to surface, so the debris I'm handling up here is almost as interesting as that on the lower levels. I particularly like the smooth, carved mani stones—there must have been millions of them here once, engraved with prayers and piled into walls. I've found probably two hundred already and it gives me satisfaction to replace them in a wall together, as they once were. And the shoots of blossoming weed that spring up beneath the stones please me too. Surely the growing things must indicate that the mountain has been dug down to its original soil?

This outdoor work also gives me an opportunity to study the other prisoners. Yesterday I worked with an Indian or perhaps Pakistani woman on one side, a couple of Chinese men uphill from me, a young boy who looked vaguely Mongolian to my right and another Caucasian woman, blond and sturdy, downhill from me. She grunted a lot, deliberately chose the biggest stones to carry, and swore copiously in Russian. More of these various sorts of people were scattered down the hillside, along with Danielson, Merridew, Thibideaux and Marsh. It's been good being with other female prisoners, seeing that they seem confident and in quite good shape despite the fact that at least two of them are pregnant. One carries a baby on her back, and, most unexpected of all, there are about ten children from the toddling age to that of the young Mongolian water boy interspersed with the adults. The children also carry rocks, some with great diligence, some chiefly lifting the stones to throw at each other or imaginary targets, playfulness benignly ignored and even smiled at by the guards, as long as they aren't the targets. One little girl seems to belong to the scowling female guard, but she nevertheless dutifully carries an occasional stone if she can lift and deposit it with one hand. With the other hand, she supports the baby she carries on her hip. I think the baby belongs to the Indian woman, since she is the one who has brought it to the field every morning and sets it on the ground beside her. The first time it squalls, however, there's the guard's little girl, hoisting it onto her hip and wiping its snotty face with her forearm.

Of course, I didn't want that fetus I lost. It would have been terrible to bear the child of rape into a prison and besides, I'm too old and having it probably would have produced a monster and killed me all at once. Still, watching these children, I think that at least it would have had company—at least I would have had company, selfish thought—and children have had even uglier places than this prison camp to grow up in. Not farsighted of me, I guess. Stupid really, but I can't help wondering, as I watch those other kids.

NEW JOURNAL, DAY 35

Today Lobsang and a guard came to fetch me.

"And how is that hitch in your getalong, pardner?" Lobsang asked me. "You are feeling less like a sick cat? Very good. We start today on another passage . . ."

I'm not sure how he managed it, but I'm back on the underground crew and I know he must have missed me because after we spent a few hours of coughing through dust and debris and searching uninteresting tiny cells, he said, "Viveka, I am thinking you could be better used somewhere else. Large hombres and I are handling engineering shit with great adequacy. I am thinking you are handier back up in room three of passage five-A. I will send Private Miss Dolma Yangzom with you to guard you from desperado tendencies and to help you."

Private Miss Dolma Yangzom turned out to be the nice female guard who had helped me clean up while I was in solitary. She and I proceeded back to the room designated as three in passage five-A, which turned out to be (oh, joy!) the library. Private Miss Dolma Yangzom, who wears thick spectacles and carries a couple of grenades in her belt along with the bandolier across her chest and the rifle slung over her shoulder, is a kindred spirit. She was both as cheered by the sight of all those books and as aghast at their sorry condition as I was. We took one look at the dark, disheveled room and the amount of work to be done and, as one woman, marched back down the hall to tell Lobsang we needed at least two of the work lamps in order to accomplish our mission.

We made quite a bit of headway, just today, grouping pages by language, or at least characters used. Dolma Yangzom seems as interested in languages as I am and although English isn't one of her best, we can communicate on a fairly elementary level. And, more important, we've found over a hundred books perfectly intact. I could have stayed there forever, but since I'm here, I want to make a private inventory of the day's finds. The books are an interesting assortment, not what I expected in a lamasery. Of the titles, mostly in English, that I recognize:

Plato's Dialogues
The Rubáiyát, Omar Khayyám
On the Beach, Nevil Shute
The Bible
The Koran
The Talmud
The Bhagavad-Gita
The Time-Life editions of the complete works of Joseph Campbell
The Foxfire Books, Volumes 1–14
The pseudoleather-bound, gilt-edged Doubleday edition of the complete works of Agatha Christie. These were much worn and only about five volumes were intact.
The complete works of Zane Grey
The complete works of Louis L'Amour
Isaac Asimov's books on the Bible and Shakespeare
The Complete Mechanic
The Complete Electrician
The Complete Carpenter
The Complete Plumber
Some weaving books (in Danish, I believe)
Two dictionaries and three thesauruses in English

I wonder if Tea might let us borrow the computer again to log in our discoveries as we unearth them. Surely such a fund of knowledge is a valuable enough resource that the camp will want to keep a record of it?

I'd better close for now. My fellow prisoners are watching me ever more intently with some of the suspicion I am beginning to realize masks rather kindergartenish hurt feelings at being ignored in favor of my journal. I'll simply have to persuade them to let me write about them, I suppose.

LATER: MARSH

Since I'm already a prisoner, I see no reason not to develop light fingers, so I snuck a paperback out of the library. I just grabbed—didn't even notice what it was until I got back to the cell and could look at it. Fortunately, it was in English, a science fiction novel called *A Canticle for Leibowitz*. I snuck my butter lamp in to read by, but before I could settle down, Keith Marsh wandered over to lean against my bunk and nonchalantly look over my shoulder. He emitted an "uh," and I couldn't decide if it was an introductory "uh", as in a clearing of the throat, or literary criticism until he said, "I don't suppose I could borrow *Huckleberry Finn* while you're reading that? And maybe have dibs on that when you're done?"

"Of course," I said. "Anything in particular you want stolen from the library, provided it's in the inventory?"

"Yes, I saw Taring come back for you today. You seem to have made quite a hit. I was hoping I might get drafted for that job after all but apparently he intervened with Wu so that he could keep you. I'd watch out if I were you. He's Wu's husband, you know."

"Tea and Wu?" I asked. "I'll be damned. I'd never have guessed. I suppose opposites do attract. How do you know?"

"Wu told me. She and I used to talk quite a lot, back when I was under the impression I was negotiating my release—that the organization I worked for really was on the other end of the letters I wrote. Later, I made friends with this one guard and she told me the letters never went anywhere."

This is the first time Marsh has ever had much to say to me. He's more solitary than the others, and most evenings squats with his back to the wall, twitching his mouth occasionally but mostly staring and thinking, I suppose. Sometimes he closes his eyes and pretends to sleep, but I think it's subterfuge to avoid having to talk.

Now he talked so fast I couldn't keep up with him. "Wait, wait, slow down," I said. "What organization? Why would she tell you to write letters and then never send them?"

Marsh has something wrong with his eyes—he blinks constantly, like someone whose laser surgery has gone bad. He also tends to drum his fingers against his knee, which makes him seem fidgety at times, though usually he moves very little and seldom changes expression unless the men are having a particularly lively sports debate. His voice, as I have mentioned, is soft and quiet, although his opinions seem pretty original for a guy whom I might ordinarily mistake for someone's accountant. Certainly I wouldn't have taken him for a lady's man, though there is something reassuring about him—not paternalistic, like Merridew, but more as if he understands everything I say to be perfectly sane and reasonable and even admirable at times.

But he blinked at me twice and said without changing expression, and without surprise, braggadocio or false modesty, merely with matter-of-fact candor, "Oh, she took a shine to me for a while there and was just stringing me along while she was trying to decide if I was her type. And she probably wanted to read the letters. She knew where the military boys were coming from but she was still curious about me and my organization."

"You're not military." I said, remembering he'd said as much when I first met him.

"No. I'm—I was—with the World Peace Organization. Flood relief in India, the last time the Brahmaputra wiped out northern India and Bangladesh. Thibideaux was escorting me into a border village with a decontamination team while he took in some cholera vaccine. The Chinese had captured the village since the last time we looked. I think it was a mistake, me getting rounded up with the military escort, but not a bad enough one for anybody to try to correct it. Thibideaux and I are the only ones who were brought here. It's a top-security facility you know—POLPOW Advocates have no record of it, I can tell you that, I used to work with them."

"What, were you an administrator or something?"

"Something. I got degrees in geology and engineering but I wanted to do work that counted. I'm good at languages too and I've used what I learned working my way through school."

"Tell me a little more about yourself—where you grew up, how you got interested in the peace organization, that kind of thing."

"I'm from Alaska. For the first few years we lived on Minto Village Corporation land along the Yukon. Mom helped her in-laws selling fireworks and cheap cigarettes and whiskey to construction workers and tourists. I think I was about eight when the money men foreclosed on the Native Corporation's loans.

"We had to abandon the villages—no war, no broken treaties, just some fine print and crooked lawyers—but while Mom was trying to convince the older ones they really had to leave—the village had been there since before gold rush days—Pop took off, joined the army, just in time to get his ass shipped to Honduras. He had the honor of being in the vanguard during the Latin American massacres. Of course, we didn't know that was what was going on at the time. The press was pretty cooperative with the government about keeping it shut up.

"My old man was reported killed in action but a cousin from Nenana came to see us later. He'd checked it out. Seems Pop was down in Brazil, got careless and stayed out past curfew in civvies and was mopped up with a bunch of half-Indian musicians. Later, when they were going over the bodies, somebody saw his dog tags. Of course, it was hushed up officially, but a guy from Huslia was with the disposal team and he saw the dog tags, recognized the name and told my cousin. Mom had moved us to Fairbanks way before that, and then over to Whitehorse. I was about ten or twelve, I guess. I'd thought my old man was a hero but my mom kept telling me Arnie said it was a stupid drunken accident. Every time I saw 'Brazil' on anything, I'd read about it. And by the time I was fifteen I had a better idea about the massacres and the drug wars and how come there's only gringo park rangers down there now and nobody else except tourists and why that's one place where so much wilderness area has grown back, making, as the government brochures say, the Tropical American Park Service one of the largest tracts of wilderness, original and 'reclaimed,' in the world.

"I worked my way through college but one summer after my mom's dad died—he was one of the lawyers who had made a lot of money 'helping' the village corporations with their lawsuits—he left me a little money. A buddy and I went down to Brazil and later to Chile on a geology field trip and to interview with one of the oil companies that was hiring down there. We heard there were gemstones in the streams. We found a couple of agates and a piece of human skull. A little farther down we found more pieces of bone. We walked upstream a ways and found a dam, crumbling away after all these years, of human skeletons jammed together and packed with clay. Made a real pretty little pool up above it. One day we got a little turned around, messing around in the jungle, and came upon this ruined city. I think maybe it might have once been Santiago. There was other stuff too—" He swallowed and blinked again and I waited for several minutes, about to make some comment to smooth over the silence.

"We had to come back before we planned. I got so I couldn't sleep down there. Couldn't eat."

"Dysentery?" I asked.

"No . . ." he said. "No, maybe some kind of respiratory thing. I felt as if I was being smothered all the time, couldn't breathe properly. Maybe I wasn't getting enough oxygen because I had trouble moving too—I felt weighed down all the time, like I was swimming in mud. My buddy chalked it up to the heat but . . ." His voice quieted to a sigh, then gusted. "The day we walked through Santiago—the stadium is still standing."

"What stadium?" I asked.

"Well, the one where they used to have ballgames, concerts. We passed it in broad daylight . . . ruins, half of what it used to be, of course, as impressive in its own way as the Mayan and Aztec ruins. Except that there's no park ranger there to sell you pamphlets about the site. There was nobody there but us, so when I heard the singing, I was surprised, to say the least. I thought maybe it was a radio somebody had left behind somewhere. What we heard was singing, in Spanish, not really professional enough for radio, I thought, when I really listened. The guitar work was okay, but basically just that beguine-type rhythm you hear a lot on California ethnic radio stations, not much embellishment. The central voice was good too, very strong, but there were too many other voices, some good, some trying to sing harmony and getting it wrong. A crowd being led in a song by one reasonably competent musician. Just one song, over and over again until some other voices started talking loudly in the middle of it, in Spanish I couldn't understand because it was spoken so quickly, but it was loud, bossy and mean and broke up the song the way static would a radio transmission. There were some thuds, a sick, kind of gasping sound like someone so hurt he can't get enough breath to scream, and the song dribbled away, one moan, two cries at a time . . . although a few voices always kept singing like background music in some movie."

"What did you make of it?"

"I definitely think it was a relic of the problems the government used as an excuse to wipe out the people down there to begin with. You know, when they were subsidizing supposedly right-wing dictators to get rid of any 'undesirable' elements. 'Undesirable' to those bozos meant people who tried to think for themselves instead of following the party line. You had to have heard about it at some point, how they rounded up not just the politicians from former regimes, but the teachers and college students, the journalists, artists, musicians, anyone from kindergarten teachers on up who could loosely be considered intelligentsia. The death squads rounded up all those people and took them to the sports stadium for 'questioning.' Of course, what they really did was murder them, at first singly, after torturing them down in the offices below the bleachers, and later on, just opening fire. But when they first gathered the people up, at least once, one fellow who had been a nationally recognized poet and musician, who had written a song that was sung all over the world, tried playing his guitar and getting the crowd to sing with him so they could focus on something other than being terrified. I read later that the goons cut out the guy's tongue and cut off his hands before they killed him, although some sources claim they only crushed his hands. It didn't really matter, there was a lot of that going around."

He shifted position and spread his hands on his knees. "My buddy heard the song too. I suppose it might have been a tape, but there aren't any radio stations down there anymore, except the official bands. But on the plane coming home, we met a ranger who was on leave. He'd been having a hard time of it, he said. He was an agronomist and was trying to find the right chemical balance to counteract the residue of the defoliants that were used during the mop-up. Though jungle was growing back over the clear-cuts from earlier ranching and timber industry, the war had left a lot of the area barren. He said that some compounds the Vietnamese had developed counteracted the defoliants okay, but that his department was having a hell of a time in some places trying to make any sort of consistent growing pattern, the kind that would buffer hills and streams and trails from erosion. In spite of the antidefoliants, some patches of ground simply wouldn't grow anything, and when the rangers dug down to take soil samples, they ran into mass graves. The guy said that of course these would have been okay for the vegetation except that the bodies had been covered with chemicals to destroy them and where the chemicals had been sown into the earth, nothing could take root, not even grass."

I nodded, saying nothing because there was nothing to say. You heard the stories, of course, from the media, saw photographs, occasionally might see something disturbing from the air, as I saw the formerly sacred lake Siddons pointed out to me, but it was never so immediate or personal as it was for Marsh, or even secondhand, for me, as I listened to him.

"It's not like the ghost of my old man came pointing

a finger at me, warning me or anything, but I knew I didn't want to be like him," Marsh continued. "I also knew I was going to be drafted as soon as I got out of college. The Terrorist Wars were going on then. So I skipped graduation and called a woman with the WPO in Vancouver. They found a place for me out of the country, in Haiti, and from there to the Middle East. They were glad to have my skills. Most successful engineers had cushy jobs in the States or in Toronto or Vancouver, other big cities. Most of the less successful were in the military."

"And you mentioned they needed those other skills you had used to work your way through school too?"

"Oh, yeah. It was part of the engineering, in a way. I picked it up back home, when I was a kid, with the gold miners and oil boomers. So when I took the courses in demolitions, I already pretty much had an acquaintance with and some skill handling explosives." He smiled a very small, brief smile, a little embarrassed. "And I like it—the edge, I mean, being right there where you could die at any time. Go analyze that if you want to but I finish disarming something and realize I'm still here and want to go have a huge meal and fuck something . . ."

"Yeah—well, so what did you disarm?"

"Bombs, unexploded mines, 'dud' grenades and later on, after a lot more training the organization paid for, nukes—that's how I started working with the military after all, especially in remoter regions where they didn't consider it cost-effective to send in their own people on the basis of unsubstantiated reports. We'd swap favors and get hospital supplies, food, in exchange for taking out a hidden device."

"I see. Were you really helping with the flood relief or was it something to do with that when you were captured?"

"Does it matter? A nuclear device isn't any better for people's health than cholera."

I couldn't dispute that. "So how long ago was that?" I asked.

He rubbed his forehead, and his voice was dimmer,

as if he'd worn it out telling me his story. "I'm not sure, really—you know how it is."

I did. I had thought I was feeling much better but perhaps the dust from my day in the library was getting to me because now that I no longer had Marsh's story to distract me, that damned recurring headache pounced again.

"Sometime after I flew to Bangladesh . . . I really remember. The Chinese had an iron grip on Tibet at that time—had had so long everybody took it for granted, though there was talk that the Soviets were going to make a play for the 'workers' of Tibet and drive out the imperialist Chinese. There was also talk that the last Dalai Lama was inciting the Indian government to a so-called Holy War, although that sounded fishy to me.

"And, of course, time passes quickly when you're having fun, as they say. After we were first captured, Thibideaux and I spent some time being 'reeducated' while we waited for execution in a Chinese camp. I was dying of dysentery when I met that young woman doctor. I think she must be this one's granddaughter. She started questioning me. I didn't think it would do much good, but I told her about Thibideaux. He was military, of course, but—I don't know, maybe because of professional courtesy, maybe because she thought the WPO might come looking for us together—she found him too. Only later, when she had us shipped from the prison hospital, did we find out just how good her connections are. Later, when I met the old woman, she knew everything about me. I guess some heads must have rolled for keeping us in that other camp without letting the granddaughter know. Anyhow, the old gal seems to be a good influence and I'm glad to see her. She's a good influence on Wu, who's not exactly stable."

"So I gathered," I said.

"Oh, I've seen worse," he said so mildly that I believed him and had no desire to question him further about it. After a moment he said, "And it seems to me they're lightening up a little around here. Danielson half killed a guard once trying to escape, back before I came here, and said they beat him up pretty bad. The Colonel said some people were injured back when he first came here and they made the prisoners work through the night. And then, Two-Gun Tsering and Samdup, that pair of guards—you know, the woman looks like she eats bullets for breakfast and the man looks like he's still asleep—after their kid was born, they haven't been as bad as they used to be. Tsering used to have a great time drawing a bead on us, one after the other, while we worked, just for fun. Then she'd pop off a shot close enough to make you jump, drop a rock on your foot, adolescent stuff like that. Really bothered me when they had me dynamiting boulders and she'd pull that shit on me while I was setting charges."

"I guess it's probably gotten better as they rotate personnel too," I said. "Probably some of the older guards get tired of the isolation and the new ones—"

"Oh, they never change them," he said. "Didn't you know? Nobody leaves this place, except dead. Not even the guards. Not even Wu. The only one who leaves is the old woman, and she keeps coming back."

SPRING?

My days have become varied and interesting. Normally, I'd have preferred to spend them all in the library, but Tea needs my help with the computer for at least a few hours a day in the lower excavations. I can't take much more than that before my cough starts to erupt, so lately he's been having me tap in quick notes and cross-file them in the library, later in the day. Even at that, after a few days below, I need a couple of days aboveground with the chain gang to keep my cough under control. Hauling rocks in the open air, with slanting rain, rainbows, and the grunting expanded society of prisoners to enjoy is really no tougher than lugging armloads of books from one place to another in an enclosed dusty, airless space with only one other person for help.

What's amazing is that anyone *cares* about my health. I suppose I'm lucky to have attracted Tea's favorable attention, because he must have a lot of influence with Wu for my schedule to be organized so that it is healthful and enjoyable for me—though I'm not sure anyone is fully aware of how enjoyable it is. I certainly try to keep a lid on it when I'm around the men, since they would no doubt mistake even a lack of misery, much less the sneaking pleasure I derive from the work and the setting, as disloyalty.

As a matter of fact, I have no loyalties one way or the other. Certainly I wouldn't think of betraying the men in my cell or causing them to suffer on my account, but neither do I feel any particular antipathy for my captors, which is not to say I'm not extremely wary. Tea, as I've mentioned, is very decent to me and I would go so far as to say I would like him under any other circumstances. Dolma is as bad as I am about getting absorbed in one manuscript or another and totally forgetting everything else, including her role as my guard, for hours at a time.

Today she is gone altogether, helping unload provisions from a pack train that's just returned. I have the computer to myself, here alone in the library.

LATER

✂ I've come across something very strange. I was trying to access the blueprints again, with hopes of sketching out a general floor plan which I planned to surprise the Colonel with to help with the ongoing escape plan.

I was playing around a little, since I had time. If one of Tea's codes was EARL GREY, in English, I wondered if his sense of humor prompted him to keep other files locked under other tea-named codes. I tried DARJEELING and got a three-column list of names in three different languages. At first I thought it might be the books and then I spotted my own name in each column, then Danielson's, Merridew's, Marsh's, and Thibideaux's. On two of the lists, Wu's, Dolma Yangzom's and Lobsang Taring's names also appeared.

None of the guards' names appeared on the list that was in Chinese, although all of our names and those of people who were presumably fellow prisoners did. Not all of the fellow prisoners appeared on both lists, however. Tatiana (Tania) Alexandrovna Enokin's name appeared on both the Chinese list and the one in Hindi, but not the Russian one. Also, while most of the names had a rank and serial number beside them, Enokin's did not, nor did Marsh's.

The Russian column was headed "United Soviet Socialist Republic Top Security Detention Facility for Incorrigible Enemies of the State"; the Chinese column was headed "People's Reeducation Camp, Clearance Utmost Secrecy"; and the Indian column designated the prison as "Top Secret Intelligence Gathering Center, Code Name Kali."

ANALYSES

⋏ I informed the Colonel of my discovery this evening, before momos and yoga. He shook his head. "Sounds like disinformation to me, Vanachek. Doesn't make sense."

"No, it doesn't, does it?" Marsh said. "The business about the guards being on the same list with prisoners, though. In some camps, the guards are trustees themselves—prisoners who earn special privileges by guarding others. I wonder if this place was set up like that originally?"

"I'll bear it in mind, troops," the Colonel said. "And if I can come up with any ideas I'll let you know. Meanwhile, I think Ms. Vanachek had better try to find out more."

"I will, sir. I had to give it back then, though. Dolma Yangzom came for it and said there were new files to be added."

"Try to get a look at them," the Colonel said, as if he needed to. "Meanwhile, I wouldn't give this too much thought. Probably just a trick to keep NACAF from finding out about this place. Kind of camouflage."

OUTSIDE

Marsh and one of the guards set charges under some of the remaining larger boulders today—just enough to break up the boulders, not enough to start another avalanche, or so it was hoped. Just in case the charge was too powerful, everybody stayed aboveground.

The explosion shattered the rock, and we prisoners converged on it as if it was a meal and carried bits of it away to shore up the walls.

I continue to enjoy the outdoor work despite the backaches and feeling nearly hamstrung by the steep climbs. The corrugated hillside is still so full of boulders and rocks even after all our efforts that in places it is like walking on giant eggs, although increasingly my foot touches patches of grass or weeds daring to crop up between the rocks. In some places clusters of tiny purple or yellow flowers peek out between rocks, and in the valley below, twisted limbs of rhododendron scrub snake past rock and ruin to thrust multicolored flowers and greenery toward the light.

A light rain began as the charge was set this morning. When the blast crumpled the stone upward in a huge thump of blossoming dust, the clouds, unconcerned, sailed by as if propelled by secret motors, jabbing the snow-covered peaks with quick-healing bruises of blue shadow. The sun broke through the slanting rain, creating a crystal-beaded curtain between us and the peaks. The dust of the explosion quickly settled in the rain, and Dolma signaled me that I was to return underground.

This was one of the days when I worked with Tea in the lower excavations. The explosion above had loosened a pair of fallen beams obstructing another passage, and with Tea on one side of the hall, I on the other, we explored a series of little cells hardly bigger than the one I had occupied while in solitary confinement.

When I opened one of the doors, I smelled, beneath the usual incense—rancid yak butter—human sweat—smell a scent that took me back to springtime and Grandad sharpening stakes and Grandma tearing up strips of rags while bright-colored packets lay in rows on the kitchen table. These seeds didn't come in packets but in huge canvas bags and had somehow stayed dry throughout what must have been years. Stacks and stacks of the bags rose from floor to ceiling. On a few shorter stacks, nearer the door, I saw little seed packets marking each bag. Atop one of the stacks a Burpee seed catalog lay, awaiting the next order. I held the catalog next to my candle. The date was November 1, 1974.

"Very interesting," Tea muttered across the hall, and closed a door behind him.

I grabbed the packet-markers from atop the bags nearest me and stuffed them into my pockets. The markers were not just pictures, but packets of actual seeds for cauliflower and nasturtiums, the first things I picked up.

Tea never checked that room and I made sure to remember its location, three down past the crossed fallen beams, on the left-hand side of the corridor.

Tonight I showed the seeds to the men.

Thibideaux grinned at the pilfered seeds and said, "Hey, dollin', we'll make a supply sergeant out of you yet. You're catchin' on. Think you can get any more?"

I nodded, feeling ridiculously pleased that I had finally stolen something that they considered worthwhile. "Sure. Taring didn't even notice. Besides, I don't want to embark upon a criminal career for nothing and I hate cauliflower."

"Atta girl," Thibideaux said, applauding my newly displayed outlaw spirit. "I ain't that crazy about cauliflower either but one thing about it, you can mostly just throw it in the ground and it'll grow up good. Try to find some zucchini too. Zucchini'll grow where you can't grow *nothin'* else."

TWO DAYS LATER, AFTER OUTDOOR DUTY

The secret garden has begun and, hard to believe as it is, I think I already see sprouts in the areas the men planted while I was working below. I had to be very casual to keep the guards from noticing how eager I was to get out on the slope and stake out an area to plant with the zucchini seeds I recovered from the storeroom yesterday while running an errand for Tea. The men have fine spots a foot or two in area cleared already, but they've been out on the slope every day. I had to work slowly, scooping off a little vegetation at a time as I hauled rocks away. The women working on either side of me, one an Indian and the other a blonde I thought might possibly be the Russian Enokin kept walking back and forth across my cleared patch. Finally, I decided to let them in on the secret to keep their feet out of my vegetables.

I asked them casually how they felt about fresh vegetables, what they liked, what they missed.

"Cabbages," the blonde, who I decided then and there is definitely Enokin, answered in English with a heavy Russian accent, said. "Big beautiful cabbages full of flavor and rich-smelling. And beets . . . and potatoes."

"Beans," the Indian woman said, also in English, as thoughtfully as an American civilian would say "diamonds" or "sables." "And potatoes and cabbages and peas . . ."

"How about cauliflower?" I asked, skipping the nasturtiums for the time being.

Danielson caught up with me the next time I hauled a rock to the wall. He deposited his own armload of stone, then detained me by gripping my elbow hard. "That was dumb, Vanachek," he hissed angrily. "That was really dumb. You shouldn't have told anybody else about the seeds. They'll squeal and we'll all be in for it."

"No talking!" Two-gun Tsering barked before I could respond. Danielson released my elbow and veered away. I thought about what he said the rest of the day. I hadn't really considered that anyone was likely to tell that I'd given them something. Why should they? But then, from what the Colonel said, sometimes people in these camps looked for things to report so they could improve their own situation by currying favor with the guards. We had been kept isolated from the other prisoners. In our cell the Colonel maintained discipline and kept strict watch to be sure we maintained the mutually protective pact he'd outlined for me my first night in camp. The men in the cell seemed to be strong characters whose loyalty had been tested. Mine hadn't undergone any of the tests they'd talked about, and I had been given a great deal more leeway than any of them had in the past. I was being well treated and given access to the rooms in headquarters and the computer, and I was not under heavy guard most of the time. It could, I saw, be a setup, to lead me into some major indiscretion that would be discovered, whereupon I would be questioned and we could all suffer. On the other hand, if I didn't take advantage of the opportunities, or was too afraid to communicate with the other prisoners for fear of betrayal, I might as well have remained in solitary. For that matter, I might as well be dead already. Because I was here now and here was where I was likely to remain. This was my whole life and maybe my future and I had to make the best of it. Probably I'd change my mind if and when I was betrayed and beaten or tortured or brainwashed or any of the other horrible things they did to people in these places, but so far I had escaped all that and *after* I was beaten, tortured or brainwashed, I probably wouldn't exactly be in the mood to figure how to use my opportunities, if I still had any, to good advantage. So I had to do it now and I had to use my own judgment, despite the warnings and the fears of the others.

Back in the cell, I said to everyone, "I gave some seeds to the women working beside me. Some of the other prisoners have kids and I don't think it's fair to keep something as important as food to ourselves."

Marsh simply raised his eyebrows at me, Thibideaux shrugged, and the Colonel gave me a long, searching, slightly suspicious look, then turned away and began yoga postures.

All during yoga I couldn't relax because I felt Danielson staring holes through me.

I lit the butter lamp after the yoga session and pulled out my journal to write the first part of this entry. Thibideaux's voice made me look up. "Du, what's your problem? Stop starin' at Vanachek like she's an enemy sniper and snap out of it."

"She breached security," Danielson said.

"Yes, she did," the Colonel put in, "and she should have discussed it with us before acting on her own initiative. But it's done and it may be for the best. We'll just have to wait and see. Danielson, you do nothing without my order and my order will be given only after a vote, understood?" And when Danielson continued to stare at me, the Colonel repeated himself, more sharply. "Du, I asked if you understood? You will not attempt to silence her without a general agreement from the rest of us. Do I make myself clear?"

Danielson continued to stare stonily at me then nodded once, slowly, in answer to the Colonel's question. His expression, calculated to frighten me, instead induced a hot flash of anger.

"Wait a minute, wait a minute," I said. "Silencing me? What is this? You guys don't wait for the so-called enemy to do me in? You just decide among yourselves whether you like how I'm conducting myself and if you don't, you save the bad guys the trouble? What the fuck *is* it with you?"

"Now, cher, you heard the Colonel," Thibideaux said. "Du's a little upset but he'll follow orders."

"*Du's* upset?" I asked.

Marsh cleared his throat. "Du has seen a lot more action than most of us, Viv."

"Let me see if I understand, then, Keith," I said. "Colonel, Doc, Du, correct me if I'm wrong. Because you've seen more action than the rest of us, Du, you've become this crazed killer who will snuff out life without a qualm and you are ready to snuff out mine because you don't like me talking to other prisoners? Only I'm lucky because the other guys aren't going to let you kill me unless they *say* so? Is that the deal?"

Thibideaux watched Danielson carefully, then ran his hand over his mouth and turned away. Marsh grunted, smiled sweetly and pretended to go to sleep. The Colonel stared first at Danielson, then me.

Danielson glanced at the Colonel, then back at me and shrugged, saying without anger, "Yeah, I think that's about it. You seem to understand."

LIBRARY, NEXT DAY

I awoke from a dream of the mountain collapsing last night to feel the weight of a shadow and a pair of eyes pressing against me. From the men around me a chorus of snores and the light breath of sleep let me know that I was effectively alone with whoever stood over me.

A hand pressed against my mouth and the figure bent low, so that his lips were against my ear. "If I was going to kill you, I would put my arm around your neck like this," he said, doing so, "and my other arm around your head and snap, that'd be it. No time to peep."

"I don't have to peep," I told him, not afraid of him particularly, although I had no doubt he was dangerous. "You're doing plenty of talking. Why, Danielson? What's on your mind?"

"I'm sorry, Viv. I don't want to hurt you, really. But you have to know that's what I'm like. I believe you that you only wanted to share the seeds with the other women and their kids but you don't know what these places are like, how they can turn somebody against you for an extra bowl of rice." He'd sunk to his knees beside my cot and I rolled over to face him, incidentally removing my head from his incipient hammerlock the way I might once have gently but discreetly removed another guy's hand from my thigh.

"You've got a family, Du," I whispered back to him, my face a scant two or three inches from his, but still I could see very little of his features. The cell was chillier than it had been when I went to sleep, and I curled in a ball on the side of the stone cot, my hands cupped together under my cheek. Danielson's posture was not so threatening now, but even if I wanted to, I wouldn't have felt safe going back to sleep when he wanted to talk. "If your kids were on a steady diet of momos and someone had a means to grow fresh food, wouldn't you want them to share it with your wife so she could keep your kids from getting deficiency diseases? When you were a kid, don't you think your mother would have wanted those seeds for you?"

He snorted derisively, "I didn't exactly know my mother, but I think if she'd known how I turned out, she wouldn't have given much of a damn."

Now we were getting down to it. Psychology 101, childhood, the whole nature and nurture business. "Well, why do you think you've become somebody she wouldn't give a damn about, Du? Was it at least partly her fault? Did you have a bad childhood? Were you beaten? Molested? You seem like an old-fashioned sort of man, Danielson, but that kind of thing is so common. All of my friends had war stories about growing up and even I got groped by my great-uncle's old guru when I was six. He was way too old to do me any real harm, but I had no way of knowing that."

Danielson was smirking to himself and emitting more little snorts I took to be laughter. Psychology 101 also says the would-be shrink should ask the leading questions and shut up. I wished I hadn't said that about myself. I didn't want to give him ideas. Maybe he was a kiddie-porn freak himself, this father of two. It wouldn't be the first time someone who loved children loved them a little more than they were supposed to . . . My heart was beating hard against the stone beneath me. While I waited for his answer, a long time coming in the dark, the breath of the other men came slow as the chants and I caught the steady, reassuring rhythm of it and felt my own bounding pulse quiet a little as I slipped back, only slightly, into the dreams of this place as it was before.

It could not have been more than seconds before Danielson answered, but real time was hopscotching between flashes of dream. "It's just you saying that about me being old-fashioned," he said, rubbing his face with his hands, his breath wheezing a little so that I couldn't tell if he was nearly laughing or nearly crying. "Lady, you don't know how funny that is. Fashioned is right. And no, I wasn't molested—at least not any more than most men who grow up in a barracks and there they call it toughening you up. See, I didn't exactly have a mother.

The army has been mama and daddy both to me, but my original parents, I guess you could say, were the research laboratory that incubated my test tube and the chemical corporation it belonged to."

He waited for me to react to that but I just nodded and waited for him to continue. My psych instructor would have been proud of my nonjudgmental demeanor. To my knowledge, I hadn't previously met anybody who'd been born in a test tube. But in sociology classes they told us that at one time predictions were that a great majority of babies might someday be born that way. The convenience of preselected genes and sex appealed to many adoptive parents who were in some cases also the donors of genetic materials, making them also the natural parents. Besides circumventing the usual complications that prevented people from having babies, saving genetic material and incubating it at the time in the lives of the parents when they were ready to be parents, rather than when biology dictated, was extremely convenient, I suppose.

Of course, the born-again neoconservatives had as much of a fit over that one as they did over abortion. Couldn't seem to make up their minds about life, those people. Eventually they put up such a stink and brought so many lawsuits to bear that the research labs had to abandon the project.

"Anyhow, I got born but I never got claimed," Danielson continued. "Later, I got ahold of company records and tried to research the people who ordered me. I didn't find anything—they could have been from anywhere. But I did discover that right about the time I came along another one of those ultraviruses swept the country and took a big body count. The company was stuck with me for the first five years or so and I grew up in their daycare center with all these little brothers and sisters who got to go home at night. I don't know what they did with me. Maybe the security guards kept an eye on me. Then I got lucky and the Defense Department decided to take a bite off old Mao's apple and see if by raising some children themselves they'd be able to make better soldiers out of them. So I was brought up in the most extensive military academy yet. A lot of other tube kids and I guess some unwanted babies born the regular way were raised from infancy by the army but I was already a little older by the time they thought of it. I still remember the lab. The smell of disinfectant and formaldehyde always makes me homesick.

"The army school I went to was okay—heavy emphasis on sports, of course. It wasn't officer candidate school, you understand. More like a trade school—we learned about choppers, explosives, firearms, and of course computers. I always tested high and kind of thought they might send me on to officer school but then my class got sent to Belize when I was fifteen." He paused, took a deep breath, and said, "I—um—I was the only one who graduated."

I took a deep breath too. He'd spent ten years with those people, the only family he had, probably hadn't liked them all but they would have been like siblings, and at fifteen he was alone again. "So what did you do?"

"Followed orders. Went to Libya with a strike force and spent four more years as a desert guerrilla. Went back to Bahrain on leave and met Sherry—she was visiting her parents, who were both officers. They wangled a peace-type assignment for me in Europe, and we had our twins. And I loved it—God, I really loved having a real, honest-to-God family. I was thinking, you know, football with the boys, Christmas presents, all that stuff. But when it came right down to it, I just couldn't wait for them to stop bawling all night, like they were some wog brats trapped in bombed-out buildings instead of kids with two parents and everything. Sherry was always doing something for them, forgot about me. I had a lot of time on my hands after I spent the day trying to tell people who'd been civilians since they were kids how to stay alive in the real world, which was what I did, that and push papers and take orders from more civilians. I guess what it all boiled down to was I just can't hack peacetime. I got bored, started drinking. But the first time I took a swing at Sherry, she ducked away and cowered against the wall, and I saw her turning into some spic hooker-terrorist, just for a minute there. Then one of the kids toddled in with his diaper around his knees and a bottle in his mouth and she ran off with him into the bedroom and locked the door against me. I wonder if she knew how close I came to killing her. Probably. I did. And I figured if I ever touched her again, being me, I'd probably finish her off, so I walked out of the house and drove to HQ and asked for another combat tour. I'm not much good for anything else, I guess.

"They wouldn't send me right back into combat so I went to school and became a helicopter mechanic, but that bored me too. I took leave, went back to HQ in Japan and talked to Sherry. She met me at the PX cafeteria, didn't even bring the kids. Brought the picture I showed you, though. I told her it wasn't working out, that I wanted more action, but I was sorry and I'd keep supporting her and the kids and I loved them, but they were just better off without me around. They can do pretty well by themselves living on post. I said I'd like to visit sometime. She said maybe later. But then she did kiss me before we left and I thought, maybe I'll try to get something closer, you know? But the next day I got orders to go to Tibet to train natives in hand-to-hand and small weaponry.

"I got to know those little gooks pretty well. I liked 'em even. Tough little buggers and hell, you know, ever since Belize I have not been able to stand letting anybody else walk point or check out an ambush. I guess I don't want ever again to be the last one left alive. I mean, shit, I'm no good for anything but killing people anyway . . . I've read stuff where they call that survival guilt but the way I am, I think it's just plain loneliness. I don't want to be left to bail out alone. Anyway, we were out on a training mission one night and it turned into a firefight with some of the Chinese. They had some of my people pinned down, so I went in after 'em. My people got out, I think, but I was taken. It has even crossed my mind that maybe I was set up, but at any rate, I spent seven months nursing my frag wounds in a cage.

"Then they marched me for a long time until I got to what I guess might have been a salt mine or something and put me to work. I kept trying to escape and they kept beating me. That's where the kid I told you about came in. Later on, Wu told me that they had learned enough from what they beat out of me to find my records and discovered that I was what she called an 'artificial person' and in view of what a ferocious war criminal I was they thought they'd better send me to this place for further study. I've been afraid they were going to dissect me or something but so far the only time they really let me have it was when I killed a guard the first time I tried to escape. They questioned me a lot, and had me in solitary and all that stuff—sleep deprivation and so on—but I never could tell them why being an 'artificial person' makes me any better or worse than anybody else. Maybe it does, maybe it doesn't. The Colonel doesn't think soldiers ought to have families. He doesn't. But I wonder if Thibideaux or even Marsh would have an easier time trying to be civilians or peacetime soldiers, trying to live with civilians. It's a different world." I felt him grinning at me in the dark. "You're the closest any of us have come in a long time to a civilian, Vanachek. I guess it's been tough for me having you here to remind me that as much as I miss Sherry and the kids, if they don't need me to actually protect them from something, I'm no fucking good for them. I'm just not worth a damn in peacetime . . ."

I thought he'd gone to sleep but I asked, "Du, I'm wondering about something."

"Yeah?"

"You guys all seem pretty healthy and yet you've had all these beatings and been living on momos all this time. Weren't you ever as sick as I've been when you first came here?"

"Well, yeah. But we got over it."

"You just got better all on your own?"

"Mostly. Yeah, mostly on my own. Wu claims it's the air around here, because it's so pure and everything, but I think I started getting better when I began having these dreams."

His voice softened and even through the darkness I could see his features relax.

"See, I had these dreams for a long time. They're pretty hazy, but I dreamed about guys in long dresses coming and taking care of me. There were these noises. Damnedest thing. But they did a good job. My feet were deformed and raw from all the beatings and in the beating I took here after I killed the guard, my hands were crushed. I thought I'd never be able to use them again. Now look," and he closed and opened both fists and made claws with both sets of fingers and thumbs.

FIRST HARVEST

The mountains are less white, cataracts tumble down their sides, the tangled rhododendron brush is flowing pink, red, purple, yellow and all shades in between, and tonight we enjoyed our first smuggled new vegetables—beautiful, crunchy, fresh-tasting things that smelled of the ground and greenness: beans, carrots, cauliflower, broccoli, potatoes and onions. The vegetables have grown at a speed that astonishes me, when I remember the careful nurturing Grandad's garden used to take and how long it seemed between planting and eating. I regret not planting tomatoes particularly, since they would have been better than raw beans, but tomatoes need stakes and tying up and special pampering to keep them from cutworms, and that would have been impossible to do clandestinely. Du as it turns out is very fond of onions, which Thibideaux ate but did not like. Marsh grazed indiscriminately and the Colonel closed his eyes and chewed in orgasmic bliss. Amazing how a dab of onion flavor improves a momo.

It promises to be one of the more gala evenings here in the heart of the Kun Lun Mountains. Our sumptuous meal will be followed, if all goes as predicted, by the arrival of another pack train.

Tea mentioned earlier in the day that the train had been spotted returning by the sentry posted at the pass. He seemed overjoyed and anxious at the same time.

"I am thinking they are returning very late," he said.

"They were supposed to be bringing the router you wanted, and some other tools, weren't they?" I asked.

"Yes, but the Terton went with them. She is my concern."

"The who?"

"You are calling her the doctor. Dr. Terton then. She is going with the pack train this time, you know."

"I know," I said glumly. Ever since the pack train left, taking the old woman with it, Wu has been her old high-handed and suspicious self. She keeps popping into the library as if hoping to catch Dolma and me smoking dope or doing something equally immoral. I have had very little time to read or write since the train left. It seems Wu is always lurking by the headquarters entrance when the day ends watching my pajama pockets for unauthorized bulges. Maybe she's monitoring Tea by keeping an eye on me. Anyway, I've sorely missed the old woman.

I've picked up enough Tibetan to augment my Chinese that I understand much of the conversation around me now, enough to realize that the camp is too isolated by mountains and distance for the usual long-distance devices. Making use of the orbiting satellites would give away the camp's position, so for security reasons as well as practical ones all of us, including Wu and the guards, are cut off from quick and easy communication with the rest of the world. Every time we find something like the bathtub or the ruins of a piano or the particularly large ivory Buddha we recently uncovered, Tea always turns to me and says, "Are you not finding it remarkable to think that everything, *everything* is being carried in on someone's back, Viv?"

But now he said, worrying, which is not at all usual for him, "The Terton was intending to take two days to conduct some business by helicopter and be returning with the train. But even so they are returning much later than we planned. The sentry is watching many days in vain."

Tonight as we came down to the cells, the sentries scanned the horizon constantly, their postures alert and tense. Usually they laugh and call to each other or hum to themselves or sometimes even play cards together at the more closely spaced duty stations. Tonight each stood ready to greet the night with a trio of unlit torches stuck in the rock wall next to each sentry post. Most nights they carry flashlights, but the vigil is too long between the time the train is first spotted at the head of the pass and the time they arrive, and it takes too much juice from the precious batteries to use the flashlights as beacons.

DAY OF PACK TRAIN ARRIVAL

The pack train straggled up the hill this morning, but they carried no tools for Tea and no computer disks for Dolma. Their backs were empty of anything except clothing.

This is apparently an unprecedented disaster. Wu called a general meeting of the camp this morning, under the beak of the canopy overlooking the slope. The doctor stood slightly behind her, slumping from exhaustion, her eyes hooded instead of fiercely boring into everyone around her as they usually did. Whatever she had had to do in civilization had remained undone, apparently. Tough luck. She would just have to be stuck with the rest of us.

During the meeting, I realized for the first time that what, or rather whom, I've seen is apparently whom I get. All the camp was present but there was no one there

I did not know either from headquarters, the cell or the field. While I hadn't consciously imagined vast catacombs of groaning cells, filled with the fallen fruits of the war, I somehow thought there were more of us than I've met. But there are only we few prisoners, and far more guards, most of them of Tibetan appearance, but some Chinese or Indians. Tea was there, of course, and Dolma, looking very martial except when she pushed her glasses up on her nose with the tip of her rifle barrel. A prison with a better than one-on-one guard-to-prisoner ratio. We must all be very desperate characters indeed to warrant such precautions. I really must have another look at that three-sectioned computer file.

Wu paced back and forth, as if she was about to deliver a long-winded speech and then said, first in Chinese, then in Tibetan, Hindi, English and finally Russian (I had no idea that she, as well as Dr. Terton and I, knew so many languages), "The supply helicopter did not come at the arranged time. The pack train waited an extra week and still it did not come with fresh provisions. Consequently, rations will be cut to half portions until the next appointed time. Do not feel that I am being unnecessarily harsh. The staff and administrators will also be on half rations. That is all. Back to work."

Today I've been working with Tea deep in the tunnel, the work lights shining through the silt and dust sifting down onto our faces, hands and clothing as we slowly dug and sorted our way through a new barrier to rooms beyond.

I would have preferred less confining work, boxed in with Tea as I was with onion still on my breath from breakfast. He noticed and said all too aptly, "You are being very closemouthed today, Viv. What is eating you?"

"Other than being a prisoner of war with rations running low, you mean?" I said, not exactly snapping, but trying to keep him from delving any further. I had distributed only about twenty-five packets of seeds, not enough to make a difference in the level in the room, not enough to make a bulge in my pockets, and not enough, I feared, to keep even us prisoners fed, let alone the guards, during the month or so until the helicopter was scheduled to return.

Tea laughed. "You are thinking you will be hungry because the pack train returned empty? Instead think how the other ladies back in North America will be envying you, who are already so much more slender than you were on arrival, and now have the chance to be going on a new enforced diet that they would be paying thousands of dollars to be nibbling on."

"I was just wondering if Wu is going to cut back to eating half of the fresh fruit I saw at her table once when she questioned me instead of wolfing down the whole bowl." He frowned. He doesn't like it when I criticize Wu but he never threatens or corrects me. I get the oddest feeling that it isn't so much that he doesn't agree with me as that he objects to my unkindness in pointing out her shortcomings.

I wish he had checked the seed room himself, so I wouldn't be in such a quandary about other, more urgent shortcomings of a nutritional nature. We have gentle rains cooperatively falling mainly at night lately, and the vegetables grow so fast I'm pretty sure we could get in another crop before the growing season ends. But if I let him know about the seed room, surely Wu will take the matter out of his hands and work us all to death planting food for her to hog for herself and the staff, leaving the rest of us still on short rations, without our hard-won new secret supplement.

Of course, before long probably one of the guards will spot our crops among the rocks for what they are.

At least some of the guards must come from farming families, although I wonder how many generations back has it been since Tibetans have been allowed enough peace to grow food. The country has been in the middle of a war all of *my* life. According to my geography texts, the Central Plateau used to be rich farming land but you'd never know it by looking at it now. Still, you'd think somebody would have recognized cauliflower when they saw it. Or was cauliflower indigenous to this area? Never mind, they haven't noticed yet, the cauliflower grows up between the rocks as fast as the weeds it replaced, and the problem remains. We've been very lucky thus far with having our haphazard plantings take root, but some things really flourish best if planted a certain depth down. It's a shame they have to go to waste because I'm afraid to share them.

TWO DAYS LATER

I've been going to laughable lengths to avoid having to make a decision. I accidentally left the door to the seed room open when we were in the lower corridors yesterday. Tea was still explaining to me how he intended to shore up a side passage as he crossed to the door and shut it behind him without looking inside the room. Today I went so far as to ask him to hold the flashlight while I looked for "something" in the room, but he's so preoccupied with his work that he continued telling me about how rich in various minerals this area once was without even glancing at the riches around him. He is a dear fellow in all other ways and not a bit stupid but is, as I first noticed, a little goofy, though now that I'm learning Tibetan I realize he speaks perfectly well not only in Tibetan, but in Chinese and Indian, and the funny-sounding tense mistakes he makes are only because he loves Western slang and insists on speaking English to me so that he can use it. None of the other English-speaking Tibetans make that sort of mistake—it's more the kind you hear from Indians occasionally. I don't have enough linguistics background to quite understand why.

Anyway, he can be remarkably obtuse. I find it hard to believe the seeds have been here undetected for so long. I guess it's just that Tea is so into minerals, he is oblivious to vegetables and animals. I wonder if that Earl

Grey program labeled rooms as to contents? You'd think if it did, he would have remembered this one. But then, it was a big place.

THREE DAYS AFTER LAST ENTRY

⚕ Damn, I wish I was able to keep better track of the dates. I gained access to the computer again, and I'm even more confused than ever. I have had a roaring headache most of the day—probably from staring at the screen.

Tea borrowed Dolma back this morning and left me alone with the computer in the library, supposedly cataloging books. He doesn't realize, of course, that I've memorized his access codes.

The Earl Grey files, now that I see them again, bother me, especially in light of the other little goodies I've uncovered under the code name of CONSTANT COMMENT (a favorite tea brand at my grandmother's house when I was a little girl). On the one hand, it's hard for me to believe that Tea is making it so easy for me to get this information, which seems to be important, at least to us prisoners. On the other hand, maybe he is as oblivious to its importance as he is to that of the seeds. Or maybe, as the Colonel says, it's disinformation. But the Earl Grey files, which bother me most deeply, have empirical data to support them. The Constant Comment files could possibly be disinformation planted for me to find just so I can make everybody else miserable when I divulge the contents. But why doesn't Wu tell my cellmates this stuff herself if she wants them to know? Part of it is just case history. It's the hero business that would boggle their minds.

It certainly boggles mine. I seem to have been keeping excellent company, here in the prison camp. I am surrounded by heroes immortalized in the history of NAC. Not major history, perhaps, since if it was mentioned in my military history classes at all, it wasn't presented as material required for testing, as I don't recall learning any of it. But it's history nevertheless—always presuming it's true, of course, and actually, I hardly see how this particular kind of information could be used to break down prisoners. On the contrary, the fact that it *hasn't* been mentioned indicates to me that perhaps Wu felt it would be too *good* for morale.

I found it by accident. Before I accessed the Earl Grey program I tried the Darjeeling one again, and it was exactly as I remembered it, with the three columns in Chinese, Hindi and Russian and our names among those of the other prisoners and guards listed below. This time I noticed that a cursor was flashing at the head of the Chinese column. I tapped the DOWN arrow until the key reached the first name I recognized, which was Danielson's. I pressed the RETURN key. For a moment, I thought I'd blown it. The screen flashed, went blank, and flashed again. What would happen if I'd erased something important? It would be discovered I'd been messing with unauthorized programs and then—what?

Before I had a chance to work up full-fledged masochistic fantasies about it, the screen filled with a file neatly headed "Danielson, Du Poindexter." Poindexter? Any guy born in a lab should have been spared having what sounded like ugly family names. A nice clean code number would have been more the thing. But there in Danielson's file was all of the history he had already related to me, followed by the cursor prompt "Access Constant Comment?" So I pressed again.

A portion at the beginning, where the date would have been, was deleted by a heavy black bar. I wished I knew how to get inside the thing and get rid of that bar. It seemed to be a press release.

Today—years after he was reported missing in action by the platoon he singlehandedly saved from destruction, Master Sergeant Major Du P. Danielson was formally honored at the dedication of the crematory mound where the ashes of NACAF troops and their allies are blended in a last testament to the brotherhood of humanity and the worldwide fight for peace. The assault led by Danielson not only saved the lives of all other personnel involved, but prevented the destruction of a nearby medical mission and village of civilians and led to the discovery and disarmament of a concealed nuclear device. Secretary of Defense Robert E. Grant, in a moving dedication speech, regretted that Danielson's remains had never been recovered so that his ashes could be among the first to blend upon Danielson Mound with those of his fallen comrades in this profound tribute to the bravery of one NACAF fighting man in particular, and to all NACAF fighting forces all over the world.

Much as Danielson disliked being a prisoner, I somehow doubted he would share General Grant's regret that the Danielson ashes were not handy for scattering.

I pressed ESCAPE and was back in the three-column file. Alphabetically, the next one of us to access was Marsh. I pressed RETURN and waited to see what the Constant Comment about him was.

The date once more was blacked out but the news release said:

The North American continent was spanned today from the Gulf of Mexico to the shores of the Arctic Ocean, as well-wishers formed a human chain to express solidarity with captured World Peace Organization activist Keith Irwin Marsh. The government of the People's Republic of China has denied knowledge of Marsh's whereabouts. The Free Marsh Fund has accumulated billions of dollars over the years, and WPO spokesmen say that if Marsh is not located within another year, the money will be used to help free other hostages and prisoners, and to train other individuals to continue Marsh's work. Marsh was known not only for his willingness to negotiate under extremely perilous circumstances, but also for his skill in deactivating nuclear and other explosive devices. It is feared he may have met his death performing such a service for his captors after he and a military corpsman disappeared after crossing into China, where Marsh had been dispatched to assist the locals devastated by northern China's worst flood in recent years.

I switched back to Earl Grey to see what they said about the Colonel and Thibideaux. I was also curious to see if, unbeknownst to me, I hadn't somehow or other been immortalized too, but I hadn't gotten that far and was interrupted before I could investigate further. Dolma stood in the door. I tapped the key and accessed Darjeeling again as she walked across the library to the table where I worked.

"Viva," she said, as it seemed easier for her to say than Viv with a short *i*, "Viva, I am assigned to the pack train that leaves early in the morning. I will not see you again for a while."

"I don't envy you the trip. How will you manage out there in the snow without your glasses fogging up?" I asked, smiling. I was touched she had come to say goodbye. We were less like guard and prisoner now than like co-workers and I felt like a rat for deceiving Dolma, though I realistically figured what she didn't know wouldn't hurt her. Still, I would have hated for her to be blamed for any of my transgressions.

She pulled off her glasses and began wiping them. "I have good far vision," she said. "I say to you, 'Don't get sick again, my friend.' "

"I'm not the one going out there in the snow and wind," I said.

"No, but you are still weak from the loss of your baby. Sometimes ladies very weak for a very long time after that."

"I suppose so."

She sat down on the floor beside the table—which was an old tabletop propped up on two big stones. Brushing her thin black hair back from her face she said, "I have to tell you something. I have to tell you I am sorry I did not come to see you earlier that day, the day you lost your baby. I was on duty. If I had come sooner I maybe save the baby."

I shook my head. "Dolma, that's all over with. Don't worry about it."

"But, Viva, I know how you feel. I too have lost my child. I cannot have more children." She sniffed and wiped her nose on the back of her wrist. "I never have spoke to you how it was with me before I come to this place. I am from a good family that lived in Shigatse. My father was a relative of the Panchen Lama. We were not wealthy people, for the soldiers had taken all wealth from every Tibet person, but even so, we are a good family and when I fell in love with an interpreter for the Chinese, my family was angry with me."

"I can imagine."

"They dared make no objection to my boyfriend, though, because they feared the soldiers. My family lost many people already to the soldiers—three of my brothers and my father's brother's entire family were killed in the rebellion after the Panchen Lama was murdered. So, although I knew they did not want me to, I married my interpreter and moved away with him, and quickly became pregnant with my first child. I was very frightened. My mother and sisters were far away. No women in the city to which we moved would talk to me for they feared my husband would inform on them. All people were afraid of each other for fear of informers. I was so afraid. Who would help me with my baby, I asked my husband? The midwives were forbidden to practice on pain of death. Our Tibet doctors were killed or sent to work in the mines or forests where hard work calloused their hands so that they could not diagnose illness by the pulses anymore. The medical colleges were teared down and all the books burned—many years of knowledge gone in a few years. All of these things I said to my husband and he understood and held me and told me that all would be well. He would find a Chinese doctor for me. My husband did not know what would befall me, Viva. He had been working with the foreigners in important government affairs and he knew little of day-to-day things, of what our conquerors were doing to the women of our people. Because I was cut off from my friends, and had been a maiden before, I knew nothing of the danger myself and went blindly into the office of the Chinese doctor who was supposed to examine me and see if my baby was all right.

"He had a table with many instruments but I thought little of it until he began to examine me, to poke at me inside with things. And all at once I felt a horrible, tearing pain. I momentarily thought this was because I was pregnant and so tender in that region, but then I felt a rush of blood and something come out of me and I fainted. My husband came for me, and the doctor was very angry with him but when the doctor had finished speaking to him in Chinese so rapid I could not follow, my husband was very angry too. He did not stop to clean me, but carried me home. I knew before I left the office that the doctor had killed my baby. I saw it lying there, in a basin, not yet a child. I would have taken it to bury but this was not permitted. Later my husband told me that we would have no more children, that the doctor had changed me so that I no longer would be able to become pregnant. He said the doctor told him this was population control, the same as had been practiced in crowded parts of China for many years.

"My husband begged my forgiveness, weeping with shame and rage as he told me these things. He was also afraid that I might die. The doctor was wrong, he said. The rule was that each couple was allowed one child but I had had no children. Our only baby had been murdered that day. And besides, Viva, there were always too many Chinese and always too few Tibet people. Always we have too few people to work our land. But the conquerors treated us as if we were animals spawning without thought or care. And now I can have no children. I have not forgiven my husband, although I know it is not his fault, but that day, I did the same thing to you—by accident—but by my neglect I caused you to lose your child. It is possible I may not return from this trip and I wanted you to know this thing before I go. I wanted to ask your forgiveness, as I have no right to do."

Her glasses were a salt-streaked mess by that time

and her nose red and soggy. What could I do? Tell her
my baby had not meant to me what her baby had meant?
She'd never understand. Besides, I would have had some
trouble talking. My throat kept constricting, seeing poor
Dolma on the table, her baby in the basin, my baby on
a cold stone floor, both in pools of blood, neither having
had a chance at life. I didn't want that baby. I am glad
not to have to deal with it and I would have prayed to
be relieved of it if I had known I was carrying it. But
just the same, some of my tears were for poor little
Buzzard Junior, whatever he or she would have been.
Women in NAC had fought for the right not to bear
children if they chose and here was Dolma, not allowed
to give her baby life. I didn't know what to say to her,
what to do, so I did what Grandma and Grandpa would
have done and gave her a hug.

About that time we heard the muffled report of the
rifle. We stared at each other for an instant. Dolma's
face was naked and pinched, her black hair spiked up
on her forehead from rubbing her face with tear-wet
hands, her nose bearing red marks where her glasses,
which she'd pulled off to polish on her shirttail, usually
rested.

Another shot, the sound like that of a bone breaking
inside a pillow. We sprinted down the hall and to the
surface.

Guards and prisoners both were running, jumping
up and down at the foot of the compound, beyond the
canopy. Someone was shouting, "Fools! Fools! Catch
them!"

I ran forward, surer with each step that my room-
mates had made their break without me. And then I saw
them, tall men in orange pajamas, running with armed
guards before and behind them, toward a panicking clus-
ter of shaggy brown animals.

The yaks darted this way and that in a panic, and
bolted down toward the valley floor.

All I could think of was meat. Fresh meat, hot fresh
meat, and it was escaping. I was so intent on the herd
I didn't see Thibideaux snatch the rifle from the nearest
guard, didn't pause to wonder that he aimed the rifle

not at the guard, but ahead of the yaks, at the opening to the pass, turning the beasts back toward us again, as he and the guards and the other prisoners went whooping down the hill like so many wild Indians on a buffalo kill.

We pelted after them, slipping and sliding down the hill. Three carcasses lay amid the boulders and ice chunks remaining from winter.

The guards who tried to fire into the herd were blocked by those with sense enough to circle it, so that guards and prisoners soon had the frightened animals captive within a small ring. Thibideaux calmly handed the gun back to a guard, snatched a knife from another guard, and began skinning out one of the killed yaks before the guy whose knife it was realized what he was doing and put a rifle against his neck, just to remind him he was still in custody.

Samdup, Two-Gun Tsering's husband, took charge and ordered the women and children to keep the herd circled, which we did, while the men hefted the largest rocks they could carry into a circle, making a corral for the animals.

It was quite a day, and that night we all feasted on fresh yak and were able to send Dolma and the pack train off the next morning with full bellies.

PART FIVE

TEA, EARL GREY, AND SNOW LION

Of course, it was the yaks and the blood that must have drawn the snow leopard that mauled Merridew down from the mountains.

Within a couple of weeks, Dolma's train returned empty and starving, and minus three of the guards, who had taken the rations of some of the others to hike back into the guerrilla camp and try to learn what had happened. Dolma sat with me in the library, moving awkwardly from exhaustion and the pain of frostbitten fingertips and cheeks. Behind her thick glasses, her eyes were dull, too tired to focus on the pages of the books. We had one wall of shelves restored by then, with some gaps to fill in as we found volumes to fit them. But there was a clear space on the floor about six feet square and since I hadn't had computer access in Dolma's absence, I had been taking notes from the Foxfire Books on gardening. Dolma licked her cracked lips now and then. The yak her party had taken with them had been wolfed down, the people were so hungry for meat. We had been on strict rationing of the remaining meat, and of course it would have been folly to kill the other animals, since they could be used, once they settled down to breeding, for butter, cheese, milk and eventually more meat. Yaks were very rare in Tibet now, Tea had told me. It was miraculous that these had found their way into our valley. Consequently, Dolma, who had gone back to half-ration momos in one week, was hungrier than I was, since I had had a small piece of yak with my supper momo every day since she left. Even at that it did not amount to as much food as a full ration, and I felt like shit for holding out on her about the vegetables, and wished I could find a way to share them with her without betraying the other prisoners. It was us against the guards, after all, I kept telling myself. But it didn't help.

I had sifted out most of the English books but there were others—loose, ripped pages of rice paper and parchment, on which were handwritten or block-printed letters, and interspersed among them were splintered and broken boards I took to be covers. Two walls in the library room were devoted not to shelves but to foot-deep cubbyholes in the wall, about two feet square. Dolma was no help with the text. She did not read Tibetan, she told me, only Chinese. Although her native tongue was still spoken among her people, it had been forbidden by the Chinese to teach Tibetan in school, so while she spoke only very little Chinese, she read and wrote better in that language, and in several others, than she did in her own. Her English had improved tremendously since we'd started working together, as had my Tibetan.

The library almost looked like a library again. Sorting loose pages by language, I was able to collate most of the English-language books by title and page number and some of them, the whole ones, I had alphabetized, wrapped with thread, and replaced on the shelves. The same with the German, French, Russian, and Japanese texts. I was rather hopeless in Greek, but at least had all the texts together, and the Hebrew was likewise just a jumble of pages. The Sanskrit texts I fared a little better with and thought I had the Upanishads pieced back together.

I would have slept there if I could. The night after I found the files, everybody was full of yak meat. My grandma would have claimed it was all that blood in the red meat that made my cellmates so feisty. The Colonel jumped me almost as soon as I walked in the door. "Warrant Officer, I saw you come out of headquarters with that woman guard. You looked mighty chummy. Have you been fraternizing with the enemy?"

"Sororalizing a little maybe," I told him. "It's a little difficult for two women to fraternize."

"Don't get la-di-da with me, soldier," he said.

"What the Colonel really wants to know, Viv," Marsh translated, "is if you've been sleeping with Taring."

"Why? Do I look especially well rested? As if I've been sleeping all day?" The sarcasm was acknowledged by Marsh and Thibideaux, ignored by the Colonel, and missed by Danielson, and I added, "Boys, the only one who's been on top of me lately is the Colonel here, who is on my back, and I sure do wish you'd get off it, sir. There are women guards too. I could accuse you of the same thing."

"That's preposterous and you know it," the Colonel said.

"Yes, Viv, don't be ridiculous," Marsh said. "You know we're out there in the field in plain view of everybody. Now, if we were working inside rooms away from the rest of the camp, we might consider . . ."

He was being sarcastic too. He'd already told me he'd done his best, within safe limits, to discourage Wu's interest in him.

The Colonel wouldn't let me alone, however, and lectured me on loyalty throughout yoga. Finally I snapped, "Dammit, I'm not fucking Taring or anybody else and have no intentions of doing so. I sleep down here and if you don't mind, I work all day tomorrow too, the same as the rest of you, and I'd like to *get* some sleep now." I abandoned my cobra position, turned over and ignored them, feeling like the guest of honor at a bear-baiting. I did not tell them what I found on the computer and decided, that if the Colonel thinks, when I do tell them, my withholding information is also betrayal, he could go fuck himself.

As for my supposed dallying with Tea, that was ridiculous. Tea had not visited the library for any length of time since Dolma and I began working there. He spent most of his time on the restoration work and although I helped him with that a couple of days a week, I usually spent my below-ground time with Dolma.

But today he came to visit, looking carefully around and threading his way through the piled pages and covers to the table. Dolma rose, stepped over three of my piles to one she had sorted before she left, fished something from the middle of the pile, and handed it to him. He accepted it with a little bow of thanks and a murmured "Much obliged," as he tucked the largish, brown-covered book under his arm. I couldn't see the title, but it occurred to me that I was not the only one with secrets.

Tea looked pityingly at Dolma and asked her in Tibetan if she was not allocated a rest day after returning from the pack train. She said she was but she had thought I would need her help. She hated to be away so long, but now she realized—this as they exchanged rather covert glances with the barest flitting of the eye in my direction—that she was too tired to remain. He nodded and she left the library.

His back was to me as he surveyed what we had accomplished with the antique Tibetan books, which were short rectangular pages sandwiched between slabs of wood. The deep cubbyholes in one wall were intended, I discovered, for stacking these odd-shaped (for a Western book) volumes, and Dolma and I had stored all of the intact Tibetan books we'd recovered so far on these shelves.

He lifted one of the books in both hands, as if it was a small injured animal, and stroked the words with one finger. His face was very intent and I felt as if I was interrupting something private. I found myself almost whispering, as if I was in a church or a real library, the old kind with all books and no taped or filmed information, "Do you understand what that says?"

"No," he said, "I am not understanding, but I do recognize this language. It is an ancient and secretive one, being used in past times by scholarly religious persons for the transmission of arcane knowledge and holy wisdom."

"Really?" I asked, leaning closer to study it, though

of course it looked like complete gibberish to me. "I wonder if anybody here understands it?"

He shrugged and tenderly replaced the book not on one of the piles but on the shelf from which it must have come. "It is possible."

"If there was a book here that explained how to learn this from regular Tibetan, and I could learn to read regular Tibetan, maybe I could figure it out . . ." I said.

"You would want to learn of dead religions and superstitious mambo-jumbo?" he asked, his voice both teasing and sad.

It was my turn to shrug. "It's not like I had any pressing appointments, unless the commandant has made one for me with the firing squad. I haven't noticed the cavalry riding to my rescue . . . Tea, tell me, is it true that once you guards are assigned here none of you ever leave either?"

"Yes, it is so," he said.

"But why? I mean, doesn't the isolation get to you? Don't the guards miss their families?"

"All soldiers here either have no families or their families are with them here."

"Still, the deprivation . . . Is this a punishment post then?"

"Oh, no, it is a privilege to work here. Great selectiveness is practiced in choosing those who come to this place."

"Even among prisoners?" I watched his face closely when I asked this.

But he didn't seem to take it seriously. He patted me on the shoulder and said, "Oh, yes, indeed, Viv, only the very finest from all the prisons are chosen to come to this place. To lift the rocks on this soil is a very great honor for all foreign demons."

"This foreign demon is extremely honored then," I said, bowing with mock ceremoniousness, "especially since I was pulled right out of the field without going to another prison first."

"Ah, but it is your destiny that you are meeting our good doctor and she is seeing at once that you are belonging here."

"As opposed to belonging back home in Tacoma, as opposed to belonging in another prison camp, or as opposed to dead?" I asked.

"Why, as opposed to all," he said, as if surprised that I should ask. "For right as rain you are here, right?"

That was indisputable.

"Well, do you think anyone is going to mind if I have a shot at these?" I asked, nodding at the pile of pages. "I know it's not supposed to be as ennobling an activity as hauling rocks and your bosses have been trying to destroy books like these for over a century but surely even they are a little curious . . ."

He looked as if he was about to argue with me for a moment then said, "Oh, you bet your bottom dollar they are being curious, okay. Go right ahead. But be providing written transcripts of your translations. We are an information-gathering endeavor here."

"Speaking of which," I said. "I'd like to get another look at the graphics files of this place in earlier times. I have trouble relating the rooms we're uncovering to the landscape outside."

"Wal, I can be doing better than that, little lady," he said. "I can be taking you topside and be scouting out this terrain with you."

That wouldn't get me computer access, I thought, and might set my cellmates' tongues to wagging again, but on the other hand, maybe Tea would know a cauliflower if I arranged for him to trip over one.

After he paced with me around ruins and boulders, showing me where the rooms we had already uncovered were, where the still-buried medical college had been and so on, we trudged down the hill and he pointed out when we stood above the isolation cells and the storage rooms. For a change the rain had not confined itself to nighttime, and a light drizzle put a chill in the air and hung curtains of mist over the valley and in patches on the hill, so we almost bumped into other prisoners and guards periodically on our trek. The mountains might as well have been prairie for all we could see of them.

"There was a shrine, there, on the shores of the sacred lake," he said, pointing his chin to the bottom of the hill. He had switched into Tibetan as he guided me, and he sounded much more intelligent and less goofy than he did in English.

"Can we walk down there?" I asked.

He shrugged and we half slid down the wet path toward the bottom of the slope. Since we couldn't see the ground in most places, my hopes of helping him find the vegetable patches were unrealized.

As we neared the foot of the hill, Tsering's daughter was carrying what appeared to be a mani stone to a large boulder, beside which she had begun a pile. The Colonel was working about ten yards from her pile, breaking up rocks with a sledgehammer. Wu and the doctor promenaded nearby, although their attention was not on the Colonel but apparently on another group of prisoners half concealed by the mist.

I heard it first—a noise I could not readily identify—something like the whine of a plane going down, something like a cavern opening in the earth, echoing and eerie. And then a movement at the top of the boulder caught my attention, and what little light there was glinted off the bared teeth and open throat of a speckled furred face, ears peeled back. The animal had made that awful sound. Below the boulder, the girl dropped her mani stone and the Colonel stood up, taking a breath and letting his eyes rest on her just as the cat sprang.

Tea and I sprang at the same time, but I would never have believed the Colonel could move so fast. As if he had levitated, he was suddenly between the cat, poised in midair, and the child, now on the ground and shielded by the Colonel's crouching body as he swung his sledgehammer upward, at the cat's descending chest.

The lion's roar choked off as the hammer hit slammed into the outstretched chest, but the huge paws came down churning and the great teeth closed on the Colonel's head as he fell back, belly up, sandwiched between the child he was trying to protect and the mauling lion.

I leapt forward, I suppose thinking I'd pull the lion from him with my bare hands, but Tea jerked me back. I rounded on him and tried to fight him off and then heard the crack of a shot and saw Wu, poised, her pistol smoking. The lion's head lolled sideways, a bullet between the eyes, the left side of the Colonel's head still between the jaws.

I don't know who was screaming the loudest, me, the kid trapped under Colonel Merridew and the dead lion, or Two-Gun Tsering, skidding down the muddy hill to land on her knees beside the Colonel. She pushed him away and tugged at the thin little arm protruding from beneath him, extricating her daughter enough to cradle the girl in her arms and rock her.

I shrieked for someone to get Thibideaux and ran to the Colonel. Dr. Terton beat me there, using Wu as an orderly as she began examining and trying to position the injured man, haplessly attempting to disengage him, without further injury, from the squalling child and the dead lion.

Tea showed the most presence of mind. Calmly, almost as if in a daze, he pried the beast's jaws tooth by tooth from the Colonel's head. The doctor, Wu, and I began staunching the wounds with cloth torn from our clothing, applying pressure to gushing holes in the man's scalp, arms, and legs where they'd been torn by the beast's claws. Thibideaux shoved me aside and with a few hurried words to the doctor, he, Marsh, and Danielson lifted the Colonel and carried him up the hill toward the dispensary, the doctor hovering beside them.

I rose too, but Tea remained on the ground, the lion's head on his thighs, her udders quivering against his shins as he stroked the scraggly fur over her desiccated ribs. "A snow lion," he told me. "Starving. If only she had first gone for the yaks."

MERRIDEW

I wrote my last entry and waited alone in the library until I thought the medical people had had time to do the most immediate repairs, then I asked Tea to take me to the dispensary. It was a very small room set in the only remaining portion of the old medical college, separate from the headquarters rabbit warren.

I hadn't waited long enough. Thibideaux, bristling and protective, still worked over Merridew, whose wounds were many and deep. By the time I arrived bleeders had been clamped off and sutured, and a few skin flaps had been thoroughly cleaned and stitched back in place, but overall, the poor Colonel was a swollen, disfigured, bloody mess.

"Well, there's good news and bad news," Thibideaux told me. "The good news is he's alive and the cat missed his eyes, his jugular, his vocal cords and his guts. The bad news is one ear is pretty well a lost cause, we got no idea how bad his head is hurt inside, and he busted a leg. Not even mentionin' all the blood he's lost."

"Why aren't you sewing those up?" I asked, pointing to some pretty deep-looking wounds.

"So the bugs can drain. We don't have any drugs and he'll die for sure if those get infected, so we gotta leave the wounds open. We do this in the field all the time." His mouth twisted down. "They usually die anyway."

"Dr. Thibideaux has been taking excellent care of his friend," Dr. Terton said from the doorway where she stood, composed and quiet-seeming, her slight form not even significantly blocking the light. "I have a salve or two that may help the healing process as well." From a bag that resembled an old pillowcase she extracted a pair of antique plastic jars of the sort that were mostly destroyed when the means for degrading plastic was first introduced to the relief of refuse management specialists everywhere. "If you will be good enough to apply this to the wounds, I will help Colonel Merridew manage his pain."

Thibideaux said nothing, to my surprise, while she held her hands above Merridew's head, closed her eyes, and started to hum.

Although Dr. Terton seemed highly regarded by Tea and seemed to have a soothing influence on Wu that made her more reasonable than otherwise, I had not forgotten the trick the doctor played on me with her hypnosis, which caused me to overextend myself on the hike to the prison camp, and the pain that followed as soon as I reached it. So I said, "Dr. Terton, the Colonel is comatose. He doesn't need you to hypnotize him so that when and if he wakes he feels the cumulative effect of all this pain. That's the way *your* treatment works, isn't it? It's certainly the way it worked with me. Thibideaux, are you going to let her do this?"

"You're forgettin' where we are, Viv. This is the boss lady you're talkin' to now. If she wants to vivisect him there's not one hell of a lot we'll be able to do, damn her."

"There's two of us," I growled but then I realized that of course Thibideaux was right. My incarceration in solitary had been long ago. I had not been interrogated for some time. This prison had been relatively easy on me, even compared to the experience of the men. My work with Tea and Dolma was much more satisfying than the GAG program and the limited functions I performed for NACAF. Here in one place were all the books I'd been trying to check out for years, in all the languages of the world, and I would throw it all back in a fit of John Wayne pique, not so much because I wanted to protect the Colonel, which I did to some extent, but mostly because I was still pissed at the doctor for betraying my trust.

She didn't even look up at me, but asked, gently mocking, "Did you expect, having entered a profession that involves killing others, that you would personally escape pain, as your countrymen do safe on their own continent, having exported their own pain to visit it upon us?" Then she resumed her humming and Thibideaux turned his back on me to apply salve to the wounds that would most benefit from it.

When he was done, she said, "Dr. Thibideaux, I have done what I can, but we have yet a bit of a vigil. You must return to your cell and sleep, so that you may relieve me later."

"Okay. Fine. Come on, Viv."

"Viv will remain with me."

"Why?" he asked warily.

"Because I would like her company while I watch over your friend," the doctor said simply.

"Why do you want to talk to me?" I asked when Thibideaux had gone.

"Because there are things you wish to know. You are a gatherer and processor of information, are you not?"

"That's one way of putting it."

"What else is a student? Not a seeker after wisdom, since it takes wisdom to seek it, and you are not wise."

"I know that," I said, irritated.

"I do not say this to make you unhappy, Viveka, but to enlighten you. For wisdom, you require perspective, and one reason you were brought here was that it appeared to me that perspective was something you had been seeking in your studies."

"Get real," I snapped. "You sound like you gave me a scholarship to graduate school instead of had me force-marched at gunpoint to a prison camp."

She clucked to herself. "You come from such a literal society. The result of all that supposedly Christian doctrine, you know. No argument allowed. Everything is subject to one interpretation only. Everything must be what it seems . . . It is not, you know. Has it never occurred to you that what seems to be a terrible experience may be an opportunity in disguise?"

" 'A stitch in time saves nine,' " I said. " 'Every cloud has a silver lining.' 'You can't tell a book by its cover.' 'Garbage in, garbage out.' Spare me the platitudes, please. I'd think I'd rather go back to solitary than listen to that from you." Panic rose in me as I seemed to be unable to stop these words, which definitely proved the old woman's assumption that I was unwise. She could throw me back into solitary, or worse, but although it was possible I was wrong, I felt as if she was inviting this, was even goading me into displaying the anger I had buried since I first arrived.

"Did it ever occur to you that a platitude becomes a platitude because it is often and for many people true?"

"What do you know about truth?" I demanded. "I know how you people distort it, try to get people to tell the lies you want to hear until they believe them themselves. And I'm not saying you won't get to me, but I want you to know right now that I know how you do it and this sane part of me knows that your truth is a lie." I sounded very grand even to me. It was a shame nobody was there to record it with the last words of Patrick Henry or one of the president's speeches. But I can't help wondering now if I would have blathered on that way if it had been some sadistic male officer, or even Wu, instead of the doctor.

And it was all wasted even at that. My histrionics did not impress her. "My dear young woman, perhaps I was mistaken about you. I assumed that as a seeker of information, you would at least be open to hearing it before you decided on its truth or untruth. Thus far, Nyima Wu has kept you and your countrymen fairly isolated, so if you already know all about us, I have no idea how that could be unless perhaps Lobsang told you?"

"Don't try to get me to rat on Lobsang," I snarled, part of me aware that I sounded ridiculously like an old Humphrey Bogart film. "He's just been doing his job."

"Of course he is. But you really should ask him. And the others. I'm sure that you and your countrymen have discussed how you came to be here . . ."

"Some of us, yeah . . ."

"Perhaps you should ask the same of Lobsang and others with whom you come in contact."

"They wouldn't answer, would they?"

"Oh yes, certainly they would. Why, it becomes very tedious being among others who know all about one for a very long time, so that one begins to feel there is nothing to share, that all is known, that there is no self . . ."

"I thought selflessness and identifying primarily with the group are what your Asian philosophies are all about."

"Identifying, perhaps, but not dissolving the personal identity. I'm sure everyone will be very glad to have you wanting to know about them. There is nothing so prized as a good listener after all. You have my permission, my blessing even, to talk to the others." And then I thought I heard her murmur, "It is time. Perhaps past time."

"What?"

"The snow lions and the yaks, of course. It is later than I had hoped. Because they're coming, you see. I suppose there will be others. Pity Nyima shot the lion, though . . ." she said, beginning once more to hum over Merridew.

"What about the lion? Look, if you're so anxious that I ask people about themselves, how about you? Why are you the only one who can come and go? If you're Chinese, why were you in a Tibetan guerrilla camp?"

"I will answer your questions, Viveka. But I prefer you ask others first."

"Even Wu? Shall I ask her to write me a little essay about all of her war criminal activities since she was eight?"

"I believe she started rather younger than eight," the doctor said. "And perhaps you should not ask her— Nyima has a great deal of potential but she is still uncomfortable wielding authority. Perhaps you should ask Lobsang Taring instead. And about himself, of course. And the others. Don't forget Colonel Merridew and Dr. Thibideaux."

"Shall I report back to you?" I asked cautiously. Perhaps she thought I would spy for her. Perhaps that's what this sudden permission involved.

"That is not necessary. I will know how you are progressing."

"Do you know everything, then? Do you know how long we're going to be on short rations?"

Her mouth pursed up in the first old-ladyish gesture I'd seen her make, and whirlpools of trouble stirred in her annoyingly serene eyes. She blinked several times, like Marsh, then shook her head. "No, I do not know that. Long, I am afraid. Very long."

No use gloating over that piece of information—the news was no better for us than it was for her. Maybe it would be awful. Maybe the guards would resort to cannibalism, as guards had reportedly once done in Siberian prison camps. Yaks would not sustain us indefinitely.

"The child the Colonel saved from the lion wasn't injured?" I asked a little lamely, changing the subject.

"No, she was not."

"I suppose you put her right back to work," I said accusingly, slipping back into my asinine role of "gallantly insubordinate prisoner, risking all to defy authority."

"She chose to, yes. Her mother was standing guard duty. Once Pema recovered from her fright, she was concerned about your Colonel Merridew and she was most uncommonly intrigued by the carcass of the lion. She was born here, you see. She has seen very few animals. Certainly never a snow lion . . ." The doctor's voice drifted off and she returned to humming over Merridew as if I wasn't there, so I left.

I returned to the cell without encountering a guard. Thibideaux, Marsh, and Danielson did not seem to fill the cell properly. We all kept waiting for Merridew to give us the decisive word. We did our yoga and waited for rice. Marsh and Danielson had picked a few immature green beans.

When the rice came, the guards came with it. It was Two-Gun Tsering, who had once taped my mouth when I was hysterical in solitary, who scowled ceaselessly while I hauled rocks, whose daughter had almost become lion food. With her was her husband, Samdup, who held his weapon firmly while his wife, stony-faced, gave each of us a standard half portion, except for Thibideaux, to whom she gave a full ration.

"What's going on?" he asked. Marsh asked the woman something in Chinese, so quickly I couldn't understand. She made a short answer, her face still stony.

"The kid the lion went for today—that was her kid," Marsh said.

"I knew *that*. Is the extra rice for Merridew, then?" Thibideaux asked, with exaggerated raising of his brows and wide eyes in the woman's direction as he pointed to the food.

She made what sounded to me like a grunt and Marsh said, "Nope, it's for you. You're taking care of Merridew, Merridew took care of her kid, she's taking care of you."

"Damn," Thibideaux said, rolling the rice into a ball and taking a bite out of it. "What a system. I love it."

"You could share, y'know," Danielson said.

"Make it last," I told Thibideaux. "The doctor is a little scared we've been abandoned by our suppliers, I think."

"They cannot abandon us," the guard said, in English. "We will be provided for, no matter what."

"It's been two pack trains," Marsh reminded her, gently for a captive to his warder. "And there's been no word from the party searching for the guerrilla camp, has there?"

"They will return. There is no way for us to get 'word' here."

"They could do an airdrop," Thibideaux suggested.

"No! That would betray the security." Tsering objected so strenuously that the panic in her voice surprised me. Is security as important to her as the possibility of her daughter starving to death? "Another pack train will be sent."

Her eyes darted toward the door and she looked sorry she had softened enough to express gratitude. I changed the subject. We could use all the allies we could get. "Is your little girl okay?" I asked, in my best mother-to-mother voice.

"Yes," she said shortly.

"How old is she?"

Her husband said, "It is wiser not to count such things in these times in a place like this. She was born on her native soil, and that is what matters."

"You are native Tibetans, then?" Marsh asked.

"Yes."

"A lot of the guards seem to be. I thought most of the Tibetans were gone and the ones who stayed hated all foreigners—especially the Chinese. So can you tell me why there are so many of you working here?"

"That is easy," the man said. "We have no place else to go. Less than one hundred twenty years ago this land was one rarely seen by foreigners, the people were happy, benevolently ruled by a God-King."

"Never mind one hundred twenty years ago. Your grandfather, who told you such a story, was merely nostalgic for the days when he was a rich man," the woman said sharply. "Before the wealth was evenly divided among the workers."

"You were a worker, Tsering," the man said just as harshly. "Did wealth ever filter down to you?" To us he said, "She is younger than me. All of her grandparents, her parents, her kin on all sides, have been killed. The only stories she knows, the only dreams she has, are those the invaders allowed her. Except for Pema, our daughter . . ."

"I know *other* things," Tsering objected. "But your stories are too fantastic to be true. I suspect the truth is somewhere between the lies you were told and the lies I was told. Certainly not the lies *they* were told." She was quiet for a moment, biting her lip, and then with great determination said, "But this one thing I think is true. Here within this compound are all of the people any of us will ever see again in our lifetimes. For me, thanks to your friend, I have kept for a time the most family I ever have had. For you foreigners, you have no one. I am sorry for this. Your country has sent you far, to die among strangers. I have not been kind. Many of us have not been kind. We must stay here, but there is no reason not to be kind to each other. My name is Tsering. It is my job to keep you here, for you are prisoners because of the harm your people have done to mine. But—if it is possible, if there is something you need—"

"That's real nice of you," Thibideaux drawled softly. "But it's the Colonel who saved your young'n."

"Yes, Thibideaux, but you have saved many others. We have learned of this—of the villages filled with disease you took medicines to and cared for alone . . . of how you were captured, trying to save yet another village—and of the prisoners you have healed here. You have a good heart but we have had to harden ours toward you until now: no longer."

They slipped out quietly and a short time later Thibideaux left to relieve the doctor tending Merridew. I lay down on my cement cot and closed my eyes, but no drowsiness would come, only the closed, hardened young face of Tsering, the flesh set in its sour grieving lines while the mouth tried to smile and the eyes reflected the doubts Merridew's actions had aroused within her about the validity of long-held opinions. I hoped she wouldn't be incautious about whom she let know she was getting soft on us prisoners. She wouldn't be able to help us, or her husband either, if anyone learned of their visit or understood that they had taken Merridew's deed personally. Funny about the husband too. He was the one who had looked pitying when they had taped my mouth while I was in solitary. Not a bad egg, perhaps. She had seemed to enjoy being cruel but perhaps it was just that she knew so well how it was done. He was the more human of the two. For them to come to us that way was a brave thing to do, a risk I wouldn't have taken, but I'm glad they took it. Because I believe she's right. We're going to die here, among these strangers, most of whom we can't even understand. I will never see Puget Sound, Tacoma, a box of corn flakes, an automobile or anything else familiar again. I've never exactly had the life I wanted NAC-side, but I wasn't a prisoner of war then either, with my fate nonnegotiable in someone else's hands. Although the doctor, Tea, Dolma and even—sometimes—Wu seemed less capricious than some of the bosses, professors, and bill collectors I'd had in the NAC, who were just as in control of me, though in slightly subtler ways.

The other thing that interests me about Tsering's little speech is what she said about Thibideaux's record as a humanitarian. Apparently our military careers are open books to our guards. Do they all crowd around the computer when a new disk comes in with the pack train as people in the Second World War crowded around the radio and people back home used to crowd around their televisions?

Now what in the hell can that noise be? I've been lying here writing by butter lamp now that the men are snoring. Just a moment ago there was the funniest sound—I thought it was Danielson, who grinds his teeth and speaks in tongues as well as snores, but this sound was more like a growl, or maybe a whine with a yip at the end of it, answered by more of the same. I've had my own ears cocked for a minute or two now and—shit! It's an avalanche. A slide of rocks and dirt—part of the ceiling just fell in and something is playing hopscotch on the surface above the cell, scampering and thumping around up there, with more of those weird noises. Doesn't seem to bother the men but I'm going to go rat on whatever it is to Tsering and Samdup and pray to God I'm not preventing somebody else from escaping by snitching.

THIBIDEAUX AND THE THINGS GOING BUMP IN THE NIGHT AS TOLD BY VIVEKA VANACHEK, WARRANT OFFICER, PRISONER-ARCHIVIST AND GIRL REPORTER

⊼ Thibideaux had left the door to our cell open behind him when he left to resume his vigil over the Colonel, and I groped along the wall and up the steps to the outer door. Tugging it open, I found myself staring down the barrel of a rifle, before the beam of a flashlight blinded me.

"I heard a noise," I said, very quickly. "Over our cell."

"What kind of noise?" Tsering asked cautiously. I think she was wondering if her softness on us was going to cost her immediately.

Her husband held the weapon, however, and he lowered it when I told them what I'd heard.

He disappeared into the darkness and poked around for a while but shortly returned, shaking his head.

I didn't feel like creeping back down into the dark corridor below to the cell to listen all night for the noises, so I told Tsering, "I can't sleep. I want to keep watch over Merridew with Thibideaux. Is that all right?"

Tsering nodded as if that was only proper and escorted me to the infirmary room. For the first time I felt guarded in the sense of protected rather than confined—I was damned glad of her flashlight and her weapon.

Thibideaux sat dozing on the floor, his bird beak–sharp nose and chin pointing straight down, his crossed arms resting on the low cot containing Merridew.

His eyes flew open when I stepped into the room. He rubbed them and stretched his hands toward the ceiling.

"How's the Colonel?" I asked.

"Not all that hot, dollin'. I can't be sure without a scan. May need a transfusion although his blood pressure seems to be stabilizing. He's still out cold and I'm pretty sure the cat's impact screwed up his spine. There's a couple of cervical vertebrae that are crunched together. Between you and me, given the facilities . . ." He shrugged. His eyes were bloodshot and his hair matted in tufts from sleeping in odd positions.

"Maybe there's something Tsering and her husband can do . . ."

"Look, Viv, I know that was pretty amazing, them bein' so human and all, but I wouldn't count on them. They could even be laying a trap for us, you know? You heard the woman's husband say she'd lost the rest of her family. These ain't no indulgent AmCan mamas and daddies buying their kids all the latest technotoys we're talkin' 'bout here. In this war, the allies and the enemies can be seasoned veterans by the time they're five years old. And a lot more of them are offed for target practice than are saved from animals who ought to be extinct."

"Well, okay, I know I'm the rookie in this outfit, but what kind of a trap would they be laying exactly? They have us in prison already. They have us bought and paid for. Mind you, I've only read books on the subject and have little previous experience but it seems to me that as prison guards who have us at the mercy of their every whim, they have refrained from being too terribly whimsical. They don't *need* to trap us, Thibideaux. We're already trapped and so are they."

"I don't like it anyway. They don't have to be whimsical—*life* is fucking whimsical. You never know what damfool thing people are going to do next. I mean, my daddy's people fished for crawdads and wrestled alligators way back before the alliance and then the corporations poisoned the fucking *swamps,* for pity's sake. They did in the oceans and the forests at the same time and there was nowhere to fish, nothing to farm . . . You know what my parents did for a living, cher? My mama was a bird cleaner and my papa ran a reclamation racket called Troubled Waters. He was a tanker chaser, following along with skimming rigs, waiting for a spill, promising to restore the area to life for a fee a little smaller than a lawsuit would cost. What he couldn't skim he'd burn or lace with chemicals that were worse than the oil, then he'd salt the place with farm-fish that lived until he was out of the area. They caught up with him, eventually, of course. He was one of the frontline troops in the early Lebanese-Libyan wars. You don't fuck with the fuel companies. Mama and me and my brothers and sisters—there was one for every time Daddy'd come ashore for a while—we traveled the coasts, wherever there was a spill, cleanin' up the birds. Mama's money all went to the government, with whatever Papa left, in fines and taxes. The only way we ate was, she didn't tell them nothing about some of my brothers and sisters and they kept the two bucks a bird they made for cleanin'."

"Seems like a pretty big jump from bird cleaning to medicine," I said.

"Nah, not really. To be a good bird cleaner you got to have the healin' hands too—calm 'em, like, while you handle 'em. And you develop technique. Then too, my mama and my sisters were always havin' babies and I learned to help with that. Bird cleaners can't afford real doctorin' so whatever camp we were in, there was always somebody needing me. Then when there weren't hardly any birds to clean up anymore and the price per bird got so high folks started sending their kids to school to get degrees to do it, the police started sayin' you couldn't move from one place to another and then finally they came in and cleaned up the bird cleaners, sent all of us into the wars. Mama, she did fine, took to the air force like a duck to water, you might say, cleanin' up mechanical birds like oncet she cleaned live ones. We never really heard from most of my brothers and sisters anymore—my sisters Marie and Claire, they're not far, somewhere around Afghanistan, last I heard. And I have a brother name of Gull got it in Morocco. The rest don't write so good and may be dead by now. Me, on account of I liked to heal things, I said I'd be a medic. But truth was, cher, I knew about your whimsicalness way before I got into the soldierin' business just from dodgin' your fuel companies and governments and such."

"I guess I know what you mean," I said. I was sitting crosslegged on the floor with my back against the wall, getting a crick in my neck from looking up at him.

"'Course, sometimes war brings out even more whimsicalness in your fellow man than average, I'll grant you. When I first got to Asia, I landed with an assault force on the beach at Rangoon. Thai guerrillas had us pinned down with heavy fire and I was layin' there with my nose in the dirt tryin' to be invisible when someone hollers 'Medic'—so I'm a medic so up I go runnin' toward this supposedly injured man and suddenly all the lead in the world is flyin' my way but I make it to where I hear the cries and I see that he's already wriggled out of range, back down the beach, because he got me to draw his fire. I guess after all them years of cleanin' oily birds, I musta looked to them like a sittin' duck, but after a couple three times, I learned. The injured were dead men, as far as their buddies were concerned, and medics were good diversionary targets."

"So didn't that make you want to stop trying to help people?"

"No, cher. Because what else could I do? I've got these healin' hands. The worst part of this prison thing is that I don't use 'em too often, and then I get kind of mean, like. No, what it made me do was say, fuck your patches and your 'This is our ally and this is our enemy.' I just worked on anybody I came across needed it."

"That must have gone over big," I said.

"Well, I'll tell you somethin' nobody else except Marsh knows, and he can keep his mouth closed tighter than a Republican senator's purse strings when he's votin' on a welfare bill."

"A what?" I asked and then remembered hearing the grandparents mentioning welfare—government relief programs, they said. Come to think of it, the professor with the theory about how NACAF was formed said the present military system made welfare obsolete.

Thibideaux grunted with irritation at being interrupted and I said, "Sorry. Go on."

The floor was cold under my rear and the room so dim from the one low-watt bulb granted the infirmary that I had to strain to make out Thibideaux's sharp features.

"I wasn't exactly in the army anymore when Marsh and me were caught. I was giving myself a little early discharge and fixin' to take care of the flood victims then make it over to Mandalay. I met this lady there . . . but well, I was still in uniform when we got captured so it didn't seem worth mentioning."

"Especially since if you'd been taken when you were out of uniform you'd have been shot as a spy?" I asked.

"There is *that*," he admitted. Then he added, "My turn was comin' up anyway when the old lady showed up. There were ten of us, counting Marsh, goin' into that village. The other seven, they bought it real quick."

"Did the Chinese kill them?"

"Nah, just didn't feed us enough—and there was that epidemic, remember. Them other folks been in the field so long their shots were worn out. We all got the shits and they died—me, I remember little things like shots so I just got the dysentery and I lived till the old lady come around. She's somethin', heh? Crazy as a bedbug but she's not mean like that young one. I don't know why they let her just pick people out to bring in here, but they do. She told me I told her what she needed to know while I was delirious and she was healin' me. I'm glad 'cause now that she caught me, I don't want that ol' gal throwin' me back 'less she could throw me clear to Mandalay and I imagine that pretty lady I was on my way to see there has clean forgot about poor old Doc by now."

After a moment he said, "I haven't minded it too much here except it's boring. It's not dirty like the other place and it's maybe a step up from cleanin' birds, but for some reason, people—not you, dollin', you done your share—but everybody else I mean, don't get real sick real often. I haul rocks good as the next fella but I'm better at medicine. The medical supplies from my kit are about gone now anyway, of course. You used up a lot of 'em, cher. Didn't settle down like the rest of us."

"I keep expecting things to get worse," I told him. "Or—I did. Any more though, I don't know. For draconian cruelty this is rather an uninspired bunch, don't you think?"

"What about those bruises on you when you miscarried?"

"I did that myself," I said shamefacedly. "Freaked out."

He shook his head once sharply, as if clearing his ears, "Well, that's what you said but we didn't believe you."

"True, I'm afraid. Of course, they were pretty nasty when I started screaming—came and tied me down and taped my mouth over."

"They do that. When I first come here, they knocked me around a little, trying to get me to tell 'em something they could use. When I started in to hollerin' though, they taped my mouth and I don't see how I was supposed to tell 'em anything. I figure they are still worried about the building caving in and figure screaming and such could knock something loose."

"A simple explanation would have sufficed," I said stiffly, but actually, it wouldn't have, since hysterics interfere with one's ability to be reasonable about things and anyhow, an explanation that the building actually *was* in danger of falling in on me would scarcely have been therapeutic.

Merridew groaned and Thibideaux bent over him, humming.

"What is it that you and the doctor hum to quiet him?" I asked.

"Well, I don't know about her, but I'm hummin' a little snatch of 'Jolie Blonde.' It was my mama's favorite coon-ass fais-dodo song and she set a lot of store by it, so I figure it's probably got as much power as the next thing," he admitted after a moment. "We got nothin' else to help him with right now, and these folks got different ways of curin' I haven't heard of before. If hummin' helps, I just hope the Colonel likes Cajun music."

His humming was interrupted by a light scrabbling on the roof overhead, and a heart-rending yowl like the one I had heard in our cell. After a moment there was another, more unearthly than the first.

"Spooks?" Thibideaux asked, only half joking.

"You figure the monks they murdered to take over this place come back on the anniversary of their massacre to haunt it or something?" I was jeering, but I was shivering while I did it.

He mulled that over for a moment. "Nah," he said, and whisked to the door, and lightly left and closed it behind him. I didn't hear his footsteps at all, but in another moment he ducked back in and gestured to me to follow. I did, as quietly as possible.

The mist had all blown away and the moon nestled in the cleft of the mountain, which glinted white and horned as the crown of Isis. I saw my way clearly and moved as noiselessly as I ever have, following Thibideaux. Despite the moonlight, the top of the infirmary lay in deep shadow cast by the canopy. As my eyes adjusted to the darkness, Thibideaux put his finger to his lips and pointed to a rock on the top—a rock which wriggled, squirmed, and opened white sharp teeth to yowl again. Not ghosts. Demons? The Tibetans at one time had been very big on demons, which may have explained the lack of guards rushing out to investigate. I leaned closer and saw that the rock was blurred and furry in outline. Then another portion writhed and yowled, outlining ears and a muzzle and one foot, pawing at the moon.

Thibideaux had been quietly pulling off his pajama jacket and motioned me to do the same. I did, shivering in earnest now and feeling embarrassed as well. The prison wardrobe didn't feature institutional brassieres or even T-shirts and although I had seen women working barechested on the hill on warm days, that sort of *National Geographic* local color was their bag, not mine. As soon as I held the jacket in my hands, outspread like a matador's cape, Thibideaux nodded to me to emulate his movements and dove for the toothy pile in front of us. I dove too, and momentarily I even made contact with something, until it bounced in the air, taking me with it, and when the stony ground rared up to jar my teeth loose and bruise me from neck to kneecap, there was nothing underneath my shirt but rocks.

Thibideaux's training as a bird cleaner came in handy at catching other slippery things and as I raised my battered body from the ground, he knelt triumphantly, juggling a bulging pajama top. It churned from within, the whole thing alive, spitting, hissing, growling and yowling furiously, throwing claws and teeth out the openings of the shirt.

"Come on, baby lion," Thibideaux said to the squalling bag of spit and claws. "Ol' Doc's gon' be your daddy now."

I retrieved my pajama top and pulled it on, pulling the sleeves down over my hands as I helped him haul the cat down the little slope leading to the door of the infirmary. About that time, the guards showed up, Tsering, Samdup, and two others from the perimeter I hadn't noticed before.

"What is it? Shoot it!" one of the newcomers said.

"No," I said, since I didn't want them to do that, especially since Thibideaux and I were wrapped around it.

Thibideaux disregarded them entirely as I freed a hand to open the infirmary door while he carried the bundle inside and the guards crowded after.

"What is it?" Tsering asked.

"A demon," someone else said authoritatively.

"It's no demon, it's an orphan," Thibideaux said. "Somebody go get me a box to pin it in."

Samdup opened the door again and slipped out but Tsering raised a pistol and aimed it at the bundle howling bloody murder in Thibideaux's arms. "Are you nuts?" I screeched in English, because my brain wouldn't translate quickly enough to stop her. "You'll bring the house down for sure," and pointed at the ceiling. Someone swept her gun aside and someone else closed in on Thibideaux, trying to take the bundle away from him. Thibideaux, of course, didn't want to let go and the pajama shirt came loose and a flash of pale fur streaked away from them, straight toward the guards, jumped into the air, onto Merridew, up to the top of the cabinet where the few supplies were kept and back down the side, bounding from wall to wall, shedding fur and spraying spittle in its wake.

Like the players in some sort of pajamaed basketball team, we hopped stiff-legged from side to side, trying to corner the cub in the small room while it yowled, spat, and took warning swipes at us with claws splayed into ninja stars.

Its ears laid back and its eyes wide with anger and fear, the cub screamed at us and kept screaming until suddenly I was shoved aside by a plastic milk crate. Thibideaux took the crate and, with the rest of us as a human pen, cornered the cub and held it down. Paws shot out in all directions, teeth gnawed at the plastic, but the cat was trapped.

Tsering once more leveled her gun at it but the weapon was knocked aside and Dr. Terton stepped in front of her. As calmly as if she was waiting for a bus, the old woman stood between the gun and the cat, which was trapped under the milk crate by a lacerated and bleeding, but triumphant, Thibideaux.

Dr. Terton knelt about two feet from the crate and, as far as I could tell, simply looked at the embattled, spitting cat. I certainly didn't hear anything over the din the creature was making, but first one claw disengaged itself from the flesh of Thibideaux's bloody palm, then the teeth closed with a mere nip to the plastic cage rather than a snap, a second paw dislodged itself from trying to disembowel Thibideaux, and the other two withdrew into the cage, to join the body in a tight crouch. After a time, the ears rose to points, the tail slowed from a rapid jerk to a quiet question mark, and the great glittering eyes focused on the old woman, who was crooning to it, singing to it, like one of those snake charmers in the stories, except this was a cat. The animal's ears pricked forward, to catch more of the croon, its pudgy, kittenish front paws slid forward and its chin settled onto them with almost a clump, the back legs sprawled out and the eyes closed. Still crooning, the old woman made an impatient gesture with her hand to Thibideaux indicating that he should stand away from the milk carton, which he did. She lifted the carton off the cub, scooped the cat into her arms and walked off with it.

"I was going to do that next," Thibideaux said. "What she did. It's an old animal-taming trick."

"Bullshit," I said, and asked Tsering for water to wash his wounds, noticing as I lifted my hands again that trickles of blood were running down my own arms from my encounter with the cub's litter mate.

Tsering returned with a Russian-style helmet full of water, half of which sloshed out when she dropped it into my hands, made a sharp about-face, and left, barking after her for the others to follow.

"You think she's pissed because we caught the cub?" I asked Thibideaux.

"Nah, she's just being hard-core again. I told you—"

The doctor shoved open the door then and Thibideaux interrupted himself to ask, "What did you do with the cat?"

"I fed her," she said. "And put out food for her brother. I have her in a cell for now. Tomorrow I will set a trap for the other."

"Some high-class camp we're in here, Vanachek, just us political prisoners and a stray cat or two—seriously, Doc, how did you *do* that? I heard of soothin' a critter down but never that fast."

"Was it hypnosis?" I asked.

"Of a sort," she said. "I believe you are familiar with the technique, Dr. Thibideaux?"

"Yes, ma'am. It's mostly thinking like an animal. But I'm not so almighty quick as you are and I thought I was one of the best . . ."

"Do not discommode yourself, my dear Thibideaux. The snow lion is the guardian beast of Tibet. I share with it an affinity which no outsider can hope to attain. I thought perhaps I might live without seeing such a creature again and yesterday, when Nyima precipitously shot the mother of the cubs, I mourned perhaps more profoundly, I admit, than I would have had the victim been

your Colonel Merridew. But you have found the cubs
and when the other is located, we shall protect them
here, as we will the yaks and any other creatures who
find their way to our valley."

"That's great," I said. "But what are you going to
feed the cats? A child a day?"

"There are rodents in abundance," the old woman
said, and added, with a rather gruesome twinkle, "and,
of course, when our food has run out, there will be
corpses to dispose of."

"You aren't expecting another pack train, then?"

"I didn't say that but we seem to have been forgotten, wouldn't you say?" Oddly, her tone was one of
grim satisfaction and I thought, The old girl has flipped
out, gone around the bend, her motherboard has bit off
half a bite more than it can chew.

"Ma'am, I've been thinkin'," Thibideaux said. "If
we're all on our way out, don't you think maybe it's going
to take more than one person doctorin' to make the end
a little easier for everybody?"

"I didn't say we were in any such condition, Dr.
Thibideaux, but your suggestion contains merit, nevertheless," she said after a deep search of his eyes with
her own.

"Well, you know and I know I'm not a real doctor,
with a license and a degree and all, but I've got a lot of
experience and maybe you could sort of show me some
things—"

"Do I understand that you are asking for instruction?"

"Well, yes, ma'am, you might put it that way . . ."

"Then perhaps you will want to return for some
sleep, Miss Vanachek? Dr. Thibideaux and I have much
to discuss and you and Lobsang have important tasks in
the morning which will require your alert attention."

Having had a great deal of experience at knowing
when I was not wanted, I took the hint and left.

SCOUTING PARTY

Another pack train, more of a scouting party this time, since they expected to be carrying nothing back, departed for the rendezvous point, taking with them the last of the yak meat. Only one cow, a heifer, and a bull remain and those are to be used for breeding stock, Wu says. We are still on half rations, although we prisoners continue to do pretty well with our vegetable supplements. The guards are so listless and tired they stay on the perimeter and sleep on the rock piles, when they're not too edgy to do so.

We're all edgy these days, as the war seems to be coming closer. Rumblings in the mountains echo back to us, sending rocks skittering and bouncing down the surrounding slopes. Thibideaux is among us very rarely. He spends all his time mixing salt water and sterilizing needles to inject the Colonel with fluids. The Colonel remains comatose, though his lacerations and deep wounds, oddly enough, are healing very well.

The day was beautiful and clear this morning as I walked to the command bunker, and I was enjoying the sight of the crystalline mountains soaring above our greenery and rocks when the guards suddenly herded everyone back in from the field. I heard a distant whine, far softer than the buzz of a bee, and beyond the canopy, over the farthest slopes, a wink in the sky. We seldom see aircraft around here, and the guards, without knowing whose plane the visitor might be, did not want it to see us.

SCOUTING PARTY RETURNS

The scouting party returned, as we thought, empty-handed, but the leader, one of the younger guards whose name I never caught, rushed right over to headquarters and was closeted with Wu and Terton most of the morning, as I know because every time I passed Wu's door it was closed.

DAY AFTER SCOUTING PARTY RETURNED

Lobsang was in the library, bent over the computer when I arrived. I was halfway across the room before he heard me, and he punched two buttons. His expression changed subtly too, from studied, grave concentration to his goofy engineer stance, and he made a little show of scratching his temple and scribbling notes and said, "Ah, Viv, I am finding something of plumb perplexity here that we should be discussing—"

"Really?"

"Yes, I am. You see here?" he pointed to something on the screen. He was in the Earl Grey program again, the screen split in half, showing rubble with a strange, semicircular space on one side and a long corridor with a bump in the middle on the other. "This is new area we are going to uncover. I am thinking that with these airplanes so near, and maybe bombings, we should be making stronger our underground so they are not collapsing again, you see?"

I nodded. "I'd see better if we could go back to the original avalanche, I think. Show me those pictures and when you first started restorations. All of the rooms." I thought I could get him to see the seed room, the storage rooms, and maybe point them out that way, but the rooms weren't labeled in the original structure, except generally as "storage cells and extra accommodation." Tea breezed right by them and I couldn't quite locate the one I knew contained the seeds. It was identical with the other rooms on that level, so much so that on two of my initial forays to that room, I'd had to open a few other doors before I located the seed room.

But Tea was flipping past, to the pictures of the first parties of prisoners arriving on the slope where the camp now stood. In the pictures there was nothing but devastation—and this time I recognized Danielson, Tea, Dolma, Tsering, Samdup and Wu, all looking very much then as they do now, though it seemed to me Danielson looked considerably older in the picture than he does now—probably, I thought, because of what he endured in that previous, crueler camp.

"You must have been working pretty fast on getting this reconstruction project going," I ventured, watching him out of the corner of my eye. His face didn't exactly close off in that hostile way some people's do when they don't want to tell you something. He just very carefully pulled down the shutters and allowed only the merest glimmer of something that could have been amusement to peek out at me. "I mean," I said, "at the rate we've been going I'd think this had taken years and"—the headache pounced with a vengeance and I leaned back and rubbed my neck and temples—"and nobody looks much older."

"Some spa, eh, Viva?" he said, fobbing me off with a joke, and I didn't press further. But it's perplexing. The men have told me that they've been here a very long time and have been busting rocks almost as long as they can remember. Of course, I realize a little rock busting can go a long way. Right then I couldn't concentrate on it any longer because of the headache, which I still have twinges of, even now, it's so ferocious.

Finally, I saw an opportunity and said, "I think we should carefully check every single room in the lower excavations, one by one, move stuff away from the walls, starting in that storage area, perhaps, until we see all the weaknesses and strengths and, incidentally, any important artifacts that we may have overlooked."

"Yes," he said, nodding in a measured way. "Yes, I see the value of this. I am now finding us helmets and flashlights and will be meeting you back here pronto."

As soon as he was gone I punched up Earl Grey but the headache and the graininess of the early vid-film convinced me that while my earlier perception was correct, I couldn't find out more at present. I tapped Darjeeling again and, passing the Colonel for the time being, accessed Thibideaux's Constant Comment file. The case history agreed with what he had told me, and the added press release said, "Today . . . a veteran's hospital in Baton Rouge, Louisiana, and an orphanage in Calcutta were dedicated to the memory of Sgt. Henri Duchamps Thibideaux. Thibideaux, popularly believed by some Indians to be the reincarnation of the saintly Mother Teresa . . ." I got no further than that because I was laughing too hard.

And something was flashing at the bottom of the screen. "Current Bulletin," it said. I wished to God they hadn't blacked out the date.

> The Liberated Lebanon Government today in Beirut declined the offer of the North American Continental Allied Forces to aid them in their struggle against the rival United Lebanese Government. The LLG, which announced last week that it had successfully acquired a major nuclear device, said that it saw NACAF's simultaneous offer to aid the ULG as a conflict of interests. Prime Minister Chaya Rabinowitz of Israel and the Ayatolla Mohammed of Iraniaq have pledged to "fight fire with fire." NACAF has called an emergency meeting of all allied nations to discuss trade embargoes and other peaceful means of controlling the situation.

Looks like everybody out there is still at the same little games, only now there are new players NACAF hasn't figured out how to control yet. I can't get too worked up about this, as long as it's been going on, but neither could I suppress a flutter of pure panic as I read. The people of Lebanon haven't known peace since before my grandparents' time. Many of them, like the Irania-quis, believe that if they die in battle they go straight to heaven. They don't seem very likely to restrain them-selves for fear of screwing up somebody else's lifestyle.

Even without the date, this had to be new infor-mation. Maybe the supply chopper had dropped some-thing after all. Maybe this was what Wu and the scout team had been conferring about and it had been put into the computer for Tea—and me?—and the others to see and ponder.

I pondered so hard that I didn't hear Tea reenter the library. Fortunately, he didn't come right up to the table again, but waited in the doorway. I punched back to Earl Grey and off.

"Just checking that storage area again," I told him, knowing, even then, that he knew I was lying, and I knew that he was, if not lying, definitely hiding some-thing—though how much I couldn't tell. "I guess I'm ready now."

I decided to end the game as soon as possible, es-pecially since I had suggested time-consumingly thor-ough searches of all the rooms. I took him straight to the seed room and beamed my flashlight directly on the Burpee packets.

Tea shone his own light onto the ceiling and said, "These shorings-up are okay, all right."

And I said, enunciating carefully and with full em-phasis and in loud ringing tones, "Oh! Look! Seeds!"

He nodded and continued to check the ceiling cor-ners. I put my hand on his arm, picked up a seed packet, and thrust it into his hand.

"Seeds," I said. "You know. For growing plants."

"They are dehydrated?" he asked, his face still turned upward to the cobwebs. "You add water?"

"Yes, and sunlight and dirt."

"And what," he asked, veering the flashlight to the opposite corner, "are we wanting with more plants?"

"We are wanting to eat them," I said, almost yelling it.

"Ah," he said, and turned his face back toward me and I saw that he was grinning, had been grinning the whole time, probably. "Then it is grub you are finding, is it?"

"It is if we get it planted."

"Then we should be telling Commandant Wu of this . . ." he prodded.

"I sort of thought maybe you could do it alone," I said. "Chain of command and all that and—uh, she doesn't like me much."

"Also, maybe, the other prisoners might think you should have kept this secret for their sake?" The bright light of the work lamp in the hall cast shadows on his pitted face that made it look full of moon craters, but his eyes glittered with a combination of humor and anger and a complexity of other, subtler things—flickerings of thought and feeling I did not understand except that in that moment I understood that he had known all along. For his own reasons he had been waiting for me to make a point of it to him. As I have previously had reason to note, while his goofiness is undoubtedly genuine, there is a great deal more to him than that.

Feeling foolish, I did not wish to pursue the subject further, but he said, "No, Viv, it is your claim, this. I will not accept credit, but will go with you to speak to my wife."

I held my hands tightly together to stop them shaking as we entered Wu's office, despite Tea's comforting presence. I was glad that he was there, even if he had set me up. I was afraid, however, that whatever other undiscovered strengths lurked as yet unexcavated beneath his craggy skin might not include the guts to stand up to his ferocious little wife and the willingness to do so on my behalf.

But there were other differences between this audience with La Wu and my previous ones. The guards on duty were Dolma, which explained her absence from the library this morning, and Tsering. Tsering looked grumpy from loss of sleep but was painstakingly careful to look past and through me at all times. That reassured me. Before Merridew saved her daughter's life, Tsering used to glare menacingly and bounce her rifle in her palms. Not being looked at was a big improvement.

Damn Tea anyway. I had trusted him and he seemed very smug and unconcerned, though no less amiable to me than ever. I didn't understand why he hadn't followed my hints earlier and taken the credit for finding the seeds instead of, as I had thought he would, having to accept the blame for not discovering them earlier. The computer was on Wu's desk and she was tapping at it when we came in, and she took several more minutes with it as if she hadn't noticed us there all along.

"Yes?" she asked frostily, though her eyes regarded Tea with several degrees more warmth than her voice indicated.

In Tibetan, Tea informed her that I had something to say to her.

She lifted a bird-wing brow in my direction.

Also in Tibetan, I told her, "One of the lower cells in the excavation is filled with seeds. We could make a garden."

"Why would we do such a thing? Who has time for such activity? Do you not have enough to do?"

"You know that as well as I do, surely. A garden would feed us." I took a deep breath and admitted even more, not only because maybe I'd just get one punishment for two crimes that way but also because I was sick of the games and if I wanted to talk straight to her, then I had to be straight myself. "The ones I"—I wouldn't involve the other prisoners if I could help it, remembering the Colonel's admonition—"have planted are already yielding well, and maybe you know that. You probably also know that I've seen the bulletin. Maybe the people out there are too preoccupied with the crisis in Lebanon to remember to feed us."

"The state will provide," she said smoothly. It was a stupid answer, in keeping with her role but not appropriate to the situation. I glanced at Tea in time to see him making a pained face at her, as I protested, "But the pack trains are returning empty."

"The pack trains are our business," she replied loftily, "and it just so happens that we have just dispatched another one which is certain to meet with success." Then with a glance at Tea she added, "However, it occurs to me that your suggestion may have merit. You prisoners have too much time on your hands these days. A garden will be a constructive project for you and also for some of the idle staff."

To Taring she said, "You will issue the contents of the storeroom only after writing down what is dispensed to the inmates and staff members. Staff will be informed that the extra food will be issued only to those who participate in planting and tending, excepting only members of the pack trains while they are in the field. Two days out of every seven should be sufficient for most. Prisoners will plant as they clear their plots and may keep a quarter of their produce for barter purposes unless I say otherwise. Yangzom, you will inventory the contents of the room and will be held accountable for it. Find those among the prisoners or staff with agricultural training—many of the Chinese prisoners have served in collectives at one time or another—and seek advice for what you do not know about where the seeds should be planted and proceed accordingly. Vanachek appears to have some opinions on the matter. She will be happy, I'm sure, to devote a few extra hours daily to helping you in addition to her regular duties. Captain Taring has more pressing responsibilities. Now, then, I have told you what to do. Everyone has plenty of work so there is no further need for you to disturb mine."

Taring nudged me and we marched from her office. I couldn't imagine what had come over her. She had never before seemed the kind of woman to let good sense overwhelm her native tendency for gratuitous nastiness. Perhaps the doctor was softening her up or maybe it was just that killing something the day before had mellowed her.

Dolma touched my shoulder briefly when she thought Tsering wasn't looking, and Tsering watched me from the corner of her eye as if she was afraid she'd need to call for a straitjacket soon. I'm not sure whether she had trouble understanding why I didn't tell about the seeds in the first place or why I told at all.

Dolma and I spent the rest of the day with the new project.

"Lobsang says that we must inventory this room anyway for our work with him, so we may as well start now," Dolma said.

I couldn't work up any enthusiasm and I worked mechanically. We accomplished quite a bit, I'm sure, because we cataloged seeds for hours, but I felt like the princess in "Rumpelstiltskin" trying to spin roomfuls of straw into gold. No matter how many seed bags we counted, we didn't seem to make a dent in the room. Toward late afternoon, Samdup arrived, escorting a fragile-looking Chinese man. "Tsering has been interrogating the prisoners. This man has been a prisoner at four agricultural work camps. He will help us dispense any seeds already covered by your inventory and direct how they may be planted. Tsering has also located four other persons with appropriate experience, but she is still convincing them to admit it."

"She's not torturing them surely?" I asked, alarmed.

"No. She wished to, I think, but instead she has instructed Pema to work beside the suspects and be inquisitive. Since the lion attack, everyone talks to Pema."

The Chinese man gave a small shaky smile and said in a voice as thin as the air. "Even me. And I pride myself on trusting no one. Is it true? Are we to have extra food?"

Dolma nodded sharply. "Yes, but you must help. Everyone must work extra hours planting and clearing more ground. Over here"—she indicated the pitifully small pile—"are the seeds we have inventoried."

He and Samdup departed loaded down with bags of seed. I watched them go and sighed.

Dolma said to me, "It is very good that you found this room, Viva. Aren't you happy that we will have more to eat? Wu was very pleased, I think, though of course she never shows it."

"She should have been pleased," I said. "For some reason she and Good Old Lobsang Tea Taring had it arranged between them that I would be the one to find

the seeds so that it would be up to me if the camp starved
or not. They knew all along that room was there. Taring
as much as told me so. I thought he was different. I
thought you were—"

She dumped her seed bag onto the inventoried pile,
dusted her hands noisily on her hips and glared at me
for half a second before lowering her bottle-lensed eyes,
her mouth set in a hard line. We worked in silence for
what seemed like hours before she said, in a voice as
tight as the rope between a mountaineer who has fallen
and the one attached to him on the cliff above, "Did it
ever occur to you that perhaps we had no way of knowing
if you, too, could be trusted?"

"Well, I can't," I told her, "so forget it. I'm a prisoner of war just like my cellmates, just like those men
out there. And you're one of my guards. Taring is one
of my guards. My loyalty is to my fellow prisoners and
I only told because I—"

"Because you don't really see the difference, do
you?" Taring asked softly in Tibetan from the doorway.
He nodded to Dolma as if to say, "You see?" and walked
off, his shoulders a little tighter than usual but otherwise
totally unconcerned.

I returned to the cell late last night to find Marsh
apparently already asleep, his face to the wall, and Danielson waiting up for me.

His voice was quiet—too quiet—and in the dark I
could feel him clenching and unclenching his fists as he
said, "They wormed it out of you, huh?" he asked. "They
found all the other vegetables and confiscated them for
the camp pot. Your momo is over there. It has vegetables
in it tonight. I hope you're happy."

The accusation in his voice matched that in my own
head but I was, of course, immediately on the defensive.
When someone who can break your neck as easily as
looking at you is peeved with you, defensiveness seems
only smart. I talked fast. "Not really, but they knew about
it already. Mmm, good momo. You've got to admit the
veggies have improved the chow." I keep forgetting Du
has no sense of humor. The fists were clenched now and
despite his quiet voice I thought he'd be pacing if there

had been room. "Look," I said more seriously, "it's not going to be so bad. Apparently they were testing me somehow or other and they were pleased that I told them about the seeds."

"I'll bet. Now they probably figure they can get you to tell anything."

"Maybe that's what they think and maybe that's what you think but what in the hell is there to tell? They know all about you guys, right down to the memorials that have been named after you since you were captured. Did you know there's a crematory mound named after you?"

"What are you talking about?" His hands remained open, though on his hips. His voice was a little louder now, more normal.

"I saw it on the camp computer. And there's some kind of peace prize given in Marsh's name. And Thibideaux has orphanages and hospitals named after him."

"Bullshit."

"I tell you I *saw* it on the computer. And you know what else I saw?" I told him about the situation in Lebanon.

He shrugged. "That kind of shit's always going on."

Marsh sat up suddenly. He hadn't been sleeping, just listening. "Sounds worse than usual to me, Du." He asked me to repeat everything I could remember about the communiqué, said, "Hmm," and rolled back over to face the wall again.

"Look, you guys are all some kind of heroes and I'm just a washed-up perpetual student," I said as Danielson continued looking stormy and Marsh feigned sleep. "They knew about the seeds already and I didn't see why people should go hungry—God, Marsh, surely you can relate to that. For pity's sake, I wouldn't tell them anything that could hurt any of you . . ."

Marsh sat up again and said in a careful, overly patient voice everybody seemed to be using with me that day, "Look, Vanachek, these people may not be quite up to the old Khmer Rouge or the SS standards as prison guards but that's what they are. The strategy for "reeducating" prisoners is very devious. There's always a trick.

Probably they'll let us plant the food and then take it away from us. Or use the barter portions to establish power cliques within the prisoner ranks and divide us against each other that way. While it's true we've never been as badly fed as in other places and have been treated pretty mildly, as these places go, they don't always use physical means to get to us. They've left us alone before except for the work but now one part of that's winding down. So maybe the game plan is changing. The thing in Lebanon worries me a little."

"I told you, Marsh," Danielson began, "new countries are always getting nukes."

"Not anymore, Du. I told you about that part of my work. Even NACAF doesn't have the nuclear force it once had, and neither does the PRC or the Soviets. Disarmament took care of the overstock and NACAF has been taking care of the situation in the allied countries—and that's nearly everybody, for quite a while now. I should know. I don't like the idea of a wild nuke in a place like Lebanon, where there is a tradition of not giving a shit."

"I guess a lot of water has gone under the bridge since I got taken out, huh?" Danielson asked.

"I guess so."

Danielson lay down too. "Vanachek?"

"What?"

"A crematory mound? Named after me? I wonder if Sherry was there. I guess she must think I'm dead."

Sleep did not come easily. I lay awake listening to Danielson breathe lest he change his mind again and decide to kill me after all just to be on the safe side. As I listened, my own breathing and heart rate slowed to match his.

I lay on my left side, facing him, watching the silhouette of his rib cage rise and fall, deeper darkness in the darkness surrounding us. My ear rested on the stone of my cot and as I lay there watching, I began to hear the echo of my heart, my breath, Danielson's breath, rising through the stone, reverberating in my ear.

I had one of the sort of dreams I had when I was in solitary, and afterward, when I was sick. I haven't had any in a long time. I've missed them. This one wasn't exactly like the others. There were no people this time, only an awareness of a vast place filled with something that started out as a heartbeat, a respiration, and swelled to become not just a chant but a song. Visually, I don't remember much except for a pattern of many interlocking segments shifting slowly, realigning into something that caused me to wake up smiling, before the men, to jot all of this down in my journal.

PLANTING THE GARDEN, DAY 1

I spent today aboveground with the other prisoners. Marsh was setting charges, blowing up boulders under the supervision of armed guards, and the other prisoners and I hauled the fragments away. The ground is mostly clear now. The huge boulders were the last of it. Many had been broken up before with sledgehammers, and there's a good open space to plant. Soft waves in the ground remain where ancient terraces held garden before.

The terraces puzzle me. Much of Nepal is still sharply terraced in places where it hasn't been farmed for years. Perhaps here it's because of the avalanche ripping away so much of the soil and piling it up in other places that the earth has begun in such a short time to regain more natural contours. But that's just one of the things that puzzle me. While it's not inconceivable that so much work would get done in such a short time with the technology available NAC-side, all of this has been done by hand. It must have taken a long time, though I admit I'm unaccustomed to hand-done processes and have no clear idea just what kind of time would have to be involved.

And it's not just Danielson's picture that bothers me. There's the business with Marsh too; the Tropical American Park Service (TAPS) was established before I was born. Marsh remembers his father being killed during the depopulation. And there's Thibideaux's story too. Although eco-reclamation is still definitely the top domestic industry of NAC, there have been no oil tankers in my lifetime. What little oil is needed these days is piped underground and underwater with the best technology money can buy.

I'm a little more aware of the reclamation stuff than many people because it's how my grandparents made their money and the reason they lived in a cabin in the woods—they planted the woods. Grandad put in the first seedlings on the site of a former state forest clear-cut by what he called the lumber maggots of the previous century. Technocrats and the military may have little use for wood, but civilians like it, both cut and growing, as a status-building and landscaping component. All of which meant—what? Danielson's picture, Marsh's father, Thibideaux's bird-cleaning youth—none of them fit in with my knowledge of what NAC was. Maybe it was a regional thing. Since I come from what was traditionally timber country, maybe I only knew about timber. But Puget Sound had once had its share of oil spills too, and Washington soldiers had helped with the "mopping up" of what was now TAPS, and Washington peace activists had been arrested and even executed for aiding refugees. Something else too. Something about the memorials.

I'm too tired to think about it anymore and my head still aches from being out in the sun all day. It was a beautiful day, the mountains sharp and frosted as etched glass. Since I failed to conveniently find a storeroom full of hoes, shovels, rakes, harrows and such when I found the seeds, we dug furrows with our hands, and hauled water from the pond located where the lake used to be. My hands and back are killing me, have been killing me all day, but I must say I enjoy coming out of the closet with this farmwork business. I've had lots of worthless jobs in my life and studied a lot of subjects that prepared me for absolutely nothing, and by contrast it's a pleasure to make lovely rows and feel nice warm dirt still gritty from the dust of the stones.

Everyone else seemed to enjoy the change of pace too. At first some of the guards seemed to feel a sense of lèse-majesté about performing the same task as the prisoners, and stood around posing with their weapons as usual, but then Dr. Terton strolled out among us, grinned as if somebody had given her a huge present, and squatted down to scoop out a row of her own, calling to Tsering, who was guarding the seed bags, to bring her some spinach, adding that she was partial to spinach and hoped it would grow quickly. Tsering took the spinach seeds to her, then began digging another row with the stock of her rifle, barking at her little girl Pema to move the stones in her path. The stones that were too big for the child to move, Tsering detoured around.

And then another plane overflew us within hearing distance and one of the guards who was still guarding yelled and pointed us all back up toward the cover of the canopy. We didn't make it, but Dr. Terton and all of the guards hit the ground and we prisoners automatically did the same, as if we were no more anxious to have the camp discovered than the guards and wanted the plane to perceive us, if at all, as corpses strewn on a fresh battlefield. I felt the sudden coolness as the plane's shadow obscured the sunlight but it flew heedlessly on and since I was lying facedown I didn't see how near it came.

PLANTING, DAY 10: Fresh Corn and Merridew's Miracle

Maybe that comparison with Mother Teresa in Thibideaux's file isn't so farfetched after all, since he seems to have wrought a miracle cure. I got permission to take some vegetables to the infirmary today to make a broth for the Colonel, thinking he might be able to absorb a little if I trickled it into his mouth. The vegetables are growing like bad weeds, at an accelerated rate I don't recall reading about in any horticulture books anywhere, so I was able to claim onions, carrots, celery and some of the first of the doctor's spinach, which sprang up as if at her command.

Thibideaux, wearing a rather stunned grin, met me at the door and when I looked around him, I saw why. The Colonel, who was supposed to have two crunched cervical vertebrae, which should have paralyzed him, and a broken leg and scrambled brains, and who has lain immobile on the cot ever since the lion attack, painfully propped himself up on one elbow and rasped a hoarse greeting.

"My God," I whispered to Thibideaux, "what did you do to *him*."

"I told you I got the healin' hands, dollin'," Thibideaux replied, sounding as if he didn't quite believe the explanation himself. "Ol' Doc Terton, she's got 'em too. I guess this time what with the two of us and all, we put a little more juice into it and—uh—well, you see how the Colonel is. Course, I suppose I could have been wrong about how bad hurt he was to begin with but I'da sworn on a stack of Bibles I was right." He shook his head wonderingly and stepped aside so that I could greet Merridew.

"Hello, sir. Welcome back to the land of the living," I said with sickroom cheeriness, setting down my vegetables and kneeling beside the cot, so the Colonel wouldn't have to strain his voice to talk to me.

He gave me a long look out of eyes that on a Caucasian would have been black and blue but on him were a deeper, swollen dark purple stain on his brown face. Around his irises, both eyes were red and yellow as eggs that had been incubated too long, but as direct and intelligent as they ever had been. His head was much less misshapen and the places where Thibideaux had sewed his scalp back together were healing so well he looked less like something out of a horror vid and more as if he had a touch of mange.

"God, Vanachek," he said after returning my scrutiny. "You're filthy."

I smiled at him. He was definitely returning to normal. "We farmers are like that, sir. Nevertheless, as I'm sure you've heard, we're the salt of the earth. Speaking of salt, I forgot it, but I've brought something for a recovery celebration dinner."

I prepared the broth, allowing it to become vegetable soup since the Colonel could now eat in the regular way. Thibideaux stayed on long enough past his usual shift to eat with us, and with the soup to supplement our normal ration of momos, the three of us ate sumptuously, though we made sure the Colonel ate most of the soup himself. Thibideaux had been collecting the Colonel's ration of momos every day from a guard who didn't have the wit to think that an unconscious man had no need of his food ration.

The Colonel insisted that Thibideaux take some of the extra food back to the others, although Thibideaux kept half of it back so that the Colonel would have a full, rather than half, ration during his recuperation.

"Good to have you with us again, Colonel," I said, a little awkwardly, when Thibideaux had gone. Thibideaux has an intense energy about him, especially since he's been caring for the Colonel. Without him, the atmosphere grew uncomfortably quiet.

"Thanks, Viv."

"I hope you weren't in much pain?"

"Not much, no. Actually, I was just telling Thibideaux, I had the damnedest dreams."

His voice sounded as if he was drawing it out of a deep-dug well.

"Of your home, sir? Your family?" I asked the conventional questions, although I wondered right away if the Colonel's dreams had been anything like mine while I was in solitary, sick, and just lately. Until I knew, it seemed best to remain conventional with a man whose straight and narrow rigidity of purpose had been his backbone through all he'd suffered.

"No, not my family," he said. "I don't like to admit this, even to you, but I stopped dreaming about them years ago. I think they're all gone now, if you want to know the truth."

"Why do you think that?"

He sank back onto the table and ran a hand over his eyes, trying to rub but lacking the strength. "Well, they were old to begin with. And my dad, he never was in very good shape once he switched to a command post in Lebanon."

I considered telling him about the current situation in Lebanon and decided to wait until he was stronger, instead saying, "That's right. You did mention that your father was career military too."

"He certainly was. My grandfather too. An officer, Grandfather. A general. I meant to make it that high myself but I got captured first."

"Cheer up. Maybe you've been promoted while you've been in here."

"Long as I've been here, I should be Commander in Chief by now if that was so."

"How long *is* that, Colonel?"

He waved his hand around vaguely, then dropped it. "Dunno. Can't think. Long time. Years. I know that. Help me get settled here, will you? My head hurts like a sonofabitch. You know, you can say one thing for these people. Lotsa prisons you get sick, you keep working or you're dead. I'm surprised they let me live."

"It's hard to farm while you're unconscious," I said.

"Farm? They found the seeds?"

"Well, yeah . . ."

"You didn't tell them?"

"Not exactly . . ."

"They didn't torture you?"

"No sir, don't worry."

"They should have had to torture you to get that out of you. I'm sorry, soldier, but you collaborated with the enemy. You offered aid and comfort . . . My old man always did say no good would come of letting women in the military same as the men. Okay for you to be clerk typists and nurses and so on but you got no pride, no loyalty, no sense of place. I'd have to have you shot if we were back home, and I will testify against you, make no mistake of that, but I understand it. I read a few books in my time too, you know. Anthropology, history. Got to know your past and know your enemy. See, you women were always getting carried off to live with other people—wives, slaves, spoils of war, what have you. Women are practical people—have to be, I suppose, with children and all. You don't really have a country, just switch sides to be on whichever one your family's on. That's your loyalty. No patriotism in women to speak of. Not that some of you don't defend your country once you decide to but by and large there are just some jobs you shouldn't hold."

"Like being a prisoner of war, for instance?" I asked. "I didn't exactly sign up for the position, sir. And I'm not the only one who's practical and thinks about children. You set the example by saving little Pema. If you can save one person, I didn't think it was such a stretch to save all of our lives by making sure we have enough to eat until the supplies arrive."

"You know what our troops used to do when they came through the villages, young lady? Strip and burn, that's what."

"Yes, sir, I majored in history—among other things. But somehow that policy didn't seem appropriate in this case. Besides, as a result of your action and maybe mine, it seems to me they're a little more lenient. The guard whose child you saved was very grateful and has been helpful."

"I didn't intend to do that, you know," he said. "It was just reflex."

"You would have wanted someone to do as much for your children, sir."

"I don't have any children, soldier. A good commander's 'children,' his sole responsibility, should be his troops, not some civilians left behind the lines in the care of a woman he sees once a year and who is around to draw his pension if he's killed."

"Good thing your own father didn't feel like that," I said a little hotly. Merridew's command posture, his certainty, had been used to bolster everyone up, hold them together, and I appreciated that, but this inhuman side of his personality irked me, all the more because I was sure that the rigidity of the ramrod backbone was in some respects a role. But I liked the instinctive behavior he'd shown, the flashes of kindness and perception he allowed himself, so I took his condition into consideration and throttled down to a safer subject. Arguing is all well and good but he'd been badly injured and I could see his jaw tightening and the teeth clenching that the lion didn't knock out, and I was afraid he might rupture something so I changed the subject. "You're third-generation military, sir?"

"Seventh, if you want to know, young lady. I had an ancestor who was a private in the seventh cav back during the Indian wars—buffalo soldiers they called them then, 'cause of the hair." He lifted a finger gingerly in the general direction of his partially scalped head. What isn't stitches or wounds is still covered with matted black steel wool. "Black men couldn't be officers till our country got into the international wars, and my great-grandfathers started as sergeants but worked their way up."

"But you didn't want to have a son to carry on after you?"

"No, I . . . Young woman, what makes you think there's going to be an 'after me' to carry on? And even if there is, how could I be sure my son will be like me, when he hasn't got me around to emulate? He and his mother would be in some cozy backwater in Uzbekistan and he'd get into trouble and—"

"Sir, you're tired. I think it's depressing you. You turned out all right, didn't you? And I'll bet you never got to see your father that much . . ."

"No, ma'am, I did not. My father was a true American hero; he was part of that astronaut program, did I tell you that? The high point of his career was being one of the first men to set foot on Uranus, just before the administration changed and they called the whole thing off for good except for those little spies we all got up there in the sky. Like I said, he was a hero. Whereas I only made Colonel. And I let myself be captured. I wouldn't say that's living up to the old man."

Why had the old woman picked such an odd crew to be in her high-security camp? I wondered. A Cajun bird cleaner and medic, an orphaned test-tube baby who'd grown up to be a wife-beating infantryman, an Indian peace fighter whose specialty was demolitions, the last descendant of a family of black military aristocrats and son of the last man to set foot on another planet, and me. Why no scientists? Theirs would be the top secrets you'd think they'd want to extract from people in a top-security camp. Surely the Chinese had medics, demolitions experts, pilots and airplane mechanics of their own. Even if they didn't, they had NACAF experts on practically everything to compensate. That was part of the NACAF peace plan.

The Colonel lay staring at the ceiling, the curl of his lashes casting long candlelit shadows on his cheeks. Tears as much from physical weakness as sadness rolled ignored sideways down past his ears. I wished I had a sedative or had learned the old woman's humming trick.

GARDEN,
DAY 30—Finds

𝙭 The garden is growing at a tremendous rate. There's so much food Dr. Terton has some of her spinach taken to the yaks. Today Tatiana, the Russian woman who prefers to be called 'Tania,' found an intact beam of painted wood, still patterned with intricate red, yellow and gilt designs.

GARDEN, DAY 32

𝙭 Pema, working beside me today and chattering away as usual, suddenly started making excited noises and jumping up and down. I straightened out my weary back and aching knees and turned my stiff neck to see that she was waving a string of turquoise, silver, and coral beads. Very beautiful. Her mother made her turn them in to Taring, of course. Moments later, my fingers brushed what I thought was a rock but when I tried to dig it loose, I found it was a grimy, blackened dragon figure with an elephant's trunk. One cheek is caved in and one tusk bent sideways, but when I scraped it with my fingernail, a gold streak threw the sun back into my eyes. I stuck it in my pocket. I'll show it to Taring later.

GARDEN, DAY 35

I worked with Tea today. He is as friendly as ever, though I'm still a little leery of him and answer with as few words as possible. It's hard to stay withdrawn around him, however, and I wonder if he even notices, as he dances around and mutters to himself constantly while he examines the finds unearthed in the gardening process. My little dragon was among the first, and I quietly slipped it in with the other things uncovered since the planting area has expanded to include the entire lower slope. Among the objects in the pile on the library floor are large sections of painted wood similar to the one Tania found, gracefully posed hands, arms, legs, feet, and torsos of statues, even one golden Buddha head with hooded eyes; ornamental fixtures—candle sconces, lamps, hooks, that sort of thing, usually golden or gilded, often carved; a smashed thermos bottle; gold incense burners in the shapes of animals; kitchen utensils; dishes; and even another bathtub.

These things represented the discoveries which were reported. Anything found by a guard or seen by a guard to be unearthed by a prisoner is duly taken to Wu. But I have seen many gardeners stop to wipe their brows and secretly tuck a prize into jacket pockets, sleeves, or the bands of trousers.

I caught glimpses of some of these objects. Mostly they were smaller pieces of ornament, like my dragon; or jewelry; pieces of cloth, some plain, that I thought might have been prayer flags; and some scraps of elaborately patterned and colored silk. Once I found a cache of pages from Tibetan books. Individually they would have been small enough to hide, but collectively the cache was too big to conceal and besides, I had permission to study them anyway so I reported them and Dolma came to collect them for the library.

Distractions make the concealment of the smaller finds easier. Every day now, it seems, we hear rumblings

of distant avalanches—or perhaps it's shelling, even in
this remote place? Every time something thunders or
crashes, the gardening stops, those who can straighten
their backs do so and scan the sky—and others stuff their
clothing with some new little treasure.

Today the big find was brought in by three of the
guards. Several people simultaneously had unearthed a
tangle of dirty cloth—silk brocade in once-brilliant ver-
milions and saffrons, maroons and gilt thread. Many of
the pieces, once they were dampened and smoothed
from the stiff knotted wads in which they had lain for so
long, were intact, though much rotted in places. The
pieces were as large as bedspreads, flat on the top, scal-
loped on the bottom.

Tea retrieved the computer from the office again
and switched into Earl Grey, back to the opening files.
He blocked out a portion of the "before" picture of the
compound and enlarged it. In the enlarged section, a
couple walked up a short flight of stone steps, a pretty
child between them. They looked very much like Wu
and Taring. Alarm bells went off in my head and I backed
away from the computer. Tea threw me an inquiring
look.

"Very interesting," I told him. "But I'm tired of
being manipulated, thanks all the same."

"Okay," he said sadly, closing the bright eye of the
screen. "I am getting it, partner. Tea speak with forked
tongue, right? But I am not understanding why what I
am showing you and telling you is more manipulative
than what you are getting from others."

I would have said "hmph," but I already felt a little
silly. He really does not seem to see what he did wrong.
For an inscrutable evil jailer, he gets his feelings hurt
too easily. Nevertheless, I am not going to be tricked
again.

GARDEN, DAY 37

Merridew is back at the cell and back at work, planting and picking as well as his recovering wounds will allow. To his disgust, all of the guards treat him with gentleness, solicitousness and respect. He'd be lots happier if they'd skin him alive. Pema stayed right by him all day, helping him up and down. He tried to shake her off but Pema does not shake easily. She brought him water so often I thought he'd drown.

GARDEN, DAY 40

The Colonel seems to be back to his old self again. Tonight he started in again on The Great Escape. I'm really surprised they haven't pulled it off before. I've been back on-line cataloging the new finds and the work Tea is doing on the excavations, as well as keeping up with the library (which has made my journal-keeping fairly erratic). I couldn't resist accessing the Colonel's Constant Comment.

Like the others, he has war memorials of his very own—statues of him, no less, artistically incorporated with the wreckage from his downed aircraft, *The Clara Barton*, in Washington, D.C., just across the Memorial Hall from the statue of his father and the other astronauts, and in Darjeeling, where his extraordinary efforts flying back and forth through constant enemy fire to provision a besieged base camp saved hundreds of military and civilian Indian lives.

My God. If anybody should be able to effect a simple

little escape from a remote mountain fastness through thousands of miles of snow-covered up-and-down uninhabited, enemy-riddled and probably booby-trapped terrain it should be this bunch. I didn't get to share my news about Lebanon with the Colonel. Danielson and Marsh beat me to it. The Colonel was no more impressed with that piece of news than he was with everything else I've told him.

So we stood around Marsh's bunk, heads together, voices quiet and urgent in the darkness—some filmmaker's view of *The Conspirators*, to the life.

"The kid is always hanging around you, Colonel, and everybody likes her. Maybe you could take her hostage," Danielson said.

"Very convincing," Marsh said. "He just wrecked himself to save her life and now he says, 'One false move and the kid gets it.'"

"*He* wouldn't have to do it," Danielson, the family man, said casually.

"Oh, I don't doubt that he could. But killing her wouldn't help anything and nobody's going to believe we would until we do," Marsh reasoned.

"I can be pretty convincing," Danielson argued.

"I don't think we have to go to those lengths, men," the Colonel said. I was an honorary man—on probation, to be sure, but included—for the moment. "But the little girl's parents trust me now, which is pretty unprofessional of them, letting personal feelings cloud their judgment like that. Some night when they're on guard duty, we create a diversion, take their weapons and we, my friends, are out of here."

It sounds like a good plan for leaving the camp okay. I just can't help wondering (though I know better than to say so now) where it is we're supposed to be going.

PACK TRAIN RETURNS

The pack train returned last night after all of us prisoners were tucked in. Bales of new supplies littered the foot of the garden, and all farmwork ceased while we prisoners dragged the bundles up the hill and into the command bunker, where Dolma sleepily stood by to inventory them.

We worked together in the library later that day and she kept pulling her glasses off and rubbing her eyes with her fists as if she could barely keep her eyes open. "Did you have guard duty last night?" I asked. We haven't had too much time to talk since the garden project began and she looked so worn out and troubled that I forgot to be angry with her.

"Yes, and my friend Phurbu was with the pack train. After the others had gone, she wanted to talk. She is very worried, Viva. The helicopter was not there to meet them again. The supplies were lying half buried in the snow and in that cave, you know?"

I nodded. The one where Terton had laid the double-whammy on me over tea-for-two.

"The helicopter had been gone long enough that they saw no tracks from the runners in the snow. As Phurbu and the others were loading up to come back, they heard rifle fire in the distance and what she was sure was mortar fire, although it was hard to tell. Three times on the narrowest trail they had to dig their way through a snow slide and she said she lost count in the valleys how often they had to take a long way around because the trail was buried in avalanche. She was shaking, Viva, not only because she was tired, but because she felt so fortunate to be back here. My friend Rinchen Norbu and three other young men are walking out to the guerrilla camp to try to find out what is happening to our supply lines. For although there is not yet fighting in this area, the noises of the war have penetrated, you see, and their vibrations have set up sympathetic resonances causing more and more high avalanches. We are all much concerned."

She still had her glasses off and searched my face with bloodshot eyes so myopic they were mostly pupil, wide and despairing. Neither of us wondered aloud if the helicopter would be able to find the meeting place again, should the avalanches obscure the valley, or what would become of us if it did not. But with the vegetables and careful husbandry of the yaks, perhaps we could survive longer than otherwise. I hoped. "Were there any more communiqués?" I asked. No need to be coy now. I know they mean for me to see these things.

"Only negative ones," she said. "None of the measures the other countries of the world have attempted have made any impact on the quarreling Lebanese governments."

I duly passed along the information to my cellmates that night.

"Idiots," Marsh hissed. "The Lebanese are all nuts with battle trauma-shock. They're going to waste the whole damned planet over a puny civil war."

"I have a family to protect," Danielson said. "I was never any good to them in peacetime but if the shit is hitting the fan, I want to be there to take care of them. And if the passes are closing up, like Viv says, I say we go while the going's good."

"Right," the Colonel agreed. "Now then, men, pay attention. I've been thinking this over and I think I've come up with a pretty sound plan. Next time that woman whose kid I saved from the lion is on duty, I'll distract her while you three go forage food, extra clothing, etc. A radio would be good too, and something to heat with, a flashlight, and a map . . . Viv, can we count on you for a map?"

I hesitated not because I didn't think I could get a map. I know right where to find one and it's no trick to liberate it from the pile where I've stashed it. But what use is all of this going to be with the avalanches, miles of cold and snow and more hungry days than we can carry food to cover. "Sure, Colonel," I said, knowing as I did so that it would be taken the wrong way. "But aren't you guys forgetting that we don't just have to walk as far as we walked to get in here, we'll have to walk clear across Tibet to get back to our lines—always assuming they're still where we left them?"

The Colonel glowered at me. "Vanachek, you've got a negative attitude. You lived back in the States too long and you're used to being coddled. We'll have to cross some bridges when we come to them."

Never mind that one of those bridges was a rope one, spanning a bottomless gorge, and might be gone by the time we reached it.

"Maybe she'd rather stay here with her little friends," Danielson said nastily. "How about it, Vanachek? Are you in or out?"

"I'm in," I said. What else could I say?

ESCAPE

⚔ This is it. Tonight. Over the past week we've stepped up the yoga and the calisthenics, gathered extra vegetables as they grew to maturity, and have made do by eating only our ration of vegetables instead of our momos, which will keep better. I provided the map and a copy of the guard roster. Tsering comes on duty this evening.

SUPPER

✗ We've had an unexpected development which I thought would be a snag, but turns out to be helpful.

Instead of dispensing momos as usual, Tsering announced to the cell at large, "All prisoners will eat together now, Commandant Wu says."

Instead of making it more difficult to escape, however, the new arrangement facilitated gathering the few items we've been lacking. Although we were all supposed to be marched under close guard to the dining room, the room I had first seen as some sort of a chapel, Tsering only made a pretense of it and chatted instead with the Colonel, who hastily made up some children to miss and to compare to her daughter. Long planks made tables and we sat on the floor around these, prisoners lumped according to cell, guards at their own table. Through the door I could see the bathtub from Akron, Ohio. Vegetable stew with rice and dried meat was being ladled from it.

And guess what's just around the corner? That's right, the supply room where the winter gear is stored. Through the open door we could see it hanging around the walls of the room, boots neatly paired beneath snowsuits and coats, mittens slung by straps over all.

NEXT DAY

✗ The plan has changed. We snag the winter gear first, and delay the escape till the next time Tsering or Samdup stands guard.

Last night in the middle of the night the Colonel feigned a bellyache, and Thibideaux called up the stairs for Tsering. As she entered the darkened cell alone, Marsh slipped out the open door behind her. She is very relaxed around the Colonel now, poor woman, and had we been ready, and if her trust was not more valuable to us for the way we planned to betray it than her death was right then, Danielson would have killed her.

"He's mighty bad off," Thibideaux told her as the Colonel moaned and clutched his stomach and acted far sicker than he had when he was injured. "You best go get old Doc Terton, ma'am."

Then from above several people began shouting at once and two shots rang out, echoing in ricochet against the wall. I thought, My God, they're shooting Marsh.

Tsering turned on her heel and bounded up the steps and we listened to more shots and more shouting and running footsteps. Then one set of footsteps clattered down the staircase outside the cell and Marsh half fell inside, dumping an armload of clothing onto the floor. His teeth gleamed in the dark, he was grinning so widely.

"I thought they'd got you for sure," Thibideaux said.

"Nope. I just let the cat out. Tsering hates that cub, you know. I've seen her poking at it with her rifle barrel and I know she'd kill it if the old woman and Wu would let her."

"Seems like a dirty trick to play on the animal, settin' 'em all on it like that," Thibideaux said, grinning back.

"That cat can take care of itself. Have you seen that sucker lately? The old lady's been nursing it with yak milk and Taring brings it rats and now it's plenty large enough to fight back. They'd better move fast or it'll get one of them, or maybe have yak for dinner." Marsh chuckled to himself.

We stuffed the clothing into emptied sandbags in the hallway, the dirt from which we spread beneath the other bags. The other things we hid between the wall and the bags, piling the bags with the clothing in them in front.

ESCAPE

"Another pack train is leaving tomorrow," Dolma
told me today. "This time I will be with them. This time
there surely will be the helicopter and we will learn what
has become of Rinchen Norbu."

Her voice is strained. I also see strain in Tea these
days. He works frantically on the lower excavations.
Even Wu has seemed distracted and the doctor works
every day with the rest of us in the garden.

Tonight I dutifully reported Dolma's news about the
pack train's departure to my cellmates.

"Then it's tonight," the Colonel said. "We have to
leave tonight. We'll be the ones to meet the chopper
instead of the pack train. We'll leave tonight, ahead of
them, wearing their gear. They won't discover it missing
until we're gone. The helicopter pilot will think we're
the pack train, bundled in their gear as we will be, and
we'll hijack the chopper and fly it back to our lines.
Besides, the kid's father is on guard duty tonight, which
makes this the most perfect possible opportunity."

I don't know whether to take my journal or to leave
it. Because I must admit now that I will miss this place,
that I will not forget Tea or Dolma or even Terton, I'll
leave it behind. I don't really think I will survive this
journey, to tell the truth. I'm in better shape than I used
to be and maybe in better shape than the Colonel, who
I also don't expect will survive. We'll probably be the
first ones to die. The men may even ultimately leave me
behind, although I think for all their rough talk they are
less likely to do so than they'd have me believe. Nevertheless, I have to try, I suppose, even if there's nowhere
to go. But I prefer to think of this part of me in the hands
of people I may not be able to call friends, exactly, but
who feel as much like friends as anyone I'm likely to
have the rest of my life. There's no one back on the NAC
to whom this last record of me might be carried. Elo-
quence eludes me. Goodbye.

PART SIX

JOURNAL, PHASE 2

✟ I write the above heading as if something has changed, though in many ways it seems as if nothing has, as if what we saw, or thought we saw tonight, was some horrible collective nightmare. Here we are—most of us, all but Danielson—once more in our butter-lamp-brightened cell. We're still in our prison uniforms and on the surface—well, maybe nothing *has* changed. But I think that maybe *everything* has. Tonight. In the space of—hours? minutes? I don't know. I just don't know. It seemed like seconds and it seemed like forever and the sky is so fucked up that even if we were topside, I wouldn't know if it was day yet.

But if it was nothing, if nothing is different, why is quiet, self-contained Marsh sitting on his bunk babbling away like a guest physics lecturer about how to safely disarm nuclear weapons, how so-and-so from such-and-such a country should have done this or that?

Why is Thibideaux sobbing and shaking, moaning as if he's in mortal pain? Why did Danielson bolt and leave the rest of us for—what? where? And why is the Colonel sitting there on his bunk with his legs crossed, pumping the top leg up and down with his bottom knee, grimacing to himself.

And why am I so cold? My fingers feel frozen around this pen and I'm sure I'll carry its imprint on my hand for the rest of my life—let's not think about that. I only wish they hadn't taken away the winter gear again. It's so cold. I can't stop shaking. I don't want to be here. I want to go home. I want my grandma. I want a joint. I want hot and cold running water and junk food and I want to sit in Sammy's bar and drink tequila and analyze everybody else in the whole fucking place. I want my worst worry to be whether or not I pass some stupid test or the other. But Grandma's been dead for years and home's been plowed under a long time ago and Sammy— well, if my guess is right, Sammy's long gone too.

What I don't want to think about is the sky. I don't want to think about that noise out there, that chugging gush of a noise. Poor Danielson. Poor jerk. Out of the frying pan into the fire, as they say. Jesus, I'm funny. A goddamn scream.

Okay, so instead of sitting here babbling across my paper and freezing to death I'm going to get coherent now. As you may gather from the above, dear diary, we did not escape. We were recaptured—sort of. All but Danielson.

In the beginning, everything ran as smoothly as planned. More so. Samdup did not need persuading of any sort. He was asleep and he'd left both doors open. He'd had a hard day in the fields and he was pooped, I suppose. I was glad. Danielson smirked down at him and crept past on feet padded with layers of fur boots and wool socks.

Marsh pulled his parka hood close to his face and melted into the boulders behind Danielson. It wasn't so cold then and I was sweating with excitement. I carried my gear, as Thibideaux carried his and the Colonel's, not just because I was too warm but because the extra clothing would make me even slower and clumsier than I already was. The Colonel hadn't worn his for the same reason, I suppose.

I had just passed Samdup when the earth hiccuped, buckling beneath my feet, and my knees gave way so that I sat down abruptly.

Samdup fell face forward onto the ground, snorted and awakened. "Eh? What?" he said in Tibetan, pulling himself up and staring at me with sleep-bewildered eyes.

The Colonel and Thibideaux melted back, out of

sight, and I dropped my gear to the ground, stood up and dusted myself off and said, "Wow, did you feel that?" first in English, then switching to Tibetan. And I thought, right then, that maybe the others would just escape without me. That I could stand staying here without them. I wasn't afraid of being tortured or punished particularly and though I had no burning desire to stay, I just decided I wouldn't mind—possibly, I'll admit, that revelation came as a result of dreading freezing to death in the mountains and being left behind abandoned as a grisly, frozen corpse.

Samdup looked confused to see me. I tried to pretend that nothing was wrong, that I'd just popped up to see what was going on, and everyone else was still down below, where they were supposed to be. I didn't want anybody to have to kill poor Samdup. He's been as decent to me as circumstances allow.

A rock in a black fist reached out of the darkness, aiming downward toward Samdup's head, then stopped in midair and dropped to the ground with a thud. Involuntarily, I glanced back at the Colonel. The whites of his eyes shone all around his irises as he stared out beyond us, and beyond the mountains surrounding us to the sky.

Samdup might have actually been hit by the rock from the expression on his face, mouth and eyes both wide as he stared out at the shooting stars, one after another, a veritable meteor shower curving across the night sky.

But something was wrong. The bright arc of light pointed in the wrong direction, from earth to air.

"Oh, sweet Jesus and all the holy saints above us," Thibideaux whispered.

Soft footsteps behind me, and at my back I felt Marsh's breath on my scalp, heard his individual heartbeat added to the Colonel's, Samdup's and mine, smelled his particular brand of B.O., very sharp, extra pungent with fear, as we watched those meteors rise, not in the random, chaotic fashion of a true meteor shower, but very calculated: one, two, three, four to the northeast, Beijing way; one, two, three, four, to the west, where

Ladahk lay; one, two, three, four, fainter, far south, and southeast toward Pakistan and Nepal.

"They're going in the wrong direction," I said and Marsh said, "Wait."

I waited. We all waited. And in a moment the sky to the north, beyond the great horned mountain where the moon rose, flashed a brilliant and barbarous rose-orange that glowed brighter and brighter until it was beyond color, beyond sound, blotting out the moon with its brilliance, and although I closed my eyes it burnt right through my eyelids.

"There goes Tashkent," Marsh said, as if with satisfaction, to himself.

The next flash was to the south and he said, "Good-bye, Katmandu," and to the east, "So long, Chungking," and when the whole sky was on fire so that it seemed the mountains themselves would melt and fold into pudding from the heat, a final, searing bolt of light rent the western sky. "And that's curtains for Kashmir." His voice had a manic edge to it.

I couldn't see anything anymore but soon I heard other voices, and felt hands shoving me down the steps again, felt the others stumbling after me, heard the cell door close behind us.

Thibideaux's teeth were clicking like a keyboard tapped by a mad typist, and I tried to hold him to stop his shaking but he cried so hard he shook me off. The Colonel halted his mumbling monologue once and asked quite clearly where Danielson had gone and Marsh halted his own monologue long enough to answer, "He kept going when I came back to see how the rest of you were doing."

"Good, good," the Colonel said, and kept mumbling. My sight returned to normal here in the darkness and after a while I lit my lamp and saw that somewhere along the way the Colonel and Thibideaux had lost their winter gear too and Marsh had also been stripped of his. So the camp officials knew about the escape attempt. It hardly matters now, I suppose, except maybe they'll find Danielson before he goes too far and has to die alone.

There have been tremblings in the earth all night and I'm afraid this place will fall in on us—or I would be more afraid, except that I know how thorough Tea's "shorings up" have been. What worries me the most is that sound—the gushing and chugging have become a roar now, and underneath is a steady rhythmic pumping.

PART SEVEN

FLOOD

My eyes feel as if they've been sandpapered and my mouth is sour with the taste of blood, every muscle and bone as tight and sore as if I'd tied on a good one and been flattened in a barroom brawl. I awoke thinking, "God, what a nightmare," until I noticed Danielson's empty cot next to me and saw Marsh sprawled, snoring noisily against the wall, the Colonel up and walking back and forth the two paces across the room. Thibideaux's body was knotted in sleep, his forearms over his crown as if he was fending off frags, as indeed he had been.

Sometime in the night the wind rose and my stone cot quivered. Pieces of stone and clods of dirt rained down from the ceiling. Once I awakened to a series of sliding thumps that I thought were fresh explosions until I heard the hiss and dry rattle of small gravel and realized that the thumps were probably caused by the sandbags in the hall falling from their perches.

My last dream of the night was again of a room full of robed men and women, chanting, praying, the ghosts of this place. No one came down with momos this morning, however, and the cell door swung easily open with a slight tug. We—the others awakened shortly after me and the four of us moved for once as if we had a collective mind—had to climb over the fallen mounds of sandbags to reach the stairs and haul sandbags away from the entrance to open the outer door. Samdup was not there, but sunlight bored through the canopy and birds wheeled and cried above the valley in the shadow of the mountains.

We stood for a moment looking out at what seemed a perfectly normal sunny sky, although the distant mountain peaks were more blurred than usual. No sign of preternatural brightness. No meteor craters. No melted mountains. Just the usual landscape and the half-ruined walls down the hill to the fields.

The pack train party poured out of the command bunker, intercepting us on our way down the hill. They were dressed in winter garb, including the bundle I had been carrying, and except for looking hot and uncomfortable in the warmth of the valley they seemed like a normal group of winter sport fans ready for an outing. I didn't notice the particular navy blue parka Danielson had been wearing, however, which was a relief, because if I had seen it it would have meant he'd been killed or recaptured.

Merridew scanned the sides of the mountains as well as he could under the canopy, looking for a lone dark figure moving against the snowy streaks on the raw stone slopes. My eyes followed his, but I also looked down over the sides of the cliff as we passed near that, wondering if Danielson, temporarily blinded during the first burst of light, might not have fallen.

But then we rounded the last of the ruined wall and boulders that lay between the upper compound and the lower slope and the valley. I'd been hearing it all night, of course, for that was the noise that penetrated the walls, the roaring and gurgling, the murmuring and the chanting.

The guards from the night before stood at the foot of the hill, staring into what had once been the valley. I saw Samdup's back and Terton, Wu, Tsering, and Tea, who may have been, like the guards, up all night. The people in the pack train first stopped dead ahead of us, staring, then began running down the hill at breakneck speed.

The noise was not very loud now, merely a little bubbling and churning as the tiny pool that had formed the eye of the valley expanded, flooding the valley floor with steaming silver water that rippled quickly over the blossoms, the rocks, the lower row of garden, toward the stone yak corral.

At one end the refilled lake lapped the mountainside, at the other it sluiced into an abandoned stream bed which ran alongside the hill containing the compound.

The greatest strategist in the world couldn't have come up with better diversionary tactics than those covering Danielson's escape. Dr. Terton nudged Wu, who turned toward us from contemplating the lake. She was smiling as I'd never seen her smile before, and she almost sang an order to the pack train, who were still so stunned that none of them thought to obey until the first one finally had the presence of mind to throw off her winter parka and run toward the yak pens. The other guards followed in demolishing the wall of the corral and driving the yaks up the hill, through the garden, tearing up careful plantings.

And so the lake has returned, more beautiful than the computer simulations, more beautiful than in my dreams even. It was the best thing that could happen. Its appearance seemed to wash away the confusion and fear of the night, which no one has commented on directly and only a few experienced anyway. The pack train was sleeping extra soundly with a draught the doctor had made, apparently, and the guards must have been too stunned to report what they saw in time for anyone else to see it. Or maybe we imagined it? The smell of the water is real and fresh and you can almost hear things growing. It does not breed an atmosphere conducive to thoughts of death on any scale.

Besides, it posed problems that forced everyone to work so hard we could shut out thoughts that are unthinkable anyway.

The pack train put off its departure to help us prisoners and the remaining guards dig up the seeds, shoots, and plants and replant them farther up the hill. By midday the water seemed to have reached its high point, the stream carrying the runoff through the boulders and rocks in the rest of the valley floor, and by nightfall the yaks were repenned within the waist-high walls of one of the ruined structures. Nothing was said by anyone about Danielson, and Thibideaux, Marsh, Merridew and I returned to our cells when it was finally too dark to work. We were too tired to eat and fell onto our cots half asleep before we were fully prone.

I arose before the others this morning. Rereading my last two entries, I can hardly believe myself all that has happened. But the only evidence I see that anything extraordinary occurred is the lake—maybe the other was not what we thought. Perhaps some kind of atmospheric disturbance, nocturnal sunspots or something? It didn't seem to affect us here, except to bring back the lovely, lovely lake.

LAKE DAY

⚸ The pack train left yesterday morning, the day after the lake appeared. I arrived at the command bunker as they were suiting up for the trek. Outside the wind scoured the surrounding mountaintops and sprinkled secondhand snow over the compound to land like sparkling confetti on the camouflage canopy. I skipped aside three steps and took another long gander at the lake. It sloshed gently in its reclaimed bed, as if settling in, its cobalt and aquamarine waters patting its shores into place. Avalanche grumblings keep the air from ever being still these days. Thank God the horned mountain already deposited most of its payload on the compound long ago or we'd probably be goners by now.

It was my usual day to work with Taring, though I thought I might ask to be relieved of my duties so I could help with the replanting. As I set out to find him at his usual tasks in the lower excavations, I passed the pack train, equipping itself once more for the long trek ahead.

The corridor was crowded with people pulling on boots, extra pants, and layers and layers of sweaters, quilted vests and coats, felt hats and mittens. One bundled figure fell against me as it struggled to pull on a boot. I staggered back, caught a quilted arm, and stared into the lenses of Dolma's glasses. They were steamed from her breath and I wiped them with my sleeve.

"You're going?" I asked.

"Yes," she said. "A man will stay in my place. The lower rooms are filling with water. Their contents must be moved. Captain Taring needs the men to help him. Don't let the flood ruin the books, Viva."

"I'm on my way," I said. "Don't let any rocks fall on your head, Dolma."

"Don't worry," she said, breathless and sweating now from the extra layers as she lifted the flap of her nylon hood to reveal a layer of heavy knit and a layer of felt. "Three hats. The stones will bounce off my head. Also two scarves and gloves beneath my mittens. Goodbye, Viva." Her mitten touched my arm and I wiped her glasses again.

"Goodbye, Dolma," I said.

"Yes," she said, replacing her glasses and looking at me as if she was going to be tested on my appearance later.

I turned away and quickened my pace on my way to the lower excavations. As I passed the branch leading to Wu's office, I saw her and the doctor, walking rapidly in my direction. The doctor caught my eye for a moment. Her expression reminded me of my grandmother's when she was about to ask me something, but she didn't.

Men carrying armloads of seed packages hurried past me, and we got in the way of each other, the corridor not being wide enough for even two of the Asians to stand abreast, never mind a large-boned American like me.

The library and the corridor outside it were still dry, as were most of the upper rooms, but deeper inside the maze, water at first made itself known as mud, then an inch or so of tepid dampness until, by the time I reached

Tea, it sloshed and steamed around my ankles, warming my feet to an almost uncomfortable degree.

"Viveka, be having a gander at this, will you! Here are the pipes—the ones we are seeing in the simulation," he said, indicating ceramic tubes with circumferences the size of automobile tires. "Unfortunately," he added unnecessarily, "they are broken."

Buried in the walls and beneath the floor, the pipes had been exposed by the digging and the water. Through the holes and gaps in them, water poured out onto the floor.

Taring seemed quite pleased about it, hopping around like a cat pouncing from one delectable mouse to the next, as if the water was not about to ruin all of our work. "Feel, it is hot water—a hot springs used not only for hot water but also for a heating system beneath the floors and walls."

"I wish you could find the Off faucet, then," I told him.

He took me seriously. "Hmm, perhaps such a thing exists, though I have never heard of it. Meanwhile, we must be funneling this water back downhill. This beneficial water will be most unbeneficial to our finds if we are not stopping it."

Just then one of the men rushing from the seed room with two bags under each arm knocked another one down and he slid in the mud, rupturing a bag and sending seeds flying everywhere.

"Let's do a relay line," I suggested, and when the guards ignored me, I went into the packet room, handed a sack of seeds to the man outside the door, and when he tried to go, stopped him and indicated that he should hand them to the next one. The line formed quickly. It was not, after all, a foreign concept to them, they just hadn't thought of using it yet that morning.

Tea finally found a way to staunch the water, but not before it flooded the generator. Most of the afternoon we worked in the glow of flashlights and oil lamps, until batteries and oil gave out. I wonder if anyone still knows how to make yak butter?

None of us slept that night, laboring to mop up the spill, to lay the seeds which had become wet out to dry, and repair other water damage. Those who were working in the field had to replant half of what we had planted already, and haul rocks and hand-plow soil accordingly.

When at last we were allowed to return to our quarters to sleep, the water had risen to cover the floor of the passageway containing our cell to the third step from the bottom and was rising. I waded in and rescued my journal, but last night we and the other prisoners, as well as the guards, slept under the canopy, between the rocks. Sometime last night I was shaken roughly awake and hauled to my feet. "You go to commandant's office now," said the guard. I was too sleepy to even see who he was but he was not one of the ones I knew fairly well.

He stopped outside the door and gestured for me to go in while he stood sentry.

Wu and Dr. Terton waited for me in Wu's office. The computer sat open on the tarp-covered desk and Wu frowned into it. Terton, I could have sworn, had been pacing until I entered, when she turned, dropped her hands to her sides and smiled at me, arranging her face into convincingly serene and benign lines.

"Ah, Viv," she said. "It has just come to our attention that one of your comrades, Mr. Danielson, is missing. We must locate him at once."

"Have you asked Colonel Merridew?" I asked. "He *is* the O.I.C."

"We're asking you," Wu said. "Where is Danielson? He is in grave danger."

"That's what he thought. I imagine that's why he left," I said and pointed at the computer, "Which side are you reporting his disappearance to anyway, Wu? The Indians, the Chinese, or the Soviets? Or is this a NACAF operation?"

"Don't be insulting," Wu said, looking and sounding genuinely offended at the mention of a possible NACAF association.

"It has that sort of cosmopolitan flavor about it, you must admit," I said.

"The information is classified," Wu replied coldly.

"Also," Dr. Terton added, "I think it matters very little now."

My heart skipped a beat and although I wanted nothing confirmed—nothing—I asked casually, "What do you mean by that?"

She shrugged and smiled the ingratiating smile of a pickpocket who hasn't seen your wallet but will certainly inquire of all her friends if they have done so. "Why, only that we have lost all contact with our supply lines apparently."

"Still you sent out another pack train."

"*We* are conducting this interrogation, Vanachek, not you," Wu said coldly.

Just as coldly, I said, "This is a prison camp. We are prisoners of war. It's our duty to escape and Danielson escaped."

"My word, child," Terton said, "have conditions here been so terrible that you would flee alone to what is out there?"

"I didn't go, he did. No, you know me, Doctor. No mountain climbing without one of your little spells. To tell you the truth, if this was any other kind of an establishment, I'd be happy enough to stay here instead of ever climbing another mountain pass or wearing an NACAF uniform again. You may not know this but they don't usually let anyone below the rank of major back into the country again, once you're on active duty. I can't go home again . . ." I didn't even want to think about how true that probably was so I hurried on. "But the food is improved, and your guards are surprisingly human, for prison camp guards—or are they really just prisoners too? Your rosters confuse me."

"They are supposed to be confusing," the doctor said.

"They are supposed to be top secret," Wu added.

"Then you shouldn't leave your top-secret information lying around for me to find along with the stuff you and Taring put there for me to find," I told her.

"This is important, Vanachek," Wu said, and for a change, when she said it, it sounded important. She'd dropped the cold, haughty bitch routine, dropped the off-with-your-head tone, and sounded merely annoyed and also, oddly, anguished. "I confess I do not much care for Sergeant Danielson but neither do I wish him to come to harm and his life is at stake. We need to know when he left and in what direction."

"I'll bet his life is at stake," I said. "If you find him, that is. And I don't know when he left or *if* he left and if so where. Away, I suppose, as fast as he could go." Merridew would be proud of me, I thought. But I realized that Wu had just stepped out of her role as commandant in time for me to escalate mine as wronged and indignant POW. That particular persona had not figured greatly in my relationship with the camp personnel to date but I felt it necessary, if I was not to break faith with the Colonel and the men—maybe Danielson in particular—to behave as I imagined they would have. Still, something about Wu's sudden change of demeanor and Terton's face, suddenly showing every year of her age and probably more, stopped me from reciting name, rank and serial number to them. "Since when have you been so worried about our lives?"

"Since the beginning," the doctor said simply, as if surprised I had to ask. "We are concerned about the lives of all of the people here."

"Were you concerned about the monks who lived here before the avalanche, before you turned this lamasery into a prison camp?" I asked. "What happened to them, anyway?"

"What monks?" Wu asked. "What do you know of monks?"

"I know that they haunt this place. I've heard them chanting, praying. Call me a crazy superstitious kid if you will but I think their ghosts helped Danielson escape by conjuring up that lake you're so fond of, Commandant. They called it up with their chanting to confuse and distract you. I heard them."

Now I knew I was losing it but I was too tired to care. I figured I'd gone too far when Wu and the doctor exchanged glances.

"You heard monks chanting?"

"Yes, I did. And lots of other times. And don't tell me I'm nuts because I've read about what this country was like before you people took over and it was fucking *full* of magic."

"Before your people made it a perpetual battle-ground," Wu shot back automatically.

"Before the Chinese invasions and occupation," I countered. And then I was off and running with every real grievance I had against my captors—not anything they'd done to me, or the Colonel, or any of the others, but all of the things I'd heard about in casual conversations within the family (our family's casual conversations were more political and less casual than most) and, later, as historical wrongs in school. I couldn't seem to shut up. "I know who tore down the monasteries and shipped the art and the timber and everything they could lay hands on, back to China. And I heard how they burned ancient holy books and killed and tortured monks and nuns, not to mention your average citizen. Wu, you're married to a Tibetan. How can you care so little what happens to this country? Doctor, I can't understand how people like those guerrillas can keep from shooting you on sight. But you didn't figure on something. This country used to be the most spiritual place on the face of the earth. Now you may laugh at that, but in my family it meant something. My grandmother kept a picture of the Dalai Lama over her futon and Grandpa Ananda flew prayer flags from the garden fence. They weren't Tibetan Buddhists but they had great respect for Eastern religion and for what this country used to be. You people have destroyed it physically, and I read about how you tore up the people's books and paved the streets with the pages from sacred works so people would have to walk on them if they wanted to go to work or get food. I know how you strip-mined the mountains for minerals, pol-luted the streams, cut down all the trees, killed the animals and used the place for a toxic-waste dump. And I also know, God help me, that my country helped you do it but I personally sure as hell did not, so don't tell me I don't hear ghost monks when I hear ghost monks. They're what make this place bearable and the only thing that helped me survive the humanitarian treatment you dished out when I first got here."

I ran out of wind then, and I also jolted myself into the renewed realization that the humanitarian treatment I sarcastically referred to was not necessarily a thing of the past and could be reinitiated at the whim of the women I was haranguing with my catalog of ancient historical wrongs.

But as I tried to stare Wu down, she grew more and more crestfallen and finally failed to meet my eyes at all, cupping her hand over her own eyes. It couldn't be my display of historical rhetoric, I thought. She let her hand fall to the table and looked up at Terton. "She's heard them," Wu said. "Why her?"

"Perhaps you've been under too much stress with your job here, Nyima. Don't take it so to heart. As for Mr. Danielson, perhaps the pack train will reach him in time."

I remembered with satisfaction how much of a lead he had on them.

"Thank you, Viv. You may go now," the doctor said, and bent over Wu as if to comfort her.

A WEEK? WEEK AND A HALF? MAYBE TWO WEEKS AFTER LAKE

We've been using hand pumps to clear the buildings. Tea works as hard as anyone on his turn at the pump. He actually seems to enjoy it. The harder and grubbier the job is the better as far as he's concerned. When I'm not pumping, I continue collating, cataloging and putting things back in order, working in the garden as if nothing has changed.

For a while I expected to be locked up again or even shot but no further mention was made of Danielson's escape or my nocturnal visit to the Commandant's office. The nights remain fairly pleasant, the garden producing at an even more fantastic rate then usual thanks to all of the readily available water, the weather warm despite the wind which howls all night around us and yet never seems to come inside the canopy. Its noise and the grumbling of the avalanches is the only manifestation we've had since the lake's emergence of the restlessness of the surrounding range.

I know firsthand about how the weather is all day and all night because since the flooding, we've continued to sleep outside, guards and prisoners alike. Taring insists that until his repairs are complete we are in danger of being buried alive if we sleep below. I don't find his cautions awfully reassuring, when I have to work below during the day.

The repairs are progressing, however, and a group of the Chinese prisoners built a kiln from a plan in one of the Foxfire Books and began shaping replacement pipe to Tea's specifications.

The relief guard sleeps in the dining room during the day, but otherwise the guards and prisoners are working together now. Needless to say, discipline has become so lax it's pretty much a thing of the past, at least for the time being.

One of the guards, a young fellow, didn't see why we shouldn't use the books to sop up the water, and since he was illiterate nobody could make him understand and I had to physically wrestle with him to keep him from destroying the Agatha Christies. The doctor was passing by just then and gave him a gentle but thorough chewing out. He helped me shelve for three days and I ended up promising to let him study Tibetan with me as I learn to read it.

Marsh and a crew of other prisoners and guards have been digging shallow irrigation ditches and channeling the flood waters from below into them as Tea's crew pumps the water to the surface. The barley crop is knee-high.

The present sleeping arrangements relieve me of the necessity of discussing anything with Merridew or the others. Even though we don't sleep too far apart, they never try to talk to me. Ears are everywhere, the Colonel told me once when I tried to tell him about the interrogation, and even if no guards are nearby after so many years of incarceration, some of the others prisoners identify more with their jailers than with each other.

I'm sure he's absolutely appalled at how the rules have been relaxed, and must be highly suspicious of the way the doctor and even Wu are encouraging the guards and prisoners to talk together. I confess, I'd dearly love to talk to Tea again. Somehow everything that's happened since I confessed to finding the seeds has sort of diminished his little deception to relative insignificance and I miss him. Though I see him several times a day, he's always much too busy to do more than nod in a distracted sort of way. I'd hate to think that if what I think I saw, actually occurred something might happen to the compound and or to one or both of us and I wouldn't get to tell him that I understand he was only trying to make peace, to give me a contribution to make of my own volition. Although there is a great deal I don't understand about this place, I really never believed that Tea was glorying in manipulating me. I hope I get the chance to say so soon.

TEN DAYS LATER

⚴ The work load has lightened, the flood is contained, the pipes are installed, but still we sleep aboveground until, Tea says, the rooms below have a chance to dry out properly. This will take most of the summer, I gather, since the buried passages are difficult to ventilate properly. Then too there are the little tremors, shaking the slope beneath us as if a large truck had just driven past, though of course there are no large trucks.

These days we do not automatically fall into bed after spending the day working. Sometimes we socialize, strolling by the lake or playing cards, gambling for those few bits of treasure so many of us had secreted that no one, not even Terton or Tea, took offense that some of the things were kept as personal property. Sometimes the gambling is for an extra onion from the next day's ration, or a portion of someone's personal yield from their garden plot. At first, people were rusty as they tried to simply relax together. On the other hand, prisoners become very good at hiding their anger, out of fear, and after a while it became apparent that this was all in fun, that there was no need for anger, since there was plenty of food to share and we could all *see* each of the treasures and it wasn't as if they were worth anything here, where there was no economy, not even in cigarettes, since there were none. So the games progressed with a great deal of giggling and laughter that had only a slightly hysterical edge to it.

Although no one refers to the night the lake reappeared, not even Samdup, who has said very little to us since then, every once in a while when I have settled down for the night, I'll see one of the sleepers or the gamblers rise to his or her feet, stroll over to the cliff edge, and look out at the mountains and down onto the lake, as if waiting.

The pack train has been gone for a very long time. As I count the entries in my diary and try to figure the days between events, it seems to me that the trains take about two months to go and return.

NIGHT OF TORCHES

Tonight I was playing cards with Thibideaux, Merridew, and Tsering's daughter when the child lay down her hand and walked to the edge of the cliff. I did the same. I felt twitchy. Though the crops have been as abundant as ever, the night air has gone from springy and soft to almost too warm and now is almost too cold for the brocade hangings to be adequate protection. Tania noticed the hangings among our artifacts and suggested their use as blankets, rinsing them out in clear water, which took two days alone. The fabric is silk brocade, double and triple thick and fairly warm. Wu surprised everyone by donating half of her personal soap supply to wash the hangings. After that we had rather elegant blankets, though lately these have not been quite warm enough.

This is not really a long-term problem. The flood was not from the lake, as we supposed, but from a hot spring which was apparently also unplugged by the subterranean activity—I try not to think of it as an earthquake—that freed the lake. Soon Tea will have a new valve made and will be able to channel the hot water through the new pipe to form a heating system similar to the original one. But I don't much like the thought of going below again. The distinctions between guards and prisoners and between prisoners of one cellblock and prisoners of another will spring up once more, I'm afraid. And I'm also afraid that we all, very badly, for whatever time remains, need to stand together.

So I stood behind Pema, looking out across the valley, my gaze craning upward to follow hers around the ghostly white peaks looming over us, as overpowering to me as I must have looked to an ant. A phantom of snow trailed its sheet as it leapt from a cleft in the ridge opposite our guardian mountain.

"Did you ever hear what they call that mountain?" I asked the girl in Tibetan.

"Karakal," she said, and suddenly gave a childish hop and pointed. "Look."

As the veil of snow swept away on the wind, spots of light appeared within the darkness, one, two, three, four, stretching out longer and longer until it seemed a ribbon.

"It's the pack train!" I told Pema, totally unnecessarily since she simultaneously let out a screech and yelled to everyone that she had been the first to spot the train returning from the outside world with all the things we wanted.

And everybody left their games or their hammocks and came to line the cliff edge, watching the light spots bounce down the distant mountainside.

"There's too many," Pema said, counting with her raised finger. "Eighteen, nineteen, twenty—there were only nine people in the train, Dolma, Norbu, Kunga, Trungpa, Jamyang, Pema Jamyang . . ."

"Hush, we know," her mother said, holding her by her shoulders and stroking her hair as the girl continued counting.

There were many more than nine lights, many more than nineteen or twenty. Hundreds of the spots formed a serpentine ribbon of light dancing from the top of the ridge, winding in a circle along the cliff sides, spiraling down until, as its tip reached halfway down the mountain, we started moving en masse down the trail to greet it.

Behind each brave and beautiful light was a foot-weary, soul-sick traveler. Many new faces, and only a few of the old ones were among them, some reached the edge of the canopy while the rest brought up the rear, still high in the pass.

How would we feed them all, how would there be enough blankets? Where did they all come from? I was relieved when I saw that each of them was carrying, besides a torch, as many personal belongings as they could carry, including animals in baskets and cages, clothing, children—these were refugees, then, rather than more prisoners.

And then I recognized, or thought I recognized, a

coat I hadn't seen for months, since it had walked out of camp on the back of one of the youngest guards, one of the ones who had stayed behind when the rest of the pack train returned. He was one of the ones who would have walked out to the guerrilla camp to learn what had become of the supply helicopter. He had returned with this party, or at least his parka, bordered with distinctive rainbow-stripped ribbon, had returned. I definitely remembered that the parka belonged to a very young guard, just beyond boyhood, but now the parka was on the back of a middle-aged man who resembled the boy enough to be his father.

I had not seen Dolma until I spotted this man, but she was right behind him, bearing one end of a litter.

The chest of the body on the stretcher still rose and fell, although the head was covered for warmth with one of those reflecting synthetic blankets.

Dolma hefted her end of the stretcher more securely and filed past me, unseeing without her thick glasses. Behind her shuffled more civilians, lugging everything from cooking pots to chickens, driving some of the more surefooted animals, chiefly goats, before them. Everyone looked like a sleepwalker.

LATER

I suppose ignorance really was bliss in this case. We saw the missiles fired and we saw them explode in return, in the distance. We knew damn good and well what it meant. But it is still stunning to hear about the obliteration from the lips of these few survivors, led through the mountains to the rendezvous point by the team who had walked back in to investigate.

The newcomers spilled out from under the canopy,

sitting numbed and quiet while we passed among them with soup and extra coverings, and helped them shed their packs.

Sometime later, after the bathtub soup kettle bore nothing but a greasy film where the soup had been, after the hangings had been torn in half to cover more children and infants, after the chickens and pigs and goats had been penned and the night of torches had turned to day and then into afternoon, I found Dolma, sitting beside the litter, tears streaming on her cheeks. I sat down beside her, my bones creaking wearily. A full soup bowl with a spoon in it sat at the head of the litter. The occupant's face was turned away, with only a straggle of fine white hair on an age-speckled bald scalp showing clearly.

Tea threaded his way through the crowd to join us and looked down at Dolma's red-rimmed eyes, much magnified by her salt-stained glasses.

"So," he said to her. "So, just how bad is it?"

"It's over," she said. Her voice quavered. Her hair was matted to her head from wearing a cap and a hood for so long and she absently brushed it out of the frames of her glasses. Tea watched her intently the whole time. They both knew what they were talking about, another part of a longstanding secret. I could only guess at that point. "We are alone," Dolma said. "Only these few were saved, and they found their way only because Rinchen Norbu and his companions met them when they walked out to try to find the helicopter. You can see from Rinchen's face what it cost him." She nodded to the middle-aged man wearing the youth's rainbow-trimmed parka. He sat looking over the heads of squalling children and the stony-faced adults who mechanically went about the business of settling in. He was staring at the lake as if by drinking it in with his eyes he was somehow healed. "These people lived in the settlements and camps near our border. When they saw the flash, they were far enough from ground zero to have time to begin walking in, with the guidance of Rinchen and the others. Three villagers, plus Sonam and Phurbu from Rinchen's party, were lost in an avalanche and later, the wind blew two people from the top of a cliffside pass."

"Little Sonam?" Tea asked. "She is gone? And Phurbu?"

"The world is gone, Lobsang. Save for these few. Their fate was to be there for the arrival of our people and to follow them here. At first many were reluctant to come, since they could never leave, as a few of them had heard in tales of this place from their great-grandparents and grandparents, who remembered us from days when trade was easier. Within five days of our border, Rinchen spotted this one." She indicated the person on the stretcher. "He recognized the parka," she said sadly.

I followed her gaze to the mottled scalp and the ragged motion of the chest as it labored to breathe and couldn't believe someone so ancient had been wandering out in the mountains alone. Perhaps, as I had heard the Eskimos once exposed their elders, someone had left the poor old thing to die?

Dolma started to glance up at me once and lowered her eyes to the stretcher again.

"So tell me," I said. "Why did all these people spend their last few days mountain climbing to come here?"

The doctor had been moving, stepping over each person to reach another, her bag in her hand, Thibideaux behind her carrying an assortment of bandages and ointments, Pema tagging behind to run errands. Terton bent slowly over the figure on the stretcher, pulling the blanket down to reach for the wrist.

Nobody answered me. Everyone seemed to be holding their breath as Terton examined the man. Thibideaux stood well away from her and her body sheltered that of her patient.

I had thought that the big secret between Dolma and Tea had to do with the missiles, with the night the sky lit up with fireballs and explosions. I thought they were talking around that, pussyfooting really, so as to avoid panicking the rest of us, which seemed an exercise in futility. I was trying to be direct, to let them know that even though we had not said anything, the prisoners—in my cell block at least—had an idea what had happened beyond the mountains. "I think I get it. They came to escape the radiation, didn't they? Because we're so far from everything. I guess they figure the fire storms and the nuclear winter and all that might not hit us up here." I paused, tried to swallow, found I could not and that I suddenly felt very shaky as I asked more calmly than I thought possible, "But even though we seem to be spared so far, all the fallout and stuff is bound to catch up with us pretty soon, isn't it?"

The doctor pulled the thermal blanket back up over her patient, turned slowly around so that she sat on the ground facing me beside the stretcher and said in a low, measured voice, "No. I don't believe so."

"You *don't*?"

"No. The rest of the world may die but in this one little place, we will continue. If I did not believe this, this place would not be here."

"But who wants to continue forever in a prison camp?" I asked, and added, a little wildly, "I mean, for a prison camp you've all been swell but it's a prison camp nevertheless."

"Does it matter what it is? You have no home to return to."

"Sherry—" The voice on the litter crackled like static, and Dolma hushed it and pulled the covers gently away.

"It is all okay now, Sergeant. We have brought you back. You see? Here are your friends Viva and Thibideaux."

The withered little figure under the blanket was sweating, so she peeled back his outer parka. He wore orange pajamas, like me.

"Sherry, I'm sorry. Coming back to—help . . ."

"Du?" Thibideaux asked and then, louder, "Du? What the—Colonel! Marsh!"

"Doc?" the old man on the cot asked and the bottom dropped out of my stomach, a boulder lodged in my throat.

"Danielson?" I asked.

"Sherry—"

"No, Danielson, it's Viv Vanachek."

"Sherry. Sorry, babe." A gob of phlegm had to be suctioned from his lips before he could continue but for a brief moment he looked up at me with Danielson's piercing blue eyes sandwiched between wrinkled, drooping lids. "Sherry, I can help. I—more than a killer."

"My God," Merridew said when he had fought his way through the refugees to reach us. "This can't be." He leaned over Danielson as tenderly as a mother with an injured child. "Sergeant Danielson?"

"Colonel, tell Sherry—"

"It's all right, son," he said, and although nothing was all right and the figure on the stretcher looked old enough to be his great-grandfather rather than his son, he didn't sound inane.

The Danielson on the stretcher fixed the Colonel with one of those fierce looks he had, exhaled as if he was sighing, and didn't inhale again. The doctor had her fingers on his pulse and shook her head, and finally Thibideaux closed the sagging lids over eyes from which the fierceness had faded.

"What did you do to him?" the Colonel demanded, his voice grinding the words to iron filings.

"Could it be some kind of radiation poisoning?" I ventured.

"I never heard of rapid aging as a sign of radiation poisoning," Thibideaux said slowly.

"It is not radiation poisoning," the doctor said. "Your friend is a very old man. You are, Colonel, Doctor Thibideaux, Mr. Marsh, all of you, all very old men. So old that it was necessary when you were first brought here to give each of you posthypnotic suggestions so that the passage of time would not alarm you."

"The headaches?" I asked.

She nodded. "Yes, a deterrent implanted in your subconscious to make time a literally instead of merely a psychologically painful concept for you to deal with. But believe me, Colonel, you and Mr. Danielson particularly are very old men indeed. When Mr. Danielson strayed beyond our borders, the beneficial effects of this place no longer protected him and within a few days he reverted to his true age."

"That's a load of horseshit if I ever heard one," Thibideaux said.

I'm not sure how long Marsh had been listening. Long enough to get the gist of the conversation anyway. He knelt beside the body and pulled back the cover and after a moment said, "It *is* Danielson. And he *is* old. This isn't radiation poisoning."

"No, no, hold on," I said, feeling as if another avalanche was about to sweep my life away. The bomb had got the world and the doctor had disposed of my sense of time and personal history with a wave of her magic wand. Still, I had put together a few things for myself and if I could make sense of those, I'd be much less a puppet, I'd have regained some control. "Thibideaux, the oil spills were cleaned up when my mother was a young woman—say twenty. She had me when she was forty-three—I remember that because Grandma had her when she was forty-three and I was forty-three when I was captured so it's"—the doctor nodded encouragingly and this time the block that I had unthinkingly grown accustomed to when I tried to puzzle out time dissolved—"2069." I could see the chronometer on my map display in Siddons's aircraft as clearly as if I was sitting before it. "September twenty-ninth, 2069, I was captured. So if you cleaned birds as a boy, you must be—"

"Nearly seventy," he said, sitting back on his heels with his hands dangling limply over his knees, the equipment he'd been carrying for Terton falling nervelessly from his fingers.

The Colonel took up the game as grimly determined as if he was biting into a cyanide capsule, "And my father took his flight when I was twenty-four years old. That was in 1991."

At length I said, "Does anybody know what year this is?"

The doctor smiled. "It is 2070 by your calendar. But it no longer matters, you see." I didn't see and neither did any of my cellmates. We all looked at her blankly and she added, as if it explained anything, "Now that you are here, I mean to say."

"But where *is* here?" Merridew demanded. "What kind of trick is this? We can't be as old as you say and even if we were, we won't be getting any older. There's been a major nuclear incident so close that I saw the flash with my own eyes. We should all be dead now, and not of old age. This has got to be some kind of trick."

"There's Danielson," Thibideaux reminded him. "He's no trick."

"Please do not concern yourself, Mr. Merridew," Terton said kindly. "We will not perish here. We are protected by the power of this valley and this place, shielded by Karakal."

"What's that? Some heathen god?" Merridew demanded.

"Karakal is the mountain, Colonel," I filled in, remembering what the little girl had told me and then remembered something else. "It's a famous mountain, isn't it, Doctor, although it isn't the highest in the range?"

"We enjoyed an uncomfortable amount of notoriety for a time," she said. "Fortunately, the explanations given in Mr. Hilton's popular novel and the subsequent film were not scientific enough to convince the world of our existence and so we remain. The model for the hero of the book was one of my grandfathers, although he was not an Englishman, as Mr. Hilton had it, nor did he in any way resemble an American film star, since he was actually an Indian diplomat. But he was able to return, finally, and he and my mother remained here through two of my incarnations, until at last the avalanche killed them. By that time Tibet was occupied by the Chinese. The task of this place has always been as a haven for those besieged by the world, as a repository for the finest treasures of art and literature. My life has been stranger than I can easily tell you, but it has always been clear to me that the greatest treasure, and the most endangered one, is the human spirit. That is why I have gathered you here."

"You're preserving us by force?" Merridew sneered.

"Had I not done so, others would have killed you by force. Would you prefer that, Colonel?"

"And the names I found on the computer," I said. "All the names of this place. None of them were the true name, were they? The name of this place is not Russian, Indian or Chinese?"

"Well, it is derived from Sanskrit." Terton said. "Which is vaguely Indian."

"What the hell are you two talking about," the Colonel asked. "Whose prisoners are we anyway?"

"You are time's prisoners, Colonel Merridew," she said softly. "And destiny's. But please think of this place as a prison no longer. From now on, we must all help each other adjust to the terrible consequences that have befallen the outside world. In the meantime, we will make our home here, in this place we have known from ancient times as Shambala, although your Mr. Hilton for some reason refers to it as Shangri-La."

PART EIGHT

OLD YEAR 2070,
NEW POST—BIG BOOM YEAR 1,
WEEK 2, EARLY AUTUMN
(Late August? Who's to contradict me? So be it.
Late August)
DAY 14

At last I have time to write at length again. For the past two weeks it has been far too busy to do anything more than make a note of the date. I don't want to lose track of time again, advisable though the doctor seems to think it would be to do so. I am only forty-three. If the atmosphere cleans up in time, some day I may be able to go outside again. Not that I can tell you why I'd want to. But maybe some day at least some of these children would want to. At least one has already expressed his opinion that Shangri-La, (or Shambala—when in Tibet, etc.) is not all it has been cracked up to be.

"I thought there would be golden pagodas, like in the stories," the boy complained as he helped me hang the chimes from the outer edge of the command bunker. Laundry flapped from the poles and protrusions like the prayer flags at Danielson's grave. People are still camped so thickly under the canopy that it's hard to walk from one end of the compound to another, but stone lean-tos have blossomed among the flowering jungle covering the valley floor and if there are more mouths to feed, there are also more hands to work on the garden. And of course, there is all the new livestock the refugees brought with them, and some very welcome small farming implements.

It took us three days of tending to the immediate survival needs of the new people before we got around to burying Danielson. The delay was partly because there was some question as to how the funeral should be handled. The wood supply was insufficient for a cremation, especially now that we were using so many campfires at night for warmth. We have continued to sleep aboveground since there are not enough cells excavated yet for everyone and we're still concerned about aftershocks, which may be able to reach us even if direct contamination, according to Terton, cannot. So when there was time, Marsh and Thibideaux helped Samdup dig a grave at the foot of the pass at the far end of the mountain.

I helped Merridew, who still limps from his cat wounds, down the mountain, where he planned to say a few words over the grave. On the way down, we passed Tea and Dolma, who each carried armloads of mani stones, smooth, with rivulets of rain dripping from the carved prayers. I have hauled so many of those stones from the garden, some whole, some broken. The ones Tea and Dolma held were whole.

"Something will be needed to keep the snow lion from taking your friend," Tea said. "In the old way, we would have let the animals have the body, but there are few animals here now and giving the only wild one the taste of human flesh doesn't seem a good idea. These seem—appropriate."

Using one hand to steady the Colonel, I could only carry one stone myself—the small ones weighed at least five pounds or so apiece—and I thought it would be a long day, carrying enough stones to form a cairn over Danielson.

But then Wu and Dr. Terton threaded their way toward us through refugees and the radish patch. On the way, Dr. Terton squatted down and lifted a stone. With a put-upon sigh, Wu did likewise and Tsering, who walked behind them, picked up three more. Meanwhile, one of the refugees who had helped Dolma carry Danielson's litter spoke a word to her, pried a stone from the dirt and brushed it off and handed it to a child of about nine, who handed it to his sister. In a hushed babble, people told each other what the stones were for, and soon there was a straggling procession to the grave. Thibideaux and Marsh were just about to lay Danielson in it when Dolma stopped them, set down her stones, and began gathering blossoms. Soon others were gathering them too, until the area was denuded of wildflowers for half an acre around, and Danielson's grave was half filled with them. Then he was lowered down and Merridew mumbled a prayer that sounded to me like "The Battle Hymn of the Republic," but he stopped when he got to the part about "loosed the fateful lightning of his terrible swift sword." He got as far as "lightning." Then Marsh cleared his throat awkwardly and said, "Walk in beauty, Du."

Thibideaux tossed in a shovelful of dirt and handed the shovel to me. I would never again need to fear Danielson looming over me at night, or have to explain myself to him. But he had died trying to escape, which was the right thing according to what he had been taught to believe, and while trying to redeem himself to his family. I'm sorry he never got the chance to be the man he might have been, given the sort of home he wished he could provide for his children and a more peaceful world.

As I tossed in my shovelful, a child in the crowd wailed and buried its face in its mother's skirt. Another child screamed a word I recognized as meaning "father" and I wondered if that child belonged to one of the people lost on the trail. But the kids weren't the only ones crying. The adults keened and clung to each other, mourning loudly. It seemed funny for a moment, since Danielson, far from crying over their graves, would have killed any one of them with his bare hands and whistled while he worked. But I guess they have a lot to cry about and maybe Danielson's funeral is the first chance they've had to do it without worrying about falling into a bottomless ravine or being shot at or having to outrun radiation.

But it seems okay that Danielson, who was not born to a family and who couldn't keep the family he tried, should become the ultimate stand-in for the families of all of these people he'd have considered enemies.

When the grave was filled with earth and flowers, mani stones clinked one atop another until they produced a pile tall enough and broad enough to shade five people.

Thibideaux walked the Colonel back up the hill, leaving me to walk alone. I felt oddly empty inside, and so incapable of crying myself, for Danielson or the world or anything else, that my eyes felt as dry as the lake once was.

I guess I have a hard time accepting that life outside does not go on as I remember it, since life here in Kalapa does continue, although it has changed since I was first brought here. If Dr. Terton is to be believed, and when I remember the strange manner of Danielson's dying and the chanting of the monks, I can't disbelieve her; extraordinary things have happened here in the past and extraordinary things are still possible. I reluctantly admit that despite the grief around me, the possibilities this place presents fascinate me.

Marsh worked with Tea on the plumbing, devising a plan to provide an energy source for the valley from the gas produced by the unending abundance of night soil. Thibideaux and Terton worked to cure physical ailments, and the excavation crews, led by Dolma, continued to unearth new caches of objects that would be useful in supporting the community. So if the ancient kingdom of Shambala is no longer an earthly paradise, it is at least no longer a prison camp.

"The golden pagodas are in the past," I told the boy, who still didn't think that the chimes Thibideaux had found in the garden and restrung sounded just right and who was staring up at me critically. "Since the avalanche, Shambala has come down in the world." It wasn't a very good joke and I'm not even sure I said it correctly, since idiomatic expressions often don't translate very well. At any rate, the boy did not give me the smile I was trying to coax, but then I remembered that the child, like the rest of us, had seen enough to knock the levity out of anybody, and I tried a serious question instead. "Why would you want them to be gold?"

A cranky-looking woman, who is probably younger than she appears, hissed to him in Chinese, "Watch what you say or these people will think you haven't got the right karma after all to come here and they will throw you out."

"I have so got the right karma," the boy said. "I just thought it would be like the stories said."

The woman looked to me as if she was arguing with him because she too was disappointed. But that may be the result of trying so hard and being very tired and having lost a great deal.

Dr. Terton emerged from the door beneath the chimes, almost knocking me off the rock on which I was standing as I tried to hang them. "Everyone's karma is fine, I'm sure," Terton said to the woman and boy, and to me she said, "If you use a longer nail, Viveka, the chimes will ring more freely."

I hopped down from my stone. "This was the longest one I could find."

"I will ask the guardians for another nail for you," the cranky woman said. Our former guards are referred to as guardians, short for the Guardians of the Gate of Shambala, by the newcomers, not as soldiers. These people have no love of soldiers or uniforms, though many of them were guerrillas themselves. The woman's spurt of cooperativeness was a form of apology, as if she was a little afraid that her harshness had cast a dark shadow on her own karma.

"If you wish to see our golden pagodas," Dr. Terton told the boy, "wait for sunset, when the last rays kiss the bowl of Karakal."

"Sunsets are very common," the boy said.

"Not anymore," I said. "Not if the rest of the world is having nuclear winter." I felt a pit yawning inside me and the wind howl through my heart as soon as I spoke and regretted that I had reminded myself, as well as everybody else. Sometimes moments passed when I forget to try to imagine what it must be like out there now. What's gone? What remains?

"None of that will touch us," the doctor said.

"Excuse me, but with all due respect you can't know that, ma'am," Thibideaux said, voicing my own feeling. He and Merridew had been in the dispensary. The Colonel's hair is growing back and his scars are barely noticeable, though he still limps a little.

"Ah, but I can," Terton told Thibideaux, smiling.

"I've lived more lives than the fabled cat to take the precautions that ensure the security of this place. You see, it really is a top-security area, even if I meant something a bit different by the phrase from the way it was interpreted by others."

"I'm glad you get such a kick out of being mysterious," the Colonel told her, "but what we need right now is a little less hocus-pocus and a little more hard data. I have a man dead of old age who was certainly no more than thirty-five when he left here, we have a compound full of homeless people who claim they had a bomb dropped on them, in which case according to all scientific calculations, it is only a matter of time before the aftereffects descend on us, before the food we are growing and the water we are drinking are deadly and we will be just as dead as if we'd been sitting on ground zero."

"That is of course unless you're a top expert from the Pentagon's ultimate survivalist school," Thibideaux added. "In that case, you probably brought us here as a food source for yourself." He was teasing the doctor and the Colonel at the same time.

Terton acknowledged the attempt at lessening the tension with a warm flicker in her eyes but said, "There is much you don't understand, I know. We have had so much to do and so many to care for there has been no time for explanations. Besides, what I could tell you is not the kind of thing one can explain to multitudes over a portable loudspeaker. The Tibetan people, the Indians, even the Chinese are not so impatient as you Westerners. They don't know the details, of course, but for hundreds and hundreds of years they have known that something of this sort would happen. And, of course, one always believes in one's own survival, no matter who else is to die. Your culture actually has had stories of this time also, including the one about this place passed off by Mr. Hilton as popular fiction. But your people ceased to believe in such stories years ago, and so took no pains to prepare a haven or avoid the consequences of the collective karma of the world. That is, of course, an oversimplified and in some respects misleading statement, but nonetheless I believe I am correct in saying so."

"That would be just fine, ma'am, if we knew what the devil you're talking about," Merridew said.

"It would help if we could just *hear*," I said. The chimes, agitated by the wind, were clanging in one of my ears while the babble of voices and the clamor of cooking pots, the banging of hammers, the chopping of knives, the slapping of clay, the hiss of fire and water and the distraction of a half-naked brat bowling me over as it ran around trying to work off energy it should have expended many times over on the hike to Kalapa, made the doctor's soft voice difficult to hear.

The sky above the canopy was still blue, the snow still bannered from the mountaintops, and somewhere out of sight rumblings and mutterings still issued from the range, but the natural sounds were all but lost in the human cacophony.

Also, it seems to me that the doctor's voice has grown fainter and more quavery than when I first met her. Her movements are also somewhat less sure, though they have a surprising grace I failed to notice before. Her skin is less like leather now than onion skin. Of course, she is an old woman, and has not lived her whole life within these boundaries, and if anything could knock the stuffing out of anyone, I suppose the end of the world ought to be it.

"Come with me to the lake," she said. "It is good to see it between its shores again."

"There's a lot of work to be done, ma'am," Thibideaux said. "Lots of these folks are still in pretty poor shape."

"Their faith in Shambala will do more for them at the moment than your ministrations, young man," she said. "Come along."

The lake glittered beckoningly, children of the refugees splashing naked in its waters, whose colors mingled pale silver to cool aquamarine, rippling into clear turquoise, teal, and to a deep navy in the center. The lake is so broad and long that its entirety is visible only from the very crest of Kalapa, which is both the name of the city that once stood on this lesser mountain and the name of the mountain itself. Already the scrubby rhododendron bushes suck up the lake's moisture and have grown to four times their former height since the lake appeared. Though the lake filled the valley such a short time ago, it is as if the valley exists only as a vessel for its waters. The lake reminds me of an Arabic saying quoted often in *A Thousand and One Nights,* the Sir Richard Francis Burton version Grandma Viveka had kept from college. When something was very beautiful, the desert dwellers said, "It is cool to my eyes." The lake was like that in that figurative sense, as well as literally. It changed the entire character not only of the valley but the compound, and I understand now a little of Wu's bitterness toward us as the people she blamed for its loss. Well, now a bigger bomb has brought the lake back to her. It is a glory to behold.

Dr. Terton sat on a stone and motioned us to be seated around her, her gestures displaying a dancer's suppleness of wrist, palm and fingers. I sat between her and the lake, the breeze fluffing the hair off my face, tickling my neck with the tendrils that escaped from my braid.

The breeze smelled like flowers and fresh water. As the doctor talked, I fingered smooth pebbles, jade, amber and agate brown. I wondered if the stones had been there before the lake emerged or if they had gurgled up from below, riding the crown of the spring.

Soon the doctor was circled by Thibideaux, Marsh, Merridew and me and by some of the children, who stopped splashing and squealing, sensing a story. Tsering's daughter, Pema, was among these, and she sat as close to Merridew as she dared. She remembers who saved her from the lion.

Terton took a deep breath and began. "What has befallen the world must have come as a great shock to all of you. I know there is much you would like to ask and much you would like explained. Have you any particular questions?"

"Yes, ma'am," Thibideaux said. "Do you mean to tell us that what happened to the world did *not* come as a big shock to you too?"

"Not in the same way as it came to you. There were

warnings. Humanity has been preparing itself for this fate for quite some time, as you cannot be unaware. Also, according to our histories, all of this has been foretold. The only question for many years has been "When?" For us it is much as if a beloved but troubled friend has succumbed to a long illness. You know death is inevitable, and yet when the end comes, you are not really prepared for it. You never realize how much you will miss your friend, or what exactly he has meant to you until afterward. That sounds a bit like a poorly written popular love song, does it not? But without your friend's troubles to distract and instruct you, without *his* symptoms to contemplate, you are once more compelled to look at your own life, to dwell only on your own growth, without the mirror your friend provided or the insight you gained by seeing his progress on the paths he chose when you selected others."

"Yes, ma'am, that's just fine," the Colonel said. "Real poetic and all that, I'm sure. But we're talking about the whole *world* here."

She nodded. "Unfortunately, yes. More than one friend, then. Many. All of us here have had great losses, many losses. And you in particular have had so little preparation or teaching. There was no time, you see. I had to locate you and have you brought here, almost one by one. There were so many who might have come but they were not within my grasp. The most immediate necessity was to relocate you and to prepare this place once more as the haven it was intended to be. But there was no time for more than the most profound tests of your ability to bear this task, no time for instruction and training which you, Colonel, would no doubt have interpreted as 'brainwashing.' I had to arrange supplies and protection for us all. Just as I thought I could return and begin your instruction, when I at last had thought of a way to help you understand—" She shrugged. "The end came. I who have prepared for it through many lifetimes and who expected it generations ago was taken by surprise at how swiftly it fell upon us."

Merridew said, "This is a lot of crap. For all we know you could have set off fireworks back in the hills.

We don't know who you are really or who these people are. We've seen no signs of devastation, nothing to support your claims."

"Unless you count Danielson, sir," Thibideaux reminded him.

Marsh cleared his throat. "I can assure you, Colonel. What we saw wasn't fireworks." To Terton he said, "But what I'd like to know, ma'am, is just who in the hell are you really? What kind of damfool Chinese officer behaves the way you have?"

"Damfool Chinese officer is cover story of Ama Terton. She also has cover story that she is Mongolian Soviet officer and Indian army officer," Tea said, crawling out of a piece of yard-wide ceramic pipe that opened into the lake. He sat down between Terton and me, wiping his face, which needed it, with the tail of his shirt. "Ama Terton is the *Terton*—she is the finder, the gatekeeper. She is Bodhisattva—compassionate saint who stays in this world through many incarnations to help others."

"I've heard of them," Marsh said, looking bemused. "But I thought all of them got rich selling wisdom during the 1980s New Age craze and moved to big estates near Banff."

"If they got that rich, then they really must have been wise," I said. Nobody laughed. I knew all about bodhisattvas though—Grandma had always claimed she must be one to put up with Grandad. "Anyway, why don't you guys just shut up and let the woman talk? I for one would like to hear what she has to say, how and why she did this, why she brought us here, and just what this place is."

"Vanachek," the Colonel said wearily, "why don't *you* shut up? You've been compromised already. I know you don't understand; you're just out of your depth. You're a nice enough lady and all that but you're no trooper, you're a fucking civilian somebody had the stupidity to stick into a uniform. You can't tell the difference between infiltrating these people to get information and falling for the line of bull they put out. You are, excuse me, just too damned *female* to bear in mind who's your enemy."

Dr. Terton beamed at me. "Yes. It's one of her better qualities." But when her smile fell on him again, it changed and she looked from one of us to the other, anxiously for someone who is supposed to be serene (although, really, how easy would it be to be serene if you were supposed to be compassionately helping everyone to enlightenment? If your heart was really in it, it seems to me like a good way to be a nervous wreck). "Oh, dear," Terton said, "I can see this will be difficult to explain. I'm sure that although most Western theology doesn't include reincarnation, you are all familiar with the concept?"

Three curt, impatient nods.

"Good. You're probably also aware that many times a person is not reincarnated as a human being, but as some lower form. Or sometimes, if the person has worked through many lifetimes to a sufficiently enlightened state, they may achieve nirvana. There are other options as well—if you are a rather sociable person, as I have usually been throughout my lives, you may wish to have lots of company in enlightenment. I've always felt it would be so much pleasanter that way. And so some of us choose to keep returning in human form even though we have nothing to gain in a personally spiritual sense. The highest leaders and lamas of Tibet have always been bodhisattvas themselves, who as they die reveal clues as to their next incarnation. In the next body, they recognize aspects of their former lives that enable those who need them to identify them. Probably the best-known case, of course, was that of the Dalai Lama.

"There is also the matter of *tulkus*—or a partial transference, as you would say—"possessing" another body, or even a manifestation created from no material substance, but that is not what is happening here. No, since I gained enlightenment, I have been charged with a single duty throughout my lives and that is to prepare this place, once the Kingdom of Shambala, currently reduced to the city and valley of Kalapa, for this time of crisis.

"In order to accomplish this task, to empower, preserve, people, and rebuild this place as necessary, I have had to use many methods you might think unbecoming to an enlightened being. All I can say to that is, twaddle. When you have lived as many lives as I have you'll think nothing of it.

"The most unusual aspect of my mission has been that although I am always born in this place, most of my lives have necessarily been lived outside of it, where I age as any person ages. I wish I could say, as did the priest in Mr. Hilton's book, that I am hundreds of years old, but as a matter of fact I'm barely seventy, and I've had a rather stimulating rough life and show it, as do many of my countrywomen in comparable circumstances. In previous lives I have sometimes been able to return here and live for many years until duty drove me forth again, but often I've died young, having gathered at great peril certain persons and objects in need of preservation or needed by this place for its own preservation."

"How did you do that?" Marsh asked. "Why are we supposed to be 'preserved' here? Do you have one of those shields like the spaceships use in the science fiction vids?"

She blinked apologetically. "Nothing so easy for you to understand, I fear, Mr. Marsh. It would help so much if at least one of you was a more religious person. Then you might be more inclined to believe me when I tell you it has something to do with what you would call the 'power of prayer.' "

"You must remember that this place is very ancient. What we have uncovered since the avalanche is the merest crust of what it once was. Even in my first life, growing up here, I had no idea how deep the catacombs went or what was in the outermost rooms. But for hundreds of thousands of generations the holiest and best of my people have been chanting and praying for the preservation of this sanctuary. Which is fair, since the people who were here were all that time chanting and praying for the preservation of the human race, and most especially for the human spirit.

"Certain people, and you among them, have been

led to me and to this place by their particular path. That they, and you, have come here has been as much your own doing as mine. You three gentlemen, in placing the need to care for the souls and bodies of others above the need to preserve your own life, showed a certain aptitude for this sort of thing."

"But I'm no hero," I said.

"No, Viveka, but you are possessed of both a trusting and a giving nature, although your society rewards neither of those traits, and you have an inquiring mind which seeks to know things that many have forgotten. You were an unusual case. You did not first go to some dreadful torture camp like the others, but your dharma clearly led you straight to me and to this place."

I was glad it was clear to her. Here all this time I'd thought it was the plane crash that had brought me to Kalapa Compound.

"Can you not see, Mr. Merridew, that your suffering and isolation, once vital to your survival, now stand between you and the peace for which you have fought at such great cost to yourself? For a time it was necessary to your psyche that you regarded us as enemies, perhaps, but that time is now past. Perhaps you might consider that you are no longer acting from your own observations of us and your own best judgment so much as you are acting from the military tradition of your family. You are the latest, but I hope not the last, of a long line of honorable, selfless men who have given much to benefit others. In the past, the dharma of your ancestors and yourself has made your family valiant warriors, but the principles you uphold are equally valuable in our situation. Do you not find it foolish to continue to regard us as enemies when there is no longer a war?"

"My country right or wrong," Merridew muttered. In another minute he would have given her his name, rank and serial number.

"Your country right *and* wrong, I'm very much afraid, though the whole question has become rhetorical. But tell me, Mr. Merridew, you were a pilot. When you flew from one country to another on your airlift missions, did you notice as you flew over the land that it had great lines where boundaries were, or that the color changed, as on a map, as you flew across borders?"

"You said you would tell us what you were up to here, not ask a lot of damned nonsense . . ."

Like Marsh, the Colonel seemed to be reacting badly to our emancipated status.

"Colonel, if you'd just let her talk," I said.

"Vanachek, put a lid on it. You've been subverted."

"Come off it, sir. Don't you get it? There aren't any sides anymore. We're it. When I was hurting, you guys helped me. When you were hurting, we helped you. What did politics have to do with any of that?"

Marsh's voice was all the more bitter for its soft reasonableness, "There is the old trick of putting a woman in as a mole, getting everybody to talk. You've been pretty inquisitive, Viv."

"You don't think they could have come up with somebody a little more like Marlene Dietrich for the job?" I asked.

His mouth twisted into what was almost a smile. "Maybe there was no Marlene Dietrich with the right karma. Besides, anyone would look good after a while."

"That's why the men had strict orders not to touch you," the Colonel informed me.

"Is that it?" So I was an outcast by command, was I? And *he* was always making noises about me being friendly with the enemy. What did he expect if nobody else was supposed to have anything to do with me? So I responded in the way that kept me out of corporate boardrooms back on the NAC. "Gee, sir, and here I thought it was my deodorant. Or saltpeter in the momos. Just joking. I actually thought it was all of our scruples. If we find out they're telling the truth and the world has ended and we're pretty much immortal, can I at least have a hug? Two or three hundred years is a long time to live without being touched."

"Yeah. If you accept that this is Shangri-fucking-La," Marsh said with a cynical grin, "it sure is."

"Well, there's Danielson," Thibideaux said. "We need to bear in mind what happened to him. No gettin'

'round it, fellas, somethin' definitely irregular, unauthorized and plain fuckin' weird happened to Danielson
and that it happened because this is Shangri-La makes
about as much sense as anything. I think we may just
be having ourselves a little credibility gap here, if you
don't mind my saying so, because we thought when it
ended it would be with a big bang and not, as whoever
the famous sonofabitch was that said it said, with a whimper."

The Colonel glared at him, stood, and marched back
up the hill, his chest stuck so far out his shoulder blades
were in danger of meeting at his spine.

"He's not always like this," I apologized to the doctor, as an upper-class wife might explain to her hostess
that her husband generally held his substances better.
"I can't think what's eating him. I mean, all this time
we've been prisoners and now all of a sudden we're
free—relatively speaking."

"I suppose it was too much to hope he'd be pleased,"
Terton said.

"I don't think he believes you," Thibideaux said. "I
wouldn't myself, except for some of the things you've
showed me since he was injured and Danielson, of
course."

"He's in denial," Terton said, falling back on the
jargon of what was apparently only one of her professions.

"Nope," Marsh said, getting to his feet. "He's in the
same place he's been for the last you-only-know-how-
many years and has been thinking of it as a prison camp
and now you tell him it's paradise. How do you expect
him to react? It's like playing tug-of-war, hanging on to
your end of the rope as hard as you can and having the
other guys let go of their end. It's a little hard for any
of us to take. I just want to know a couple of things right
now. One, if this was supposed to be paradise, how come
you left a martinet like Wu in charge?"

"She had to learn to use her authority better than
those who once had authority over her, and also she is
a performer, and acting a role came more easily to her
than it did to the rest of the people who remained here
to receive you. I saw to it that none of the rigors you

suffered were more than would have been asked of a monk seeking enlightenment. The more difficult tests were not of her devising."

"She doesn't seem like much of a candidate for enlightenment to me. Why bring her here anyway? Did you do it to protect her? She's not your daughter, is she?"

"No, she's not my daughter. She has been my mother, however. She was once a very idealistic young woman, a television journalist, in Beijing. She had the courage to publicly support a student movement demanding government reform. When the soldiers overwhelmed the students, she was captured, tortured, slated for execution. I happened to be a private in the Chinese army at that time, a lowly Tibetan recruit, but I was her jailer. I freed her, and together we fled the city. I was wounded as we drove through a roadblock. It was a small wound, but in the days and nights that followed as I attempted to take her to friends on the Indian border, the wound festered. I spoke to her of my birthplace, of the friends who would help her, and told her how to find them. Finally, when I was too sick to move, she took the last of our food and left me to die. Later, she found Lobsang Taring and he led her back here. Within a few months, she gave birth to my next incarnation and I was once more born here."

If this startled Marsh, he didn't show it. "Okay," he said. "So Wu's your mama. Now, my next question is this. If we are in the only safe place left on earth, we're the last of the human race, right?"

"That has not been revealed to me, though logic would seem to suggest—"

"That's just what I thought," he said, and started walking back up the hill.

"Where you goin'?" Thibideaux asked.

"I'm going to get started on my traditional duty as one of the last men on earth. The war's over. Time for the repopulation part."

"I think I'd better get back to those sick refugees too," Thibideaux said. I rose and caught his arm and we took a few steps, out of Terton's earshot.

"Wait," I said. "Don't you want to hear what she has to say?"

"Cher, that old lady is a mighty fine doctor and there is somethin' funny happenin' here, I grant you. But all this stuff about the power of prayer and her rescuin' Wu and Wu bein' her mama after she died, that's a little crazy. I think all this has been a little strain on the old girl, you know? I don't know what happened to Danielson but I begin to wonder if Marsh is wrong and what we saw was really nuclear missiles."

"But why would they stage a hoax?" I asked.

"I don't know but I don't know why anybody'd deploy nukes either. Ain't nobody asked my opinion on any of this. So I'm gon' go back to my patients and think it over some more. Between doctorin' and that repopulatin' Marsh mentioned, I reckon to have my hands full for a good long while, and that's just in this life. I ain't thinkin' no further than that right now."

The doctor watched Marsh and Thibideaux leave with a somewhat pained expression and Tea, who had quite successfully made himself invisible after his initial comments, raised his eyebrows quizzically at me.

I shrugged. "They're upset and they're joking to cover it up, I think."

"No, no, it is a good idea," Terton said. "To think of conception instead of destruction. Very natural, very healthy. But I am afraid they do not entirely believe me."

"Well, as you said, doctor, it's easy for your people to believe in this stuff. They were raised on it. Most of my people are steeped in a belief in logic and reason. We aren't quite ready for the truth as you know it. You should have softened it up a little maybe. Given a little white scientific explanation of everything so it would have made sense to them." I appealed to Tea. "You're an engineer with a Western education. You know what I mean."

"Oh, yes, I know. But you, Viv, you are also a Western person. Are you believing Ama Terton?"

"I do believe in fairies, I do believe in fairies," I mumbled.

"Pardon?"

The doctor smiled at him. "Your education was neglected, Lobsang. She quotes the famous death scene of the Tinkering Bell from the child's story *Peter Pan*. In my fourth life, it was very popular in all Western countries and once a stage version was shown in Hong Kong. To save the Tinkering Bell, all children must aver their belief in fairies. The force of their collective will goes into the Tinkering Bell so that her soul is restored to her same body. It is very moving."

"It helps, Ama Terton, that you understand some of our stories too," I said. "These stories were already old and much disused when I was a child, but my grandparents and my mother held rather anachronistic views for their time and had many unfashionable books and videos for me to study. Would you understand the reference if I told you I feel now like Alice after she fell down the rabbit hole?"

The doctor thought for a moment, then shook her head. "That story too I may have heard in another life but this body's mind does not recall it."

POST–BIG BOOM,
DAY 40—REPOPULATION
(Late September or Early October 2070)

The doctor so far hasn't found another opportunity to tell me her complete story, though pieces of it come out on walks, in brief anecdotes, and in the stories told by the other former prisoners and guards. Sometimes the children pester her for stories about her past lives and she welcomes my listening, if I have time. But she's often busy in the evening and although I'm sure she has told some of the other former prisoners at least a portion of what she told us, I haven't talked about it to her or to them. As for the refugees, the legend of Shambala seems to be enough for them now, probably because dwelling in the more recent past is too painful, and thinking of the future impossible. Thibideaux, Marsh, and Colonel Merridew haven't discussed the doctor's story with me since the day by the lake.

Marsh and Thibideaux earnestly pursue the repopulation campaign, and Marsh in particular has been steadfast in his determination that the maximum number of possible mothers be the recipients of his efforts. This has presented a few problems.

I found him one day in the far end of the valley sitting by a streamlet that fed into the lake. The late rhododendrons were in bloom—something blooms all the time in the valley now, and I thought I would pick a bunch to please Dolma, whose spirits had failed lately, perhaps because of the presence of so many children. Marsh sat in a spot so well sheltered by rhododendron tangle that I almost missed seeing the flash of his orange uniform until I heard mysterious splashing sounds. Parting a few more tangled branches. I saw him sitting on the bank throwing rocks at the fish, trying to stun them.

"Cease fire!" I called out, ducking through the brush. He shushed me, and with exaggerated stealth looked around. "You weren't followed?"

"Not that I know of. I didn't exactly know I was coming here until I got here. What are you doing killing these innocent, and possibly rare fish? Don't you realize they should be encouraged to spawn or whatever it is that fish do so we can get more fish? God only knows how they found their way here. You don't suppose they've been nuked, do you, and will have mutant swamp monster offspring? Speaking of which, how's the repopulation program going?"

He groaned. "I hope you're not here to volunteer. Not that I'm turning you down, you understand, because at least I'm dead sure that you're female, but I really think you and the other women ought to get together and straighten out that refugee group. I can't be sure, but it looks to me like all the boys under the age of forty are gay. At least after I approached a couple of women I thought might be interested, I started getting these languishing looks from those guys. I'm as broad-minded as the next guy but seriously, if we are going to colonize this place, everybody is going to have to do his or her part and that means laying aside—"

I couldn't help it. I giggled.

He grinned. "Bad choice of words. I mean that I think we should set aside personal predilections until we are knee-deep in squalling brats."

"What an attractive way you have of putting things," I said. "But you know, from something Dolma told me, even going on the assumption that every woman producing lots of children is going to be a good thing, there may be a problem."

I started to tell him about how Dolma lost her baby when rattling brush announced the arrival of two boys who looked slyly at Marsh and tittered behind their hands.

He stared pointedly in the other direction. I had the funniest inclination to avoid rudeness at all costs and began trying to chat with the boys, but my conversation was of no interest whatsoever to them. One started to touch Marsh on his deliberately turned back and I said quickly, "Perhaps I can help you. Mr. Marsh is—uh—deep in thought. What was it you wanted?"

They tittered some more.

Marsh turned around, having apparently had time to gather patience, and asked in Chinese, with all the diplomacy he no doubt had gathered on peace missions, "How can I help you fellows?"

In English I smirked, "Remember, Marsh, studs are a dime a dozen but you're a remarkable person," and started to leave the young folks alone but Marsh grabbed my elbow in a bruising grip. I pretended to shrink from him and to the boys said, "Oooh, watch out, guys, he's an animal."

"We want make babies with you," the bolder of the two said.

"Me? Or her?" he asked.

"Do you suppose 'make babies' is the local euphemism for copulation of all descriptions?" I asked, tickled with my own owlishness and his discomfort. Marsh is always so in control, so deliberate, that it was great cruel fun to see him squirm.

"Who is she?" the bold boy pouted.

"You can speak freely in front of her," he lied. "We've been living together for some time now, haven't we, honey?"

"Right, my poppet, but there's no need for me to be selfish about it. These boys—"

One of the "boys" abruptly pulled "his" shirt off, displaying more-than-adequate-for-nursing breasts. "Not boys," she said, in case the gesture hadn't already amply proved her point.

"I guess not," he said, whistling appreciatively, which was more than usually effusive of him but I suppose was intended to make up for his former lack of enthusiasm. "Which of the many perils females imagine they face that men don't were you two avoiding with this ruse?"

The women looked at each other and shrugged. He had forgotten himself and lapsed into English.

"Sterilization?" I ventured, using a complex mixture of the Tibetan words I knew that I thought might mean that. The girls nodded.

"Yes," the shirtless one replied in Chinese, in which she seemed more fluent than in Tibetan. "Many other ladies also pretend to be boys. It has been the custom in our villages for some time. The *philing* invaders wondered once how there came to be young ones when there were so many men and so few women. Someone said we must be hermaphrodites and so our village has been jokingly called since." To Marsh she said quickly, "But we are not hermaphrodites. We are normal women. We want babies and there are few men among us who are not close kin. You aren't bad, for a Westerner. And you're sure not a relative. How about it?"

I excused myself and left Marsh to defend his own honor.

PBB, DAY 45 (probably mid-October 2070 by old reckoning)—THIBIDEAUX

Most of the time I stick to my old prisoner schedule, spending every other day belowground helping Tea excavate, and alternate days in the garden, clearing my lungs and thinning vegetables. The plants grow in greater profusion all the time, like the bottomless purse in old fairy tales. Another small herd of yaks, six in all, and five deer have somehow found their way into the valley. They are kept in pens and guarded carefully from the snow lions, and one of the yaks and several of the domestic animals have been carefully sacrificed to leave as offerings for the cats so they won't starve. Tsering wanted to recapture them but Terton, familiarly called Ama-La by the Tibetans, vetoed the idea. The cats are half grown now and wouldn't survive, she said—which is certainly true, especially if Tsering has anything to do with it. The valley looks like an old nature film, fast forward from planting to harvest, exaggerated animated springtime quickening to life over and over.

Tea works harder than ever, and every day we make new discoveries which add to our resources. Last week we opened another passageway and found, not another series of storage cells, but two huge rooms. In one were spinning wheels and enough bales of wool, bowls of cotton, and bats of silk to satisfy Rumpelstiltskin. The raw fleece basketed in one corner still smelled nauseatingly strong of lanolin and ancient sheep shit. In the other room looms hulked up like robotic monsters and shelves and baskets were filled with yarns so dusty the colors were impossible to tell apart, bits of vegetable matter and a witch's laboratory full of what I imagine were dyes and mordants, since they were shelved near a hodge-podge of large ceramic and enameled pots. Further along, oh joy, oh happiness, was the longed-for room of farm implements and gardening tools. Why they were not put next to the seeds is beyond me. So much for the all-knowing wisdom of Shangri-La.

Still, my chief consolation, recreation and hiding place remains the library. Last night after a long day in the garden (I had to weave myself a hat of barley stalks— my nose is brighter red than the reddest of the rhodies in the valley) I crept down the cool foot-worn stone stairs of the command bunker, previously so frightening, and with my butter lamp in hand slipped down the chilly, dusty passages which smell less like incense and sweat and more like freshly butchered wood and mildew these days. No one forbids us to go anywhere now, although most of us stay within the compound at night because of the snow lions. I needed to flee from that mass of people crowding, jostling, crying, arguing, laughing and screwing, and lose myself in a nice sane book.

It was not to be.

The glow and distinctive stench of two butter lamps greeted me as I opened the door. A figure huddled in the shadows between the lamps and the shadows jumped like jack-in-the-boxes as pages flipped in the book the figure held before it.

I was greatly tempted to ignore the figure and isolate myself behind a huge stack of Tibetan language reference books, but then I noticed that the hand nearest me was making big sweeping gestures across the surface of the table so I walked a step closer and Thibideaux glanced up. He looked no happier to see me than I was to see him, so of course I had to make conversation.

"Hi. What are you doing?"

"Trying to find something that shows the order of colors on a peacock feather," he said. Once a bird person always a bird person, I thought.

"Oh?"

"Yeah. I got to thinking about it. Something reminded me, I don't know—oh yeah, the colors on the lake this evening—and I thought, that's just like a peacock feather only the colors are in another order. But I couldn't remember the order and none of the books here seem to have a color close-up."

"Too bad."

"Yeah. Ain't it? Because there are no peacocks here and if the rest of the world is kaput, there are no peacocks anywhere anymore. Shame for a kid to never know about somethin' as pretty as that. And the same kinda thing is going to make it hard to talk to them about other things, unless it's in these books. Maybe they won't miss it but . . ." His voice trailed off.

I nodded slowly. He was right. The children born here would have a totally different frame of reference, even, than the children born in the villages. The generation gap between them and the adults would be a doozy, even though we wouldn't look too much older than they would once they grew up (I'm sure they do grow up—Pema's been growing as fast as the crops), since we supposedly will age very slowly. The world we knew is gone, I suppose, and the proper attitude with the kids should be "Long live the world" as we'll come to know it. But it's going to be a tight little, constricted little world, limited even in the memories of those of us who are left, and that makes me sad.

"I guess there's not much we can do about it, is there?" I asked.

"I dunno," he said. "I always been real good at art. I'm goin' to start drawin' everythin' I can remember. Maybe get the rest of the folks to do it too, or help me draw things for them. Give me somethin' to do once everybody gets well. Doctorin' is pretty slow around here most times. Somethin' else. These underground rooms are fine but I can't help feelin' like this place is still a prison because it *looks* like one. Soon as things settle down a little, I'm goin' to make me some plans and see about buildin' some proper houses and such around here."

I think Thibideaux's attitude is commendable as hell. I admire the industry of the refugees. I respect the stated motives of Dr. Terton and the other compound administrators, but right now I'm downstairs in our old cell, writing by the light of my little lamp like I used to do. Sometimes I just need to stay the hell away from everybody. I'm happier working by myself these days, without even Dolma or Tea around. When I'm not needed I study or read in the library, though sometimes I find myself weeping uncontrollably over a book for no apparent reason except to think that Huck's river and the island and Agatha's and Sherlock's London and all of the other places and people are gone forever. Which is silly because they were gone forever by the time I was born, in the sense that they appeared in the books.

Perhaps in some ways it would have been easier if the loss was more personal for me, but I have no one specific to grieve for, unless you count Sammy maybe. But I don't think of her dead but still wearing that stupid hat, conning me with her Calvinist-rooted no-nonsense psychology into enlisting. My mother, my grandparents, have been dead for years. I believe I mentioned earlier that a virus killed my grandparents. I always wondered about that virus. It seemed particularly to hit people in their late sixties and early seventies, people with good minds and still a lot to offer but who continued to embrace an outdated value system. My mother didn't outlive them by many years. I had barely enough money to see me through four full-time years of college and graduate school before they upped the fees, and from then on I was always scrambling for cash. No real friends. No long-term lovers.

But even though nobody special is left behind, everybody seems special now. I wish I'd known them better. I wish I'd told that one history prof how illuminating I found his remarks. I wish I'd told Sammy to fuck off. I just can't help thinking what their faces must have been like when they saw the flash, not from a protected distance, as I did, but close up, just before they turned into human X-rays and ashes, in that moment they had to realize "This is it." The big one. Surprise, surprise. You didn't have to be in the military after all to be at risk. Or did you? Was NAC, somehow, shielded? I guess I'll never know. So. What do I do? Live out my elongated span in this small place enclosed by mountains among a lot of very strange people.

I guess I know how the Colonel feels, at least a little. Somehow, it was easier to keep going in the prison camp, where even if my life was limited, it was still just one kind of life in a big and varied world—some people were much better off than I was, some not as well off. But that this is *all* there is, maybe all there will ever be . . .

PBB, DAY 60—TARING AND THE TERTON

I've stayed aboveground lately, and I suppose I've overdone the gardening bit. Guess it's part of my grieving. I keep seeing my grandfather's hands doing what mine do and find myself bawling into the radish bed. This morning was warm and hazy and I kept working, hours it must have been, until once when I reached up to wipe my eyes, in the moment that they were closed, I heard a roaring in my ears that sounded like the foghorn chanting I'd heard so long ago in my cell, and behind my closed lids points of light glittered in a deep maroon darkness. Not keen on being the first case of heatstroke in Kalapa, I washed my hands in what was left of the water for the plants, dumped the rest of the containerful on a grateful bean vine, and decided to retire to the library for the rest of the day. Lately when I've read I've sought a rock by the lake or headed for the cheerful solitude of the stream in the rhododendron jungle, but today the idea of the library's darkness and cool seemed more attractive.

Once more, someone had beat me to my sanctuary and sat laughing softly at what lay between the widespread covers of a largish book. But this time the light was better and even if it hadn't been, the laugh was a giveaway.

"Tea, what are you up to? Research?" I called as I walked toward him.

"Of a sort," he said, swallowing chuckles long enough to answer me. "Come and look. Look at this funny fellow."

I looked. He pointed to one of several head-and-shoulders portraits in what appeared to be a yearbook. The one he indicated had a shaven head, prominent cheekbones, a distinctly Asian cast to his features and a bad case of acne.

"You?"

"Yes. From Montana School of Mines. Not a former life, you see, but it is sometimes seeming so."

"Might as well be," I said, unable to match his mood. "The Montana School of Mines is no more. Like everything else."

"Almost everything else."

"Tea, how can the doctor be so sure the aftermath of the bombs won't reach us here? I mean, prayer is all very well but there was one avalanche already . . ."

"Yes, the one that is occurring when His Holiness, the last Dalai Lama died, and Shambala was more needing than ever of protection and concealment. We believe that this was a beneficial occurrence—anyway, Ama-La and some of the rest of us so believe. It was coming as a great shock to Nyima. She wants everything to be unchanging, always. Me, her, Ama-La, the lake. Like your Colonel Merridew, she is liking to keep her enemies in their place and her friends as well."

"Do you believe all this karma stuff and people living a really long time or one life after another? I mean, I know it's your religion and Dr. Terton is one of your leaders, your lama I guess, but do you really believe all that stuff?"

In answer he turned the cover of the yearbook toward me. Across the padded fake leather it said, *Montana School of Mines, Class of 1969.*

"Well, the long-life part, I guess you do," I said, pretending that the revelation didn't affect me at all, that I really didn't care that the man was almost as old as my grandparents and looked no older than I was. "But I just don't understand all this karma stuff. Who came and why.

I mean, why Danielson, for instance? Why should he be chosen to come here and be a prisoner until he died trying to get out?"

"We don't always know why, Viva," he said just a little impatiently. "We are just people, you know. Not some sort of gods or Superman heroes. Maybe Danielson was here so he would not kill other important people. Maybe he was here to learn something vital to his soul before he died. Maybe he was here just to be what he was to those people at his funeral—the representative of all they had lost and the death of the glory of war. But I know that he was here preparing for his next incarnation, as we all are for ours."

"Is *that* why I'm here?"

He surprised me by turning to me and taking my shoulders in his hands and saying with a laugh, "You are here, my dear Viv, to be asking a lot of questions everybody else is wondering and no one else is asking. Your purpose is very clear, and has always been very clear to me. You are a bridge, and though sometimes you sway in the wind as you try to take the weight of the world upon you while spanning all the time of this place and all of the lives and concerns of the people, you have been a very strong bridge. And you know, do you not, that a bridge is a very dear thing to the heart of an engineer?"

We talked all afternoon, sitting in the deep shadows of the library, paying no attention as the kitchen crew trudged back and forth from the old dining hall with food for the people outdoors, sitting in darkness for a time when the generator droned to a halt for the night and the work lights blinked off. A little later, I lit a butter lamp so that I watch it gleam on his eyes as he talks and cast shadows across the moon craters of his face.

He had been born in Kalapa, as he told me, and studied to be a monk of the religion of Shambala, which is not precisely the same thing as Tibetan Buddhism, but a mixture of that and a sort of universalist creed born out of a powerful respect for all other faiths mixed with an intellectual study of how spirituality affected people living in the world.

"But I was curious about many things practical as

well as spiritual, and when the Chinese invasion looked as if it was going to be a permanent thing, my lama and the Terton who now wears the body of Ama-La told me that I must leave the lamasery, at least in an exterior sense, and depart Shambala for a time to be an emissary to the Tibetan people, an ally to the Dalai Lama. I would assist the Terton in bringing to Kalapa those who were necessary.

"To that end, shortly after the Chinese takeover in 1959, at the age of eighteen (give or take a year or two, time sense being blurred as it is here in Kalapa) I walked over the pass and continued walking until I met a band of immigrants. They thought I was a bandit at first and feared me, but I had grown so skinny that as soon as they got a good look at me they decided that if I was a bandit I was certainly not very good at it, so they allowed me to travel with them."

On the journey to Dharmsala, he encountered death for the first time, when a child and then its mother died of hunger and exhaustion. "It was much a surprise to me," he said simply, staring into the flame of the lamp. "I knew that they would return but somehow, that did not make me feel better, then, when her other children cried for their mother and her husband grieved for his wife and the infant, who was his only daughter. More died of hunger, and of the change in climate when some of us were moved to the southern plains of India to farm. More died on road gangs. I myself was rescued from this by the intervention of foreigners. Kalapans are naturally somewhat taller than average for Tibetans and when the American CIA found it expedient for a time to assist the Tibetan cause, I was chosen to train as a guerrilla."

He laughed ruefully. "I very much enjoyed flying above the clouds as if I was much more advanced spiritually than merit had earned me, and your Colorado Rocky Mountains were very nice, what you would call a homey touch, although of course I was not supposed to know that was where we were training. What I did not care for was the shooting practice and the suspicions they wished us to entertain of everyone, even of our own families. Avoiding the aspects I disliked, I made myself useful instead as a mechanic of airplanes and jeeps and displayed a great interest in the flora and fauna and the minerals.

"One of the Americans who was training us, the first to call me Tea, was also most interested in minerals, particularly silver and gold. I told him we had much gold and silver where I came from and he thought I meant Tibet.

"Later I returned with the others to Dharmsala but when they were selected for a mission, I was not. To tell you the truth, I hid from those who came for us. I preferred to work on old automobiles. As a guerrilla I was a failure. But then I was found out and one day while I was beneath a car, a man came to talk to me. I only saw his feet. His shiny black shoes were muddy from the road. He said to me that it was arranged that I would go back to America to study geology, engineering and mining, that this had been arranged by interested parties and that it was the wish of His Holiness that I serve him and Tibet in this fashion.

"At that time, in the Montana School of Mines, no one knew where Tibet was so I wore a T-shirt made by one of our little home industries. It said *Free Tibet*. One of my classmates asked me where a person could acquire a free tibbet and what it was. This was also during the early years after the American involvement in Vietnam, you understand. Many of your people were very mad at Asian people of any country. I spoke to my classmates of how it was for my countrymen in Tibet and of my journey and life in exile in India and they came to know me and to understand a little so that by the time I graduated, although I missed my people very much, I was sad to leave the school too.

"When I returned to Dharmsala, I wondered why I had gone to mining school, because instead of working as an engineer, I was instructed to train a new guerrilla group which was to infiltrate Tibet behind the Chinese occupation lines. I spent many years waiting for something to happen, losing one friend after another as our team dwindled until finally I alone waited, ostensibly as a Tibetan interpreter for the Chinese. I should have paid

closer attention in spy school because despite what was
going on around me I was still very trusting. Then one
day, I learned firsthand one of the many hardships to
which my people were subjected. I decided I should
have a wife and I married a young girl in Shigatse, of
good family connected with the Panchen Lama. Our
child was butchered by the Chinese, my wife mutilated . . ."

His voice wavered as he said this and he stared hard
into the candle flame.

Wonderingly, I realized that I had heard that story
before from another viewpoint, "Dolma?" I asked. "You
and Dolma were married?"

He nodded.

"But your names are different. You call her Miss."

"Naturally she felt I had betrayed her and when she
was stronger, after her ordeal, I used both the sages who
dreamed of Shambala and my guerrilla connections and
returned with her to a family I knew within one of the
villages that were the vestiges of the eight cities surrounding Kalapa. We have provisions for divorce, although they are not frequently practiced, and it was her
wish that we divorce, so we did. Since then, she has
come to see that I was as ignorant as she, and we are
very good friends and family of a sort. But she cannot
forget entirely, of course. We are not Buddhas here yet."

"Then you never really became a monk?"

"No, it was not my destiny. When I brought Dolma
back here, I learned that the Terton had died in the
Golmo labor camp, beaten to death by his fellow prisoners in a *thamzing* session.

"When next I saw the Terton she was a little girl,
only six years old, and it was my task to help her return
to Beijing, from which her mother had come before she
was sent to Golmo, where she had tried to aid the previous Terton. The little girl was already very wise, and
clearly, although her body was still a child's, her spirit
was that of our Terton. She did not weep when I handed
her over to our Chinese agent, but her eyes searched
each pore of my face and every feature of the landscape
along the trail, memorizing it.

"She did not find me again until fifteen years later and by that time she was a dying young woman and the soul of the Terton drained from her eyes before I could speak to her.

"With her was another injured girl who did not talk and who moved very little, but who lived. The Terton had given her life to deliver that girl to me so that I could take her to Shambala, so once more I made the trek through the mountains.

"By that time I was nearly fifty years old and it was much more difficult. I came here and have not left from that day to this.

"The girl slowly awoke from her shock and grief and would trust no one but me. Her friends and her husband had been executed. I think she had had to help kill some of them, perhaps including her husband, as part of her torture. And then the others who had shared with her such a faith that their government would not harm them and so many ideals, these friends were turned loose on her. On the eve of her execution Terton, who had hidden herself in the army and become the girl's jailer, smuggled her away and brought her to me, though, as I said, at one point they were nearly captured and the Terton received the mortal blow that in time claimed her life.

"I failed to understand for some time why Terton had brought the girl to me. However bravely she had once behaved, her spirit was broken, she would not speak or cry and had to be fed and taken to the toilet. She cringed if anyone but me came near her. In time, however, she grew a little better. Her wounds healed, the beauty of Kalapa soothed her, and her own beauty grew. I began to love her, and she would have no one else near her. She was a very glamorous woman in China. She had a career in media, was both an intellectual and a celebrity. She had been married three times, divorced twice. He third husband was the one whose execution she was forced to witness. All this came out gradually, and the last came out when she asked me if I would marry her and stay with her, so she would not be alone and afraid again. I married her. We had a daughter, and with her, the Terton returned to Kalapa."

"So you're Ama-La's father?"

He nodded. "She was with Nyima and me in the country visiting Dolma when the avalanche occurred."

It had occurred to me more than once from the tender way they behaved toward each other that Tea and Terton might be related, Tea her grandson perhaps, but now I began to see the whole timelessness concept in a very personal light. Despite what great assholes they are sometimes, I do care very much about the other men, my countrymen, my fellow prisoners, but I quite simply like Tea better and always have. It's partly his gentleness and his humor, and even the disarming goofy accent, but it's also because he has been the one since the beginning who explained things to me and shared things with me. I've identified less with the other prisoners because Tea at least has never treated me like a prisoner. Well, hell. I loved my grandparents a lot but I never thought I had such a thing for *much* older men. A great-grand-Electra complex?

"Does it disturb you that such a venerable person is my daughter?" he asked.

"Umm, aspects of it, yes," I admitted.

"There then, you see why I have not been able to tell you everything before this? Before there was a need for you to know about Shambala it would have been very confusing to try to explain. The Terton is simply not like the rest of us. Though in different bodies, she is always the same child, whether male or female, the same young person, and if she lives so long, the same adult. Her soul has been incarnated so many times it needs very little refinement. It is her task that keeps her among us. So although biologically I am her father, she is still my most revered teacher and leader. And yet I still remember that little body trembling in my arms that day as we ran as fast as we could back toward the city, to see it sliding with pieces of the mountain into the lake. We did not dare go closer. Those who could flee had fled and the whole valley was full of stones bouncing like a child's ball and the dust and water spraying high into the air. Our mountain, our protector, which had shielded us since the earth first cooled enough to sustain life, toppling in upon us, its crown falling as effortlessly as that of a sand dune in a high wind.

"As soon as the earth settled enough to risk it, we began digging out our friends and relatives but we could save very few. We had no heavy equipment, you see, since we could never use aircraft to bring things here— it all had to be packed on the backs of men or animals. Those who were injured healed very slowly and that was when our little Terton understood that in this incarnation she was to be Ama-La. Our medical college was destroyed and all of the doctors, save one, were killed. The one remaining had been pinned beneath a building, crushing one of his arms and severing the other arm at the elbow.

"Our climate is such, so healthy, the water so beneficial, that he survived, but he was no longer able to diagnose by the pulse or to use his hand for healing. The little one learned all he had to teach before he died, a few years later. By the time she announced she would study in Dharmsala, she already knew more than most of her teachers.

"You have seen the simulation of the damage and the earliest photographs so you have some idea of what we were up against in trying to dig out our city. We were so few. Our lake, not just a water supply but the Jewel in the Eye of the Lotus, was swallowed by the earth, the most dire of all possible omens. If we could not somehow repair this damage, our mission had failed and we would be able to save no one. I feared we were doomed, that more bombs would weaken our borders and that we would die as Tibet was dying, without accomplishing our purpose, without saving a piece of the world and a remnant of humanity to begin again when the world destroyed itself.

"Nyima mourned more deeply, perhaps, even than those of us who were born here. She wandered among the ruins and rocks like a forlorn ghost, her eyes ever staring at the cleft in our mountain or into the barren moonscape where our shining jewel had been. Her eyes reddened and grew dull as if they actually, physically thirsted for a glint of water where water should certainly be. Ama-La, when she visited, tried to comfort her, but my wife would not be comforted.

"At last Ama-La, already playing mother to her own mother, helped Nyima to cry and then to become angry at those who had destroyed her second home even more thoroughly than her first had been destroyed. 'They should have to pay,' Nyima said. 'If I could, I would make them fix this.'

"Ama-La just smiled at her and said, 'Your idea has merit. I'll arrange it.'

"When next we saw her, she was leading a group composed of a few of our young people who had gone to serve Tibet and so missed being killed in the avalanche, along with two or three uniformed Soviet soldiers, all very sick from the altitude, and six half dead Chinese she had, in her capacity as a high-ranking Soviet officer, 'transferred' from the abysmal conditions in their Siberian camp to this place, for which she had forged papers to indicate that it was the top-security death camp you know and love so well." His mouth twisted ironically but his eyes smiled as he rubbed the back of my cold hands with his own work-roughened palm.

"She brought us weapons too, to maintain the cover, but also medicine and food, since our storage cellars and our tillable soil were buried beneath the peak of our sacred mountain and the ruin of our sacred city.

"The newcomers took a long time to recover enough to work. The Soviets had come as guards and at first seemed to feel that it was expected that they bully the rest of us, particularly the Chinese prisoners. That was when Nyima assumed her role as commandant. Because of her ability as a television actress, as a journalist for the People's Republic had to be at that time, she could speak very harshly while at the same time discouraging harsh actions. She made the rule that only our own people were to carry weapons, most of them not loaded with live rounds, though her own sidearm and a rifle or two were kept ready for attacks by wild animals, more numerous at the time and attracted by the odor of death that still hung like poison gas over our valley."

"I'm surprised we haven't found any bodies," I said.

"The rooms we have uncovered so far are all surface rooms," he said. "The people ran outside, as you saw. There are many bodies, I am sure, beneath the lake, beneath the jungle in the valley. But those who died on the slope we recovered at once, or else they were so utterly destroyed that you have dusted their bones from your hands without realizing it. We lost a few more people during the initial efforts to locate bodies, for any loud noise would cave in new sections of ceiling. That was when Nyima issued strict orders against firing the weapons, yelling or screaming—or causing anyone to scream—when beneath the surface."

I grunted noncommittally. Wu could single-hand-edly reverse the damage of the avalanche by divine intervention and I still wouldn't think of her as one of my favorite people, but maybe she does have a few redeeming qualities. Subtle ones. At least her background explains why I had such mixed reactions to her role as a martinet. She may be an actress but she's particularly convincing.

"With the help of these people we were able to clean out some of the underground rooms and make quarters for ourselves and for them. The Terton established the helicopter route and those of us with the training for the trek to the edge of Shambala formed the pack trains to meet the shipments at the drop-off point.

"Later, the Terton returned many times, sometimes as a Russian, sometimes as an Indian, sometimes a Chinese. Always bringing a few more people when she came and sometimes simply sending them to us, with the supply train, having hypnotized them into making the walk. This she did with you and most of your friends. The first one she brought was Sergeant Danielson, followed by the Colonel, then Mr. Marsh and Dr. Thibideaux."

"How long ago was that?"

"Sergeant Danielson came to us with the second batch of prisoners, the first among the group she brought from the Chinese camp. He was not, you understand, a young man when he came to us. Our climate was quite healthy for him and he appeared much younger than his true age when you met him. I would guess he was in his mid-fifties. And he was with us many many years. The Colonel was not a young man when he came here either . . ."

PBB, DAY 46—MERRIDEW

Crisis time. Merridew had just enough understanding of our new freedom, apparently, to take advantage of it by finding out that the blond Russian woman, Tania Enokin, is a former mountain climber, quizzing her on the hazards of this particular sport getting her advice on which equipment to use, swiping the gear she recommended from the locker room, and abducting Dr. Terton. Apparently, when Tania witnessed the abduction and objected, he knocked her out and left her in the coatroom.

Dolma first discovered the missing gear when she did her weekly inventory. Then Tsering and Pema, who had been looking for Merridew, couldn't find him—or Samdup's side arm. Finally, Wu could not find Dr. Terton to ask her advice on all these irregularities and when Tea and Dolma rushed back to the coatroom to don enough gear to try to follow Merridew, they uncovered Tania hidden under the blanket where scarves, hats and mittens are spread out to dry.

Tania was the one who confirmed, most indignantly, that Merridew had taken the old lady hostage. "He left last night," she told us. "He wanted me to help him but after I gave him advice on what to take, how to tackle the rough spots, he said to me, 'I am traveling light or I would take you along, young lady.' As if I cannot go by myself if I wish! I am at first very angry but then I think, foolish man to try it alone, with his limp and those other recent injuries. Still, I go with him to help him pick out equipment. But the old lady interrupted us—not as if she was going to stop us, just in that curious way she has about her. He pulled a gun and pointed it at her, ordering her to attire herself to accompany him. I tell him that this is crazy, and he says that no one will follow him if she is his hostage, and that I should not worry, he will bring help that will release all of us. I try to talk to him, to make him relinquish the gun, but he looks at me as if I am the one who is crazed and then he *hits* me."

"We must stop them before they reach the border of Shambala," Tea said, tucking his snowsuit pantlegs into the tops of winter boots as he talked.

Marsh and Thibideaux, who were there because we had asked them to help us find Merridew, grabbed parkas and snowsuits from the racks and pulled them on too, insisting that Tea shouldn't go after the Colonel alone. "You'll have better luck talking him down if we go with you," Thibideaux said.

"And I will go," Wu said. "If necessary, I will exchange myself for Ama-La. It is me that the Colonel blames."

I like her a little better for that, especially now that I realize that so much of her frostiness is because she's skating on such thin ice, mentally.

"And I will go," Tsering said. "I am a good climber."

Pema insisted on coming too. She all but worships the Colonel and I think she's afraid he'll be hurt. And he might.

The upshot of it is, I'm going too, in case Tea's right about me being a bridge. I would prefer that nothing happen to the Colonel or Terton or Tea—or anyone else—and if there's anything I can do to prevent it, I want to be there to do it. I never thought I'd do that trip again unless someone was chasing *me*. Anyhow, there's only time to write this down while the others are dressing and then we're off.

PART NINE

PBB, DAY 120 (Approximately)—
NEW YEAR'S DAY, OLD TIME 2071

⚸ It's over. It was a long chase and a long, sad return trip, but it is, beyond a doubt, all over.

They had a good head start but they were, after all, a limping man and an elderly woman. We almost caught up with them several times, or rather the front runners did, and those of us farther back heard about it by relay. Tania, Tea, Thibideaux, Tsering and Samdup, the fittest and fastest, led and were soon miles ahead of all of those of us who trailed behind, including Wu, Dolma, and me. Dolma could have traveled with the advance group but Pema was with us and would not be left behind. Dolma stayed behind to help her. Long ago, back on the NAC, I would have locked her in her room and told her to shut up, but Dolma swung Pema up piggyback and I strapped the child to her. Dolma trotted along with her as if the little girl was a sack of barley.

Once when we stopped for a few minutes, I looked up to see Pema pointing at something with one hand while patting Dolma's shoulder to get her attention with the other; meanwhile, Dolma was pointing in a different direction with her walking stick and gesturing with her opposite hand. I had the oddest feeling I was staring at a picture of one of those multiarmed statues come to life.

The trip was both harder and easier for me this time. Harder, of course, because I was doing it consciously, without the mixed blessing of Ama-La's hypnotic spell, and also harder because we pushed ourselves to keep going before and after the best light of the day and through the strongest winds, trying to catch up with the Colonel and Ama-La. But it was also easier this time because I was in better shape—I breathe easily in the thin air now, and the gardening has developed my legs so that with little more than a pleasurable stretch in the backs of my legs, I can climb inclines which once would have stopped me cold. Also, this time I was among friends and we helped each other, if in no other way than by our very intensity reminding one another of the gravity of the reason we were traversing ridges of blowing snow and long, avalanche-blocked valleys rather than remaining in the relative safety of the compound.

On the third day of the trip, we paused to drag our midday ration from the folds of our clothing and to eat a few hurried bites while Pema gave Dolma's back a rest. She had remounted and Dolma was adjusting the pack straps when Tania came sliding down the snow meadow into which we were about to ascend. It had snowed the night before and the tracks of the forward party were half filled, and Tania looked legless as with each step she took she slid down, hip-deep, another few feet closer, snow spraying in high wide arches on either side of her body.

"We've spotted them," she told us. "I am supposed to let you know and to lead you forward. The pass is very treacherous. A small slide half buried Keith Marsh this morning and there are whole sections of trail missing." To Dolma she said, "The child must walk by herself now."

Dolma shook her head and deliberately tightened the strap binding Pema to her. Tania shrugged as elaborately as she could, bundled as she was, and turned her back on us, returning through the ditch her body had made as it plowed toward us.

Once we climbed the meadow and into the pass at its head, I kept my eyes glued on the trail, glancing away only far enough to note the position of Wu, who preceded me. Dolma and Pema preceded her.

When the path narrowed even farther Dolma un-hitched Pema and we roped ourselves together and inched sideways down the steep face of the mountain.

Straight across from us was another peak, a monstrous fang looming above the abyss yawning beneath my toes, which curled out over the eroded edge of the trail as if trying to meet my heels. I scraped my backside along, one centimeter at a time, baby step by baby step, my heels barely shuffling, my ankles and calves shoved firmly against the cliff face.

All the time the wind tried to sweep us from the mountain, bowing the line between us if the least slack occurred, the wind-borne rope tugging the person on either side toward oblivion.

Even when no fresh blizzard assailed us, blowing snow whipped into our faces on the shrieking wind, blinding and deafening us at the same time.

So I didn't hear the first shot. All I knew of it was when the face of the mountain began tumbling toward us and Wu lunged half off the cliff as Pema slipped down the side. I grabbed for Wu and just at that moment my foot lodged in a crack, giving me enough stability to haul on Wu's arm as she reached for Pema with her free hand.

We would have all gone down then, except that Tania and Dolma had reached a broadening in the trail and sat firmly down, grasping each other, Pema, and Wu. For a moment I toppled forward, but my trapped heel held until first Pema, then Wu, could be half dragged onto the broad part of the path and I dislodged my foot and followed, shaking, as the cliff side above rained rocks on our heads.

We were halfway down the ridge when another shot rang out and this time all of those in the forward party dove into the snow for cover. We hunkered against the hill, our arms over our heads, and continued to scuttle to firmer ground. We'd known the Colonel was armed. Why hadn't we brought weapons too? Well, because it was stupid shooting at things in avalanche-prone country for one thing. Okay then, crossbows or something. Anything to avoid being sitting ducks. Fine. But if we'd brought weapons, we'd have had to shoot someone and just who was it I wanted shot? The Colonel? He might be crazy and stubborn but he was still a good man and for all I knew one of the last of my own people in the whole world. And I didn't want Dr. Terton hurt either. Or any of us, God forbid. So I crouched and scuttled and prayed the Colonel would run out of ammo before he hit anybody or brought several of the more prominent peaks down on top of us.

On the trail below, Marsh called out to Merridew. A broad straight path stretched out before us and Tania unknotted her rope, lay on her stomach, pushed off with her mittened hands and body-sledded down the rest of the mountain. The rest of us followed. I wore a fiberfill suit of slick, water-resistant silon and slid much faster than I could control, headfirst at a dizzying speed down the mountain to land in a pile with the others.

Now I could hear Marsh coaxing the Colonel to give up his weapon.

"I can't do that, son," the Colonel said. "Got to make it back to headquarters with my prisoner. You could come with me. You and Thibideaux and even Viv, though she may have to face charges when I file my report." The doctor looked tiny and fragile beside him.

"We'll come with you but the old woman will never make it. Headquarters is too far. Come on, let's go," Marsh said and stepped forward.

The Colonel fired in the air and the shot ricocheted, repeating over and over again, the single shot striking first one surface and then another, a veritable fusillade, and soon afterward it was followed by the artillery-like rumbling of a mountainside tearing loose. The usual small and medium-sized stones skidded down upon us, but the source of the rumbling became apparent as an outcropping just above the two lonely figures standing near the opposite peak broke off, fragmented, and fell. The Colonel was struck with the first large rock and the gun went flying. The doctor could have run clear but she knelt to help him, starting to pull him free, and another rock struck her down.

The worst of the slide bounced to a halt in a few seconds and during that time the forward party ran the distance between themselves and the pile of snow and rock where the Colonel and the doctor had been. They had already uncovered the doctor, who had fallen on top of Merridew, by the time I reached them. She was not badly hurt and had shielded his head from the worst blows. Most of what had fallen on them was snow. Thibideaux used the stock of the broken weapon to dig.

Merridew clawed his way to the surface and sat up, shaking off the snow, then dragged his legs clear.

"We better make a campfire and try to warm these two up," Thibideaux decided.

"No time for that. We have to make it behind the lines," the Colonel said firmly. "Come on, men, help me."

"Nah, Colonel, I don't think we better do that," Thibideaux said. "That trip might make an old man out of you in a hurry and besides, there ain't anything out there anymore."

Merridew gave him a pitying look. "For Christ's sake, Doc, these people are the enemy. They're just telling us that to keep us here."

"There was Danielson."

"Some kinda trick. Torture maybe. Who knows what those people did to him? Damn shame, too. He was a damn good man."

"Yeah, but he tried the same dumb stunt you're trying to pull and you notice he ain't around no more."

"You're not turning traitor on me too, are you, Doc?"

"No, sir, I'm not, but I'm tryin' to talk sense to you. What'd you think you was gonna do, blazin' away like that besides killin' that little old lady, your own self, and a whole bunch of us?"

"So it's 'us' now is it, Doc? You have turned against me too."

"Excuse me, please," Dr. Terton said, "This divisiveness is not good. There are no longer any sides. If Mr. Merridew so fervently desires to reach the border, then he shall. I will be happy to take him there and perhaps it would be a good thing if some of you came as well, as you have come so far already. In this way we can all travel at a more leisurely pace and be assured of arriving and returning safely."

Merridew clearly thought that was a trick too, but there was nothing he could do but go along with it, and since we were headed where he wanted to go, he steeled his jaw, set his eyes flintily on the path ahead, and persevered, as did the rest of us in a somewhat less determined fashion.

Now we could have a fire and rest for longer than a few hours at night. Three of our party had given their food to someone else to pack and had themselves hauled bags of synthetic charcoal, since there is no other fuel available in the high mountains in the winter. Even had there been enough animals around to leave burnable droppings, we'd never have found droppings beneath the snow.

In another few days, after several more narrow escapes, we crossed over another precarious path and descended into a basin that didn't look the least bit familiar to me until Terton led us into the mountain face, which contained the cave I remembered.

The cave offered shelter and nothing more, as the refugees had stripped it of supplies on their way to Kalapa.

"Why have we stopped already?" the Colonel wanted to know. "We need to find civilization. Don't try to fool me, Doctor, with this pretense that you're cooperating. You have committed crimes against the people of the United States of America and I intend to see that you pay for them. Her too," he added, nodding in Wu's direction.

Wu glanced at Lobsang and I saw him shake his head. Wu had been subdued during the trip, particularly after our near catastrophe. She bit a piece of her cracked lower lip and watched the Colonel warily.

"The boundaries of Shambala extend until the next pass and no farther," Dr. Terton said. "Beyond that no one can travel without returning to his natural age. You, Mr. Merridew, are very much my senior, I'm afraid. You may recall that when we met I was scarcely older than Nyima appears now."

The Colonel shrugged. "It's not my lookout if you should have used a better grade of skin cream, lady. I need to get me and my people back to our lines without interference and you will help me do it."

"The other danger, of course, is radiation. Beyond our borders we will be as susceptible as those who have already perished. Our new residents fled before the effects of the bombs, but those conditions, the fire storms, the radiation, will be surrounding Shambala on all sides now. Many years must pass yet before those effects dissipate sufficiently to allow us to venture beyond the pass."

"That's your story," he said. "I just don't buy all of this. If you people were so benign and interested in our own good, why did you have a prison camp with the Dragon Lady here in charge? Why not just tell us where we were and let us have the freedom to decide whether to stay or not?"

But Dr. Terton's age had caught up with her and her stamina was not up to more arguing. So she didn't answer except to yawn at him, give him a sleepy smile, and curl up against the wall of the cave for a nap. Wu took up the argument instead. "But if you had decided to go, you might have told your people, who would return and destroy us."

"If you had behaved like a friendly nation they would have had no reason to destroy you," he replied.

"They didn't need a reason to destroy us," Wu said bitterly. "And need not have done so on their own behalf. Since the beginning of Tibet's troubles your country's position has been that all of Tibet is part of China. Shambala is technically within the borders of Tibet, although actually it transcends them. Your pilot needed no particular reason to bomb our mountain—"

"This is all in the past," Tea said sharply. "The real issue, Colonel, is that whatever has happened to you has happened so that you may fulfill your destiny with us. You were one of the Terton's earliest choices. There was a good reason for you to be among us."

"Not good enough for me," he said. "I think it's about time we got going again, unless you're going to try to force me to stay."

"No, no," Lobsang said. "It would be a great waste

of energy to have to chase you clear across the mountains again. The Terton has said we will go to the boundary, as you desire . . ."

The Colonel grunted, but otherwise said nothing, and rolled onto his side to sleep.

People were already up and out of the cave when I rose but since all I had to do was stand up and grab a handful of dried vegetables from my belt pouch, I lost no time joining the others. The sun rises late so deep in the mountains and the fading light that seeped between peaks threw the whole valley into an eerie moonscape of shadows, glowing brightness and deeper, blacker shadows. We trudged toward the pass, half awake.

Once from the corner of my eye I thought I saw something pale and shaggy flitting past us on one side, but if it did indeed flit it flitted away so quickly that by the time I turned my head no sight of it remained.

Dr. Terton led the procession, followed closely by the Colonel, Wu and Lobsang. Pema tried to keep up with the Colonel, but he would have nothing to do with her and she quickly fell behind, to be hefted this time onto her father's back. From that vantage point she watched Merridew as if he was her pet cat or dog who had contracted rabies and become vicious but who, because she loved him, she hoped might still remember her and be saved.

Watching her, I stumbled and fell flat on my face, and floundered for several minutes in the deep snow, sinking first one foot and then the other in to the hip as I tried to gain leverage to rise again. Finally, Dolma pulled me out and after that I watched where I was going instead of watching the other climbers.

We climbed the pass single file, paying strict attention to our relative positions and I did notice then, looking up to see how far we had yet to climb, that the mountain before us was glowing with pale lime phosphorescence, dulling to mustard gold where it touched the sky. The higher we climbed, and the more of the pass that was revealed, the brighter this light became, until the valley below us was lit with it.

At the crest of the pass Dr. Terton stopped. "Look,"

she said unnecessarily to the Colonel, who had stopped dead a few feet behind her, staring past her in stricken silence. She pointed outward, toward a smooth bit of trail that connected the pass to a nearby peak. The peak was suffused with the greenish glow and as I crowded closer to her, I saw that beneath the trail was a great deal of thin air, what looked like a desert made of snow, and a vast lake or river of incredibly deep blue, tinted slightly turquoise by the greenish glow, with oily-looking rainbows dancing across its surface. A snowfall that more resembled the snow of static interference on a video device than real snow blurred the whole scene, and a piercing wind shrieked up from the water. The odd thing was that nothing moved except for the pulse of the glow and the crackle of the snow. "This is the southern boundary of Shambala."

"Surely even you can see that it is dangerous out there," Wu said, her voice breaking between an argumentative declaration and an awed whisper.

The Colonel squared his shoulders, glared at her, and declared, "It's dangerous here too." He limped forward to close the gap between him, Ama-La, and the bridge.

"Very well, then, if you are determined," Ama-La said and stepped out onto the bridge.

The Colonel started after her but before anyone else realized what was happening, Wu let out an anguished "No!" and pushed past him.

Ama-La continued to walk calmly across the bridge, but looked back once when Wu shouted and I saw that where the snow touched the doctor's face great sores erupted and froze. She stopped walking just before she reached the other side of the bridge and sank down, the hood of her coat covering her face so that we could not see.

Tea grabbed for Wu as she plunged past him. "You can't help her," he screamed, but Wu broke loose from him and ran onto the bridge herself.

Marsh and Thibideaux meanwhile held tightly on to the Colonel. Wu rose as far as her knees and crawled toward Terton. I heard something snap and one leg collapsed under her, and she dragged it, her sobbing broken up by the snow and the glow. Her face and hands were shielded by clothing, as was the rest of her body, but her movements were pained and slow for all of her urgency. When at last she reached the Terton, she removed a mitten and stretched out her hand. Before the sores covered it I saw that it was clawed and knotted. She touched Ama-La's face and screamed, cradled her in her arms, still screaming, as the wind caught her hood and ripped it back exposing the seams of age and the spreading lesions ravaging her doll-like face. Her thin white hair tore from her skull in patches as the sores spread so quickly I almost could not be sure of what I saw before she died.

The Colonel was sure, however. "I see," he said. On the far side of the green-lit path, Wu's skull crumbled and the bodies of the women visibly shrank inside their clothing, until the next blast of wind carried away first a coat, then a boot, then the rest, so much used clothing blowing down toward the electric blue lake.

Pema escaped her mother and slipped between the adults to take Merridew's hand. He glanced down at her, unseeing, for a moment, then followed the tug on his hand and allowed her to lead him back down the mountain.

PART TEN

EPILOGUE: PBB, TENTH YEAR—JUNE 15, OLD TIME 2080

⚶ Today, while methodically building shelves in yet another of the old cells to hold our preserves and dried produce, I found myself suddenly panicky and fearful, and realized that the dark stains on the floor of the cell in which I was standing were probably my own blood. I had miscarried and almost died in that cell. That part of this life happened so long ago—no, to be honest, I have made, as we have all made, a conscious effort to forget about it. We have all become different people. I thought I had no interest in the old, sad past except for the stories we tell the children about the Terton.

So I surprised myself by standing in that claustrophobic little room and bawling my eyes out, sobbing and gulping and sobbing again, sinking to the floor, leaning against the old cot for support as I grew exhausted with crying. I heard the "clink" as my head lolled against the stones and that was when I remembered the loose stone and found the first section of my old prison diary.

I finished the section about the journey the day we arrived back at Kalapa, in the library. Tea came in while I was writing and sat quietly, watching, until I laid down my pen. Then he came over to the table, gathered my pages together in a neat pile, sandwiched them between two empty wooden covers from one of the ruined Tibetan books, and tucked my diary in among the other books on the shelf. "Now you must write new things," he told me. And I have. Mostly I have written descriptions,

329

catalogs of all of the sights and sounds, objects and animals, institutions and inventions I remember from my past. I also write down the stories the others tell me of their lives until they came here. But, like everyone else, I have other duties as well, including many of the same tasks I have been performing since I was first assigned to assist Tea.

Others chose new paths. Shortly after we returned, Thibideaux closeted himself in the library for several days and when he emerged, he began work on his first chorten. Dolma, who had been closeted with him and who helped him find the books he needed, told me he had decided to model the structure on the one that once formed the main gate of Lhasa. The structure would be stepped below four smooth, rectangular walls, then steps would lead to a dome topped by a ringed spire. The superstructure would be of stone for all but the dome and for that he would use the clay from which Lobsang and Marsh had fashioned the water pipes.

Dolma and Lobsang remembered details from other chortens they had seen and offered help and advice. By the time the chorten was done, Dolma decided that there was more to a pairing than producing children, and she and Thibideaux are designing several more buildings. He wants the camp to look as much as possible like the ancient Kalapa about which people used to dream and tell stories to their children. "I don't want to be livin' in no prison camp the rest of my life, but we are stuck here in this valley. Make the best of it, cher, my mama always used to say and that's what I mean to be doin'."

That first chorten stands now atop the old command bunker, and though it has no relics, it evokes our varied memories of Ama-La and Wu. Marsh and his wives and children and the other husbands of his wives and their children bring flowers every day.

I think Marsh has missed Wu in a way that none of the rest of us, including Tea, have missed her. For a man who dedicated his life to peace, he needs a sparring partner more than most, but he has to settle for playing chess or wrestling with his children, because nobody else is fond of conflict.

Ama-La chose well. We have potters and weavers and farmers and breeders of animals who have increased the stock from the wild things that wandered into the valley. We have carpenters and electricians and makers of candles and carvers of stone and wood. We all have to be farmers if we want to eat, although some of us are better than others. Dolma and I are the archivists and Tea has prevailed on Dolma to help him write a little book of Ama-La's aphorisms in her most recent lifetime, while Tea has added a few more sayings from previous lifetimes.

But although everyone has a contribution and we were presumably chosen for this community so that none of us are deadweights on its resources, physical or spiritual, the one position no one has yet seemed overly eager to assume is that of leader. Maybe it's because we have all been in the center of so much strife for so long. Maybe it's because we have each seen how the most failsafe plans by the wisest people with the purest possible motives can be misconstrued or misrepresented by one flaw in the character of one person. So by and large we each tend to our own business, and larger projects which involve all of us are put to a vote. If there's less than unanimous agreement, we wait. Time is something we either have a great deal of, or none of at all, depending on how correct the Terton was about the magical shield of Shambala and how well all those prayers and psychic vibrations will hold up to the onslaught of the disaster raging around us. We will either outlast the disaster or it will outlast us, but meanwhile, we continue as if we will continue. We have no leaders, for we are all leaders of ourselves, the people that the Terton led to Kalapa to live in the ruins of the last sacred place on earth while the rest of humankind destroyed every other thing natural and human-made that it should have held inviolable.

I have made one other contribution to our society besides my histories, my work in the archives and on the farm, and now, this written record of our beginnings which lies before me. My other, very important contributions are my children.

Forty-three is not so very old in Kalapa, and as

Marsh says, if the human race is to survive, there is a need to repopulate. Tea is enjoying fatherhood, and actually spends more time and attention than I do on our daughter, Nyima (no, I didn't like Wu, even after I knew about her, but Nyima means Sunshine and our daughter lives up to it to an almost irritating degree at times) and our son, Mike. (Growing up in a family of odd names has made me appreciate what sounds to me like a nice, solid, ordinary boy's name, although the other children tend to call him Meekay, which just demonstrates what I was saying about good intentions.)

Tsering and Samdup have four more children, Tsering has two others by one of the Indian prisoners, Pandit Singh, and Tania is expecting her first child by Samdup and hopes it will be a sister to the son she bore with Marsh.

Pema is a good young mother to her own daughter. Colonel Merridew insisted that Tea, who is as close to a clergyman as we have here, marry them in a proper ceremony. It took Pema until she was eighteen to convince the Colonel that a man who had never enjoyed a childhood needed a young wife to show him how to play with his children. The Colonel and Pema, like Tea and I, are so far monogamous. Dolma is the natural person to keep the census, since she goes with Thibideaux to help deliver babies and everyone confides in her. Even Shambala could not heal her enough that she has been able to have her own babies, but she is what amounts to a youthful grandmother to every child born in Kalapa. Though she and Tea set up the classes, we all take turns teaching the children our special skills, and if one child or another shows a particular aptitude for what we do rather than for what its own parents have become, then the parents will allow the child to be trained by the person who can teach them the best. It's a good theory. I hope it works. As the kids grow up, I'm afraid they'll become bored and restless. I'm afraid that a lot of the peace we have now is only because so many of us adults have known so much war. The kids didn't grow up with it.

They only know a few of the stories and stories

always sound glamorous whether you mean them to or not. The valley will be too small for them in time, and too familiar, despite the wealth of treasures yet to be uncovered and the amount of work to be done. Even Tea admits that the stories and myths surrounding Shambala predict that it will decline from being a haven to once more being in the midst of the world and conflict. Well, it makes sense that if the world doesn't revive and intrude on us, at some point, when it's safer to do so, at least some of our people will want to go out into the world. Like the past residents of Shambala, once our children reach maturity they will age slowly, as we age slowly. I see no reason why, if our natural death rate continues to be so low (the chorten and Danielson's mound mark the only new graves since shortly after the avalanche), we will not become overpopulated in a few generations. Also, if we are truly repopulating the world, then some of us, at some time, will have to go out into the world. Our children will not be like us, peaceful because they are tired, lacking a broader inquisitiveness out of fear.

Just the other day Pema brought her eighteen-month-old, Chime Cincinnati (the middle name is for the Colonel's birthplace—it was Pema's idea, not his, that the name reflect something of his past) to the library. She and Tea and I were talking about the dance classes Tania is organizing, which will help condition us all better for mountain travel. Mike was riding herd on Chime, when suddenly she let out a howl that none of us could ignore and scuttled after him while he tried to keep a book out of her reach.

"She's very good with books," Pema said, half apologetic and distressed and half defensive on her child's behalf. "She sits quietly for many hours with them."

"But, Mama, it's the book of the Terton," Mike said. "Father won't even let me touch it without him there, much less a baby."

He held it up and I saw that he was right. It was one of Ama-La's medical books, an indecipherable one in ancient Tibetan we hoped someday to decode and so kept in the library instead of redistributing it with the rest of her belongings to the newcomers. Chime waited for a moment, her eyes lingering tearfully on the book, then wiped her eyes and fixed first her mother and then me with a bright, beseeching stare. When we did not immediately chastise or support her, she calmly stretched out her chubby little cocoa-colored hand for the book and said sweetly but firmly to Mike, "Mine."

A Note from
Elizabeth Ann Scarborough
on her new novel,
LAST REFUGE

When I read from *Nothing Sacred*, I introduce the book by telling the audience, "There's bad news and good news about this book. The bad news is, I end the world. The good news is, there's a sequel."

If *Nothing Sacred* is my take on an apocalypse book, then *Last Refuge* is the obligatory after-the-bomb book. I got interested in science fiction and fantasy to begin with because of these kinds of books. Growing up during the Cold War, being drilled on air raid procedures every week in school (which meant we hid under our apparently nuke-proof desks), gave me a very personal interest in what would happen after the bomb dropped. Books which postulated that anything would still be happening were extremely comforting and hopeful. I kind of always thought all of us would just be dead.

While that's certainly not desirable, the horror of it somehow exceeds the fears I have about my own death. Why is the idea of everybody dying at once more terrifying than us going one at a time? Why is the idea of the fast death of the planet more terrifying than the idea of the planet slowly asphyxiating? As I explored Tibetan Buddhism and some of the assumptions it makes about reincarnation and so forth, it seemed to me that maybe the saddest thing about everyone going at once with few or no living entities left to carry on is that the continuation of spirits would be lost. No one would survive, culturally, spiritually, physically or in the memory of anyone else. Works of art would not be immortal. Wise words would not be remembered. Everything we like to believe is important would be wiped out.

The Shambala myth addresses that fear. James Hilton wrote of Shangri-La, his westernized take on the legendary Tibetan refuge, after WWII, when the world seemed in danger of ending. Since then, with Tibet occupied by hostile Chinese forces and the Dalai Lama in exile, many Tibetans still living in their own country probably feel the worst *has* happened and if Shambala really exists that it should have manifested itself for them by now. But of course, the Tibetan government in exile continues to survive and the Nobel Peace Prize-winning Dalai Lama continues to try to forge a course that will free his people and *not* end the world.

The worst has not yet happened. If it does, I hope that Shambala still exists, is still hidden, guarding its karmically suitable inhabitants (and maybe taking in a few of us, of course), its spiritual and cultural treasures. I hope that the decimation of animals by the wanton sports hunters of the invaders, the strip mining of the mountains, the erosion that has been allowed to take over the land, and the forced sterilization and genocide of Tibet's native people has not also reached and destroyed Shambala. I would like to think that such a place can remain hidden and secret and emerge when it is needed. I would like to think that if the worst happened and some of us were still left alive, the inhabitants of Shambala would come out and get us and take us to safety. I don't want to live in a survivalist world of the kind some of my colleagues describe (a very good reason not to go crazy with nukes, as far as I'm concerned). I don't know what would happen after a massive multinuclear strike, but if the Buddhists are right and our less-than-saintly souls should be blasted abruptly into the limbo of the bardo awaiting reincarnation, and the only living beings capable of helping us live again are sequestered safely in a place like Shambala, I hope a Chime Cincinnati or a Mike will exist to help the rest of us lost souls find that last refuge.

Elizabeth Ann Scarborough
Port Townsend, WA
May 21, 1991

Racial strife: up
Poverty and homelessness: up
Moral decay: *way up*
Mistrust of the government: off the scale

So when would the world end already?

The Songkiller Saga

Volume One:
Phantom Banjo
Volume Two:
Picking the Ballad's Bones

---

by Elizabeth Scarborough
Winner of the Nebula Award

The devils had it all planned nice and neat: a little human degradation, a little mutual misanthropy, a little social chaos and humanity would be on its way out. But something had thrown a monkey wrench into their demonic plans, and for all the wonderful evil they'd conjured, humanity just kept plugging away. So what was the problem?

Music.

And not just any kind of music, but folk music. The kind of music that shores up the human soul in times of trouble: songs people sang when chained in slavery, or working in dark and dangerous mines.

The answer was clear: Folks music had to go. But the devils didn't count on the power of the music or the strength of the human spirit.

On sale now wherever Bantam Spectra Books are sold.

AN226 -- 1/92